"It is clear you ... ...guishing for a man. Permit me to show you," Ranulf murmured, his voice stroking Ariane's senses like dark velvet. "Let us see if we can make your lovely body turn traitor."

He cradled her against him with a gentleness that belied the dangerous determination in his eyes. Then, to her complete startlement and dismay, he bent and kissed her, his lips warm and incredibly soft. The shock sent a wave of heat streaking through Ariane, a shock so powerful it paralyzed her.

It seemed she had waited nearly half her life for this, to know the taste of his kiss.

Long moments later Ranulf drew back, but only to whisper against her lips, "Let me show you pleasure, Ariane. Let me please you as I would have you please me . . ."

Praise for
THE WARRIOR

"EXHILIRATING . . .
Ms. Jordan proves herself a marvelous storyteller.
THE WARRIOR is a winner!"

Rendezvous

The Warrior

Nicole Jordan

AVON BOOKS ◆ NEW YORK

THE WARRIOR is an original publication of Avon Books. This work has never before appeared in book form. This work is a novel. Any similarity to actual persons or events is purely coincidental.

AVON BOOKS
A division of
The Hearst Corporation
1350 Avenue of the Americas
New York, New York 10019

Copyright © 1995 by Anne Bushyhead
Published by arrangement with the author
Library of Congress Catalog Card Number: 94-96275
ISBN: 0-380-77831-9

First Avon Books Printing: March 1995

AVON TRADEMARK REG. U.S. PAT. OFF. AND IN OTHER COUNTRIES, MARCA REGIS-TRADA, HECHO EN U.S.A.

Printed in the U.S.A.

RA   10   9   8   7   6   5   4   3   2   1

To Sandra Chastain—
friend and supporter *extraordinaire*.
You deserve a book dedication all your own,
even if medievals aren't your cup of tea.

Every lover is a warrior,
And Cupid has his camps.

—Ovid

A NOTE FROM THE AUTHOR

A kingdom in turmoil . . .

When King Henry I of England died in 1135, his nephew, Stephen of Blois, usurped the throne from Henry's daughter Matilda and plunged England into a civil conflict that lasted nearly two decades. Mighty earls and barons chose sides and waged private wars for land and power, until even King Stephen's supporters decried the anarchy and lawlessness of his ineffective rule.

At last defeated by superior forces, Matilda retired across the Channel to Normandy, where she continued to plot to regain the English crown for her eldest son, Henry Plantagenet of Anjou. Young Henry made several unsuccessful attempts to claim his throne, but not until 1153, when Stephen named Matilda's son as his heir, was a peace agreement reached.

Yet not all of England's ruling nobility approved of the plan. Although most swore oaths to Henry (now duke of Normandy) as their future king, some rebellious barons supported Stephen's brother, while others thought to raise Stephen's bastard son to the throne. Thus, upon King Stephen's death the following year, England was once more plunged into turmoil . . .

Prologue

Claredon Keep, England: June 1150

His gift of a rose bewildered her. Bloodred, perfectly formed, the fragile summer bloom seemed too delicate for the ruthless warrior's hand, which could wield a sword to deadly effect. The Black Dragon of Vernay had plucked the bud for her as they strolled in the castle garden, and now stood offering it to her in his long, sinewed fingers.

Startled by the tender lover's gesture, Ariane gazed up at the powerful, harsh-visaged Norman knight who towered above her. Amber eyes as piercing as a hawk's surveyed her intently beneath heavy black brows, a question in their golden depths.

"Have I rendered you speechless, my lady?"

She felt color flush her cheeks, yet she raised her chin bravely. "I . . . was merely surprised."

When she did not immediately accept his gift, he shook his head. "Ah, but I overlooked the thorns," he murmured, his deep, masculine voice soothing and low.

Ariane watched in amazement as Lord Ranulf slipped the dagger from his belt and trimmed the savage thorns from the flower's stem in silent concentration. Scarcely daring to breathe, she studied the man who was shortly to become her betrothed.

Sun-bronzed and starkly chiseled, his proud features were striking rather than handsome, his thick, untamed raven hair overlong and falling nearly to his shoulders. But one forgot even such notable considerations in his formidable presence. Superb in physique, awesome in his raw power, the Black Dragon possessed a commanding bearing that would alarm

1

and intimidate his enemies and arouse respect and confidence in his allies.

In all her fourteen years, Ariane had never met any man quite like him.

The ladies and serving women of Claredon alternately envied her and trembled for her, although this morning envy had begun to prevail. Ariane was inclined to tremble. *She* was the one who would celebrate her betrothal in merely a few short hours. She was the one who would someday take this dark stranger as her lawful husband. Who would receive him into her bed and body and bear his children.

When Ranulf looked up to meet her watchful gaze, her heart fluttered.

"Do you fear me, demoiselle?" he asked softly, as if reading her thoughts.

Did she fear him? Ariane wondered. Until this moment she would have said yes. Ranulf was a fully grown man, nearly ten years her senior. His great height and powerful, broad-shouldered frame towered over other mortals, while his exploits in battle and tourney were already legendary. But it was his fierce repute that alarmed her most. Spoken of in hushed tones, the Black Dragon of Vernay was the subject of fearsome tales and scandalous rumors that had followed him across the Channel from Normandy.

She would have preferred not to leave the safety of Claredon's great hall or the vast number of guests that were already gathered there for the betrothal celebration. But when the lord of Vernay had invited her to walk with him alone in the garden, she hadn't dared refuse. To her dismay, she who had often been scolded by her lady mother for her bold tongue and irreverent wit could think of not a single word to say, clever or otherwise.

He will wonder if he is to wed the village idiot if you continue to remain speechless, Ariane scolded herself as she gazed up at him.

To her complete surprise, Ranulf lifted the rose to caress her cheek, brushing the velvet petals along her skin with a gentleness that seemed totally incongruous coming from such a man.

"Such innocence," he murmured almost absently, his gaze far away. "I wonder how long it will last."

She was not certain if he spoke of the rose or herself—but then the powerful knight seemed to collect himself. "I believe you have not answered my question, demoiselle."

"Q-Question, my lord?" she repeated, caught by the quiet intensity of his amber eyes.

"Do I frighten you?"

Yes, she wanted to answer. She understood why men trembled in fear of him. She would never forget her first sight of Lord Ranulf yesterday as he approached Claredon. Mounted on a massive destrier, dressed in full chain mail armor, he was a forbidding figure with his banner and shield that bore his feared device, a black dragon rampant on a scarlet field. Since his arrival, his manner had seemed distant, even unwelcoming; until this moment, she had thought him cold, hard, dangerous. But he did not seem so fierce or ruthless when he was wielding a rose instead of a sword.

"No, my lord, you do not frighten me," Ariane replied finally, and realized with surprise that it was true.

"Then will you accept my humble gift of a flower?" A faint smile curved his lips as he made her a courteous bow. "You must, demoiselle, if only to protect me."

"Protect you?"

"Aye. The theft of a noble's rose is considered a crime in most parts, but if I give it to you, then I have no need to fear reprisal."

Her eyes widened in startlement. Was he teasing her? Yet it made her smile to think of so mighty a knight needing her protection from anyone or anything.

"That is much better," he said with soft satisfaction.

She took the rose from him and buried her nose in the scented velvet petals to hide her flushed cheeks, grateful for his effort to ease her fears. "I thank you, my lord," Ariane murmured. "These roses are my mother's pride, but I am certain she will not begrudge you a single bloom, since we are soon to be betrothed."

It even seemed natural, then, for her to voice the question that had been preying on her mind as they turned to continue their stroll along the garden path. "Was there some reason you desired my company, my lord?"

He seemed to hesitate before casting her a brief, enigmatic glance. "Yes, demoiselle. I have a question to put to you."

Another pause. "Is a marriage between us what you wish for your future?"

"I am not certain I understand what you mean."

"Are you in full agreement with the betrothal?"

Her eyes widened slightly. "Yes, my lord. I know my duty. I am prepared to obey my lord father." When Ranulf frowned, Ariane realized her answer was apparently not the one he sought. She hastened to add, "I understand that Claredon needs a strong lord. And now that my brother is ... gone and my father no longer has an heir, he wishes to make provisions for when he is no longer able to rule—to leave his lands in capable hands, as well as to give me the protection of a strong husband."

"That is not what I asked, demoiselle. I understand Lord Walter's reasons for promoting the union."

She gazed up at Ranulf, not knowing what he wished to hear from her. She had been raised to put duty and responsibility above personal consideration, and her brother Jocelin's death earlier this year had made her the heir to Claredon, with all the solemn obligations such a vaunted position entailed. If her father wished her to make a political marriage to ensure Claredon's future, then she would do so, and willingly. But she did not think Lord Ranulf needed any such explanation, since their union would be a political alliance for him as well.

It was another moment before he spoke, and then his voice sounded strangely constrained, almost taut. "I have no desire to force a reluctant damsel to accept my suit. I have seen more than one marriage where the lady was unwilling end in calamity."

Still watching him, Ariane noticed the way his strong jaw had hardened, caught the faint note of bitterness in his tone, and wondered if he was speaking of his own experience.

But perhaps she mistook his intention. Perhaps he was attempting to renounce the betrothal and searching for the kindest way to tell her.

Impulsively she reached out to touch Ranulf's sleeve, a gesture that seemed to startle him and made him halt in his tracks. "Do you wish to be released from the betrothal, my lord?"

His amber gaze searched her face intently, and for a moment as she met those arresting golden eyes, she thought she saw a bleakness in their depths, a flicker of something almost like torment. But then it was gone. "I want to be certain you harbor no objections to wedding me."

Was he actually asking if she consented to their marriage? In her admittedly limited experience, no warlord would seek the approval of a mere girl but would be solely concerned with gaining land and power. Surely in Normandy as well as England, land counted for everything and the consent of the lady very little, despite the Church's efforts to provide greater protection to unwilling brides. Lord Ranulf intended to wed her for the vast demesne she would someday bring him upon her father's passing, she knew.

Ariane could not read the question in his eyes. He had gone still, his expression serious, almost guarded. She trusted those eyes, she realized with a sudden conviction. They were hard, intense, but not cruel.

"I have no objections, my lord. I consent freely to the betrothal."

The taut expression eased from his features, softening the grim line of his mouth, while his powerful body seemed to relax. Only then did Ariane realize he had not answered her own question. She wanted desperately to ask him if their marriage was what *he* wished for—but Ranulf was a powerful landed knight who could afford his choice of bride. If he objected to the union, surely he would never have accepted her father's proposition in the first place.

"Is that what you wished to know?" she asked uncertainly.

"Yes, demoiselle. I was merely interested in discovering your opinion." He seemed suddenly discomfited by the subject, or by her, for he looked away, across the garden toward the bailey wall.

Yearning to put him at ease as he had her, Ariane smiled wryly. "My lord father would say daughters have no right to opinions, and that I have too many for my own good. I daresay he is right."

Ranulf glanced back down at her sharply, as if in surprise. "And do you always agree with your father, my lady?"

She wrinkled her nose. "No, seldom, in truth. He claims it is my greatest failing."

Ranulf chuckled faintly, a rough, rusty sound that made Ariane certain he was not a man who laughed often.

"Indeed, I suspect Father is so eager to be rid of me, he is grateful you are here to court me."

"Court?" The tall knight grimaced slightly. "I am a soldier, demoiselle, not a poet." The smile that played on his lips was self-deprecating, endearing somehow. "I know little of wooing a lady."

She was certain he was wrong. If this strong, charismatic man put his mind to it, he could seduce the birds from the trees, Ariane suspected.

"Well, I know even less about courtship," she answered boldly, "so you need not fear I will judge you harshly. You are my first suitor."

"Your first? I cannot credit it. Can it be that the men in England are blind?"

Now she *knew* he was teasing her and being kind. She could make little claim to beauty, with her ungainly height and freckles that accompanied her fair skin and hair. She well knew her noble birth and the rich demesne of Claredon were her prime advantages.

"Alas," she replied with a rueful laugh, "my appearance has little to say to the matter. My father refused to entertain the idea of suitors for me until he was certain which way the political winds blew."

Ranulf studied her speculatively. "You are not afraid to speak your mind, I see."

Wondering if his remark were a criticism, Ariane found herself flushing. Her lady mother had always warned that her wayward tongue would plunge her into trouble someday. Perhaps she *had* been too bold with Lord Ranulf, but her intuition told her he would not want a meek bride. Her chin rose slightly. "No, and I am not afraid to wed you, either, my lord."

He smiled then. Fully. A slow, tender, sensual smile that softened his harsh features and made Ariane's heart suddenly trip over itself. Unprepared for the intimate rush of warmth that suddenly rioted through her, she blinked at the dazzling sight, feeling as if the sun had burst from behind the clouds.

Was *this* what her women had admired and envied earlier? This bold, masculine appeal that held all the shock of a lightning bolt? Was it possible for a single smile to win a damsel's heart?

Then Ranulf raised a gentle hand to brush her lower lip with the tip of a forefinger. He had barely touched her, yet her pulse skittered wildly, while a strange heat blossomed inside her, sending her emotions into a wild state of confusion.

Ariane stared up at him in mute bewilderment, startled by the feelings that had sprung to life at his slightest caress, the strange sensations that quivered through her body. Never had she been so vitally aware of being female than at this moment. Never before had she been shaken by a man's touch.

"Then we are agreed, my lady? The betrothal will go forward?"

"Yes, my lord," she murmured breathlessly.

When Ranulf held out his hand to her, Ariane shivered, not from apprehension, but from fascination and excitement and anticipation. She *wanted* this man for her husband, she realized. She wanted to wed this powerful, magnificent knight who cared enough to concern himself with her feelings and her fears. Who could make her tremble with merely a smile and a touch. Despite the rumors of his terrible past, she desired to be part of his future.

Hope took wing in her heart as she placed her trembling fingers in Ranulf's hand. They would have a good marriage, Ariane vowed silently, remembering the reluctance she had sensed in him. She would endeavor to make Ranulf a good wife, strive never to give him cause to regret this day.

With a tremulous smile, Ariane clutched the rose he had given her and allowed the Black Dragon of Vernay to lead her back to Claredon's tower and the betrothal celebration within.

Chapter 1

Vernay Keep, Normandy: November 1154

The warm lips nuzzling his bare skin no longer had the power to arouse him, nor did the cool, silken hair trailing provocatively over his naked back. Ranulf lay sprawled on his stomach upon the musky linen sheets, sated and spent, his body glistening with sweat after his exertions. Pleasing two lusty wenches at once taxed even a man of his strength and stamina.

Yet Layla continued her merciless assault with mouth and tongue, her lush, opulent curves pressing erotically against him, her nails sending delicate shivers racing along his spine, her teeth intermittently nipping his buttocks with a sharpness that was just short of pain.

"Enough," he muttered huskily—a command he lacked the energy to enforce.

When she bent to offer a luscious breast to him, teasing her dusky nipple against his mouth, Ranulf patiently averted his head. When she threaded her fingers through his raven hair and tugged insistently, he merely caught her wrist and pried loose her grip. It was only when Layla scraped her nails in a deliberate path over his scarred back that he finally reacted; she knew quite well such probing of his scars was forbidden, even though he had been unable to break her of the habit.

"*Cease*, wench."

At his sharp tone, the ripe young body at his other side flinched, and Ranulf had to murmur gently to Flore and stroke her soothingly till she curled against him once more.

For temperament, he much preferred the petite, fair-haired Flore to the voluptuous Layla, whose ebony tresses were as dark as his own. Flore was a sweetly submissive Norman wench, always eager to do his bidding, whereas the foreign Layla had a grasping, querulous nature. Only because of her exquisite skills did he humor the beautiful Saracen.

"I seek simply to pleasure you, lord," she said petulantly in her thick, honeyed accents. "You know well Layla pleases you far better than any other."

Ranulf could not dispute her claim. Stolen from her family and enslaved in an infidel brothel, Layla had been trained in the sexual arts of the East, and knew well how to satisfy a man and bring his desire to a fever pitch.

If he also gained a bitter measure of satisfaction in possessing the exotic concubine his detested father had brought back from the Holy Land ... well then, he would not deny himself the pleasure, even if he was perforce required to bear with Layla's sharp tongue and acid jealousy. He could have chosen from a dozen peasant wenches just as eager to warm his bed, and yet tonight he had needed the fierce release the Saracen could bring him. He needed to forget. Summoning Flore at the same time only increased the odds that he would find respite from the demons that shadowed him.

"You are cruel to Layla, lord," she complained, running her tongue over her pouting lower lip.

"Methinks thrice is enough," Ranulf retorted, his tone dry, "even for a woman of your passion."

In answer, she captured his hand and held it to the satiny flesh of her generous breast. "You dislike my passion? You desire Layla no longer?"

Ranulf grinned unwillingly as he gave her taut nipple a playful squeeze. "You would have to geld me to quench my desire for you, wench. But it is time for you to seek your own pallet." When Layla made to protest, Ranulf raised his powerful body up on one elbow. "You know my wishes. I sleep alone."

In truth, he was not singling her out for punishment by sending her away. His solitary slumber was a self-imposed rule. Though he took great pleasure in the female body, he rarely lingered with a woman. Too much sensual indulgence bred softness in a warrior; a knight who cavorted too often grew lazy and careless.

When Layla refused to budge, Ranulf gave her bare flank a mild cuff, which made her squeal in mock protest.

Defiantly, she lay back upon the dishevelled pillows, gazing up at him with languorous, seductive eyes. Provocatively her long fingers played over her sumptuous breasts, caressing the dusky crimson nipples in erotic invitation, while her lush thighs spread for his masculine appreciation. "Once more, lord, I beg you. . . ."

Despite her disobedience, Ranulf gave a rough chuckle. He was sated enough at the moment to be amused at her tactics, and wise enough to relent. Sometimes it behooved a man to let a wench win small victories so that she yielded more readily in important matters.

"Once more, then." His fingers splayed over the smooth mound between her thighs, shaved bare in the Saracen style . . . parting the damp, passion-flushed lips, seeking the tender nubbin that was a woman's delight.

Layla drew a sharp breath and closed her eyes, while her legs opened wide, giving his stroking fingers full access to her heated, dewy center. With controlled expertise, he caressed the slick flesh, sliding slowly inside the hot, sleek moistness. Layla quivered with arousal. In merely moments a throaty moan of rapture escaped her; her head fell back in ecstasy as she arched her supple back, her voluptuous, golden body undulating in the flickering candlelight.

Ranulf viewed her breathless, writhing response with gratification. Layla deserved to be rewarded for her earlier exquisite ministrations. She had provided him comfort tonight; it was only fair he reciprocate. Indeed, for the past fortnight— ever since he'd returned home to Vernay to cool his heels and await a summons from Duke Henry—Layla had succored him frequently. He should feel more remorse, perhaps, at relaxing his own strict custom of self-denial. Yet if he indulged his lust more often than usual when occupying Vernay Keep, it was because the diversion helped keep the memories at bay.

Restlessly, Ranulf lifted his gaze from the panting woman in his bed to glance beyond the open bed curtains. The solar at Vernay, where the lord slept and spent his leisure, remained a cold, stark, spartan chamber, devoid of comforts other than a roaring fire in the hearth and an occasional tapestry draping the stone walls to thwart the chill. He had refused to change a single appointment since his father's tenancy, perversely determined to preserve the bitter evidence of his past.

Yet *he* was lord here now, Ranulf reminded himself. The honor of Vernay belonged to *him*, given to him in fief by Duke Henry, along with a charter of nobility that had reinstated him to his rightful rank. He was a disinherited, landless castoff no longer.

For all his present power and wealth, though, he could not quell the unease that always assaulted him in this chamber—the place where his father had flayed the flesh from his back. Even now, his skin turned clammy with dread each time he entered these apartments, for he could not help recalling the terror and pain of his youth. He had no need even to shut his eyes to remember crouching there against the far wall as a child, naked and trembling, waiting to endure the punishment of a vengeful sire. Not even the current consolation of heated female flesh could completely drive away the memories—although it made up in some measure for the countless hours of fear and torment he had suffered here.

The distant blare of the night watchman's horn brought Ranulf's head up like a wolf scenting the wind. At his sudden tensing, Layla's eyes flew open.

"Nay! My lord . . . you cannot cease. . . ." Her demanding tone was sharp and insistent—and breathless as well.

He smiled faintly as his brutal memories faded. "We have time."

And they would. Any new arrival must first await the lowering of the drawbridge, then ride through the outer and inner baileys before seeking entrance to Vernay's tower.

He had the leisure to bring Layla to fulfillment.

Yet even before the grateful, sobbing woman had collapsed against him, Ranulf's thoughts had already moved ahead to review his plans. If the new arrival was indeed the duke's messenger with a summons, it meant King Stephen had died and Henry was preparing to claim his rightful crown as king of England. And since Henry was certain to be met with resistance, he would need to raise adequate forces to ensure the successful assumption of power.

Ranulf felt anticipation swell at the promised conflict. Not only was he willing to supply the knight's fees he owed his liege, he was impatient to take up arms for Henry. He had remained idle too long, his battle sword and lance growing rusty with disuse. For the past three months and more, peace had reigned in Normandy. There had been no rebellions, no skirmishes, not even a nearby tourney where he could hone his skills and exhaust his frustrations in the melee or increase his wealth by capturing enemy knights for ransom.

For the past fortnight all had been in readiness for the forthcoming journey: the armor polished, the weapons sharpened, and the baggage wains staged for loading. His knights and men-at-arms had engaged in daily practice, sparring in swordplay, tilting at the quintains, shooting archery butts, and yet, they too were restless at the delay and eager to begin the campaign.

And now it seemed the moment was at hand.

As Ranulf expected, a lengthy interval passed before a rap sounded on the iron-banded door—time which he spent attending to Flore's pleasure in reward for her sweetness and patience. At his command to enter, Ranulf's vassal, Payn FitzOsbern, strode into the solar, half-dressed in an unlaced tunic and grinning broadly.

"Duke Henry?" Ranulf queried as he eased his body over the Saracen wench to sit on the edge of the massive bed.

"Aye, the duke—soon to be king of England. He rides for the coast in two days' time and expects us to accompany him." Payn made no apparent attempt to keep the glee from his tone. "The messenger would speak with you."

Flashing his own grin, Ranulf solicitously twitched the linen sheet up over the two nude women in his bed. "Bid him enter."

The messenger had obviously ridden hard from the duke's court, for his cloak was spattered with mud, while grime and weariness lined his face. He confirmed what Payn had already announced, adding more details about the departure plans and composition of Henry's forces, and warning of the resistance expected from the late King Stephen's supporters in England.

Satisfied, Ranulf dismissed the man with orders to seek food and rest in the hall, then strode naked to the table where refreshment awaited. Pouring wine from a flagon into two pewter cups, he handed one to Payn and raised his own.

"On to England, then!"

"Aye, on to England! May we find a vast supply of English rebels to vanquish—before your impatience renders your temper even more vile than of late."

"I?" Ranulf's black eyebrow rose in amused mockery. "My disposition has been sweet as honey."

His vassal gave a snort of laughter. "And what of the three quintains you destroyed yesterday? Had their straw forms been infidels, we would have freed the Holy Land by now! I vow I've encountered wild boars less dangerous than you after you've been caged here at Vernay for any length."

Ranulf's sole response was a shrug as he drained his cup. "Perhaps."

"Yet I see you have been laboring at a cure for your foul mood." Payn grinned wickedly as, with a nod of his head, he indicated the women in his lord's bed. "By the rood, two wenches at once, Ranulf? Could you not save some for the rest of us?"

Ranulf surveyed the handsome, chestnut-haired knight with wry amusement. "I much doubt you lacked for company yourself."

"Nay, but for some reason I find utterly unfathomable, females seem to favor you, despite your black scowl."

"Simply because I take the time to ensure their pleasure instead of seeking merely my own." At Payn's grimace, it was Ranulf's turn to grin. "Less selfishness would stand you in good stead, my friend."

"Doubtless you are right." Tilting his head back, Payn swallowed the remainder of his wine, then glanced at Ranulf with a measure of slyness. "And wise, as well. Best get your fill of your lemans now while you still can. Your bride will be none too pleased to share you after the wedding. A lady of her rank will expect you to devote your attentions to her, at least in the beginning."

Ranulf's good humor faded at the reminder. His betrothed awaited him in England—the sole reason he would not find this campaign entirely to his liking. "With the opposition we undoubtedly will face," he said stiffly, "it could be months before I can manage time for a wedding ceremony."

" 'Tis likely you'll not be able to put off your nuptials much longer, though," Payn observed, laughter lacing his tone.

To hide his thoughts, Ranulf pivoted abruptly to refill his wine cup. His friend had long known of his reluctance to visit England but only lately begun to suspect the cause: *The Black Dragon of Vernay had misplaced his vaunted nerve.*

Ranulf shook his head ruefully. How was it possible? He was a warrior, a powerful knight who had earned his spurs at the youthful age of seventeen. In the eleven years since, he had proven his valor countless times over. His remarkable achievements in combat had earned him the name "Black Dragon," a dreaded appellation that made his foes tremble. And yet the thought of wedding the Claredon heiress unnerved him.

He feared a mere girl.

Payn would think it a great jest—uproarious, in fact. It would indeed be humorous, if not for the possible repercussions, Ranulf admitted wryly. If his men learned of his trepidation, not only would he suffer untold ribbing, but their respect for him would diminish, a consequence that could prove detrimental to his leadership.

As if sensing his discomfort, Payn gave a guffaw of laughter and cuffed him on the back. "Take cheer, my lord. As you said, it could be months before you must face your bride. With luck, Stephen's defenders will not surrender England easily, and your time will be spent fighting and subduing rebels. Perhaps you can manage to delay your visit to Claredon through next spring and even into the summer."

"Aye," Ranulf said, swallowing a long gulp of wine. What he needed was a good fight to take his mind off his impending nuptials. War, sport, and tourneys—those were his passion. Not women. Not his heiress bride. He was eager for battle, for confrontation, if only so that he might escape the affliction of matrimony for a short while longer.

"You can count on me to see to the final arrangements for the journey," Payn assured him. "We shall be prepared to march at first light."

Ranulf nodded, but scarcely noticed when his vassal departed. His thoughts were too wrapped up in the fate that awaited him across the Channel. While he anticipated the forthcoming military campaign with relish, he was not at all anxious to set foot in England.

More than four years had passed since the betrothal contracts had been signed, time which he'd spent fighting and serving his liege. He had permitted the seasons to slip past one by one, too occupied with his duties and obligations here to fetch his young bride; convinced that she would prefer to remain with her family in England rather than be dragged off to Normandy as his wife, to the fearsome lair of the Black Dragon. Even when an opportunity had arisen, though, he'd made no move to claim her, but instead found reason to tarry in Normandy. He had not even accompanied Henry to England last year when the duke met with King Stephen to secure the succession.

Absently, Ranulf moved to stand before the crackling fire in the hearth, his gaze engrossed by the flames.

At the time, his betrothal to Ariane of Claredon had seemed a sound idea—a politically expedient maneuver that would provide him land and heirs and cement an alliance with a powerful family who held fiefs throughout England. And after living much of his life without land or even a name, he had leapt at the chance to increase his wealth and extend his power base to England, where he possessed only minor holdings. He'd been eager for the connection offered him, driven by a fierce determination to become more powerful than his despised father, to forge for himself a dynasty that would rival any lord's in the land. That a noble wife came with the transaction had not seemed too great a price to pay . . . at the time.

Her father Walter's reasons for wanting the marriage were just as mercenary and perhaps more political. Walter supported King Stephen yet knew Empress Matilda and her son Henry might one day prevail. Shrewdly the lord of Claredon had betrothed his fourteen-year-old daughter to a Norman warlord who supported Henry, with the intent of leaving her well protected by a powerful husband should the English crown change hands.

At the time, Ranulf reflected, the scandal of his birth and his doubtful lineage was no longer much of an impediment, for he had just been reinstated to his inheritance and the honor of Vernay, which, added to bounty already gained from tourneys and wars, made him one of the wealthier knights in Normandy.

It had seemed a good match on both sides.

Except that the ink was scarcely dry on the parchment before he had longed to be free.

In these uncertain times, a betrothal pact could always be broken, for who would enforce the law? Civil rule in England was in shambles, while King Stephen had virtually lost the power to control his subjects or dispense justice. Yet as the years passed Ranulf had found no good reason to dissolve the contract. What could he say? That he feared such an advantageous marriage? His enemies would delight in his faintheartedness and he would appear a fool. Her brother's death had made Ariane of Claredon a great heiress, a prize any nobleman would fight to possess.

Idly Ranulf rubbed his bare chest as he stared at the leaping flames, vaguely aware of the heat warming his naked loins.

He had met his intended bride only once—for the betrothal celebrations. Ariane had been a mere girl then, but he remembered her still: a long, thin body that held a coltish grace; pale hair a hue between flaxen and copper; plain, sharp-boned features dusted with freckles; and huge gray eyes that seemed to see more than he wanted to reveal.

Ranulf considered her youth an advantage. He had wanted a meek bride, someone young and malleable whom he could train to do his bidding, who could be taught obedience if not loyalty. He'd taken great care to ascertain her willingness for the marriage, desiring no repetition of his mother's faithlessness to his father.

Ariane had seemed innocent enough, even possessing a virginal sort of charm that had surprised and enchanted him. Time would have changed her, though, Ranulf suspected regretfully. By now she would have had ample opportunity to learn the talents that were so prevalent in her sex—the arts of cruelty and lies and betrayal.

Her birth and station alone gave him cause to be wary. From the cradle, his ordeals with noblewomen had marked his soul, just as his father's scourge had scarred his back. His own adulterous mother had condemned him to a life of torment, sentenced him to the hell of his father's rage. Because of her infidelity, he had been forced to fight for his birthright, his identity, his very existence.

In truth, he had little use for women, other than the pleasure their bodies afforded. He was a man with strong appetites, but he preferred a simple peasant instead of a highborn lady. A lusty wench whose base and modest needs were easily fulfilled, who made no pretense of understanding such principles as honor and constancy and faithfulness. Who would not scorn him for his ignoble origins.

Give him someone other than his betrothed, Ariane of Claredon.

Ranulf exhaled a reluctant sigh, reminding himself it was far too late for him to withdraw his suit. He would honor his word regarding the contract. When England was won and Henry's rule secure, then he would journey to Claredon and submit to the nuptials he had delayed for too long. Even if he would prefer to fight an entire enemy army rather than face his betrothed.

Realizing the absurdity of that thought, Ranulf laughed softly at himself. How had he been caught in this dilemma? His courage held hostage by a mere girl half his weight and a tenth his strength? What could she do to him, after all?

Deliberately, he shook his head, forcing himself to clear his mind. What need had he to concern himself with his bride—or with any female, for that matter? All he knew was fighting. All he wanted was a good battle or three. And yet . . . And yet his future was at stake. The moment he set foot in England, he would seal his fate. The only delay he could hope for would be revolts against the new king that needed quelling—

Ranulf was brought out of his unpleasant reverie by silken arms that entwined his waist from behind, by a lush, familiar, feminine body that pressed suggestively against his. Her delicate, stroking hands felt cool on his fire-warmed skin. Ranulf felt his tense muscles relax.

"She will not pleasure you as I do," Layla purred, nipping the corded muscle of his upper arm with her teeth.

"She?"

"Your English bride."

Ranulf grimaced. He had no desire to dwell on his bride, or discuss the subject of his marriage with his leman. "She is not English, but Norman, as are all the ruling families there."

"Norman, English . . . she will not delight you as Layla will."

"Enough." His hands came up to unclasp the concubine's

arms from around his waist. "I have no wish to speak of her."

Moving sinuously to stand before him, Layla pouted up at Ranulf. "Forgive me, lord. Layla had no desire to anger you."

His mouth curled in knowing amusement. "No? You delight in rousing my temper, wench, as you well know."

Unabashed, she leaned closer to press her lips against his breast, swirling her wicked tongue over his nipple . . . lower, through the mat of curling ebony hair covering his chest . . . and lower still, along his flaccid member . . . arousing him deftly as she knelt on the stone floor at his feet. "Only because I also know how to appease you afterward, my magnificent stallion," she throatily whispered against his swelling flesh.

"Aye," he agreed, his tone husky. Already he could feel his groin stirring, his organ stiffening, throbbing. "So why do you delay? Appease me now."

His hand on her shoulder, he drew Layla to his pulsing arousal. She knew what he wanted, what he needed from her. Her mouth curving in a feline smile, she closed her caressing fingers around the base of his burgeoning rod, now huge and thick, and took him in her hot mouth.

With a grimace of pleasure, Ranulf shut his eyes, his buttocks tightening rigidly as he thrust with slow, shuddering restraint into her slick heat. This was his last night at Vernay and he would make good use of it, of the exquisite skills the exotic Saracen possessed.

His hand rode her dark head as he tried to lose himself in the sensual pleasure she provided, as he tried unsuccessfully to forget his laughable dilemma. He, a powerful Norman warlord and one of Duke Henry's most able vassals, had turned craven.

Yet it was not his mighty enemies and their armies who were to blame, but a young noblewoman. A mere girl.

Absurdly, beyond all reason, despite all rational arguments with himself, he feared his own bride.

A bride he could not avoid facing very much longer.

Chapter 2

Claredon Keep, England: April 1155

His first response when Ranulf spied his winsome bride on the battlements was supreme wariness, followed swiftly by unwelcome surprise. The plain, skinny child he remembered from five years before bore little resemblance to the tall, regal beauty he was looking at now.

God's wounds! The recent reports of Ariane's striking loveliness had been exaggerated perhaps, but not overmuch, Ranulf admitted grudgingly. The setting sun turned her fair, plaited hair to palest flame, while her fine-boned profile could have been carved from alabaster.

His loins tightened instinctively—a stirring he abruptly quelled. He was never invulnerable to a comely woman, but this was no time to be lusting after his bride, certainly not if she was contemplating treason against the crown.

Ranulf voiced a quiet oath under his breath as he stood watching Ariane from the shadows. He had spent the past months quelling resistance to the new king throughout the length and breadth of England, but rebellion from this quarter was entirely unexpected. King Henry had counted Walter of Claredon one of his firm supporters, which made his betrayal all the more treacherous. Walter had joined Hugh Mortimer's revolt at Bridgenorth, thus earning Henry's legendary rage. Ranulf had been sent here to Claredon to seize the traitor's estates—and to apprehend Walter's daughter.

At present, she stood, cool and defiant, on the wall-walk overlooking the entrance gates, directing the preparations for the castle's defense. Everything below was chaos, the milling crowds and herds emitting a clamor of sound—shouts, thudding hooves, the squawks and squeals and brays of farm

20

animals—as they poured across the drawbridge into the outer bailey. No fools, the serfs and villagers of Claredon sought refuge behind the thick stone curtain walls of the keep, all fleeing the wrath of the Black Dragon.

All were unaware that the Black Dragon himself had entered the gates with the first wave of refugees hours before and now stood in the shadow of a stone alcove on the battlements, a mere pebble's toss from their lady.

"My lord?" his squire, Burc, whispered at his shoulder. "Do we arrest the demoiselle now or do we wait?"

"We wait."

He would allow his betrothed to prove her intentions. Her father was in open rebellion against King Henry, which warranted her detention as a political prisoner, but it would go easier with her if she denounced Lord Walter's treason and voluntarily surrendered his castle. It was still possible she would yield, although her current actions suggested otherwise. Judging from appearances, the Claredon heiress was girding for war.

Ranulf would have preferred to question her at once, but he would not risk approaching his bride yet, not until dusk fell to aid his disguise. The cowled monk's robe he wore concealed his face and untonsured hair, but his great height and powerful frame were difficult to mask. He had stooped his shoulders and broadened his girth with a cushion tied over his belly, but he preferred to avoid recognition. Having to fight his way through such a motley crowd would not suit his purpose.

Already the armored knights and archers arrayed along the battlements made the vulnerable flesh between his shoulder blades itch. He had left off his chain mail and sword when he'd donned his coarse brown monk's garb, and carried only a dagger as a weapon. His best squire, a lad chosen for his quick mind, would scarcely provide much support should the Claredon forces discover an enemy in their midst. Yet he'd elected religious garb as the least likely to arouse suspicion, while affording him the best opportunity to observe his betrothed—and put him in a better position to act should she defy the king's command and close the gates against him.

A development that seemed imminent, judging by the frantic preparations going forth.

Ranulf's jaw clenched. If his bride forced him to lay siege to the castle and risk his men's lives, she would feel the vengeance of his sword.

Narrowing his eyes, Ranulf studied Ariane with unwilling admiration. Her tall, graceful frame gowned in rust-red bliaud and gold-linked girdle appeared as slender as a willow, too delicate to lead a retinue of knights and men-at-arms in defiance of her new liege, King Henry. She would not be the first of Henry's subjects to attempt it, though, nor the last. Henry had been confronting unruly English barons since his first moment of arriving from Normandy four months ago. After being crowned king, he had moved swiftly to restore order in England, demolishing unlawful castles built during the late Stephen's reign, crushing revolts, and defeating any of Stephen's supporters who refused to swear fealty to their new ruler.

The current uprising was led by Hugh of Mortimer, who wished to set Stephen's bastard son William on the throne in Henry's stead. At this moment King Henry was besieging Mortimer's castles in Shropshire. And Ranulf had been sent to Berkshire to take possession of Walter of Claredon's demesne and to deal with his daughter.

At the moment she appeared deep in contemplation, a pose that only increased Ranulf's wariness and mistrust. In his experience, females of her noble class who thought overmuch were intent on mischief and scheming.

He watched as Ariane raised a hand to her brow and bowed her head. Was she weeping? Praying?

No matter. He could not be swayed by tears. And God could not save her from his wrath if she was intent on treason. If she chose to support the rebellion against England's lawful king, she would pay dearly for her betrayal.

The choice was hers to make.

"Shall we raise the drawbridge, my lady?" Simon Crecy asked quietly of his mistress. "Most of the villeins are accounted for."

"A few moments more," Ariane answered. "There may still be others who wish to seek the safety of Claredon."

She felt Simon move to stand beside her. As her father's chief vassal and commander of the garrison at Claredon,

Simon had been left behind with a force of knights and men-at-arms when Walter rode to join Hugh Mortimer. Ariane was grateful for his company, for it helped ease the great burden of responsibility she shouldered.

"Simon?"

"Aye, my lady?"

"You have done well. My father shall hear of your efforts."

Stealing a glance at him she saw him flush at her praise. They were of a height, but Simon was older than she by some dozen years and far more experienced in political and military matters. Ariane trusted him implicitly. She had always wondered if he might have sought her hand in marriage if not for her betrothal.

My perpetual betrothal, she thought bitterly.

Her fingers clenched as she forced the reflection aside. She had vowed not to dwell on her lost hopes, her faded dreams.

Lifting her chin, Ariane gazed out over the parapet wall at the newly sown fields of Claredon, at the shimmering river winding sinuously toward the horizon, golden in the fading rays of sunset. The scene looked so peaceful—an illusion, to be sure.

She had never known true peace. She'd been reared during one of the most turbulent periods in England's history, and while her father had managed by strategic combat and judicious political maneuverings to shield his estates from the devastation wreaked on much of England during Stephen's reign, no aspect of their lives had remained untouched. In the past ten years, Walter had spent a fortune erecting new stone curtain walls around Claredon in place of the wooden ones, yet no walls could stretch far enough to shield the surrounding countryside from an invading army. If the lord of Vernay laid siege to Claredon, he would first destroy fields and stores and the rude homes of the peasantry in an attempt to starve the castle inhabitants into submission.

And his army was on the march. The distraught messenger who had ridden frantically in from Bridgenorth this morning with the incredible news about her father's treason had also warned of the approach of the Black Dragon's forces.

Mother of God, how she dreaded the possibility of war. Was there a way to prevent it short of surrender? How could she spare the lives of her people and yet remain loyal to her father? She had promised to hold Claredon Keep in his absence, and she would sooner be drenched with scalding oil than fail him. She would not destroy what little faith he had placed in her.

"Simon?" Ariane asked in a troubled voice. "Think you we take the right course?"

Simon shook his dark head. "I know not, my lady. Yet I believe this is what my Lord Walter would have wished. You know your betrothed better than I."

"I doubt it. I met him but once, for a brief while, and that when I was a mere girl." Her mouth twisted in a joyless smile as she recalled her one startling meeting with Ranulf de Vernay.

He had been a fully grown man then, nearly ten years her senior. When he invited her to walk with him alone in the castle garden, she dared not refuse, but his sheer presence had awed her, rendered her completely tongue-tied. Those amber hawk's eyes had scrutinized her intently, as if she were his prey, driving her heart to her throat.

Yet, astonishingly, the lord of Vernay had seemed to understand her agitation and he had taken the time to ease her fears, indeed to charm her, chasing away her wariness, seducing her with his gentle teasing. To her utter amazement, he had asked if she consented to the betrothal.

Then, even before she had overcome her bewilderment, Ranulf had suddenly smiled at her, with a heart-stopping tenderness that incredibly, magically, melted the harshness from that cold, hard countenance.

She had lost more than her fear of Ranulf in that moment. She had lost her heart. She deemed the lord of Vernay a magnificent suitor, the embodiment of every girlhood dream. And she had vowed to herself then and there to make him a good, faithful wife.

What a fool she had been!

"I thought him kind and gentle," she murmured to Simon. "Can you credit how poor my judgment was?"

"I have heard fearsome things said of him."

She had heard the tales, too, over the years—of the Black Dragon's prowess in combat, of his merciless vengeance. His very name, taken from the device on his shield and banner, struck fear in the hearts of lesser men.

"Some say de Vernay is Henry's best field commander," Simon murmured. "And his most brilliant tactician. He is known to have challenged and defeated his own father in battle. A most unnatural son."

Ariane fell silent. Those tales of Lord Ranulf were the most shocking. His lady mother was said to have taken a peasant lover before Ranulf's birth, so that he might well be a lowborn freeman's offspring. Certainly Ranulf's noble father doubted his parentage. Yves de Vernay had refused, even after his two older sons had died, to acknowledge Ranulf as heir. The Black Dragon had claimed his inheritance at the point of a sword.

"We should fare well enough," Simon was saying. "Our forces are in position. We have adequate supplies—due to your own efforts, my lady. We can hold out for some time against a siege."

"And you sent word to my father at Bridgenorth."

"Two separate couriers, lady, to improve the chances of gaining through. If Lord Walter is free to come, he will."

If he is free.

Ariane shook her head. Her shock at the recent turn of events still had not faded. Her father had been charged with high treason for conspiring with Hugh Mortimer against the crown. She simply *could* not believe him guilty; she knew him too well.

"The drawbridge, my lady?" Simon urged gently, interrupting her troubled thoughts. " 'Tis dangerous to tarry longer."

"Yes." Gazing down at the approach to Claredon, Ariane realized that the final stragglers had entered the castle bailey. "We should proceed."

Turning, Simon called down to the keeper of the gate. Almost at once a tremendous grinding of chains sounded as the huge wooden bridge was slowly raised.

The action came none too soon, for in the far distance a golden swirl of dust could be seen on the horizon—the kind of cloud kicked up by a rapidly approaching army. Ariane felt the muscles of her stomach tense with dread.

The Black Dragon. Her betrothed. The man who should have been her husband long ere now.

The warrior who had never come to claim her as his bride.

Her nerves were shredded raw by the time the horde came to a plunging halt a safe distance from the castle walls. The sun had nearly set, yet she could see a force of some two hundred strong—a quarter comprised of fearsome Norman knights garbed in conical steel helmets and long tunics of chain mail, mounted on snorting destriers, with gleaming lances and tall shields at the ready. The rest were archers and foot soldiers wearing bullhide armor. A banner waved over the throng—a black dragon rampant on a scarlet field.

Before long, a single mailed knight broke from the ranks of horsemen and rode slowly forward, bearing a white pennon, seeking to parley. Ariane flinched when a short blast sounded from an enemy trumpet, even though she had known to expect it. She was grateful to have Simon Crecy standing beside her.

The rider halted his bay charger within hailing distance of the stone wall and called up to the defenders on the battlements:

"In the name of Henry, duke of Normandy and rightful king of England, you are commanded to open the gates!"

Taking a deep breath, Ariane answered, although her voice was neither as strong nor as clear as she would have liked. "Tell me, good sir, why should we open our gates when you plainly come prepared for war?"

There was a pause, as if her question had surprised the knight. "Because to refuse is treason. King Henry has ordered Walter of Claredon's arrest and awarded his lands and possessions to the lord of Vernay—who demands your immediate surrender. I carry the king's proclamation." His gauntleted hand raised a scroll for her to see.

Ariane forced herself to unclench her fingers, which had curled into fists. "I am the lady of Claredon. Do I have the honor of speaking with the lord of Vernay?"

"I am my lord's vassal, Payn FitzOsbern, demoiselle. Lord Ranulf has charged me with arranging the terms of your surrender."

She felt the slightest measure of tension ease from her body; this was only the Black Dragon's emissary.

"Your lord could not spare the time to come himself?"

she asked. "I should think if the disposition of Claredon were important to him, he would have ridden here with all due speed."

"My lady . . . he . . . has been delayed."

"Indeed?" Her tone was heavily laced with irony. "Yes, I can see how five years might be too brief a term to permit a visit to his intended bride."

FitzOsbern hesitated, obviously searching for words. "Demoiselle, will you open the gates?"

"I will discuss my course with Ranulf de Vernay and no other. You may tell him so."

A pause. "He will not be pleased with your answer."

Ariane forced herself to return a cool smile. Her betrothed's refusal to come to Claredon himself was a calculated insult, perhaps, but she could use it to her advantage. "Nonetheless, that is the answer you will give him."

She could almost feel the knight's frustration. "You refuse to surrender the castle then, my lady?"

"I repeat, I will gladly discuss the subject with my Lord Ranulf. Please convey my regards to him. That will be all, sir knight."

FitzOsbern gripped the haft of his pennon more tightly with his leather-gauntleted fist, clearly reluctant to accept his dismissal. Ariane remained watching until finally he wheeled his prancing destrier and rode back to join his lord's forces.

Slowly she let out the breath she had been holding. With luck she had managed to buy some time until the siege began—a day or two perhaps, and any delay could prove vital to her father's chances. As long as Walter possessed Claredon, he remained a force King Henry must reckon with. Even a convicted traitor might use his rich estates to bargain for his life.

Her response just now had not directly defied the king's command, Ariane consoled herself. Soon she would have to commit herself, though. The Black Dragon would doubtless be irate when he learned of her refusal to surrender the castle to his emissary, but in truth, she had no choice. It was imperative that she retain possession of Claredon in order to aid her father. And she would not disappoint him as she had so many times before. If it took her last breath, she would not fail him.

"Their actions suggest they are making camp, my lady," Simon observed.

Ariane nodded in weary resignation. In the gathering dusk, she could see knights dismounting, their squires scurrying to tend horses and weapons, while their archers positioned themselves in a defensive line opposite the castle. Soon they would erect pavilions and build cookfires—and Payn FitzOsbern would likely send a courier to his liege lord. Then Lord Ranulf might very well come himself.

Ariane shivered in the evening breeze. She would rather deal with a hundred of his envoys than the lord of Vernay himself.

"You are cold, demoiselle? Allow me to send a serf to the tower to fetch your mantle."

"Yes, thank you, Simon." Spring had come early to England this year, and yet the damp air held a bite she could feel through her fine woolen overgown and undertunic and her linen shift. No doubt, though, her apprehension sharpened the chill.

As Simon left her, she found herself bemoaning the frailties of a woman's body. If she were a man, she could have ridden out to challenge Ranulf's knights in combat . . .

Her lips compressed in a bitter smile. If she were a man, she might never have become acquainted with Ranulf de Vernay in the first place. Certainly she would never have been pledged to him in marriage so that her father might gain an ally for Claredon.

Sweet Mary, why could she not have been born male? How much better to be a son whom her father could count on to assume his barony and protect his hard-won holdings, rather than a disappointing daughter. What freedom to be a knight who could take up arms in defense of his demesne, rather than a pawn of men's political games! Or worse, a neglected bride required to suffer the whims of a reluctant bridegroom.

Of their own accord, her fingers curled into fists. Only to herself would Ariane acknowledge a deeper truth: that her hurt over Ranulf's long neglect might also be driving her resistance.

It hurt to be unwanted. To hear the whispers. She was the forgotten bride, the rejected one. *Is there something wrong with me that not even the promise of great wealth can overcome?* For years she had pondered that question, had agonized over her inadequacies. For five long, wasted years she had waited and worried and pined—until finally hope had dwindled, leaving only anger and bitterness and despair. Until her resentment against Ranulf festered like a poisoned wound.

Yet that was not her primary reason for defying him now. Her father's very life was at stake. If she surrendered his holdings, everything he had striven for would be forfeit. Worse, he would be rendered powerless, at the mercy of the king's justice. And in his absence, she was responsible for Claredon and its people, their lives and welfare. On her shoulders alone rested their fate.

As in countless times during the past, Ariane's gaze shifted to the east, focusing on a deep forest glade of birch and oak, some quarter league from the castle walls. The wood was said to be haunted by evil spirits and ruled by man-eating wolves, but she knew better. Only a handful of people were privy to the secret of those woods. *Will the inhabitants there be safe from the Black Dragon?*

Her eyes blurring at the sight, she forced her gaze away, focusing again on the enemy forces. She could still see the fierce black dragon on a red silk field boldly waving above the invading army. What would her mother have done in these difficult circumstances?

Why, Ranulf? Why did you never come for me?

Swallowing, she fiercely brushed away the tears of anger that stung her eyes. She could not afford the luxury of weeping, or the indulgence of self-pity. Her regrets would have to keep for another day. Now, more than ever, she had to be strong.

Defiantly, Ariane lifted her chin.

Let Ranulf de Vernay come to Claredon now. She was prepared to defend the castle and people against her vengeful betrothed, if need be.

And she would remain loyal to her father, even if her defiance made her guilty of treason.

Safe behind his concealing monk's robes, Ranulf watched his intended bride with increasing ire and bitter disappointment. A flaming torch had been set in a bracket in the parapet, casting an angelic glow about her as she stood in deep reflection. The innocent image was misleading, he was certain, as was the weary, troubled frown on her clear brow. No sweet, biddable wench, this. Her cunning ploy earlier was worthy of any sly deception perpetrated by the ladies of the Norman court—refusing to surrender the castle to FitzOsbern while at the same time not openly declaring her rebellion. Clever but mistaken. She would not succeed in evading the king's wrath by such tactics, Ranulf promised silently, or escape penalty for her defiance.

Ranulf's eyes narrowed as the knight called Simon drew a fur-trimmed mantle solicitously about her shoulders. There was evident intimacy and affection between the two of them. The affection of lovers? An irrational surge of jealousy speared through Ranulf. Ariane of Claredon belonged to *him*, just as her father's castle now did. She was his betrothed, soon to be his political hostage. If she was being faithless to him with her father's vassal, she would suffer the consequences. Just as she would pay if she chose to challenge his authority.

He had been charged with quelling resistance and imposing the king's will on the land, and he would not be gainsaid. Not by a woman. Most definitely not by his own bride. If she forced him to resort to violence, he would crush her without mercy.

Almost as if she had divined his thoughts, her head lifted slowly and she half turned, her troubled gaze searching the shadows where he stood.

Ranulf froze—and drew in his breath sharply at the vision of loveliness Ariane made in the glow of torchlight. Nay, the reports had not exaggerated, he thought as a shaft of desire shot through him with startling intensity. Where once she had been all bones and eyes, now she was slender curves and eyes, with gleaming tresses of pale copper that shimmered and rippled with life. An enchanting, beguiling combination.

The change disturbed Ranulf greatly. He might have forgiven a child her faulty judgment, for being misled by her advisors, but Ariane of Claredon was no longer a child. She was fully a woman. A noble lady quite capable of aiding a rebellion and supporting her father's treason.

And she was his to deal with.

He could not control his body's hard response at the thought of having such a defiant beauty in his power, yet before the stirring in his groin could swell to uncomfortable proportions, Ranulf set his jaw and tucked the cowl of his clerical garb more tightly around his face. Then he stepped forward, taking care to remain away from the circle of torch-light, keeping his gaze trained on his bride and her armored protector.

"A monk seeks audience with you, my lady," Simon advised her.

Ariane gave a start when the vassal's voice interrupted her brooding. With a sigh, she turned to greet the intruder—and halted abruptly. A dark shape had condensed out of the shadows ... tall, powerful ... ominous.

Her hand went to her throat. For the space of a dozen heartbeats she remained frozen, while the night sounds of the castle faded. The presence of her own soldiers, the plight of the refugees, the threat of an enemy army, were forgotten. She was only aware of the towering, motionless form shrouded in a blanket of darkness.

A frisson of fear ran down her spine at the obscure figure looming so threateningly near. The shadows thrown by the torchlight cast such a strange spell she could almost imagine the giant silhouette to be a menacing dragon.

It was simply fancy, she told herself with desperate calm. A deceptive trick of the light. Willing herself to show no fear, Ariane took a faltering step closer—and the fearsome image thankfully vanished. The light barely licked at the foot of his robes, but Ariane let out her breath in relief as she recognized his garb. It was only a monk. No danger here.

Her paralysis faded, yet her uneasiness remained. A man of such height and bulk would be powerful, strong; such a giant could easily be a warrior. Even across the distance that separated them, she could feel his towering masculine presence.

Wondering at her strange awareness, at her sense of fore-boding, she reminded herself that she had her own men to protect her.

"Greetings, demoiselle," the shadow said softly.

Something within her stirred at that deep, muted voice. She felt the oddest sense of . . . intimacy? Familiarity?

She went still, while strange sensations shivered through her. "Do I know you, sir monk?"

"I think not, my lady."

She hesitated, divided between wariness and curiosity. He was a compelling figure, for his sheer mystery if nothing else. His hands, only partially hidden by the wide sleeves of his robe, were large, strong, long-fingered . . . capable of great violence or tender compassion?

With effort Ariane shook off her fanciful imaginings. Taking another step closer, she peered at the hooded face still in shadow, wondering why he was here and what he wanted of her.

Ranulf, imagining uncomfortably that she could penetrate his disguise, bowed his head with feigned respect, and raised the pitch of his voice to a soft tenor. "I wished to express my gratitude for giving refuge to a poor monk. I was making my way to the monastery at Frotham when my journey was interrupted by the fleeing villeins. I thought it wiser to follow them to the safety of your keep."

"You are welcome to Claredon's hospitality, sir monk." She waited politely for him to continue, but returned his gaze warily, he noted, her clear gray eyes watchful and intent.

"I wondered, my lady, if at this time of trouble I might aid you in some manner. Since your noble father is away, you might wish for guidance from wiser heads."

He saw her mouth twist in the faintest of smiles. "Prayers would not go amiss, good brother, but unless you are versed in military stratagems, I shall rely upon my father's vassals for counsel."

"Mean you to declare your opposition to the lord of Vernay, then?"

Her expression turned cool, Ranulf observed, but she avoided giving him a direct answer, saying instead, "I regret you were detained, since I fear we may be under siege for a long while. I dare not lower the drawbridge for you to leave Claredon, but if you wish, we could have you lowered from the walls, so you might safely effect an escape."

Under siege for a long while? Then she intended to refuse him entrance?

"You misunderstand me, lady. My concern was not for my own safety, but for the good people here. Would it not be wiser to surrender the castle to the lord of Vernay at once?"

"Wiser for whom?"

"For you. For your villeins." At her frowning hesitation, Ranulf added swiftly, "You may confide your fears to me, noble child."

"A comforting thought," she replied with questionable sincerity. "It is unfortunate then that I have already confided my fears to God."

He had overstepped the boundaries allowed even a man of the cloth, he realized. He glanced at Simon, noting the knight's fist resting cautiously on the hilt of his sword. "Forgive me, demoiselle. I meant no insult by my curiosity. I simply wished to offer help."

Ranulf felt her intent gaze searching his monk's cowling again, as if to read his shadowed expression. "I am grateful for your interest, truly. It is just that . . ."

"Yes, demoiselle? Just what?"

Ariane turned away, gazing out over the darkened countryside, faintly illuminated by the flickering campfires of a besieging force.

"I am unaccustomed to discussing my troubles with anyone but our own priest," she said finally.

"You have endured great troubles of late, it seems."

It was a leading remark, she knew, probing with a gentle intensity she could not resist. "No more than most."

"But this current crisis . . . Lord Ranulf's army at your gates. He is your betrothed, is he not?"

"Yes," she replied, her voice edged with bitterness. "Regretfully."

"Regretfully? You are not eager to wed him?"

When she remained silent, the monk added musingly, "I wonder that you agreed to the betrothal. Although many a bride has been persuaded by force, the Church does require the consent of the lady before sanctioning marriage."

"I had no objections to marriage once," Ariane said softly. Her hopes still had been very much alive . . . then. "Lord Ranulf was my father's choice for my husband, but in truth, I was pleased to wed a knight with the strength to preserve the holdings I will one day inherit. A woman needs a husband capable of maintaining authority, of protecting the land. There can be no security otherwise.''

"A judicious philosophy. And your father made a wise choice in knights.''

"I once thought so. The lord of Vernay is one of the most powerful barons in Normandy—by his own ruthless efforts.''

"You consider him ruthless? Was he unkind to you?''

"No." Indeed, she remembered her shock that such a fierce warrior as Lord Ranulf could be kind and gentle to a nervous young maid.

"Then why do you regret your betrothal?''

Because for nearly five years he had stayed away, Ariane reflected with silent anguish. Five interminable years during which she had been left to languish in her father's household, pitied by her friends and acquaintances. She was almost twenty now. By that advanced age other women had married and borne several children. But she remained unwedded and unbedded, a maiden still, innocent of passion, of life. "Because I discovered the truth about the ignoble lord of Vernay,'' Ariane whispered bitterly.

"The truth?''

"He is no true knight, but a grasping, baseborn pretender to nobility ... a usurper without principle or honor, who claimed his father's demesne at the point of a sword. I would that I had never heard his name.''

Going rigid at her quiet denunciation, Ranulf missed the bitterness in her scathing tone and heard only the scorn, a scorn that stung like the cut of a hundred knives—or the scourge that had once flayed his back raw. He was accustomed to the disdain ladies of her class held for his lack of birthright, but it sliced deeper coming from this woman.

Ranulf felt his fists clench with the familiar rage. "Do you mean to deny him entrance?'' he demanded grimly, forgetting his masquerade.

Ariane frowned as she suddenly recollected herself. Why would a man of the clergy concern himself with such worldly matters? And why was she speaking to him so frankly? She could tell a servant of God more than she would others, but he was still a stranger.

Uneasy about her indiscretion, she glanced over her shoulder at the shadowed figure of the monk, replying cautiously,

"My father charged me with defending Claredon in his absence. I cannot give up his castle without first knowing his wishes."

"Even though Claredon is his no longer? A rebel's estates are forfeit to the crown, and it is said Walter of Claredon has partaken in the barons' revolt, an attack on his sovereign lord."

Her back stiffened perceptibly, Ranulf noted. "Fools say many foolish things, sir monk."

"Then Walter has not joined the revolt?"

"I know not what has occurred. But when he rode for Bridgenorth, it was not his intention to declare against the king."

"Mayhap he would not make you privy to his intentions."

"Because I am a mere daughter?" Her chin lifted. "I assure you, my father would inform me of any plan of such momentous consequence. And he is no traitor."

"Yet Hugh Mortimer has raised a rebellion, which makes your father, as Mortimer's vassal and supporter, guilty of treason—unless he repudiates his oath of fealty."

"I am well able to grasp the politics of the situation," Ariane replied acerbically. "Despite my frail sex, my mind is fully functioning."

Remembering with difficulty the role he had assumed, Ranulf bit back the retort that sprang to his lips. From the silver flash of anger in her gray eyes, he thought his betrothed might be preparing to voice another scathing remark, but she tucked her clenched hands within the long, sweeping sleeves of her gown, and said with admirable calm, "My first allegiance I owe to my father. I will not surrender his castle until I have proof of his guilt. Now, if you will forgive me, sir monk, I have much that requires my attention."

He had received his dismissal, Ranulf realized with unreasoning fury. He wanted badly to take his defiant bride by the shoulders and shake her, or to haul her into his arms and commit some other more passionate, less violent act upon her person, but to touch her would immediately bring the castle guard to her defense. And to tarry would only arouse suspicion. He would have to postpone their reckoning for the nonce.

He bowed low and gave her his blessing, then turned

abruptly and made his way silently along the wall-walk to disappear among the shadows.

Ariane stood there long after he had gone, unable to shake her sense of foreboding. He had probed too many raw wounds for comfort, his bold questions only adding to the turmoil and uncertainty in her mind. Had she taken the wrong course of action? Would yielding to the Black Dragon be the wiser choice?

While she pondered, Ranulf gestured for his squire to follow him and stalked down the stone steps to the crowded yard, his jaw clenched. A cowherd scurried out of his path, but Ranulf never faltered as he strode toward the distant gate that gave access to the inner bailey. He needed to make certain he was allowed into the tower itself this night, to sleep in the great hall with the lord's vassals and household servants.

The wench had forced his hand. From her own lips he had heard Ariane declare her intentions. She meant to defy him— and her king as well. But by God's wounds, he would crush her defiance, Ranulf vowed, and exact recompense for her rebellion. He would conquer his rebel bride and take pleasure in so doing.

At the thought, Ranulf cursed silently, tasting a bitterness like bile on his tongue. Coming to a halt at the gate to the inner bailey, he stood there trembling as a dark cloud of rage dulled his vision—a black fury that was overwhelmingly familiar. He had lived this grim tale once before, when his noble sire had denied him his rightful inheritance. The pain was still raw and fresh, an unhealed wound festering inside him, unlike the welt of scars on his back.

He had fought his own father—and now he would have to fight his betrothed.

You should feel satisfaction. Your bride has presented you with sufficient reason to break your longstanding betrothal, Ranulf reminded himself savagely. Her rebellion was cause enough to repudiate the marriage. Yet instead of satisfaction, he felt an acid disappointment that Ariane of Claredon had chosen to support her treasonous father.

Such loyalty might be admirable, were it not so imprudent; she risked imprisonment and worse by such a course. But was loyalty truly her motive? Perhaps she was merely protecting herself in attempting to avoid arrest. Ariane would be well aware that as a political prisoner, she would be accorded none of the liberties and privileges she now enjoyed. A traitor's daughter would possess fewer rights than a field serf.

But her defiance seemed foolish, Ranulf reflected grimly. If she were truly clever, she would have forsaken her father and welcomed *him* as the new lord of Claredon, in hopes of securing his favor and mitigating the king's retribution.

Yet she, like Walter, was guilty of treason. By rights these entire estates were forfeit, her person subject to arrest.

And he, the Black Dragon of Vernay, would insure swift justice. Ariane of Claredon was now his enemy, her castle and lands his for the claiming.

Besieging or destroying Claredon Keep and the surrounding countryside or risking the lives of his men unnecessarily, however, formed no part of his plans. Not if he could succeed by easier means. He was prepared to take the castle, but on his own terms. Claredon boasted more knights than could be easily defeated, yet he would not need to use overwhelming force if he could turn the circumstances to his own advantage. And in this case, guile would serve him in better stead than open violence.

Quelling any inclination toward lenience, Ranulf forced himself to move. Disguised as a monk, followed by his squire, he gained entrance to the inner bailey and made his way up the outer stairway of the immense stone keep, to the second story and the great hall, now a scene of chaos as serfs and armed men ran to and fro.

He smiled grimly as he melted into the crowd.

The battle was set to begin—a battle he would win in short order.

Chapter 3

The tall night candle sputtered, its flickering glow probing beyond the parted bed curtains, sending faint shadows dancing across the pale beauty in the bed. Ranulf held his breath as he gazed down at the woman slumbering so peacefully. In the golden half-light, she was too lovely to be real.

Her fair, copper-tinged hair spilled over her naked shoulders, shimmering and glorious, caressing the gentle rise of a breast that peered beneath the edge of the woolen coverlet. His nostrils caught the subtle woman's scent of her sleep-warmed body, an alluring fragrance that stroked his primal, masculine senses and kindled a desire as intense as any he'd ever known. A muscle tensed in Ranulf's jaw at the effort to keep from reaching out to her.

He could see the faint pulse throbbing in her white throat as he stood drinking in Ariane's beauty. Pale and perfect. Delicate as a rose. Innocent and vulnerable as a babe ... Except that she was no babe, nor child either. She was a fully grown woman, who stirred his passions as no wench ever had.

He wanted to touch her.

Without thinking, he reached down to graze the soft skin of her brow with his thumb, then drew back abruptly, cursing himself for his weakness. When she awakened, the scorn in her silver-gray eyes would flay him without mercy.

And yet he could not resist the temptation. Unwillingly, he ran his fingers over the pale curve of her cheek, tracing the fragile bone and delicate hollow beneath. Her soft sigh as she stirred beneath his touch was a whisper of sound, a lover's plea.

His body hardened as heated images flickered before his eyes.... Ariane shuddering and straining beneath him....

Ariane willing and eager, welcoming him into her bed, into her body. . . .

A bitter smile twisted Ranulf's mouth. She would never be eager for his touch. She rued their betrothal, rued ever hearing his name. She would be glad to be free of him.

He is no true knight. A grasping, baseborn pretender to nobility.

He should have felt relief that she found their betrothal so repugnant. Should have been pleased that her own defiant actions released him from any obligation toward her. He had been prepared to honor his word, but now he need not feel remorse for delaying his arrival for so long, or for repudiating their union. In truth, it was fortunate he had discovered her true feelings—the contempt she harbored for him—in time, before he was irrevocably tied to her.

And yet . . . a hollow ache he could not explain centered in Ranulf's chest, along with other, less precise feelings of turmoil.

The savage rage he'd felt earlier toward her had faded, leaving behind a familiar emptiness. His irrational fury, Ranulf realized in some dark corner of his mind, had not been directed at Ariane so much as at his own despised father, for making him fight for what rightfully was his.

The battle for Claredon would be similar to his long-ago struggle for Vernay, Ranulf acknowledged, yet it was not vengeance that drove him this time, but duty. He almost felt a measure of regret that he would be compelled to take Ariane hostage, but he had no choice in the matter. Henry's orders were clear. A traitor's lands were automatically forfeit, and swift retribution against Walter of Claredon would serve as a lesson to others who would defy Henry's rule. Moreover, Ariane's own actions had sealed her fate, Ranulf reminded himself. Refusing the king's order to surrender the castle made her a traitor to the crown. He could perhaps understand her defense of the castle and her loyalty to her father, but he could not condone it, nor allow her defiance to continue.

I would that I had never heard his name.

"But you have heard my name, demoiselle," Ranulf whispered bleakly.

With a muted sigh, he settled one hip on the high bed, beside his sleeping betrothed. Carefully he lifted the pale, thick tendrils of her hair away from her ear and pressed the delicate line of her jaw beneath, prepared to wake her quietly.

Her dream seemed so very real. The gentle rasp of pressure over her skin . . . the seductive warmth against her cheek . . . the lush, sensual pleasure of a caressing rhythm . . .

A lover's stroking hand?

My beloved, have you come for me at last?

Within the drugged oblivion of slumber, Ariane arched against the unfamiliar heat, aching for some unnamed fulfillment. Her body seemed aflame with need. Her eyelids felt so heavy . . . yet she could almost see him . . . her dream lover . . . tall and powerful, godlike in countenance and bearing. His passion was just as she had always imagined it would be: fierce . . . tender . . . overwhelming. Blindly she tried to reach for him, but her arms remained frustratingly pinned at her sides.

She could almost feel his weight beside her, his voice a low murmur as his strong, caressing hand moved slowly along her jaw to gently brush her lips. . . .

The subtle pressure turned insistent. With a sense of bewilderment, Ariane forced open her eyes—and blinked in the glow of candlelight. It was yet nighttime, but the damask curtains of her bed had been pulled aside to allow in the light of the immense candle that burned the night long. Above her loomed a dark form, a shadowed face, while his fingertips pressed warningly against her lips.

"Do not cry out, demoiselle. Do you comprehend?"

Her grogginess fled with the sharp awareness of danger. Her eyes widened as she stared at the intruder. No dream lover, this. Nor was it one of her tirewomen come to awaken her. This was flesh-and-blood man, whose broad shoulders and powerful, shadowed form seemed intimately familiar.

"Do you comprehend?" he repeated more urgently, his thumb moving caressingly over her lower lip.

The deep, husky voice was familiar as well. She wondered if she had heard those harsh tones recently. A dark, cowled figure came to mind—and yet he lacked the tonsured baldness of a cleric. His hair was black as midnight, with an apparent tendency to curl, but she could not make out his shadowed features. His scent held a disturbing appeal—horses and leather and determined male, overlaid with a hint of spice.

Not answering his question, she dared to lower her gaze, trying to see more of him. He no longer wore the hooded robe, but a dark-colored tunic of fine, embroidered wool, with a jewel-handled dagger sheathed at his waist. His girth had shrunk mightily as well, although the shoulders were as broad as they had been earlier this evening.

"Sir monk?" she whispered, her voice fracturing with uncertainty.

"No monk, lady. The Black Dragon of Vernay at your service."

"Nay. . . ." Her heart, which already thudded erratically in her breast, leapt in alarm. She lay naked beneath the covers, vulnerable and unarmed, while her vengeful betrothed sat brazenly at her side, on her very bed.

Hardly aware of her actions, Ariane made a frantic lunge toward the other side of the bed, desperate to escape him, but found herself impeded by the covers and Ranulf's lightning-swift reflexes as he grasped her bare shoulder and held her fast. When she screamed to alert her women, he pushed her back down among the pillows and covered her mouth with a calloused palm.

"Do not act the fool," he ordered softly. "I shall not harm you. Not unless you resist. Do you understand me?"

When she nodded once, rigidly, he eased his palm from her mouth. Trying to calm her panic, Ariane dragged a ragged breath of air into her constricted lungs.

His searching gaze was wary. "Will you yield to me, demoiselle?"

"Do . . . do I have a choice?"

The harsh lines of his features softened in the dim light as Ranulf smiled briefly. "None whatsoever."

His arrogant assumption of superiority was as mortifying as it was valid. He could overpower her with ease, she knew quite well—a dragon striking down a kitten. If she chose to fight, she would only suffer for it. And yet she could not simply surrender meekly. . . .

Her right arm had come free in the struggle, Ariane realized dimly. Not giving herself time to think, she groped blindly for the dagger at his waist and miraculously made contact. Her fingers curling around the handle, she drew back her arm in order to strike.

The gleam of polished steel flashed in the dim light inches from his face, but he was a knight trained in warfare, with instincts honed to a razor's edge. His hand shot out to catch her wrist, halting her blow. His grip tightening with a pressure that made her cry out, he wrested the deadly blade from her grasp and flung it across the bed.

Cursing softly, Ranulf shoved both of Ariane's hands up over her head and pressed her down with his body, pinning her helplessly beneath him. Her gasp of shock was loud in the quiet chamber as she took his weight.

Her heart was racing, more in fury than fear, but she could not struggle, could not move a muscle. His angry face was so close she could feel the soft rush of his breath against her lips, could sense the tension in his clenched jaw. Then his smoldering gaze met hers.

Their eyes locked, while a strange awareness passed between them. For the space of a dozen heartbeats, time seemed to stand still ... a long sensually charged spell, tremulous, quivering. A moment fraught with tension, with danger ... and something more.

Ariane found herself drowning in the shadowed glimmer of Ranulf's eyes. They were enemies, not lovers. He would not kiss her ... would he?

His gaze had dropped to her lips, and he hesitated, as if considering. His eyes narrowing, his gaze moved lower still, raking her slowly, along the column of her throat, her collarbone, her bare chest.... She froze, her breath arrested, as his expression shifted subtly.

Never before had she questioned the custom of sleeping unclothed, a practice shared by nobles and serfs alike, but she wished fervently now that she had at least her shift to cover her bareness. Ranulf was staring at her right breast showing beneath the wool coverlet, the rose-tipped mound pale and naked in the candle's glow. Masculine speculation shone in his amber eyes, a glitter of admiration that she had often seen upon the faces of her father's men when they hungered for a willing castle wench.

Nervously Ariane tried to ease her body lower beneath the covers in a fruitless effort to hide her nakedness, but Ranulf prevented her, pressing her down with his body, subduing her movement.

When his gaze lifted once more to meet hers, his mouth was curved faintly. " 'Tis a first, demoiselle, I admit. Never before have I had a damsel beneath me in bed who sought to stab me . . . or one who managed to relieve me of my own dagger. Usually a wench is interested solely in the pleasure I give her."

Her heartbeat quickening at the seductive promise in his tone, Ariane shivered uncontrollably. If Ranulf wished to have her, if he wished to deal violently with her, she could do little to prevent him.

Not daring to breathe, Ariane stared up at his shadowed face, searching the harsh features above her. His raven hair, thick and shining, fell forward to brush his prominent cheekbones and the muscular grooves that bracketed his square jaw.

"Will you yield?" he repeated, his voice holding a new huskiness.

"Aye." Her whisper was a bare rasp of sound in the taut silence.

Thankfully, to her surprise and utter relief, he released his hold and sat up.

"W-Why have you come?" she demanded shakily, snatching up the covers to shield her body from his gaze. "What . . . do you want of me?"

The heated gleam in his eyes only darkened, while his lips curved again in that infuriating half-smile. "Your demesne, demoiselle, simply that. I've come to claim your father's holdings, which are now mine."

"*Yours?*"

"Aye, mine. Given to me by Henry's decree."

"Stolen, you mean!" Impotence made her lash out unwisely. "Exacted by guile. You crept into Claredon like a thief, disguised as a servant of God, no less. 'Tis blasphemous!"

Her furious accusation was met with a cool smile. "Mayhap. But I do not take by force what I can take by wit."

"Or *treachery*."

"Had you surrendered to my vassal, FitzOsbern, I would not have been obliged to employ such a ruse."

"You are despicable."

His dark countenance turned suddenly ruthless in the glow of candlelight, making Ariane abruptly recall how completely vulnerable her position was.

"You dare accuse me of treachery, demoiselle, of despicable acts, when you seek to keep from me what is mine by right?"

Desperately she thought back to their discussion on the castle walls. What precisely had she said to him? "My father charged me with holding Claredon—"

"So you contend. But you failed abominably in your aim, did you not? You are now my prisoner."

Fury and despair warred in her eyes. "What do you intend?"

"At the onset, to gain the surrender of the castle garrison. I doubt your men will wish to risk your life. Once they realize I have their lady in my grasp, they will quickly lay down their arms."

"Are you such a coward that you would make war on women?"

"Have a care, demoiselle." The hard voice had turned softly menacing. "You stand guilty of treason. I could have you hanged and no one would gainsay me."

When she remained silent, he reached for her again, his hand closing gently over her throat, forcing her chin up. Those long, battle-roughened fingers had the power to crush the life from her, Ariane realized with renewed fear. She could feel her heart hammering wildly as Ranulf's golden gaze bored into hers. "Do not defy me, lady. You will not win. I will quash you as I would a flea."

Ariane bit her lip so fiercely that it stung. She knew his warning was no idle boast. Within his corded, muscular frame lay the might of two normal men.

He released his grip on her throat and leaned back, bracing his weight on one hand. "Dress yourself."

"Why?" she managed to ask in a shaky voice.

"Because I command it. And because you doubtless have no wish to be paraded naked before your household for all to gawk at." He cocked one dark eyebrow at her. "Such treatment is only befitting a traitor, but I will spare you the indignity if you accept your defeat with proper meekness."

Meekness! It was all Ariane could do to clamp down on the retort that sprang to her tongue.

"Why do you tarry? I gave you a command." *And I expect immediate obedience,* his tone said clearly.

Not daring to delay any longer, she attempted to take the woolen coverlet with her to cover her nakedness, but Ranulf's hand came up to close over hers. Holding her apprehensive gaze, he deliberately tugged the fabric from her grasp. "There is no need for such modesty between us."

Her eyes widened. "Do you mean to watch?" she asked incredulously.

"Aye, I must. I cannot trust you out of my sight." That maddening grin flashed again. "Not that I consider such duty a hardship. I've always found it a great pleasure to observe a comely wench as she leaves her bed, flushed from sleep—or more arduous activity."

When she remained immobile, he added silkily, "Must I dress you myself, demoiselle? I assure you, you would not wish for my services."

Gritting her teeth, Ariane forced herself to throw off the other covers—a difficult task with Ranulf sitting on much of them—and slipped through the bed curtains on the opposite side. Her hope for privacy was short-lived, though; almost lazily Ranulf leaned over to part the bed curtains, giving him a clear vantage.

Shaking with rage and fear, Ariane gave him her back while he remained casually lounging on the bed. Never before had she been so grateful for her hip-length hair, which shielded much of her nakedness. Even so, she could feel Ranulf's gaze boldly traveling over her as she fumbled for the clothing that her tirewoman had left folded on a chest beside the bed.

Hastily she dragged on her shift before risking a nervous glace over her shoulder. The lout was grinning at her, she realized. An arrogant, appreciative smirk that made her blood boil. Sweet Virgin, how she wanted to box his ears!

"Your curves have filled out since last I saw you," he murmured wickedly. "The effect is quite appealing. Highly arousing to a man."

Her jaw clenched so hard the muscles ached. Not only was his provocative taunt inflaming for its sheer brazenness, but it reminded Ariane of the fierce resentment she'd harbored against the lord of Vernay for neglecting her for so many years. She dared not reply, though; to answer as scathingly as she wished would be to put her life at risk.

With a fervent effort at control, she reached for her woolen bliaud, not bothering with the undertunic. Drawing the gown on with a jerk, she smoothed the skirt and struggled to tie the laces under her arms. Then, shunning hose, she stepped into her shoes and turned defiantly to face Ranulf.

Her voice held the slightest quaver when she spoke. "Now what?"

"You will serve as my hostage," Ranulf answered as he retrieved the dagger she'd tried to steal from him and rose from the bed with remarkable grace for so large a man. "As surety for the good conduct of your father's knights."

To her complete startlement, he fetched her mantle from a wall peg and drew it around her shoulders. "Shall we proceed, my lady?"

"Why do you bother to ask?" Ariane couldn't help saying. "You have already informed me I have no choice. That I am your prisoner."

"Aye, you are. A pity."

For a moment he stood looking down at her, a thoughtful frown on his face. Slowly then, he lifted his hand to caress her cheekbone with the lightest of pressures, almost as if he meant to reassure her. His tone was gentle when he murmured, "When you have had time for reflection, you will agree that this is the better course."

That soft, seductive voice—his monk's voice—reminded her forcibly of Ranulf's treachery, made her recall all the years of misery and uncertainty she had endured at his hands—and why she had to resist his deceitful tenderness now.

"Better for whom?" Ariane retorted bitterly.

"For you . . . for your people. For my men. There will be less bloodshed this way. And I can better serve my king if I don't lose valuable men fighting unnecessary battles."

"And what of my father's men? What will be their fate?"

"We will discuss it further when I am in command of the castle. Now, where does your garrison commander sleep? The knight called Simon?"

"You . . . won't harm him?"

"Not unless he chooses to fight me. He is the logical man to deal with to achieve a surrender. Where he leads, the others will follow. Take me to him, demoiselle—and not a sound from you. I have no wish to alert the household."

With one hand grasping her upper arm, the other holding his jeweled dagger at the ready, Ranulf guided her to the large oaken door and slowly drew it open. As they passed by the large dormitory where her women lay soundly sleeping on pallets and in curtained slumber niches built into the wall, Ariane grimaced in dismayed disgust. Not one of them had roused when Ranulf stole into her bedchamber, intent on taking her prisoner.

Her apartments were located on the fourth floor of the massive stone tower. Directly below on the third lay the lord's solar and the large chamber which served as a workroom for the woman of Claredon, where most of the spinning and weaving and sewing was done. The second and main story was taken up almost entirely by the great hall, the center of activity of any castle, while on the ground floor, inaccessible from the bailey without, lay the kitchen and storerooms.

Torches set in wall brackets lit their way down the winding stone steps of the tower. No sentries came to her rescue, a fact Ariane greeted with mounting anger, until she remembered that the men who were awake would be guarding the castle walls in case of a siege by the Black Dragon.

She shook her head in weary disbelief. Ranulf's plan was indeed cunning. He had made use of Claredon's every vulnerability, taking shameful advantage of her weakness. She felt dazed, stunned, by the sudden turn of events; horrified and shamed by the ease of Ranulf's victory. Her father had asked her to hold this place till he returned, but she had failed him sorely, losing his castle in a few short hours.

All was quiet in the great hall, Ariane saw with disappointment. After the excitement of the day, the household folk and favored serfs were sprawled on pallets arrayed alongside the walls. When a shadow separated itself from a stone arch, she almost gasped.

It was just a lad, Ariane realized, but he held a gleaming sword in his hand.

"My lord," the youth whispered conspiratorially. "I found a weapon, as you commanded."

Sheathing his dagger in the scabbard at his waist, Ranulf accepted the sword and tested its weight. "Excellent, Burc. You may accompany me now. I have need of you."

"Aye, milord." An edge of eagerness threaded the young man's tone.

"Where does the knight Simon sleep?" Ranulf asked Ariane.

"I am not certain," she said, prevaricating.

With a rough movement, he tightened his grip on her arm and jerked her upright. "I will warn you but once, demoiselle. Never, *never* lie to me." His expression had turned harsh, vengeful, his eyes cold and merciless.

Although trembling inwardly, Ariane lifted her chin proudly, meeting his gaze without flinching. "You may find him yourself. I will not aid you."

Ranulf returned her stare with welling anger and reluctant respect. He had to admire her courage, no matter how infuriating. She had not taken fright when he'd surprised her in her bed, when many other wenches would be hysterical with fear by now. Nor had she resorted to pleading, or attempted to sway him with the artifice of tears.

"Milord," Burc offered uneasily. "The one called Simon has not entered the hall. But the armory is below in the bailey, along with the military barracks. Mayhap he is sleeping there with his men."

His jaw hardening, Ranulf nodded curtly. Allowing Ariane's defiance to pass, he ordered Burc to fetch a torch.

She exhaled slowly in relief. When he guided her toward the antechamber that led to the main entrance door, she tried to hold back, but his grip tightened cruelly on her arm, forcing her to keep pace with his long strides.

The night breeze was chill on her face as they descended the outer stair of the tower to the yard, but it was fear that made her shiver uncontrollably. All too soon they crossed the large inner court to a series of wooden buildings that housed the stables and military garrison.

Ariane approached the barracks with growing trepidation, praying Simon would be patrolling the battlements. When Ranulf pounded on the wooden door with the hilt of his sword, she took a deep breath in preparation. When the door swung open, she gave a piercing scream of warning.

"Simon, flee, I beg you! 'Tis a trap!"

She heard Ranulf's vivid curse, which instantly was echoed by the clatter of armor and the sound of booted feet. Almost as swiftly, their small party was suddenly surrounded by men bristling with weapons, outnumbered twenty to one.

A dozen archers had raised drawn bows, aiming at Ranulf's back, but he had brought the blade of his sword to rest across Ariane's throat.

"You will lay down your arms if you have a care for your lady," he ordered.

Her father's chief knight, unhelmeted but still dressed in chain mail, came slowly through the portal, his sword held neutrally at his side.

His gaze swung from Ariane to Ranulf. Evidently comprehending her captor's deadly intent, Simon demanded, "What are your terms?"

"I will spare her life in exchange for the complete surrender of the castle."

"We have an army at our gates. Why should I surrender the castle to *you?*"

"Because the army is *mine.* I am the lord of Vernay."

A murmur went around the crowd, interspersed with startled whispers of the words, "Black Dragon."

Simon stared with dawning comprehension. "The monk."

"A clever deduction. How unfortunate for Claredon that your perception came too late."

Ariane clenched her teeth at the faint amusement in Ranulf's voice. She knew Simon's expression of frustrated impotence was mirrored on her own features. And she could see him wavering.

"You will order your knights to surrender," Ranulf repeated more forcefully.

"You will spare their lives?" Simon asked.

"I will grant them honorable terms. Those who comply will be allowed to ransom their freedom. Those who refuse . . ." He let the threat remain unspoken.

"And my lady?" the knight pressed. "What will become of her?"

"If she will submit fully to me and acknowledge me as lord, then no harm will come to her."

Ariane bit her lip hard. She could not simply change her loyalties as Ranulf demanded; her allegiance was to her father.

"Simon, pay him no heed," she said with quiet desperation. "There are only two of them. They could be overpowered."

The knight shook his head. "Forgive me, my lady. I could not live with myself if I allowed harm to come to you."

Even as he said the words, Ranulf's squire gave a shout of warning, "My lord, behind you!"

With lightning-swift instinct, Ranulf half turned while shifting his sword from Ariane's throat and raising the blade to deflect the blow aimed at his head. In a clang of steel, he managed to ward off his attacker—a mailed knight who had crept up behind him—and return a blow of his own.

Urgently Ranulf spun fully to face his opponent, his weight balanced precariously on his heels. Defending himself against the surprise assault was less difficult than keeping hold of Ariane while shielding her from danger.

And yet his skill stood him in good stead. A timely thrust, a slicing parry, and he managed to regain the offensive. Another slashing blow and he penetrated the chain mail of the knight's sleeve. Giving a cry of pain, the man dropped his sword and clutched his bleeding arm.

Unfazed by his exertions, Ranulf resumed his lethal hold of Claredon's lady and directed a fierce gaze at her chief vassal. "For the last time, will you surrender?"

Simon, with a sorrowful glance at her, nodded. As he commanded his men to disarm, Ariane hung her head in anguish, unable to bare the stinging shame of their defeat.

With a dazed sense of unreality, she listened to Ranulf's orders regarding the disposition of the garrison troops present. In too short a time, his collaborator, Burc, had rounded up all the Claredon men in sight and herded them within a vacant storeroom, barring the door against escape.

"Now the drawbridge," Ranulf prodded Simon. "You will direct it lowered for my army."

Giving no argument, Simon led the way across the inner bailey by torchlight, with Ariane and Ranulf following, the squire Burc bringing up the rear. The guard at the gate balked initially, but then capitulated after a brief word from Simon about the threat to their lady's life.

Passing through the gate, the small party made its way slowly across the expanse of the now-crowded outer bailey, while serfs and animals scurried from the Black Dragon's path. Terror hung thick in the air; the rumor of what was afoot had spread throughout the castle grounds like wildfire.

Ariane stumbled once in the dark, but she felt Ranulf's arm tighten about her waist, supporting her easily. Helplessly she watched as Simon order the armed sentries down from the battlements and the drawbridge lowered and then dealt sharply with the protests. Her last hope died as, at Ranulf's command, she and Simon preceded him up the stone steps to the wall-walk overlooking the entrance to the castle. In the distance she could see the flickering lights of his army's campfires.

The grating chains screeched loudly in the night—a signal to Ranulf's men apparently, for almost at once his retinue of knights and men-at-arms appeared as a dark shadow on the horizon. As the column of prancing steeds neared, Ariane could see the crimson banner of the lord of Vernay in the glow of torchlight, waving like a bold taunt. In her imagination, she could even make out the fearsome device it boasted—the black body of a dragon rampant.

When the column came to a halt, Ranulf called a greeting down to his chief vassal and was met with a rumble of triumphant laughter.

"You succeeded!" Payn FitzOsbern exclaimed.

"Did you doubt I would?"

"Nay, lord. I know you too well."

Still holding Ariane, Ranulf gestured with his sword toward the gate below. "You may enter my new demesne. And be quick about it. We have much to accomplish before we can claim full victory."

The thud of horses' hooves echoed over the wooden drawbridge, followed by the stamp of marching feet as the army filed into the castle. When the last man had entered, Ranulf felt the rigid tension drain from the woman in his arms, felt the life go out of her as she bowed her head in defeat.

Only then did Ranulf release his prize; the lady of Claredon had served her purpose. He was acutely aware of the tears running silently down her face, but he willfully ignored them, as well as his own unfathomable urge to comfort her. He would not be swayed by a woman's weeping.

"What do you intend?" he heard her ask softly.

"To secure the castle."

"And afterward? Will you keep your word and spare the lives of our soldiers?"

He glanced at Simon, who stood grim-faced at attention. "My word is my honor. Will you keep yours and swear obedience to me, demoiselle?"

Ariane remained silent. She had never promised to give such an oath to Ranulf—nor would she. Yet now did not seem the wisest moment to tell him so. The lord of Vernay was watching her closely, his amber eyes hard and uncompromising.

"I am lord here now," he reminded her in a silken tone. "Claredon is *mine*. Now come," Ranulf added, as if impatient with discussion. "My men are weary. They marched over twenty miles today and have earned their rest."

At sword point, he urged Ariane and Simon down the steps to the bailey and ordered a man to watch over them. His knights had already begun taking control of the keep, but Ranulf summoned Payn FitzOsbern to confer about holding the entire garrison prisoner and rounding up the able-bodied male serfs for the remainder of the night, placing them under close guard.

"But, Payn, handle them softly," Ranulf warned in a voice loud enough for Ariane to hear. "I want no trouble with these people."

She was scarcely heartened by his concern. Her own guilt weighed so heavily that she could think of little else.

What she wouldn't give to relive the past few hours. If only she had never trusted that accursed monk. If only there were a way to reverse the damage she had done, a means to defy her treacherous betrothed—

But what if there were?

She could never make amends for allowing the fall of Claredon, but perhaps she could offer a measure of resistance, rather than simply accepting defeat. There was still a chance to save the honor of her house. . .

Her head came up slowly. A man had been set to watch her, yet he was paying more attention to the activity across the bailey than to his prisoners.

Keeping a wary eye on both her guard and his lord, she edged closer to Simon. Bowing her head as if weeping, she pretended to seek comfort from him, even as she whispered urgently, "Simon?"

"Aye, milady?" he whispered back.

"You must contrive to escape somehow . . . ride north to alert my father, seek his aid."

His reply held distress. "Nay . . . I cannot abandon you here . . . not and leave you to the lord of Vernay."

"You must—and quickly. We haven't much time. You heard Lord Ranulf. We will be his prisoners, under heavy guard. Now is our only chance. Go and warn my father of what has occurred. Perhaps eventually he can raise a force and return to rescue us—"

"But my lady—"

"Please, Simon! There are fifty saddled horses to choose from. You can seize one and be over the drawbridge in moments, before Ranulf's men even have the opportunity to react."

When he hesitated, she raised her head and gave him her most pleading look. "Please, Simon, I beg you. It is our only chance."

"Very well, my lady . . . but I do not care to leave you—"

"Go now!" she repeated impatiently, striving to keep her voice low. "I will do what I can to create a distraction."

Simon wasted another few precious moments while Ariane held her breath, but then he began to edge slowly backward, toward the castle gates.

Her heart pounding, Ariane followed him, while at the same time fumbling to unpin the jewelled brooch that customarily clasped the edges of her mantle together. She saw, with fervent relief, that Ranulf was deep in conversation with his vassal. Around him, ordered tumult reigned as his men took possession of the keep.

From the corner of her eye, she saw Simon pause at a throng of destriers, held by a bored page. She moved carefully closer as Simon quietly caught the mane of a stalwart bay and prepared to mount. At his nod, she said a fervent prayer and stabbed the hindquarter of the horse nearest her with the sharpened point of her brooch.

In answer to her prayer, chaos erupted. With a squeal the wounded animal bolted against its fellows, causing another charger to rise up on its haunches and paw the air, while their startled groom shouted in alarm. At the same moment, Simon leaped into the saddle. Wheeling the horse, he dug in his heels fiercely and charged the gate, lying low over his mount's back.

Ariane managed to elude the flailing hooves, but glanced fearfully over her shoulder at Ranulf—in time to see an archer raise his bow and notch an arrow. With a cry of desperation, she threw herself in the path of his aim, lifting her arms to make herself the target, her sole thought to protect her father's vassal and increase his chances of escape.

She heard Ranulf's violent curse above the tumult, glimpsed his reaction as he lunged forward and struck the bow from the archer's grip. Released with a twang, the arrow flew sharply awry, to stick quivering in the ground, a mere yard to her right.

Her heart in her throat, Ariane stood trembling as the lord of Vernay strode furiously toward her. He was barking out orders to a half-dozen of his men to ride after the escaped prisoner and hunt him down.

As they jumped to do his bidding, Ranulf came to an abrupt halt before her. Ariane stared fearfully up at him, even as she strained to hear the fading hoofbeats of Simon's mount, praying he would get clear.

"By the bones of the Saints—you fool! You could have been killed!"

Ranulf's expression was so fierce she thought he would smite her. She closed her eyes, knowing one blow from that deadly fist would be the end of her, yet he stood towering over her without touching her.

She could feel her nails painfully scoring her palms as she waited for his judgment, yet her fear was not just for herself; dread filled her as she heard Simon's pursuers clatter across the drawbridge.

"Payn!" Ranulf barked suddenly, making her jump.

"Aye, my lord?"

"Hold her firm."

Ariane felt fresh terror rise in her throat as his vassal obediently stepped behind her and gripped her arms. Dear God, did Ranulf mean to beat her to death in punishment? He stood there flexing his fists, as if only by sheer force of will could he summon restraint.

"You will take this wench to the tower and confine her to her chamber."

"Her chamber, Ranulf? Not the dungeon?"

Ranulf's jaw clenched. It would be a fitting punishment to imprison her in the castle's dungeon for her treachery. She had aided one of his most valuable prisoners to escape in an obvious scheme to send for help. That single innocuous act could have deadly consequences, could endanger the lives of his men and the success of his mission, permitting his enemy to summon reinforcements and counter with an attack.

And yet Ranulf would not permit himself to go so far as imprison Ariane—or make any rash decision regarding her fate just yet. Her betrayal had rekindled his fury, but until he was calm enough to deal with her, he would do better to allow his knights to handle the matter.

"She is a woman," he said grimly, as if that explained his reasoning. "And I would prefer not to inflame her people unnecessarily. Set a guard at her door and make certain she cannot escape. She is not to be trusted for an instant."

Payn raised an eyebrow, but nodded at the command. Motioning for two of his men to follow, he urged Ariane forward with a gentle shove, forcing her to walk before him.

It was all she could manage not to flinch as they passed the lord of Vernay. She raised her chin proudly, though knowing he wasn't fooled by her brave facade.

When she spied her half-brother, Gilbert, and the Claredon priest, Father John, hovering helplessly among the crowd of watchers, she gave them a faint smile of reassurance. Yet she was shaking visibly by the time she reached the fourth floor of the keep, where her frightened women milled. She managed to say a few soothing words, telling them to remain calm and obedient to the invaders, but the tension and fear of the past hour had taken an exhausting toll. She was almost grateful to be imprisoned in her own bedchamber, even if the mailed knight called Payn forced her to lie on her bed and was now binding her hands and feet with a length of cord and securing the ends to the carved bedposts.

He was studying her thoughtfully in the candlelight as he worked, she realized after a moment.

"I confess myself astonished at Ranulf's leniency, demoiselle," Payn said in a tone so enigmatic she knew not whether it held scorn or surprise.

"Leniency?"

"Aye. You should count yourself fortunate. If you were a man, you would be lucky to survive your mischief. Ranulf would have you flogged at the very least."

"If I were a man," Ariane retorted bitterly, "Claredon would not have fallen so easily."

"Mayhap he wants you in his bed. You certainly would not be the first woman he has tamed with passion."

The unwelcome shock of the knight's observation left Ariane struggling for breath. *Ranulf wanted her? In his bed?* Was that why he had refrained from striking her? He was saving her for his ravishment?

Never! she vowed silently, clenching her hands defiantly. She would fight him with the last ounce of strength left in her body.

Payn tied the final knot and tested his handiwork for tension, then rose to his feet. After cautioning her not to cause any more trouble, he let himself out of the chamber. Behind him, the key grated ominously in the lock.

Alone, Ariane shut her eyes in dismay, a fresh worry occupying her tormented thoughts. Her dreams of a tender lover had been shattered with a vengeance. In addition to losing her father's demesne, over and above fearing for her vassal's safety, beyond being Ranulf's prisoner, she might very well have to endure his physical assault.

Chapter 4

Not until the following evening was Ariane summoned by the new lord of Claredon. She spent the entire day incarcerated in her apartments, with but one woman to attend her and to bring her meals. Through her window she could hear the activity below in the bailey. The usual domestic din was replaced by the sounds of marching troops and whinnying horses as the Black Dragon took full possession of the keep and the surrounding countryside.

Ariane's spirits sank with every passing hour. Failure weighed like stone upon her heart, as did fear for Claredon's people. She could only pray that Lord Ranulf would not deal too harshly with them.

When the summons finally came, her despair had grown to such magnitude that she scarcely flinched. In truth, she would almost be glad to get the ordeal over with. Even the severest punishment would be better than this agony of uncertainty.

As she was ushered within by her stern-faced guards, Ariane realized Ranulf had appropriated the lord's solar as his new chambers. That he would take her father's place as lord of Claredon stung like a salted wound and filled her with renewed fury, but she dared not show her feelings. Edging to one side of the oaken door, she stood quietly near the cold stone wall, waiting for his notice, yet wishing she could make herself invisible.

The chamber was crowded. Several of Ranulf's vassals milled around him still, dressed in chain mail armor, munching on capon legs and quaffing wine, while a half-dozen of Claredon's household serfs filled a huge wooden tub for his bath. His squire, the young man called Burc, was engaged in removing Ranulf's hauberk, a long mail tunic so heavy the lad nearly staggered under its weight. Ranulf had obviously been engaged in physical exertion, for his raven hair was damp with sweat and matted from the weight of his mail coif and steel helmet.

He paid her no attention, though, a slight which Ariane greeted with relief. If he was to pronounce her sentence, she would prefer he not do so before an audience.

Lightheaded with fatigue and strain, she raised her bound hands to awkwardly rub her throbbing temple, trying to ease the ache. She had only her wits to rely upon, and she would need every ounce of energy and strength she possessed if she were to hold her own against the Black Dragon of Vernay.

It was not until his knights began taking leave of their lord that Ariane's nervousness rose again to a fever pitch.

"And Payn," Ranulf concluded as his vassal turned to go, "pray don't deal too harshly with the castle wenches. They have other duties to perform besides servicing you."

"Have no fear, lord. I shall show them merely the hardness of my blade, not the harshness."

Male laughter followed the ribald jest as the men filed passed Ariane. Their glances at her were solemn and perhaps a bit leering. Payn FitzOsbern's amusement faded abruptly when he spied her, his expression turning grim. He left the door open behind him for the serfs that still scurried to and fro carrying warm bath water.

Ariane's wary gaze returned to the Black Dragon where he sat on a wooden bench, allowing his squire to attend him. Ranulf had not acknowledged her presence yet, thankfully. His woolen tunic had been removed, and now his mud-spattered boots were stripped off, his woolen chausses unlaced, leaving only linen braies covering his loins.

Seeing him thus, Ariane drew in a sharp breath at the sight of Ranulf's powerful body. Nakedness was a common occurrence in castle life, and she had frequently seen unclothed men before. Her duties as chatelaine of the castle often required such exposure—helping the lord dress, bathing visitors of high rank, using her knowledge of medicines to dress the wounds of soldiers and serfs alike. And yet no man had ever affected her as strongly as this one did now; no physique had ever seemed as compelling as Ranulf's masculine body ... hard, muscular, battle-scarred.

His shoulders appeared massively wide, his chest broad and darkly furred, marked with badges of combat. His flat, taut belly tapered to narrow hips, while his thighs and calves bulged with ropes of muscle. But it was the force and energy that radiated from him, even when he was at ease, that commanded her attention. Somehow Ranulf de Vernay dominated the entire chamber.

He still had the power to awe her, Ariane realized with regret, yet he was a far more fearsome adversary now than ever. He looked supremely dangerous at present, with his jaw darkened by two days' growth of black beard. Cold, harsh, merciless . . .

He was no longer simply her betrothed, the heartless suitor who had left her to pine and wither for so many years. He was her enemy.

The last of the servants finished their tasks and withdrew, giving her cautious, regretful glances as they passed, as if to apologize for abandoning their lady to the terrifying Black Dragon. Ariane returned faint smiles of reassurance, trying to pretend that her courage was not failing her. When they had gone, she stood unmoving by the wall, not daring to call attention to herself.

Moments later Ranulf dismissed his squire. As the door closed quietly behind the youth, Ariane's heart rose to her throat. She had preferred to be alone with Ranulf when he meted out her punishment, but now that she was, she found herself hoping with a foolish desperation that he would forget about her.

He was toying with the dagger in his hand as he lounged on the bench, stroking the sharp steel blade with an almost absent caress. Ariane had the ominous feeling his silence was deliberate, a calculated attempt to shred her already raw nerves further.

Then suddenly he looked up, and she was pierced by bold, brilliant amber eyes. The impact took her breath away. His lean, hawklike features held a harsh look of simmering anger, while his gaze was like a lance pinning her against the wall. Quite clearly Ranulf had not forgotten her actions of last night—nor forgiven her.

Calling on every bit of courage she possessed, Ariane lifted her chin and coolly returned his gaze. She would not cower before him. The lady of Claredon had more pride.

His look darkened and warred with hers—until finally it dropped to her bound wrists. His hard mouth tightened.

"Come here."

Ariane stood rooted to the floor.

"I won't repeat myself, demoiselle," he said in warning.

Stiffening her spine, she forced her feet to move.

She had taken but a few steps, though, when the door swung open once more. A serving wench came tripping into the chamber, carrying a pile of linen towels and a carved wooden box that Ariane knew contained costly soaps.

Although grateful for the respite, Ariane found herself clenching her fingers in disapproval. Only she and the castle seneschal had keys to the storeroom containing soaps and spices and medicinal herbs. That a serf had been raiding the stocks of Claredon, now that no authority existed to exert control over the castle, raised her ire. And her raw nerves made her speak more sharply than usual.

"What is the meaning of this, Dena? You were taught never to enter a chamber unbidden."

At the scolding, the girl lowered flashing brown eyes. "I beg pardon, my lady. I thought to bathe the new lord."

"Well, knock beforehand next time—"

"What did you say to her?" Ranulf demanded, interrupting.

Ariane gave a start and glanced at him warily. She had spoken to the girl in English, the language most of Claredon's serfs understood, instead of the Norman French of England's ruling class. Was it possible Ranulf could not comprehend that tongue? If so, it might prove an advantage ... Or he could simply be testing her. . .

"I advised her," Ariane replied truthfully, "to remember her training and knock before entering a closed door."

Ranulf's hard gaze bored into her. "You would do well to remember your own precarious position. You are lady here no longer, nor do you have the right to command *my* servants. Your authority here is no greater than any serf's."

She flushed at the reprimand and fell silent. Dena's sly glance at Ranulf implied that she at least understood the import of his harsh declaration, and that she was enjoying her lady's humiliation.

"Tell her to set her burden down and leave us."

When Ariane reluctantly complied, Dena bobbed a curtsey and hastened to obey, while at the same time letting her gaze travel over Ranulf's nearly naked body. As she bent to leave the towels and soap beside the tub, the neck of her tunic slipped half off one shoulder, baring a good deal of a generous breast. And as she took her leave, she gave Ranulf a seductive display of swaying hips, explicitly announcing her availability to the new lord and her eagerness to share his bed.

He seemed not to notice. He kept his hard gaze trained on Ariane until the door had shut once more, leaving them alone.

"The wench seems far friendlier than my own bride," he said silkily.

"Perhaps she does not know you as well as I do," Ariane retorted scornfully. "Or perhaps she does not object to the stench of treachery as keenly."

Her charge cut Ranulf in the raw. She dared speak of his treachery after her own betrayal?

A muscle flexed in his jaw, while his gaze impaled her. "You have a sharp tongue, demoiselle. I advise you to curb it."

She fell silent, but a flicker of contempt crossed her features. Ranulf's jaw tightened. She should have been meek and frightened, cowering before his anger and begging for mercy, not favoring him with that regal disdain.

"I told you to come here. Do it. *Now*." His deep, impatient voice barked the word when she hesitated.

Marshalling her courage, Ariane forced herself to obey. When she halted before Ranulf, regarding him uneasily, he ordered her to hold out her bound hands, which she did hesitantly.

She knew an instant of alarm when Ranulf lifted his dagger—alarm that turned to shock as he sliced through her bonds, freeing her hands. Ariane stood staring down at him as feeling rushed back into her numb fingers. Absently rubbing her wrists, she searched his harsh face, wondering at his game.

"Why . . . did you do that?"

"Do what?"

"Set me free."

"But I have not freed you, demoiselle." His mouth twisted in a grim smile. "On the contrary. You are still very much my hostage. But I see no need to bind you. If you tried to run, you would not get far."

Ariane bit her lip at that unpalatable truth. She was entirely in Ranulf's power. She stood quietly, vaguely aware of the musky scent of sweat and maleness that emanated from him. It was not unpleasant; indeed, it was strangely, disturbingly arousing.

Summoning her failing courage, she forced herself to ask the question whose answer she dreaded. "Then . . . what do you intend to do with me?"

His piercing gaze studied her face. "I have not yet decided." Her relief at his reply was merely temporary, though. "I might have forgiven your defense of the castle, but helping a prisoner escape . . ."

"Simon escaped?" She could not keep the hopeful eagerness from her voice.

"He was not found," Ranulf replied tersely. "The guard who failed his responsibility is now chained in Claredon's dungeon." At her faint look of guilt, his black eyebrow rose. "What did you plan by your betrayal, sweeting? To have your knight seek assistance? To summon reinforcements to your rescue? To raise a rebellion?"

When she wouldn't answer, his eyes narrowed. "You cost me a goodly ransom—and his escape will no doubt cause a great deal of trouble in the future. I shall have to carefully consider what punishment you deserve." Raising a hand, Ranulf rubbed the bristle on his jaw thoughtfully. "If you were in my position, what would you do?"

The question took her aback. Ariane eyed him warily, wondering at his intent. "I suppose . . . I would hold you prisoner . . . till you yielded."

"And would you yield, demoiselle?"

"No," she replied stiffly.

"Then imprisoning you would do no good, would it? What of locking you in your chamber, starving you into submission? No? I suspect that would have no result except to reduce you to skin and bones." His bold gaze slowly swept her slender body. "You cannot afford to lose much flesh. And I would have no use for you then."

She did not care in the least for the vague threat implied in his words, or the muted smile that curved his handsome mouth. It was faintly amused, as if he were intent on toying with her, the way the stable cat played with a captive mouse. Perhaps this was to be her punishment, to be tormented by uncertainty.

"No," Ranulf said slowly. "I shall have to think of a better, more fitting penance."

Although aware he was attempting to intimidate her, Ariane couldn't prevent herself from glancing nervously, involuntarily, at the bed. Was his vassal's conjecture correct? Did Ranulf mean to ravish her? To conquer her with passion?

She took a steadying breath. "What of the others ... my father's men? You didn't harm them?"

"They are my prisoners, and no longer your concern."

"But ... The man you wounded last night? Might I not at least see to his injuries?"

"No."

His abrupt reply brooked no argument, yet she couldn't accept defeat so easily. She tried once more, striving to keep the anger from her tone. "My lord Ranulf ... Please, will you not reconsider? As lady, it is my duty to see to the sick and injured."

He returned her gaze fiercely, impaling her with his hot golden eyes. "Do you forget? You are lady here no longer."

"But no one else at Claredon has a knowledge of medicines."

"My own leech will see to him. Your man will be given adequate care."

She would have to be satisfied with that, Ariane knew.

Ranulf rose to his feet suddenly, making her shrink back in alarm. But he did not reach for her as she expected. Instead he bent to strip off his braies.

"What are you doing?" she exclaimed, unnerved.

His mouth twisted in a taunting smile as he bared his body. "I am bathing, what did you think? I intend to remove the stench that is so offensive to my lady."

He turned and strode boldly toward the tub, and to her dismay, she could not drag her gaze away from the sight of his taut, powerful body sculpted with muscle. Even his buttocks were lean and firm—

Suddenly Ariane drew a sharp breath as her gaze settled on Ranulf's broad back. It was scored with ribbons of color—the pale white of dead flesh intermeshed with welts of darker tissue. No sword alone had caused those fierce weals. She had viewed floggings before, and tended the resultant wounds, but never had she seen any so severe. How had Ranulf come by such terrible scars?

He seemed oblivious to her regard. Setting his dagger on the floor within reach, he stepped into the tub and sank slowly into the water, partially facing her. After ducking his head, he reached for a piece of soap scented with oil of rosemary and began scrubbing vigorously at his arms and chest.

Ariane stood there hesitantly, wondering if he intended for her to assist him as she might have a noble guest. Would he require her to wash his back, to touch those fierce scars?

The silence stretched out for so long that she optimistically thought Ranulf might have forgotten her. But when he had washed and rinsed his black hair, he glanced up at her. "I spent the whole of today securing the castle and the surrounding countryside. On the morrow I shall see to the demesne manor at Wyclif. That *is* the name of your father's property directly to the north?"

"Yes."

"I want a peaceful transition of power. And I require your full cooperation."

Her eyes widened. "You expect me to aid you in usurping my father's demesne?"

Usurping? Her choice of words stabbed a festering wound of Ranulf's. How many times had he heard the allegation that he was undeserving of the spoils earned by his own labors?

"You forget, demoiselle. This is no longer your father's demesne. The king gave me his holdings here. The honor of Claredon is mine."

"Because you stole it through deception and trickery."

"*Stole?*" Her heated accusation caused Ranulf's temper to explode. "By my faith!" His hands gripping the sides of the tub, he rose up half out of the water. "There was no theft here! Your father's lands and castle were forfeit because of his treason against the king—a fitting retribution for traitors."

"My father is not a traitor! I am willing to stake my life on it!"

Ranulf gritted his teeth, fighting for restraint. "A foolish wager, demoiselle. Will you deny that your father is at this moment entrenched with Mortimer at Bridgenorth Castle, which is under siege by King Henry?"

Ariane's spirited defense faltered beneath that fierce gaze. "No, that I cannot deny. But my father was called there last month to provide knight's service. He could not refuse the summons of his liege lord. Yet he took merely a handful of men, just the twenty knights fees he owed Mortimer. If he were minded to treachery, why did he contribute so small a force?"

"If he were loyal to Henry, why did he not forswear his oath when Mortimer declared his rebellion?"

"I do not *know!*" Ariane cried in anguish. "I only know that he would never have chosen to defy the new king! Not now—not when England at last has a chance for peace."

Hearing her genuine distress, seeing the look of pain in her lustrous gray eyes, Ranulf sank slowly into his bath. Her conviction actually sounded sincere. Perhaps she truly did believe in her father's innocence.

He almost envied her such faith. He couldn't remember a time in his life when he had ever believed in anyone or anything. Vengeance had been his only creed. But he was determined to quell his fury now. He refused to allow this wench to make him lose control.

She deserved punishment for her outburst, he knew, and yet his conscience already was pricking him with guilt. Seeing her chafed wrists, the welts that had resulted from his order to prevent her escape, had disturbed him keenly.

Indeed, everything about the wench disturbed him. When she'd entered the chamber a short while ago, he had become instantly aware of her presence, all his senses alive, attuned to her, his body alert, nerves strumming, like a stallion catching the ready scent of a mare. It was all he could do to rein in his urges and his temper now. And now—with her silver eyes pleading, her breasts heaving with her passionate defense of her father, her carriage as proud as any queen's—his blood stirred as for no wench he'd ever known. Lust, hot and sweet, coursed through his loins—while at the same time fury, scalding and fierce, still simmered in his veins at her perfidy in

freeing her vassal. It infuriated him more that he could still
desire her so intently after what she had done.

He could not soften toward her, Ranulf reminded himself.
She was his enemy, not to be trusted. And her rebellion
deserved some sort of reproof. She would have to learn that
she could not challenge him without penalty. He needed to
crush her defiance immediately, before it broadened.

"Such fierce nobility," Ranulf said, forcing a note of
mockery into his voice. "A pity I have no faith in your
motives, demoiselle. Naturally you would assert your father's
innocence in order to prevent your own arrest. I might have
believed you more readily had you not spurned the king's
command and refused to surrender Claredon to me."

"I had no choice," Ariane replied in a low voice.

"You had *every* choice," he retorted. "You still have
choices. Indeed, your fate depends a great deal on the path
you elect to take now."

"What . . . what do you mean?"

"Your submission, demoiselle. I would have your oath of
obedience, and your allegiance to me as your overlord."

"I . . ." She bit her lip. "I cannot give it. My allegiance
belongs to my father."

Ranulf grunted in exasperation. "This pretense of loyalty
is wearing. You cannot wish to bear the consequences of
remaining allied with a traitor."

"It is not pretense. I stand by my father."

"Such stubbornness will exact a high price."

"I know." Her reply was a mere whisper of sound.

Ranulf's jaw hardened as he fixed her with a grim stare.
He had given her every opportunity to save herself, but she
seemed intent on resistance. God's limbs, but it obliged him
to use harsher measures to compel her obedience. But what?
He suspected it would take more force than he was willing
to wield to make her back down.

"You will learn that defiance is futile, demoiselle," he
said softly.

Reaching over the rim of the tub, he picked up the dagger
he had set on the floor—and took grim satisfaction in the
flash of alarm that shone in his bride's eyes. Holding her
apprehensive gaze, Ranulf drew the razor-sharp edge of the

blade across his cheek, scraping away the stiff bristles, smiling a little when the tension left her body.

He felt little remorse in his tactics. She *should* rightly fear him, after what she had done. And the wench deserved far worse punishment, Ranulf well knew, than he could bring himself to award her.

Disturbed by his lack of resolve, Ranulf let his head fall back, rolling it from side to side to ease the tight ache in his neck. A strange depression had settled heavily over him like a pall in the past hours. He had won Claredon with ease, without bloodshed, yet the victory left a bitter taste in his mouth, reminding him of his dire battles with his despised father. His mere existence had been challenged by his noble father, but he had fought back with a determination forged from torment. He had carved a destiny for himself, driven by revenge, fired by hatred, and eventually he had triumphed.

He had thought—hoped—his acquisition of Claredon would give him the chance to start anew, to prove he deserved the overlordship of such a vast demesne on his own merits, despite his baseborn origins and the scandals that had surrounded him his life long. . . .

Recollecting himself, Ranulf shrugged off the disconcerting reflection. He was not ordinarily given to morose wallowings in his past, nor did he have time for them at present. Reluctantly he returned his attention to Ariane. At the moment he wanted simply to get this infuriating, arousing wench off his hands, and seek ease from his exhaustion. Yet he would have to deal with her.

"I will have your submission, demoiselle, one way or another. I suggest you consider your answer carefully. Your position as political prisoner is tenuous at best. A traitor's daughter has fewer rights than the meanest serf."

Ariane regarded him with disdain. "I am no traitor's daughter, my lord, or a serf. I am your betrothed, or perhaps you had forgotten?"

"I beg to differ, demoiselle," Ranulf replied with forced casualness, ignoring the sarcasm in her tone. "You no longer hold the position of my intended bride. Our betrothal is at an end. I will not be constrained to wed a traitor."

From the startled look on her lovely face, he knew he had taken her aback. "I hold the law on my side, I believe. No ecclesiastical court would force me to honor the contract now. As for the benefits of matrimony, I no longer need marry you to possess the lands you would have inherited at your father's passing. They already belong to me.''

He watched the complex play of emotions in her expressive eyes, none of which was expected. If he had to vouch a guess, he would swear she almost looked hurt.

Her reply was a long time in coming. ''After all these years . . . you intend to cast me off like a worn cloak?''

He could not comprehend her reaction, unless she was attempting to play on his sympathies. She had claimed—most emphatically—that she regretted their betrothal. Indeed, her scathing denunciation still rang bitterly in his ears. ''I have not cast you off, demoiselle. Your own actions are at fault. Had you surrendered Claredon to me willingly, I would have honored you as my wife.''

Ariane looked away, unable to bear his challenging regard. It wounded her that he could so casually dismiss the years of anguish and uncertainty he had caused her. ''I would have done so,'' she said quietly, ''had you come any time these past five years—even as late as a fortnight ago.''

Ranulf's mouth tightened. She was behaving as if *she* were the one wronged. Perhaps he *had* been delinquent in claiming her as his bride, but the revulsion and scorn she felt for him was reason enough for him to wish to end the betrothal. And she was the one who had defied a royal command and then compounded the crime by aiding her father's vassal to escape. She had declared herself his enemy, and should expect no mercy. And yet, irrationally, to his disgust, Ranulf found himself wanting to offer her explanations he was under no obligation to give, even to apologize for repudiating their betrothal.

''I regret that I never came for you,'' he said stiffly, ''but I cannot undo the past—or countermand Henry's wishes. My orders are to hold you as hostage.'' When still she remained silent, gazing at him with that wounded look of accusation, Ranulf felt a defensive anger seize him. ''You should have no complaint about the dissolution of our betrothal, sweeting. Ours was an arranged marriage. Indeed, you clearly told me of your regret just yesterday. A 'grasping, baseborn pretender to nobility' is the phrase you used, I believe. You claimed to rue my very name."

The reminder that she had been tricked into making such a statement filled Ariane with impotent fury and despair. She wanted to strike him, to mar Ranulf's harsh, handsome face with her nails; she wanted to rail at him, to wound him as he had her. And yet she dared not attempt any outright defiance, not when he held the power of life and death over her and her people.

"I will not protest your decision, my lord." Her chin lifted proudly, while her voice took on an edge of icy disdain. "I will gladly release you from the contract. Indeed, I could not be persuaded otherwise. After your treachery, I would refuse to wed you under any circumstances."

Any relief Ranulf felt at her easy acquiescence was countered by the contempt in her proud tone. With effort he clamped down on the ire her declaration aroused in him. He would not be manipulated into a response by this woman—or defied by her, either.

Yet it was a dilemma, how to punish her without being overly cruel. He dared not risk any sign of weakness, and yet he had tied his own hands in dealing with Ariane. Not only would he find physically harming so delicate and lovely a wench supremely distasteful, but he had vowed never to subject a woman to the abuse his despised father had displayed toward his mother—or the torment he himself had endured. He refused to sink to such depths of depravity, or take out his violent wrath on creatures frailer and weaker than he.

His gaze swept around the solar, seeking an answer. Having been fully occupied with securing the castle, he'd had no time earlier to inspect his new living quarters. The sight was pleasing. Norman society was enormously more sophisticated than England's, but the appointments in this chamber compared favorably with the wealthier keeps in Normandy. Far more welcoming than his own solar at Vernay, with none of the disturbing associations, it provided richness without ostentation, comfort without being overly soft for a man of war accustomed to living in army camps.

A huge curtained bed dominated the chamber, while intricately carved chests and thickly padded benches stood in the corners and before the bronze-hooded hearth where embers glowed warmly. The two tall, shuttered embrasures would allow in ample light during the day, and the cushioned seats arranged in the deep-set window alcoves would afford a restful place for ladies engaged in needlework or conversation. There were also several gilt screens for privacy and to reduce drafts, finely woven carpets on the woodplank floor, tapestry hangings to accent the whitewashed walls, and even a brightly painted floral mural decorating the stone at the head of the bed.

Slowly Ranulf's gaze returned to that bed with its rich quilt of brocade and additional coverlets of marten fur. Seeing it reminded him of the current circumstances and his dilemma. He was alone with a beautiful wench who was his prisoner, with no satisfactory notion of what to do with her.

He knew what he would like to do. He wanted her sprawled in that bed, flat on her back, her legs wrapped hard around his hips as he appeased his carnal hunger—

Ranulf muttered an oath beneath his breath. The image of Ariane lying beneath him, her slim, silky body open for his pleasure, made his loins tighten painfully and caused his body to tauten like a bowstring. Yet she was no ill-bred leman to be taken at his pleasure. And the existence of the betrothal contracts constrained him further. He could not touch Ariane, could not consummate their relationship at least, while the legal documents existed, or he would be as good as married to her. No, he would have to find another way to punish her, much to his regret.

But what? He had no desire to keep her imprisoned, and yet he dared not let her have the run of the keep, for she could too easily aid her father's men to freedom. Even if she gave him her solemn word, he could not trust her to keep it. Nobly born females, in his experience, had a inbred instinct for betrayal. His own mother ... the wife of his foster lord ... the ladies of the Norman court ... all had shown how duplicitous they could be. And Ariane of Claredon had proven the danger in trusting her. He would constantly have to remain on his guard.

His gaze narrowing, Ranulf eyed the bed speculatively. 'Twas a pity he would have to keep his hands off her. One night in his bed and he might manage to compel her submission without any resort to violence. His skill as a lover had rarely been questioned. He knew well how to pleasure a wench and make her respond to his physical persuasions. If this damsel was like the other females of his acquaintance, he could soon have her trembling at his merest touch.

Yet Ariane, he was beginning to suspect, was perhaps a woman of a different stamp. Her regal air, her cool disdain, was as vexing as it was novel. 'Twould be intriguing to see if he could make her yield, if he could melt that haughty manner and turn her scorn to gasping surrender. . . .

Testing the smoothness of his shaven jaw with his palm, Ranulf returned his attention to her, considering her with a measuring gaze. "The hour grows late. It is time to retire."

She stared at him a long moment, before warily, wordlessly turning toward the door.

"Where do you go, my lady?" Ranulf asked silkily. "I did not give you leave to withdraw."

"But you said . . . you wanted to retire."

"So I did. I suggest you prepare for bed."

"W-What?"

"You can begin by disrobing."

"You wish for me to *undress?*"

A smile curved his lips. "A clever observation, sweeting. You may make use of my bathwater if you choose. I will be done with it in a moment."

Ariane stood frozen, staring at him as if he had taken leave of his senses.

"You will remain here for the night," Ranulf explained vaguely. "I intend to keep you close, since I cannot trust you out of my sight. Doubtless you will find it preferable to being locked below in the dungeon."

"I would infinitely prefer the dungeon," she said with more heat than was wise.

"I do not mean to give you the choice. You will remain here where I can keep an eye on you. You will sleep in this chamber, in that bed, willing or no."

Their gazes warred, but Ranulf refused to relent. He *wanted* her to worry about his intentions. No doubt she would much prefer to be locked chastely in her own apartments instead of being compelled to bear his company. It should prove a humbling experience, being forced to share a bed with him, the grasping knight she scorned as a dishonorable pretender to nobility.

She had not yet moved, Ranulf noted as he forced away the erotic reflection. "It will go easier for you if you submit to me willingly," he warned, his tone casual.

"I will not be dishonored," Ariane replied at last, her voice shaking.

"Dishonor? Is that what it would be, demoiselle?"

"Yes, if you take me without the blessing of the Church."

"That presumes you still have honor to lose."

Letting his dagger drop to the floor with a clatter, Ranulf rose abruptly to his feet and stepped dripping from the tub. His nude body glistening, he strode purposefully toward her.

Ariane flinched and tried to retreat, but he reached out to capture her long plait and wrap it around his hand. Imprisoning her thus, he moved closer, crowding her with his towering body, his amber gaze boring into her. He was so near, Ariane could feel his skin's heat, could smell his clean masculine scent, spiced with the fragrance of rosemary, enveloping her.

"Are you still chaste, sweeting? Or have you played me false in that matter as well?"

"Of course I am chaste . . ." she retorted breathlessly.

"Your father's vassal, the one you helped escape. You claim you were never lovers?"

"Lovers? *Simon?* Certainly we were never lovers—"

"You expect me to believe you have never been intimate with a man?"

"Yes . . . most assuredly I do."

"You are far older than most maids, a spinster almost."

Stung by the injustice of his accusation, Ariane felt fresh anger rising within her. "And whose fault is that, my lord? You left me neglected and unwed for years."

His eyebrow rose as he searched her face. "You will forgive my skepticism if I doubt your virtue. My past experiences with noblewomen have not led me to put any faith in their protestations of innocence."

She wondered what had occurred to incite such bitterness in his tone, even as she met Ranulf's gaze scornfully. "I care not what you believe. I am still a maiden."

"There is one sure way to discover if you are telling the truth."

Her response became a gasp as his hand rose to close gently around her throat. Her hands came up to resist him, which was a mistake, she discovered as her palms encountered the granite wall of his chest. It was a distinct shock to feel the warm furred flesh still damp from his bath.

Desperately, Ariane tried to ward him off. "You will not . . . take me without the sanction of marriage vows."

"I have the right," Ranulf said softly, determined to make her understand the power he held over her, the better to appreciate the leniency he intended to show her. "I could keep you chained in my bed, forcing you to service me. I could claim you as the spoils of war, and no one would gainsay me. The king would even understand. I could take you now and no one would stop me."

Ariane felt her heart pounding in her throat as she stared up at him. His harsh, sun-bronzed face was so close she could feel his breath soft on her lips. "You . . . would rape a gentlewoman?"

A smile flickered across his mouth as he thought seriously about her question. "I much doubt it would be rape. I have never before found it necessary to resort to such tactics. The wenches I've been required to subdue eventually offered no resistance. They came willingly to my bed, even eagerly."

Her eyes widened incredulously. "You dare boast of your conquests?"

"No boast, sweeting, simple fact. Women find pleasure in my arms—as you would, I am certain."

His arrogant implication left Ariane speechless with outrage. The idea that she might actually enjoy her ravishment affronted her. "I shall *never* share your bed without benefit of marriage. I will never come to you willingly!"

"We shall see."

His soft declaration held a threat, Ariane was certain, but it was Ranulf's dangerous look that disturbed her more. His stormy countenance had softened, to be replaced by something heated and intense in his golden eyes. She had never been more aware of a man—of his body, of his nudity. When he leaned into her, pressing against her, she could feel his quickening desire, the hardening ridge of his manhood against her belly.

With a gasp of alarm, she tried once more to break free

of his imprisoning hold, but his fingers on her throat were like velvet manacles.

"The sooner you accept me as your liege, the easier it will go for you."

Ariane held her breath, forcing herself to stand utterly still, trying not to show her panic, yet she knew Ranulf could feel her pulse hammering wildly beneath his palm.

For an interminable moment, he stood staring down at her ... but then his hand abruptly fell away as he smiled tauntingly. "You are fortunate that I am too weary to properly attend you tonight, demoiselle. It is a firm rule of mine—I never take a wench unless I have the energy to see to her pleasure as well as my own. But after remaining awake for two full days, I expect the exertion would tax even my stamina."

Stepping back, he left Ariane gaping at his temerity as he turned to pick up a linen cloth and towel himself dry. To her shock, his erection was flushed and engorged, standing nearly to his belly. After a nervous glance, she dared not look further at him.

When he saw how she averted her gaze, Ranulf chuckled in wry amusement. It was sweetly satisfying to see this scornful, haughty wench disconcerted. "You should feel honored, sweeting," he prodded. "I don't usually allow my women to remain with me the night through."

"Honored!" The sheer audacity of his statement took her breath away. "It is not an honor! And I am not your *woman!*"

"Indeed, you *are,* demoiselle. You are mine to do with as I will."

The urge to slap his arrogant face made Ariane's palm tingle, but seeing the sparkle of humor in his eyes turn hot, glimmering, made her think better of it.

"You knave," she muttered heatedly under her breath, a retort Ranulf unfortunately heard.

"Such offended pride. Such righteous indignation."

Her chin snapped up. "You dare mock me."

"Aye, I do," he replied with a maddening smile. "I crave the enjoyment of seeing your temper rise."

"You are cruel."

"Cruel?" A slashing eyebrow rose abruptly, while his

smile faded. "You think you deserve kindness? After your defiance yesterday? When your actions were tantamount to treason? You should consider yourself fortunate, demoiselle. Any other lord would have had you flogged senseless, or spread your legs and used your body without regard to your station or innocence. I have not harmed you—nor will I unless you give me further cause."

She fell silent, her accusing gaze a flashing mixture of frustration and despair and impotent fury. Her reaction disturbed Ranulf's conscience far more than continued argument could have done. Deciding it time to end his deliberate attempt to provoke her, he returned her regard steadily, trying to give the appearance of indifference.

"You can rest easy, sweeting. As much as I would enjoy your body, I intend to deny myself the pleasure. Taking you would cement our betrothal contract and validate our marriage, God forbid. It would take a decree from the pope to annul, and I would not care to be put to such bother."

Her eyes widened in disbelief, and he could feel her gaze following him as he moved about the room, snuffing the candles in the wall sconces.

He had spoken the truth, though. For once he was too weary to do justice to his bed partner or his carnal nature, despite the blood that pooled thickly in his loins, hot and potent, despite the way his fiery bride—former bride, Ranulf corrected himself—aroused him. He would force her to share his bed, although naught more physical would occur between them, not tonight at any event.

Even so, her evident aversion to the idea of accepting his attentions stung his male pride. He had never before been denied by any woman he wanted. In truth, much of his trouble had always been that wenches were overly attracted to him. His female villeins often clamored for his favor, eager to bear him sons who would raise their own status and perhaps elevate them to a better life. They knew his feelings about children. He loved the half-dozen sons and daughters he had sired—he who allowed himself to care about nothing and no one. Children were his one weakness, and he was stubbornly resolved on providing his own a better life than he had known, one without the shame, the pain, the bleak loneliness he had endured.

Ranulf left the single large candle lit for the night and drew down the bedclothes before glancing over his shoulder at Ariane. "Why do you tarry?"

Her wariness had returned, as well as that proud defiance that stirred his anger and unwilling admiration.

"I tell you, I will not lie with you," she replied with feigned bravado.

She had never seen anyone react so swiftly. In two strides Ranulf had closed the distance between them and scooped her up in his arms. In three more, he had carried her to the bed and dropped her onto the soft feather mattress, following her down to pin her with the full length of his body. Ruthlessly, he captured her flailing arms and locked them over her head.

Shocked, breathless, Ariane could only stare up at him.

"You will lie with me, wench," he said with lethal softness. "You will warm my bed if I command it. You will clean my boots if I say so. And by the Virgin, you will curb your defiant tongue in my hearing, do you understand me?"

Ariane gritted her teeth, staring back at Ranulf with trepidation and seething fury. "Yes, I understand."

"Yes, *what?*"

"Yes, my lord."

His glittering eyes narrowed as they locked with hers. Suddenly feeling the softness of her body beneath him, Ranulf swore under his breath. That same stark, sexual awareness that he'd experienced last night when Ariane had lain beneath him struck him again with the force of a battering ram, exploding to pool thick and hot in his loins.

God's blood, he needed a woman. He had been celibate for several weeks now, having denied himself often during the five months of the recent campaign. And having such a winsome captive so near at hand without being able to touch her would prove a sore strain on his fortitude. Yet he had brought this dilemma on himself. God's teeth, but this close proximity was supposed to serve as *her* punishment, not his own.

Shutting his eyes, Ranulf forced himself to exhale slowly. Jesu, he was tired. Bone tired, his body stiff with weariness and need. Abruptly easing his weight off her, Ranulf reached down to pull the sheets and a fur coverlet up over them both.

Rolling over to face the far wall then, he closed his eyes and forced his body to relax, willing the tension and exhaustion to drain from muscle and sinew.

Not daring to move, Ariane stared at the back of his head, a dawning sense of relief stealing over her. It seemed as if Ranulf did indeed mean what he said about not ravishing her ... at least not this night.

Their confrontation had not gone as she expected. Ranulf had not hurt her precisely. He had tormented her with threats, yes, raising her fears with his taunts and innuendos. And yet she was still free, somewhat. He hadn't incarcerated her in the dungeon, and for that she was grateful. Being forced to sleep in Ranulf's chamber, even in his bed, was by far the lesser punishment, for imprisoned, she could be of no help to any of the inhabitants of Claredon, nor defend them against the Black Dragon. Not that she had managed to give much of an accounting of herself tonight.

Still, she hadn't surrendered to Ranulf entirely ... and he hadn't ravished her....

Shaking with rage and relief, she listened with growing resentment as Ranulf's breathing settled into a quiet rhythm. He was obviously unafraid to turn his back on her. He had not bothered to hide any of his weapons, evidently believing she would never have the courage to use them against him. Courage had little to say to the matter, though. She would not be so foolish as to attempt his life. Even if she managed to kill the lord of Vernay, his vassals would most certainly avenge his death, not only on her but on the hapless people of Claredon. No, for the moment she would have to accept his rule.

Her gaze focusing on his hair, she realized his wet, raven locks had curled into damp tendrils that shimmered softly with blue highlights. For an instant, Ariane found herself wondering if his hair was as soft, as silken, as it looked, but she quelled the urge to reach up and test it. Her gaze dropped lower. Beneath the edge of the coverlet, she could see the beginning of his broad back and the terrible scars that criss-crossed the ravaged flesh. Ruthlessly she crushed the involuntary surge of sympathy that stirred within her. The lord of Vernay was a black-hearted devil, who needed no compassion or pity from anyone, least of all his helpless prisoner.

Turning her head, Ariane stared blindly up at the canopy overhead, a dull ache constricting her chest. No, this encounter with Ranulf was nothing like what she had once expected or hoped.

This should have been her wedding night. She had dreamed of her first time with Ranulf. Countless times she had imagined lying with him, giving herself to her husband in love and honor, opening her body to him, responding to his tender caresses. . . .

Her dreams bore no resemblance to this . . . this mockery of a solemn marriage bedding. She was sharing his bed, yes, but not in love or honor.

They were enemies now. The lord of Vernay had repudiated their betrothal and refused to touch her, while she shrank from him in fear and loathing.

Chapter 5

S he dreamed of her lover again. A haunting, erotic fantasy that faded like wisps of smoke as dawn stole through the shuttered windows.

Ariane slowly awakened from a fitful doze, conscious of an incredible feeling of sadness. Only in increments did she become aware of other vivid sensations: a corded arm curled possessively about her waist . . . the searing heat of a hard, male body at her back . . . a fierce yearning within her that rose hot and formless and powerful.

Ranulf.

Sweet Mary. . . .

She froze, aware of his enveloping embrace, of his shaft, throbbing and hard, pressed against her buttocks, even through the layers of her clothing. For a score of heartbeats, Ariane lay there rigidly, not daring to move. She could hear Ranulf's breathing, soft and even, feel his relaxed pose. . . .

Merciful God . . . he still slept.

Holding her breath, Ariane eased from beneath his arm and slipped from the bed. Silently, she fled to the sanctuary of the window alcove where she curled shivering on the cushioned seat. After the warmth of Ranulf's bed, her rumpled bliaud provided little protection from the morning chill. And no garment could shield her from her shameful, traitorous thoughts. She could still feel the boldness of his body imprinting his maleness onto her, still sense the nameless yearning that had swept through her at his unconscious embrace.

Mother Mary, what had come over her? Her only excuse was that her defenses had been sorely weakened. For the second straight night, she had scarcely slept, and her nerves were strained by fear and exhaustion.

Hearing a slight noise, Ariane glanced warily back at Ranulf. He had shifted his position to sprawl across the huge bed, a starkly masculine figure against the flaxen-hued sheets. Her attention caught, she studied his slumbering form, wondering how he could look so commanding and forceful even in sleep.

His face was drawn in clean, harsh angles, the features sensuously, ruthlessly chiseled. His heavy, slashing brows were black as night, his nose strong and hawkish, the chin square with a slight cleft. Long, ebony lashes closed over eyes she knew were a shade of brown that was nearly gold.

As for his body ... Ariane bit her lip in dismay. That she found Ranulf physically appealing mortified as well as infuriated her. She was no longer the nervous, tongue-tied girl he had once awed, yet she couldn't deny her fascination with him now. Old habits were difficult to forswear. She had dreamed of this man as her lover, the idol of all her girlhood fantasies. . . .

Abruptly she shook her head. She would crush her attraction for him if it took every ounce of strength she possessed. Ranulf was a cold, heartless devil, the man who held her hostage. She had wasted five of the best years of her life waiting and yearning for him—and he had cruelly shattered her most cherished dreams without a single measure of remorse, repudiating their betrothal contract as casually as he would cast aside a cloak that had outserved its purpose.

Curse you, Ranulf de Vernay. He cared nothing for her. Worse, he considered her a traitor for closing the castle to him and for helping her father's vassal escape. The man who should have been her lord and husband was now her bitter enemy.

The only fortunate turn was that she did not have to fear his ravishment. As Ranulf had pointed out, if he were to consummate their union, they would be wedded in the eyes of the Church. And the very thought was repugnant to him.

Ariane shut her eyes, trying to swallow the bitterness that choked her, to deny the pricking warmth of threatening tears. Lamenting lost dreams would serve no useful purpose. She must focus her efforts on the future, on safeguarding the people and home she loved. They depended upon her to shield them, to fight for them.

If she tried, perhaps she could atone in some measure for her inability to defend Claredon, to somehow assuage the guilt she felt for failing her father. Walter had brought them safely through years of civil war and lawlessness, only to have his demesne fall to a warlord who should have been an ally. And to be accused of treason for taking part in a revolt against the new king. . . . Ariane could never believe her father guilty of such foolish defiance, especially not when he so wanted peace for England. Certainly he not been contemplating treason weeks ago when he'd left Claredon for Mortimer's keep at Bridgenorth.

Yet now her father's life might very well be forfeit. She had lost his demesne, the one thing that might have aided his cause and given him power to bargain with. Even if by God's mercy his life was spared, the punishment for treason was severe. The thought of her father blind or without hands or genitals caused hot tears to well up in her throat.

Ariane pressed a hand to her mouth to hold back the sob trembling inside her, yet she couldn't prevent the tears from spilling over. Blessed Virgin, she was utterly helpless to aid him. At present she could not even find the strength to fight the desolation assaulting her. . . . Burying her face in her hands, she gave in to strain and despair and softly wept.

"I do not recall granting you permission to leave my bed, demoiselle."

The husky, sleep-laden sound of Ranulf's voice startled her. Choking back her sobs, Ariane turned abruptly to find golden eyes above a hawklike nose surveying her intently. She swallowed thickly and hastily wiped at her eyes. Her humiliation at her defeat was great enough without adding the shame of weeping before him.

"Come here."

For a moment she hesitated, but the implacable look in his eyes brooked no defiance, and she closed the distance to the bed. To her shock and dismay, Ranulf reached out to grasp a handful of her gown, and with a gentle tug, pulled her down to sit beside him on the bed.

He studied her for a long moment, trying to discern if the emotion glistening in her eyes was genuine or feigned, if the soft sound of her sobbing when he'd awakened had been a calculated ploy for sympathy. He did not want to see the misery etched in her lovely face, and yet he could not completely trust it. In truth, he trusted no women and few men. And the cool, bewitching beauty of this particular wench, with her spiky-wet lashes and trembling mouth, doubly set him on his guard.

His urge to touch her was strong—and keenly disconcerting. He understood the desire that tugged at his loins. His customary morning arousal had made him hard and throbbing beneath the bed linens, but he was well familiar with waking in such a painful state—and having so haunting a wench so near at hand did nothing to cool his blood. Yet the softer feelings running rampant inside him bewildered him. The urge to draw Ariane into his arms, to hold and comfort her and kiss away her sorrow, was a novel, startling experience for him. He had never embraced a woman merely to offer comfort, without lust driving him.

Determinedly Ranulf steeled himself against the need to console her. He did not wish the wench to see how much he desired her, or perceive how her tears affected him. He would not give her such weapons to use over him, or allow her to think she could employ her womanly attributes to advance her position. At the moment she sat stiffly beside him, her delicate chin lifted at a defiant angle, her gaze wary.

"Why were you weeping?"

"I was not weeping," she replied, the tremor in her voice belying her words.

"No?" He raised a hand to brush a teardrop from her cheek with his forefinger. "What is this wetness on your face, then?" When she remained silent, Ranulf narrowed his gaze. "I cannot be manipulated by tears, demoiselle. Or swayed by womanly arts."

A flash of renewed fury shot through Ariane at his callous assumption of her motives. She had too much pride ever to use such ploys, and lacked the talent besides. Never having been to court, she had little experience in flirtation or persuading a man to do her bidding. Furthermore, her mother's teaching had always stressed honesty and principle when dealing with others.

"I doubt a man of your stamp would understand how a woman could succumb to despair in a moment of weakness," she muttered scathingly.

He winced inwardly at the scorn in her tone. *A man of your stamp.* A baseborn pretender to nobility, undeserving of the honors he had won at sword's point, she meant. Ariane knew of the scandal surrounding his birth, evidently. Knew he had been forced to claw his way up to the ranks of nobility. A highborn lady like she would not consider him good enough to aspire to her hand. Only his possession of Vernay had made it possible.

Ranulf looked at her sharply, refusing to let her see how her words cut. "I asked a question of you, lady, and I expect a truthful answer. Why did you weep?"

Ariane averted her gaze. "My father has been condemned as a traitor ... I bear the shame for losing his demesne ... I am your prisoner ... you repudiated our betrothal ... I believe I have ample cause to weep."

"You have naught to be ashamed of regarding the fall of this keep. Your defeat was inevitable."

"That is not so!" she retorted in a low, fervent tone. "You would never have taken Claredon had you not resorted to deception and guile."

Willfully Ranulf ignored her accusation, quelling his resentment in favor of logic. "The fact that I averted bloodshed and the expense of a long siege by my ruse does not soothe your conscience?"

Ariane shook her head sadly. Nothing could assuage her guilt over letting her father down. "My father depended upon me."

"And my king depended on me," Ranulf replied reasonably. "I but carried out Henry's commands. Surely you can understand that."

"You will never convince me that securing your own interests was not your chief goal."

"Indeed it was. But only consider my position. I could not have allowed you to challenge my authority. I would have appeared a fool could I not even manage to control my own betrothed."

It stung her that he would put forth so rational an argument in so reasonable a tone, but before she could think of a proper rebuttal, he quizzed her on another point she had introduced.

"You said you would gladly dissolve our betrothal. Did you speak true?"

Her chin rose regally. "I do not lie, my lord."

"Then why do you weep over it?"

"Merely because I no longer desire to marry *you* does not mean I have no wish to marry at all."

Ranulf eyed her thoughtfully, wondering what troubled her. She was still young and beautiful enough—incredibly so—to easily attract another suitor. "I see no reason you cannot still wed. Even a maid of your"—his gaze raked her while his tone turned dry—"advanced years should still be able to garner a husband."

"After your rejection? Without a marriage portion to bring to my new lord?" She looked away. "I suspect you have made a future marriage for me impossible."

He'd had little to do with the loss of her inheritance, actually; her father's treason was to blame. "Not impossible, demoiselle. Perhaps it is unfair that your father's castle was awarded to me . . . but your lack of dowry should not be an insurmountable impediment to marriage. You are not ill favored. For a noble maiden still intact, there are always men seeking a bride. Mayhap some of my own vassals might be interested."

"They would be willing to take your leavings?"

"Leavings?"

"Who would credit my maiden status after you forced me to sleep in your bed?"

His brow clearing, he laughed—confounding her completely. "Who would credit that I allowed a wench to pass the whole night with me? Especially one of your class. No one who knows me well would accuse me of defiling you. My aversion to noblewomen is well known—and so is my ability to find wenches willing to share my bed. I have no need to resort to ravishment, I assure you. No, they will consider you my hostage, nothing more. Do not fret overmuch on that score."

She looked skeptical and faintly puzzled. "How easy it is for you to mock my pain."

His gaze softened. "I do not mock you, lady." He paused, searching her face. "Is marriage so important to you, then?"

"It is to any woman. A man may fight and compete in tourneys and travel the land. A woman has only her home and family to care for." Biting her lip, she looked away. "I no longer have either."

Ranulf shifted uncomfortably. He was not accustomed to feeling guilt, yet he felt a flash of it now. He had never considered her perspective. He'd thought a girl so young would be content to remain in her father's castle, rather than be hauled off to Normandy as the bride of the Black Dragon—but perhaps he'd merely persuaded himself of her reticence to justify his delay, to ease his conscience for not proceeding with the marriage. He should have come for her sooner, certainly. Then again, Ariane professed to loathe him. She had less desire to wed him than he did her.

"You could always enter a nunnery," he suggested lamely when she remained silent.

Ariane shook her head. "I am not fitted for the church. My lady mother always said . . ." She faltered, realizing she had strayed to dangerous ground.

"Yes? What said your mother?"

"That my tongue was too barbed for the peace of a convent."

Ranulf's hard mouth curved in a sudden grin. "A wise woman, your mother. I have had a taste of that barbed tongue." He noted the flash of fire in Ariane's eyes with satisfaction, strangely preferring that show of spirit to her despair. "The Lady Constance . . . I met her but once at the betrothal ceremony, she was all that was gracious. She died some years past?"

Ariane stiffened at the reminder. "We lost her four springs ago," she said carefully, reluctant to discuss her beloved mother's passing. What the world knew was not the truth, but it would have to suffice.

"You mourn her loss?"

"Aye . . . keenly." That much was certainly true.

He heard the sadness in her voice, saw the grief in her eyes. Involuntarily, Ranulf raised his hand to stroke the elegant hollow beneath her cheekbone, but she flinched at his touch and pulled back.

Shifting his weight, he pushed the pillows behind his back and sat up, drawing Ariane's gaze to his powerful bare torso, to the soft mat of curling hair on his chest. Seeing it, she recalled the feel of him last night when she had tried to ward Ranulf off, and felt a quickening in her body that was totally unexpected.

"I would rather not be doomed to maidenhood," she murmured in an attempt to return the conversation to the subject at hand.

"Doomed? Strong words for the unwedded state." His scrutiny turned considering, gleaming with a brightness that bespoke mischief. "One would think you regret never being bedded."

Uncontrollably a blush rose to Ariane's cheeks. "You twist my words, my lord. I want children. If I must suffer the physical attentions of a husband to gain them, then I am willing to do my duty."

"Suffer? Duty?" An amused light flickered in his eyes. "Your notion of the marriage bed is a cold one, methinks. Doubtless it is your innocence speaking. If you had more experience, you would know what pleasure can be found even in duty."

"If you had *less* experience, my lord," Ariane said tartly, "you might properly value the solemn commitment of the flesh."

"Ah, but I do value it," he replied, his warmth fading. "Too much so to risk an irrevocable union. While I might desire to sample your lovely charms, I have no intention of solemnizing our contract."

"You will never sample my charms!" she retorted stiffly. "I will not play the whore for you!"

A provocative smile curved his mouth. "I would not ask you to, demoiselle. I like my wenches with more honey and less vinegar. I would have a meek maid in my bed, not a virago."

His soft taunt did more than sting; it wounded her. Ariane's indignation abruptly faded, swamped by familiar insecurities, but she took refuge in sarcasm. "Since you find me so unappealing, I wonder that you agreed to the betrothal in the first place."

Ranulf shrugged his broad shoulders. "I agreed for the usual reasons. I found an alliance with Claredon politically advantageous. And your father sweetened the arrangement with a grant of land in the south."

Intellectually, Ariane understood those reasons. For most

nobles, marriage was a matter of cold calculation, the means to gain rank and riches, land and heirs. And Ranulf had been bribed further to wed her. He had been given, not a fiefdom for which he would have had to swear fealty and provide knight's fees, but an outright grant.

"I never desired a bride, only your lands," he added with chilling honesty.

Ariane clasped her fingers together to keep them from trembling. It shouldn't hurt to hear the truth so bluntly stated, yet it did. She looked down at her hands. "Is that why you never came for me? Because my father still lives, I never inherited his demesne?"

Guilt pricked Ranulf's conscience. He could not admit to her the true reason for his reticence: that he feared betrayal by any bride, dreaded risking a repeat of his mother's faithlessness or his father's violent retribution.

"Aye," he prevaricated. "I could not gain control of the chief prize of your inheritance—Claredon—until your father's passing, which appeared to be many years in the future. And there seemed no reason for haste. Both sides enjoyed the advantages of the alliance, without the encumbrances. And Walter saw no urgency in completing the contract."

"But now that you have possession of Claredon, you need be encumbered by me no longer."

Ranulf clenched his jaw, wondering how she managed to twist the truth to make *him* the villain when she had brought about this predicament herself, by defying the king, by freeing a prisoner of the crown, and by supporting her father's rebellion. "I am under no obligation to honor a traitor with my allegiance," he replied in his own defense.

She lifted her gaze—and her chin. "I would know your intentions, my lord. What will become of me?"

He frowned. "If your father is found guilty, you will become a ward of the crown. Your marriage will be in the king's gift, for him to dispose of as he sees fit. For the nonce, I am to hold you as a political prisoner." He paused. "You cannot be unaware of your value to Henry as a hostage, or that your arrest will perhaps end the rebellion sooner. . . ."

Ranulf's explanation trailed off as he recalled the exact situation. Why was he permitting her to make him feel guilt for executing his duty, or sympathy for her plight? He should know from her recent treasonous actions that he could not allow himself to soften toward her. He could not let down his guard. "You are my prisoner, to do with as I will, demoiselle."

At the sudden harshness of his tone, Ariane dug her nails into her palms. How could he be so gentle and reasonable one moment, so cold and heartless the next? "If you mean to punish me, I wish you would do so."

"Your wishes are of little concern to me, my lady."

No, Ariane thought bitterly. She could not expect otherwise. She was naught to Ranulf but a foe to be broken and used. And when he was done with her, he would marry her to some grateful lackey or pack her off to a convent. By the Blessed Virgin, how could she ever have cherished such tender dreams of him?

He was watching her intently, his expression enigmatic. "However I choose to exact retribution from you," he said finally, "it will come in my own good time. As I informed you last evening, you can yet influence your fate."

"What . . . do you mean?"

How forthcoming should he be? Ranulf wondered. Despite his justifiable mistrust of her, despite the wisdom of caution, her cooperation would prove helpful in a successful transition of power. With their former lady's support, the castlefolk would accept him as lord more readily, perhaps even peacefully. And yet he had no wish to give Ariane the notion she could exploit his vulnerability to her advantage, or to furnish her any leverage to use over him.

"I desire your cooperation regarding the people of Claredon. I would keep their goodwill. Your father's knights can be expected to follow a code of honor, but not the villeins and freemen. I do not want them set against me, intent on rebellion. Waging war against one's own property is never profitable, and I have no intention of denting my coffers in unnecessary strife."

"Claredon is not your property as yet. My father has not been convicted or even afforded a trial. You are not yet lord here."

Calling on the control he had so mercilessly taught himself, Ranulf forced himself to temper his reply. "I *am* lord here, by Henry's orders. I hold this place, demoiselle. And what is mine, I keep."

"Then you may keep it without my aid."

Anger darkened his face. She would not bend easily, Ranulf was coming to realize.

Without warning, he threw off the covers. Startled, Ariane leapt to her feet, gazing at him in alarm.

"If you wish to retain your maidenly virtue," he said sardonically, "I suggest you step back. I would dress."

Abruptly, she fled to a far corner of the room.

His mouth curling at the corner, Ranulf rose from the bed and strode naked to the door. Opening it, he bellowed for his squire to bestir himself. Then crossing to the bench where he had disrobed the previous evening, he tugged on his braies and tied the drawstring at his waist.

"You have two days to decide your course," he told Ariane with forced evenness. "I ride for Wyclif this morn and should remain the night at least. In my absence I shall leave my vassal, Ivo de Ridefort, in command of the keep. You will remain confined here until such time as I have your solemn oath to accept me as your liege."

"I will not give it."

With effort, Ranulf held fast to his temper. The wench was sorely in need of a strong hand to curb her defiance, and he would have to provide it. He was determined to conquer her will—and he would, eventually, once he found an effective method to deal with her short of physical violence. As yet, nothing had worked. But two days should buy him time to decide.

"Meanwhile," he continued as if he had never heard her interruption, "you may have the freedom of this chamber. I shall not order you bound, and your women will be permitted to attend you."

"Your generosity overwhelms me, my lord."

"Have a care, demoiselle. My patience wears thin."

"Does it indeed? I suppose I should be quaking in my shoes?" she replied scathingly.

He pinned her with a dark look. "Were you wise, you would be. I can inflict a great deal of misery upon you."

"I have not the least doubt on that score. I would expect nothing else from a brute."

"Brute?" His black brows snapped together in a scowl at the unjust accusation. He had taken great care to treat her gently—indeed with far more lenience that she deserved. Yet he was a fool to let her goad him, Ranulf realized. Letting her barbed slurs provoke him into losing his temper only awarded her the upper hand in their battle.

Shaking his head, Ranulf exhaled a rough chuckle and forced himself to relax his rigid muscles. "Have I hurt you, lady?" he managed to reply evenly.

"Nay . . . but neither have you accorded me the slightest respect."

"You forfeited that right by your defiance. Your status now is no higher than a serf's."

Ariane glared back at him; if he hoped to see her cower, he had much to learn.

It took all her willpower, though, to resist flinching when Ranulf turned and casually strolled over to her. He stared down at her, his amber hawk's eyes unsettling with their intentness.

"You will submit to me, demoiselle," he promised softly. "You will call me lord and master."

Summoning every ounce of courage she possessed, Ariane lifted her chin defiantly. "You may be lord here, Sir Dragon, but you will never, *never* be my master."

A slow, terrifying smile suddenly wreathed his lips, a dangerous, wolfish grin that boded ill for her. "Beware, wench. I might just accept the challenge to tame you. Methinks I could find pleasure in the attempt."

Ariane fixed him with a bristling stare of fury, which Ranulf proceeded to ignore entirely as he turned away to wash at the basin.

When his squire entered bearing a tray, he broke his fast with a chunk of bread and cold venison and a cup of wine, while his squire helped him with his armor. In short order he was attired in the fashion of a knight, with his mail hauberk clinging to his broad frame and gold spurs attached to his boots.

Finally, Ranulf glanced at Ariane as he buckled on a leather waistbelt with its sheathed sword. "When I return, we shall conclude our discussion. I suggest you carefully consider your answer."

Without another word, he donned a conical helmet with a wide nose guard that obscured much of his face. Then he turned and left the chamber, his squire following hard on his heels.

The oaken door closed behind them with a dull thud, and Ariane could hear a soft scrape of a bar being set in place. Alone, she stared at the door with frustrated rage. He had locked her in—after dismissing her as if she were beneath notice, like the meanest serf, or worse—a *woman*. May God smite that iron-hearted knave! She could scarcely contain her frustration. She could see shades of her father in Ranulf. Indeed, she could accept the Black Dragon's legendary wrath better than his dismissal.

Muttering imprecations under her breath, Ariane went to one of the embrasures and unbolted the shutter. The windows of the solar boasted panels of costly glass, and from her vantage she could see the castle grounds below. A troop of mounted knights and archers attired in chain mail or leather breastplates awaited the lord of Vernay in the inner bailey, while his crimson silk pennon with the dragon rampant snapped and fluttered in the breeze.

Moments later, she spied Ranulf striding across the court, toward a great black warhorse. When he had mounted his charger and accepted his weapons from a squire, he looked positively lethal. Early-morning sunlight glinted off the twenty-foot steel lance and tall, kite-shaped Norman shield, while his newly polished armor sparkled silver. Then Ranulf wheeled his destrier, and under his dragon's banner, led his body of mounted men through the inner gates. They traversed the outer bailey at an easy gallop and thundered across the castle drawbridge without pause.

Ariane watched until they were long out of sight. Eventually, though, she was struck by a bitter awareness: The sounds of castle life had returned to normal. The squeals of animals in their pens, the irregular clang of the smithy's hammer, the cries of falcons in the mews, were no different than under her father's rule, before the arrival of the Black Dragon. Life had gone on much as before, despite the change of lordship.

Save for her, she thought with despair. She was Ranulf's hostage now, confined to these chambers like any highborn criminal. They were sworn enemies, locked in a battle of wills—a battle that she dared not lose. Too much was at stake. Too many lives depended on her.

Turning her head to the east, into the rising sun, Ariane gazed across growing fields and green meadows now hazed with a golden mist, her eyes blurring at the sight of the forest beyond.

Mother, how I wish you were here to guide me.

Yet her lady mother was not here, Ariane reminded herself bitterly. Nor was her father. She must deal with this terrible dilemma entirely on her own. Somehow, some way, she had to thwart the Black Dragon and regain Claredon. Being a woman she must fight with what few weapons were at hand, but she would defeat Ranulf de Vernay if it took her last dying breath.

Chapter 6

Midafternoon the following day, Ranulf rode with his knights and men-at-arms toward Claredon, well satisfied with his recent achievements. The wooden gates of Wyclif had opened to him without a battle, and he had taken control of Walter's nearest demesne manor with ease. Many of the vassals had sworn allegiance to their new lord, and those who refused would be ransomed by their families. The subjugation of Claredon was proceeding as planned.

Save for one small detail, Ranulf mused wryly. The lady of Claredon. His former betrothed. How to deal with Ariane was his greatest dilemma. Resentment still gnawed at his insides over her defiance, yet he could feel himself unwillingly softening toward her.

Pure madness, Ranulf thought in exasperation. Ariane had shown not the slightest repentance for refusing him entrance to the castle or for aiding her vassal to escape, nor had she displayed the least sign of submission to him afterward. Although her refusal to cower stirred his admiration, he could not allow her to go unpunished, not and maintain discipline among her people. But what to do? Choosing a punishment commensurate with her crimes was not the problem; finding one where he could live with his conscience was.

Moreover, he had no desire to continue fighting her. He wanted a peaceful transition of authority, and for that he needed the Lady Ariane. Needed and *wanted* her. Although he was loath to admit it, she stirred his blood as no wench had in years. *Witless fool, letting her play on your sympathies. At this very moment she might very well be plotting your downfall.*

Yet to his annoyance, Ranulf felt his pulse quicken in anticipation as they crested a hill and he spied the gray walls of Claredon in the distance. He was required to rein in his prancing destrier, who sensed his excitement.

Ranulf's mouth curled in self-derision. He was much too eager to return to his newest castle and confront the cool, defiant beauty who awaited him. Indeed, she had occupied his thoughts far too much of late.

When he heard a throat being cleared beside him, he turned to find Payn regarding him closely, a smile of amused understanding curving his mouth beneath his steel helm.

"You should have sampled the manor wenches last night after all, lord. There was a petite, flame-haired morsel who could have tempted even your jaded palate."

Ranulf let the observation pass. Payn knew he did not mix pleasure with duty.

"Did you bed the lady?"

Ranulf's head whipped around. "Who?"

"I know of but one woman who could be preying on your mind so relentlessly that you forget your companions at arms. You have spoken nary a word this past hour and more. Your betrothed, of course."

"I never touched her," Ranulf said grimly.

"I thought not. Your temper has been too wretched."

Few people could taunt the Black Dragon even good-naturedly without fear of retribution. But Ranulf and Payn had fostered together as boys in the same noble household in Normandy. Payn knew his deepest secrets, understood the demons that drove him.

"It is not merely my loins that pain me," Ranulf retorted dryly. "It is her manner. The wench continues to thwart me."

"If you want her, then take her. You would not be the first knight to claim a noble hostage as the rewards of war."

Ranulf's mouth curled. "You are obviously not versed in Church law, else you would know that were I to 'take her' as you advise, she would be my wife in truth. And having that traitorous wench to wife is my remotest desire."

"She is comely, you must admit."

Ranulf grunted. "The blossom of the hemlock plant holds a deceptive beauty, but its poison is deadly." He grimaced. "I thought I was pledged to a sweet, malleable girl, yet the wench has a tongue as tart as a lemon and a will as stubborn as a mule's. She will not yield. And she is dangerous, besides—not to be trusted.''

"Then toss her in the dungeon and be done with it."

"She is a *lady*," Ranulf replied in frustration.

Giving a low laugh, Payn shook his head. "Some dragon you are. I have seen you deal ruthlessly with your enemies, but with a wench you have no more willpower than the veriest kitten. I advise you to harden your heart, my lord, lest the Lady Ariane take your compassion for weakness."

"Aye," Ranulf agreed, his mouth twisting ruefully at his failing. "I must needs show her who is the lord and who is the hostage."

"You could always summon your Saracen leman from Normandy to ease your ache and keep your mind off your former bride."

Ranulf laughed outright at that provocative suggestion, his good mood restored by Payn's banter. Although not his only leman, Layla was by far the best, yet not even she was worth the price he would have to pay for her exquisite services. He had no desire to show such a grasping, greedy wench such favor, for she would take merciless advantage of his weakness. For that reason, he had not brought Layla with him during the extended military campaign—that and his refusal to indulge in too much softness.

"I could not afford the expense of summoning her," Ranulf replied dryly.

"How *will* you deal with your former bride, then?" Payn asked.

"I know not." He fell silent, contemplating his dilemma. Unless he hit upon an effective solution, Ariane could prove a savage thorn in his side.

Possessively Ranulf gazed at the stone fortress rising tall and regal in the distance. Perhaps he had been mistaken by not coming to England before now ... although even had he married Ariane, he could not have claimed Claredon, not as long as her father Walter lived. But the castle was his now, by king's decree. *His.* His overlordship of Claredon meant more to him than he wanted to admit. For the first time in his life, his future held a promise of peace. He had the chance to start anew here. This was not Vernay, with its legacy of hatred and torment. Claredon was a rich demesne, worthy of a great lord—and he wanted to be worthy of it.

Ranulf felt a burgeoning hope flare within him as he surveyed the rich countryside. He had never allowed himself to yearn for such providence, except perhaps in the secret recesses of his soul. Even now his good fortune could prove ephemeral. King Henry favored him now because he'd fought well and hard in support of the crown, but Henry could always strip him of honors or return him to bastard status on a royal whim.

Until then, however, he intended to take up residence at Claredon. For the nonce, he would treasure the prize he had been awarded.

He wanted to be a just lord, Ranulf thought with an unfamiliar wistfulness. Yet the Lady Ariane could greatly influence his ability to rule. Without her cooperation, he might be forced to deal harshly with the people of Claredon. His former bride could cause him even more trouble than she had of late.

"I shall have to contrive something," Ranulf murmured almost to himself. "I will not lose this place."

"Perhaps you should consider a different strategy," Payn observed. "As you said, your hostage is a lady—a member of the fair sex—and thus susceptible to persuasion. Why do you not put your legendary talents to good use?"

"Talents?"

"If anyone can seduce the lady into yielding, 'twould be you, Ranulf. You need not actually consummate the betrothal. And you would doubtless find the challenge of taming her pleasurable."

Seduction? Of Ariane? Ranulf fell silent at the suggestion. In truth, he had already considered such a course, although not seriously.

But perhaps he *should* change his strategy in order to win her cooperation. He knew how to persuade a wench to do his bidding. Normal ones, at any event, Ranulf thought with a rueful grin. The lady of Claredon might prove to be a far bigger challenge than he could manage. Ariane responded to him with icy indifference or scathing derision. In truth, if her contempt were not so cutting, he might even have found it humorous. At Vernay the serving wenches usually tripped over themselves trying to get in his bed, but not Ariane.

Ranulf laughed silently at himself. If he had any pretensions to vanity over his success with women, she would quickly suppress them.

But Ariane was his hostage, under his control, which gave him an advantage over her. And without actually intending to, he had created the ideal setting for a seduction. Forcing her to share his bed did not have to be a punishment, but a means to gain her surrender.

Would she be able to resist him if he truly set his mind to winning her?

His mouth curled in a smile. How he would like to break through that icy, disdainful facade of hers. To prove that he could melt that haughty scorn. And were he to succeed, the benefits would well outweigh the trouble.

"I might indeed put my skills to the test," Ranulf replied thoughtfully.

He had barely spoken the words when out of the corner of his eye he caught a flash of movement in the wooded undergrowth. They had been riding along a rutted lane, flanked by oaks and elms, but Ranulf had been paying little attention to his surroundings. Suddenly an arrow whooshed past his head, followed by a sharp cry as one of his bowmen was struck in the chest.

"Blood of Christ, an ambush!" Ranulf roared.

Steel hissed as he drew his sword. With reflexes honed by years of battle, he wheeled his destrier and charged the forest where the attackers were hidden, with Payn a single galloping stride behind him.

A hail of feathered shafts shot from the trees with deadly intent, but Ranulf's men rode directly into the fray, against a horde of bowmen and peasants armed with sickles but led by mailed knights. The forest came alive with the singsong hiss of arrows and the clang of steel on steel.

Ranulf dispatched an archer who had leveled his bow directly at him, while Payn plucked a rebel from a tree with his lance. Catching sight of a mounted knight who shouted orders to the ambushers, Ranulf spurred his steed on, engaging the enemy who was obviously the leader.

Their swords clashed, and Ranulf bared his teeth with a wolfish grin, blood lust singing in his veins.

For a time the knight held his own, but from his defensive maneuvers, it soon became apparent Ranulf's skill and brute strength would triumph. He was about to strike a finishing blow when he heard a hoarse shout to his right.

"My lord, behind you!"

He turned his head, but not in time; a serf charged him fiercely, wielding a pitchfork like a lance. Ranulf felt the twines pierce his mail armor, enter his side, his ribs bearing the brunt of the assault. Giving a war cry as he twisted in the saddle, he hoisted his blade and swung, nearly cleaving the man in two.

Breathing hard, Ranulf bent over his horse's neck, resting his weight against the high wooden pommel of his saddle. When he glanced around him, the fighting had nearly ceased. His men were in control, Ranulf saw with little satisfaction. The villains had been routed, and a number lay scattered on the ground, dead or dying, yet the enemy knight had fled, taking the remainder of his rebel force with him.

Payn gave an order to pursue the fleeing enemy, and when some of Ranulf's men had obediently galloped off, he urged his destrier beside his lord's. The forest had grown starkly quiet, save for the harsh breaths of blowing mounts and panting men.

"You are bloodied," Payn observed with concern.

Ranulf shook his head, his features dark with fury. "I will live. Which is more than I can say for that poor fellow."

One of his bowmen lay sprawled on the forest floor, an arrow having found its deadly target in the center of his chest. A low groan capturing his attention, Ranulf shifted his gaze to another fallen colleague—and let out a violent curse.

"Burc . . ."

Holding his stinging ribs, Ranulf quickly dismounted and knelt beside the lad, carefully inspecting the arrow protruding from his bloody shoulder.

His squire groaned again, gazing up at him with pain-filled eyes. "I beg forgiveness, milord. It was stupid of me. . . ."

"Hush, boy. Don't try to speak. You aren't to blame."

Ranulf cursed again, this time at himself. He alone was to blame for his carelessness, for allowing his thoughts to be distracted by a bright-haired, silken-skinned wench. He had led his troops directly into an ambush.

In a torment of self-condemnation, he sheathed his sword. Ignoring his own minor wounds, he bent and carefully lifted his squire in his arms and gave him to a mounted vassal with orders to return to Claredon at once and seek his surgeon. Fortunately the lad had fainted and would feel little of the jarring ride. Ranulf could only hope the boy would remain unconscious while the arrow was removed—and that the steel head could be cleanly extracted. He had seen more men than he cared to count die of wounds poisoned by debris embedded in the flesh.

He felt a great weariness descend over him as he watched his squire being carried away. His blood still coursed from the recent skirmish, yet deadly fury washed through him. God's wounds! His party had been attacked with peasants armed with pitchforks and led by rebel knights. The image of Simon's face came to mind, followed swiftly by that of the knight's cohort in crime, Ariane of Claredon.

"We killed five and took two prisoners, both wounded," Payn informed him. "One appears to be a knight."

"How many escaped?"

"A dozen or so, I think."

"Carry the prisoners to Claredon," Ranulf ordered grimly, "and chain them in the dungeon. And see to their dead comrades as well. You know what to do."

"Aye, my lord."

The bodies of the slain rebels would be exhibited on the castle walls, to serve as an example to others. His enemies would learn the futility of challenging the new lord of Claredon.

"And Payn, I want regular patrols sent out henceforth."

"As you wish. Never fear, lord. We shall bring the lawless brigands to heel. Defiance will gain them naught."

"Aye, they'll find what rebellion brings," Ranulf said darkly as he turned to mount his stallion.

The chapel bell had just tolled vespers when the oaken door to the solar slammed open. Ariane nearly jumped out of her skin at the crash, even though she had been alerted earlier to Ranulf's arrival by the blare of the gatekeeper's horn signaling the approach of riders. She had watched with dread as the bodies of several men had been handed down from the horses and piled heedlessly on the ground. One of her worst fears had apparently come to pass: the people of Claredon suffering the merciless wrath of the Black Dragon.

At the moment her heart was lodged in her throat as she stared at the powerful, menacing figure in the doorway. The conical helmet with its broad nose guard concealed most of Ranulf's face, yet his fierce gold eyes stabbed her, while his hard mouth compressed with fury.

"I trust you are satisfied with the devil's brew you've stirred up," he said tightly as he kicked the door shut behind him.

"W-What do you mean?"

"We were ambushed on our return from Wyclif. One of my men was slain and my best squire gravely wounded."

He drew off his helmet, which bore a large dent on the left side, as if from a sword's blow. Such a powerful blow might have killed him, Ariane thought with dismay. The helmet would need a trip to the armorer before it could safely be used again. And traces of blood caked the chain links of his mail hauberk. Ranulf had evidently been wounded in the fighting.

He tossed the helmet on a chest without taking his ruthless gaze from her. "I advise you not to be too pleased by your handiwork, wench. Two of your father's vassals sit in Claredon's dungeon—one of knight's rank. And five of your serfs lie dead in the bailey. Their deaths rest on your conscience."

"Five? Mother Mary . . ." Her heart constricted with horror.

"Aye, five. See you now what your treachery has wrought?"

"M-Mine?"

"You abetted your knight Simon in escaping, and he in turn attacked my troops, which resulted in the carnage."

Weakly, Ariane raised a hand to her temple. Earlier she had fallen into a doze after so many nights of sleeplessness, and her head felt so woolly with fatigue, she could scarcely think. "Are you certain it was Simon?"

"What matters who led the attack?" Ranulf snapped. "Your defiance incited your followers to rise against me."

"I am sorry. . . . I never wanted anyone to be hurt."

Her apology fell on deaf ears. Ranulf's granite-hewn features showed no sign of forgiveness as he pushed back his mail coif, exposing raven hair damp with sweat. "Your sorrow will not restore the life of my archer, nor aid my squire to recover from his wounds."

Ariane swallowed. "I know something of healing. Your squire . . . will you permit me to see to his care? To make amends?"

Ranulf shook his head. "You have done enough damage already, milady."

She bit her lip, wondering how she could hope to find any pity in this harsh, ruthless man, particularly when he was rightly outraged by the carnage. Stiff with dread, she moved to stand before him. Summoning her courage, she placed an imploring hand on his mail sleeve, although he shook it off as if her touch burned. "The men who died . . . will you allow them a proper burial?"

"They will receive no such veneration. Their bodies will remain on view as a reminder to those who would dare rise against me."

"Nay, 'tis barbarous. You cannot—"

"I *cannot?*" Ranulf's eyes narrowed fiercely, flashing like yellow lightning. "Do not seek to test my mettle, lady. I could crush the breath from you in an instant."

She knew he spoke the truth. He could choke the life from her with ease, or fell her with a single blow. Yet she could not give up without trying to persuade him to mercy.

"And your prisoners?" she breathed. "What will befall them?"

"For their treachery, they will pay with their lives."

She gazed at him in anguish. "No . . . please . . . my Lord Ranulf . . . Have you no compassion? Can you show no mercy?"

"I have no mercy for traitors."

"I beseech you—"

"Cease your entreaties, lady!" he roared. "I will not be swayed!"

Flinching from his violent fury, Ariane bowed her head. "I humbly beg your forgiveness, my lord."

A muscle in Ranulf's jaw worked at her transparent attempt

to manipulate him and assuage his anger. God's teeth, but she seemed determined to push him to the limits. Even now she refused to back down.

"Will ... will you not permit me to sue for their lives at least?"

He had been about to give her another blistering rebuke, but his gaze arrested. This was her first sign of weakening. He would be a fool not to pursue it, Ranulf realized. He wanted, needed, her cooperation to achieve his goals. Hitherto Ariane had responded with defiance and scorn at any suggestion that she aid him in assuming control of the demesne, deeming him a usurper and trickster. If he could win her support, though, however reluctant, the people of Claredon would accept him more readily as overlord, would confer him their loyalty that much sooner. "What do you offer in exchange?"

"I ... I have naught to give you," Ariane replied. "You claimed anything that was mine when you seized Claredon."

"There is your oath." She gazed at him with faint confusion. "Will you swear for Henry?" Ranulf demanded. "Will you accept me as your liege?"

"You know I cannot. My allegiance is to my father."

He cursed under his breath at her continued stubbornness. "Under the circumstances, you have no reason to consider yourself bound to your father."

"Perhaps ... but I will not forsake him."

"You would forfeit the lives of your vassals?"

An ache rose to her throat, and she could barely force her denial past the constriction there. "No. What do you want of me?"

"I would have your sacred vow, demoiselle. You will swear to keep faith with me, to submit to my rule without question."

"You will not harm your prisoners if I yield to you?"

Ranulf stared down at her beautiful, upturned face, into the luminous eyes swimming with tears, and something within him softened, like wax against a flame. He had to admire her courage. She had not pleaded for herself—now or at any time since he had taken her hostage—but only for her father's men.

"I will not allow them to go unpunished, demoiselle. Not

only did they dare challenge my authority, but they cost a good man, and mayhap another. But I will agree to spare their lives.''

Ariane searched Ranulf's harsh features, realizing she would gain no other concessions, not when he was so enraged by the senseless carnage. It would be unwise to press him further. Indeed, she knew what her lady mother would advise: a willow that bent with the wind would outlast the storm, though a mighty oak snapped. For now she would have to bend, would have to bide her time. It was no shame to strike such a bargain in order to prevent more deaths.

''Very well,'' Ariane said quietly. ''I make you a solemn vow to submit to your wishes.''

Ranulf shook his head. She looked so guileless, her eyes wide and full of repentance. Yet he could not allow her to escape with total impunity. She had given him nothing but betrayal. And she had caused the death, at least indirectly, of a half dozen men and nearly killed his squire, a brave lad who had shown only loyalty and devotion. ''Not so quickly, demoiselle. I will not allow you to escape retribution so easily. There are conditions.''

''Conditions, my lord?''

''You will address your villeins and vassals, proclaiming me lord of Claredon. You will offer your homage to me in a public forum, clearly accepting me as your liege.''

''But . . . women cannot pay homage.''

''It will be a symbolic gesture, merely that. I will have your people observe your submission, so they will follow me more willingly.''

''I shall do as you wish.''

''That is not all. You will serve me henceforth. My squire was wounded as a result of your actions, so you will assume his duties. You will attend me as my body servant, perform every function I required of him, until such time as he is fit to resume his responsibilities.''

Ariane nodded slowly. Doubtless it was Ranulf's intent to demean her by forcing her to play his servant in public, yet it was not too high a price to pay, not if he would spare the lives of her people.

''There is still more. I demand your unquestioning obedience. You will leap to fulfill my every wish, carry out my smallest command.''

Ariane felt her fingers curl involuntarily, yet she dared not show the slightest sign of rebellion. She nodded.

"I will have your oath, demoiselle."

Knowing she had no choice, she bowed her head. "You have it, my lord," she replied solemnly. "By my sworn word, I pledge to obey you in all things, to act as your servant, to seek to persuade the people of Claredon to accept you as their rightful liege."

Ranulf stared down at Ariane warily, reluctant to trust her, even more unwilling to trust his own senses. Her voice quavered, husky with relief or unshed tears he wasn't certain, but with a power that tugged relentlessly on his sympathies. It was impossible to ignore the compassion she stirred in him—or deny the arousing effect of her nearness, either. He could smell her scent, the subtle, sweet fragrance of oil of roses and warm woman. He was keenly aware of her body's heat, of the constant charge of attraction that flowed between them, of the primal urges she kindled in him so effortlessly. Ranulf felt his loins tighten, become heavy and full, and he swore under his breath.

Deliberately he took a step back, absently clutching his aching side as he put a safer distance between them. Yet a frown scored his brow. He had gained Ariane's promise of submission, her pledge of unquestioning obedience. So why then did he feel as if she were the victor and he the vanquished?

Chapter 7

The crowded great hall was deathly quiet, so still a mouse could be heard rustling in the floor rushes. Only the fire crackling in the immense stone hearth at one side of the long hall disturbed the silence.

All eyes were trained on the lady of Claredon as she gave her oath of homage to the Black Dragon of Vernay. Ariane knelt before Ranulf, her head bowed, her hands placed in his, and swore to serve him faithfully.

When she rose and met his wintry gaze, her carriage was proud and erect. "My liege," she said clearly—and felt like the meanest traitor. It had been her responsibility to defend the demesne, and her failure distressed her keenly.

Her vision blurred, she turned to survey the crowd, facing her people for the first time since the fall of Claredon three days ago. She saw sympathy and sorrow on the countenances of those who had served her all her life: Claredon's priest, Father John; his clerk and her half-brother, Gilbert; her ladies and sewing women; kitchen wenches and serving maids, including the insolent Dena; pages and varlets who performed the countless domestic chores. She saw no sign of the castle's seneschal or steward or any other high official. Doubtless Ranulf had imprisoned them for refusing to accept him as lord.

"The new lord of Claredon bids you lay down your weapons and go about your duties," she told them in English, in a voice she managed to keep steady. "He says there will be no further bloodshed if we give him no trouble and serve him well."

She repeated the message in French for the benefit of the Norman conquerors. Hesitating then, she glanced up at Ranulf, wishing the short blue square of silk she wore as a head covering was large enough to shield her from his penetrating gaze. His harsh visage had remained coldly expressionless during the ceremony, and now he watched her with an intentness that made her want to shiver. She could well understand how he had earned the dreaded name Black Dragon.

"Is that sufficient, my lord?"

"For now. On the morrow you will address the assembled field serfs and bid them return to working the land. I want my new estates to prosper."

"As you wish, my lord," Ariane replied quietly, making every effort to keep her manner complaisant, refusing to give him any reason to repudiate the bargain they had struck.

Ranulf called for the repast to begin and the crowd dispersed. His vassals found places at the long trestle tables erected for meals, with those of highest rank sharing the lord's table on the raised wooden dais at the hall's front end. Without being told, Ariane followed Ranulf to his seat and waited as he settled into an ornately carved, high-backed chair, one of only two backed chairs in the entire chamber. Lifting a flagon, she poured wine into a goblet for him, and then stood obediently behind his chair, at hand to attend him.

The tasks he had set her to were not so onerous, she reflected. As his body servant, she was to select and care for his clothes, help him dress, serve him at table, which included carving his meat and presenting the lord's wine cup, and generally perform whatever personal service he required. She knew precisely what was expected of her. Over the years she had watched her father supervise the training of countless pages and squires, most of whom were the sons of nobles who fostered with him. Her mother had directed the castle staff with a similar firm hand, and when Ariane assumed those duties four years ago, she was well versed in every aspect of service.

It was also a squire's duty to see to his lord's armor and weapons, but earlier Ranulf had claimed he didn't trust her to care for them properly. And that she was clearly unfit for military service.

A faint smile twisted Ariane's lips as she recalled Ranulf's disgust a short while ago when he'd commanded her to remove his war trappings. Her grimace when she unbelted his bloodied sword had earned her a quick rebuke, and he'd shown little patience with her further ministrations. As tall as she was, she had needed to stand on a stool to raise his chain mail hauberk over his head, and then she had staggered so under its weight that Ranulf had to take it from her and arrange it over the wooden form himself.

She had drawn a sharp breath when she realized his woolen tunic was soaked in blood.

"Do not raise your hopes overmuch, demoiselle," Ranulf remarked dryly. "It is a mere scratch."

When his torso was bared, though, Ariane could see he had greatly underestimated the severity of his injuries. Doubtless the inflamed gouges in his side were no more than pinpricks compared to some of the wounds he had suffered in previous battles, but they could be dangerous should they putrefy. She had offered to tend his wounded ribs and apply a herb compress, but Ranulf had coolly declined, saying that he didn't trust any remedy she supplied not to be riddled with poison—his tone suggesting that he was already regretting his insistence that she serve him in place of his wounded squire.

"You find something amusing, lady?"

With a start Ariane realized Ranulf had glanced over his shoulder at her and was fixing her with a cool stare. Carefully she schooled her features to blandness. "No, my lord. I have no reason to be amused."

"My cup is empty. Fetch me more wine."

She hastened to obey, gritting her teeth at his commanding tone, even while reluctantly acknowledging the effectiveness of his uncommon method of justice. The role Ranulf had forced her to play was designed not merely to replace his wounded squire—an eye for an eye—but to display her subjugation. By requiring her to serve him publicly, her people would clearly see his power, and perhaps realize the futility of defying his will.

And though she was loathe to admit it, his chosen form of retribution was indeed merciful, Ariane knew. After his party had been attacked, his men killed and wounded, the new lord of Claredon would have been well within his rights to exact a devastating reprisal. Other warlords in similar circumstances had been known to raze entire villages, torturing and killing even women and children in their desire for revenge.

It might be humbling for someone of her high birth to be

treated no better than a serf, mortifying in truth, but Ariane was thankful for Ranulf's measured sentence. Thankful for the opportunity to leave her prison as well; to be allowed to move about the keep, among her people, where she could keep watch on the new lord of Vernay. She did not trust Ranulf not to visit some cruelty upon them, even if thus far he had shown remarkable restraint.

Moreover, she hoped her new responsibilities would help her conquer the nerve-shredding fear of the past few days.

She would be boiled in oil, though, before she displayed the slightest hint of fear to Ranulf. She was determined not to give him the upper hand.

Keeping her head high and her resentment hidden, Ariane stood at attention behind Ranulf during the entire meal, determined to anticipate his every need, to give him no cause for rebuke. Serfs carried in trenchers of day-old bread to serve as bowls and plates. Such trenchers were usually shared by two people, often a lady and a nobleman, but Ranulf enjoyed his own, for the twin chair to his right remained empty.

He conversed idly with his knights as he ate, first a thick soup, then platters of roasted meats, and finally cheeses and sweet wine. Ariane suspected the dishes were not prepared with the care they would have been given under her management, yet the food smelled delicious. Her own hunger took her by surprise, since she'd had little appetite during the past four grueling days.

It came as a welcome relief when Ranulf at last flung her a careless glance. "You have my leave to eat, demoiselle."

Feigning indifference, Ariane withdrew before he could change his mind, and sought a place at the opposite end of the hall, as far away from the lord's table as she could get. She could feel Ranulf's gaze boring into her as she was welcomed eagerly by Father John and his clerk, Gilbert, who both jumped to their feet to serve her.

A lad of some sixteen years, Gilbert was actually her half-brother—her father's son by a field serf. By law a serf's bastard could not inherit a noble's demesne lands, but Gilbert had never appeared to resent the limitations of his baseborn status. Tall and slight of build, he was obviously unfit for the demands of a knightly life, yet he was clever and quick and had earned the notice of his lordly father and the lord's wife, Ariane's mother.

It was actually Lady Constance who had plucked Gilbert from the obscurity and grueling toil of a serf's fate, and had seen him educated by the Church, which dispensed all learning. Although it was not uncommon for a lady to raise her husband's bastard sons, Constance had been exceptionally generous in Gilbert's case, since she herself had been unable to give her lord husband more children. Claredon, as well as Gilbert, had profited. Clerking was an honorable profession in great demand. Many nobles could write at least a little, but most relied upon clerks to see to such work, to handle correspondence and to keep the accounts for their seneschals and stewards.

"My lady!" Gilbert exclaimed in a fierce undertone that startled Ariane as he resettled himself beside her on the bench. He was normally sweet-tempered and exquisitely-mannered, but his fair complexion now was flushed with emotion. "It aggrieves me to see the shame that black devil has heaped on you."

It aggrieved her as well, but she thought it wiser not to inflame her half-brother further. "It is not too unbearable," Ariane replied soothingly.

"But he treats you so ill—"

"He has not harmed me, Gilbert."

Father John scolded the youth to silence. While she ate, the elderly priest related the events of the past three days of her incarceration. It seemed that the new lord was in full command of Claredon. "Yet we have not despaired. Your courage is being hailed on every tongue, my lady."

"Mine?"

"Aye, for foiling the Black Dragon, for aiding Lord Simon to escape. You have given us hope."

"False hope, I fear." She stole a glance at the far end of the hall, where Ranulf sat with his men. "All I have done is bring his vengeance down upon our heads."

"They say he is a devil," Father John murmured in a fearful voice.

"He gives no quarter," Ariane agreed.

"Our father would have dealt swiftly with him," Gilbert muttered beside her.

A pang of remorse shot through Ariane at the reminder of her failing. "But our father is not here, so I must act as I see fit."

Her brother scowled. "What villainous means did he employ to force your surrender? 'Tis rumored he threatened to kill his wounded prisoners, and that you traded their lives for your subservience, milady."

"He was justly angered by the attack on his men," she murmured.

"But to abuse you so—the accursed devil! He should be stricken down for defiling you."

"He has not defiled me. He only denied my status as a lady."

"He has not taken you as his leman?"

Ariane felt a blush rising to heat her cheeks, knowing Gilbert's assumption was what the rest of the castle folk must believe. "Nay, he has not. He did not wish to validate the betrothal contract. He means to repudiate it—and me."

Her assurances did not appease the boy's fury. "All the same, he has dishonored you by this public humiliation. Would that I knew how to wield a sword! I swear I would cut him down where he stands!"

"Gilbert!" she replied sharply. "You must not even consider such a rash act. To challenge the new lord would be to forfeit your life."

"I care not! I cannot allow him to treat you with such disrespect."

"We will aid you to escape to the abbey at Frothom," the priest broke in with a suggestion. "The Church will succor you. Simply say the word."

"Aye," Gilbert seconded. "There are many here who would lay down their lives for you."

"I do not want anyone else to lay down his life!" she said emphatically.

"But you must seek refuge, lady."

Ariane shook her head at the priest. "I cannot abandon Claredon. I have a responsibility to the people here. How could I live with myself if I fled to the safety of the abbey while those I left behind suffered?"

Father John nodded solemnly. The noble class enjoyed a

life of power and privilege, but many, like Walter and his daughter, believed that advantage carried with it obligations.

"As for the future, you will offer no further resistance. Lord Ranulf has killed and wounded too many already, and I want no more senseless deaths. We will have to bide our time until my father returns. . . ." Ariane faltered, choking on the words, but forced herself to continue. She did not wish to stir false hopes, and yet it was her duty to comfort and cheer her people as well as protect them. "You must not lose faith. Lord Walter may yet be proven innocent. You must pass the word, Father John. No more ambushes on Lord Ranulf's men, do you mark me? He is lord here now, and must be acknowledged as such."

"Aye, milady. Though it goes against the grain to accept so cruel a knight as overlord."

"He has not been cruel," Ariane replied grudgingly. "His retaliation for today's assault was not excessive. It might be barbaric to display the bodies of his slain foes, but he has the right."

"But, my lady, I doubt he intends such. Lord Ranulf gave me the order for their burial but a short while ago."

Ariane gazed at him in relief. Ranulf must have acceded to her plea for the proper observances for the dead men. "You see, Gilbert?" she addressed her brother. "The Dragon can be reasoned with."

The boy clenched his fists. "Still, it galls me to see you treated so, my lady."

"I know. But it is not so onerous, truly. Under the circumstances, he has acted with restraint. Indeed, most men in his position would never have bothered gaining a woman's allegiance, and yet that is all he has asked of me." She could scarcely believe she was defending the Black Dragon, and yet she could not allow Gilbert to embark on so foolhardy a course as to challenge a powerful warlord. Ranulf would crush him without mercy. As it was, she could only hope the new lord of Claredon would keep his end of the bargain.

Stealing another glance at Ranulf, she found herself pinned by his bold regard, and hastily looked away. His disapproving expression boded ill for her. Falling silent, she bent her attention to finishing her meal.

She would have been even more worried had she been

privy to the conversation at the opposite end of the hall, where Ranulf was enduring a reproach from his chief vassal, Payn FitzOsbern.

"You should have hanged the culprits," Payn remarked grimly, daring to criticize his liege. "Your punishment was too lenient by far, my lord."

"If I can gain the willing obedience of the people here," Ranulf replied mildly, "then my lenience will have served a purpose."

Payn drained his wine cup. "True, but I fear you are thinking with your loins rather than your head."

Ranulf's head turned, his gaze narrowing on his vassal. "What mean you by that?"

"Merely that you seem to have been bewitched by your bride."

He stiffened. "She is no longer my bride, and I fail to see the logic in your charge."

"You returned to Claredon bent on revenge, yet she managed to persuade you to stay your hand."

"Solely because I *chose* to stay it."

"You mean to say she does not rouse your lust?"

"She stirs nothing in me save my temper," Ranulf lied. "I've no interest in a sharp-tongued vixen, especially one of her high birth."

Payn's brow shot up, while on his other side, Ivo de Ridefort grunted. "Such defiance must be beaten out of a wench."

Ranulf's jaw hardened. He would never sink to the animalistic level of his brutish father. "I will handle her as I see fit."

Ivo's cousin, Bertran, glanced down the length of the hall where Ariane sat eating. "I almost envy you the taming of her, sire. She is a beauty, no mistake. 'Struth, I wouldn't mind taking her off your hands. Give her to me for a week or so and I will have her purring at your every command."

Another of Ranulf's vassals guffawed. "You, Bertran? Purring? What would a lady such as she have to do with a ham-handed lout such as you?"

"Best curb your lust, Bertran," another knight said with a glance at Ranulf's unsmiling features, "before our lord curbs it for you."

Forcing himself to relax the set of his jaw, Ranulf allowed

his mouth to curve in the flicker of a grin. He did not care to hear his men discussing Ariane as if she were a common castle wench, yet defending her would only add substance to Payn's accusation.

Was Ariane a witch who had cast him under her spell?

Reluctantly, Ranulf found his gaze drawn back to her. She held herself with the regal grace of a queen, despite the humbling ordeal he had forced upon her by making her serve his needs in full view of her people.

He could not have said why he wanted to shield her, especially when suspicion and resentment still ate at him. Perhaps there was some merit to the charge of bewitchment, after all. Her stubborn support of her treasonous father irritated him, while her barbed wit stung; yet he had to admire her courage and spirit. And the burning in his veins was not due to anger at the wench's disobedience, Ranulf acknowledged. No, he was fiercely attracted to her, despite her defiance, despite her noble birth.

Ranulf exhaled a slow breath. He could not permit himself to care about her. Payn was right on one score at least. He would have to harden his heart and guard himself well against her wiles. Highborn ladies like Ariane brought nothing but pain and trouble. He had shown her mercy, a mercy he himself had never known. With that she would have to be content.

She was fortunate her connection to the ambush could not be proven. According to the confessions of the men they'd captured, the knight she had recently aided to escape, Simon Crecy, had not engineered this afternoon's attack. The blame lay with other loyal knights and serfs seeking to regain possession of Claredon. Yet Ariane bore some of the responsibility, Ranulf reminded himself, for refusing to surrender the castle to him in the first place, in defiance of a royal command.

Now that his fury had a chance to cool, however, he was willing to admit he might have overreacted when he'd demanded that she serve as squire. He had been angry over the pointless deaths of his archer and Claredon's serfs, as well as Burc's wounding. Ariane's servitude might serve a useful purpose, though. She would change her tune soon enough if she had to endure enough personal humiliation, would soon be pleading with him for mercy. He had no desire to mistreat her, but he was determined to make her yield to his authority.

She had surprised him a short while ago with the sincerity of her pledge before her people. No one but he would have guessed that her oath was forced, that she had not willingly submitted to him.

A jongleur who had begun strumming a viol asked the lord's permission to entertain the crowd with a ballad. Ranulf nodded but listened with only one ear as he impatiently awaited Ariane's return. He did not care for the fierce glances the handsome blond youth sitting beside her kept shooting him.

It was far too long in Ranulf's opinion before she finished her meal and resumed her duties at his side.

"You test my charity, wench," he remarked when she reached him. "I said you might eat, not dally with the castlefolk."

"I beg pardon, my lord."

His mouth twisted dryly. "What were you discussing with such earnestness? Plotting my demise?"

Ariane flushed. "No, my lord, we were not plotting."

"I trust not, demoiselle. I doubt you would enjoy the consequences."

His tone was mild, yet she clearly heard the threat underneath. Refusing to be provoked, though, Ariane raised her chin and eyed him coolly. "If you care to know, we were discussing the burial of the dead—and the plight of the families they leave behind," she prevaricated. "A subject which should concern you as well. As lord of Claredon you are now responsible for their welfare."

"I am well aware of my responsibilities, demoiselle."

"Then you will take steps to provide for them? I am certain you would not permit them to starve," she added archly. "You agreed to treat Claredon's people with mercy—or need I remind you of our bargain?"

Ranulf's eyes narrowed at her temerity, but then he smiled, a dark, dangerous smile that held a promise of retribution and made her pulse suddenly beat faster. "Perhaps you should remind yourself, lady. If this is an illustration of your 'unquestioning obedience' to me, then you have already violated your oath."

Willing her heart to settle down, Ariane bit back the retort she longed to make and sighed inwardly, prepared to endure a long evening.

Eventually the last course ended and the tables were cleared of dishes. The company appeared ready to settle in for a long interlude of wine and revelry, for already the dicing and music had begun.

"Will you give me leave to retire, my lord?" Ariane asked after a time.

Ranulf shook his head and sent her a taunting smile. "Your duties are not finished. Go and order a bath prepared for me, and return here. I cannot trust you out of my sight."

If she had begun to soften toward him, that provoking look rekindled Ariane's temper. Holding tight to her resentment, she did as she was bid, finding several of Claredon's more trustworthy servants and ordering a bath filled in the solar for the new lord.

When she returned to the hall, she was given a warm jolt of surprise—a most unpleasant one. Several of the castle wenches hovered before the high table, clearly seeking the lord's attention, and Ranulf was favoring them with an easy smile.

He was a devastating man when he truly smiled, Ariane reflected with chagrin. His harsh features softened, gentled, while his already potent masculine appeal increased tenfold. Her dream lover in the flesh, she thought despairingly, recognizing the compelling charm and heart-stopping tenderness that had earned her adoration when she was but a girl.

As if sensing her regard, Ranulf turned his head and his eyes hotly connected with hers. Abruptly his smile changed, to one of challenging, almost mocking, male arrogance, reminding Ariane more clearly than words of the conflict between them.

She had just reluctantly resumed her place at Ranulf's side when a commotion sounded at the entrance to the hall. Glancing up, Ariane saw several armed knights swiftly approaching the dais, followed by two men-at-arms who were dragging a struggling man between them.

Immediately the hall grew quiet. One of the knights bowed before Ranulf. "Beg pardon for the intrusion, lord, but a matter requires your judgment. This cur was caught stealing weapons from the armory.''

Ranulf's gaze narrowed sharply on the burly man. ''Who is he?''

''The smith's apprentice, lord, Edric by name. He took some dozen swords and daggers, including one with a jewelled handle.''

''What have you to say for yourself, Edric?'' Ranulf demanded in heavily accented English, dashing Ariane's previous hope that he could not understand the language.

The brawny Edric hung his head, and yet his belligerent stance showed little sign of contrition.

''I asked you a question!'' Ranulf barked. ''Answer me.''

''I . . . needed the weapons, milord,'' Edric mumbled finally.

''Why?''

''Shall I wring a confession from him, lord?'' a guard asked when the prisoner remained silent.

Watching the proceedings, Ariane could no longer keep still. ''My lord, if I may speak?''

Ranulf turned a piercing gaze upon her.

''There must be some mistake. I have never known Edric to be dishonest. He would not steal, I am certain.''

''Then how do you explain his theft of the weapons?''

''Edric . . .'' She turned to the smith. ''Why did you take the swords? Did you mean to work on them at the forge, perhaps?''

''Nay, milady.'' The smith glanced warily at Ranulf. ''I . . . it is just . . . I didn't want harm to come to you, milady. Someone must defend you.''

''You thought to defend the demesne?''

''Aye, for you and my Lord Walter.''

Ariane bit her lip, while renewed anger streaked through Ranulf—anger directed at Ariane. This new incident coming so swiftly on the heels of the ambush was fresh proof of the trouble she had caused by her refusal to surrender to his authority. She had endangered his men, his rule, with her brazen defiance.

''This is what comes of leniency, Ranulf,'' Payn muttered in outrage, loud enough for Ariane to hear. ''When a common smith thinks to challenge you—''

"He should lose a hand for stealing," the knight Ivo, interjected.

Ariane drew a sharp breath. Cutting off a hand was the usual punishment for thievery, but this was no normal theft.

"My lord," she interrupted, appealing earnestly to Ranulf. "I beg you to show mercy. He did not seek to steal for gain, but only to defend the castle. If you must punish someone, then punish me."

Ranulf's mouth tightened. Ariane was beseeching him again for mercy? Deliberately he hardened his heart, cursing his absurd impulse to yield to the plea in her eyes. His urge to comfort her only proved his vassal's charge, that he *was* truly bewitched—a bewitchment he had to fight with all his might. If he softened each time she merely looked at him, it could prove deadly to his command.

And yet this was the first real test of his rule. Would mercy serve him in better stead than ruthless adherence to policy?

"He sought to *defend* the castle?" Ranulf asked softly, with an edge of scorn. "From my rule? Some would consider his crime worse than theft. It is treason to plot to overthrow one's lord."

Having no answer, she remained silent.

His hard gaze skewered her. "You see what your disobedience has wrought, lady? Had you relinquished the castle instead of thwarting me, had you obeyed the king's command, I would not now be required to defend against challenges from every side."

"Aye, my lord," she whispered, her own gaze anguished.

Her show of remorse tempered Ranulf's anger only a small measure as he sat staring at her in smoldering silence.

"The culprit must still be punished for his crime," Payn said sharply, as if sensing his lord's wavering resolve. "Even if he does not lose a hand."

"Flog the cur," someone else interjected.

Wincing inwardly, Ranulf hesitated, reluctant to order a punishment he loathed. Yet if setting such an example to prospective rebels could prevent more deaths, then it would serve a useful purpose. While he delayed his decision, a spirited discussion ensued among his knights, debating the merits of various penalties. The argument continued until Ranulf finally held up a hand.

"Fetch the lash," he said tonelessly.

He was aware of Payn's sharp glance, but he ignored it. He despised the lash, was sickened by that form of punishment, but he forced himself to use it upon occasion. He could not neglect to sentence a criminal simply because he abhorred flogging. And in truth, it was the more lenient penalty. A handless smith would soon be reduced to begging for sustenance.

Bracing his resolve, Ranulf gestured to one of his sergeants. "Give him twenty-one lashes. Then confine him where he may reflect upon his misdeeds and reconsider his rashness."

Deliberately then, Ranulf rose from the table and moved to the center of the hall, where he could view his orders being carried out. He would not exempt himself from so onerous a duty.

At his pronouncement, Ariane let out her breath slowly, dismay warring with relief. Though severe, the sentence was a just punishment. So serious a crime against one's liege could not be ignored, or anarchy would reign. His authority would constantly be challenged. She knew to her sorrow the high cost of a weak ruler. King Stephen had been one, and for twenty bloody years his kingdom had been mired in lawlessness and strife. Any new lord *must* establish his authority. The good ones walked a fine line between weakness and mercy, between compassion and justice. In this instance at least, Ranulf had shown himself to be merciful.

And yet she could not absolve herself from blame for the role she had played in inciting her father's loyal followers to challenge Ranulf. Her own defiance of him, at least indirectly, had brought on Edric's punishment. Ariane bit her lip hard, her guilt flaying her as she watched the preparations.

Edric thrashed and strained against his captors' grip, but was eventually subdued and stripped of his tunic, then secured to a wooden column and his hands tied overhead. With a curt nod, the new lord of Claredon gave the order to begin.

At the hiss of the first stroke, a cold wave of nausea washed over Ranulf, yet he stood and forced himself to watch as the punishment was carried out. He winced inwardly each time the bullhide lash cracked against the man's bared back, the memory of the scourge flaying his own back making him feel faint.

Each brutal stroke reminded him of his own terrifying youth, except that his father's whip had been a scourge made of plaited steel chainwork. If he shut his eyes, he could feel himself kneeling, naked, on the cold stone floor, petrified, trembling, desperately fighting back screams of pain, his heart filled with hatred for his brutish father and the adulterous mother who had caused his torment with her betrayal of her lord.

Devil's spawn! Progeny of hell! His father's enraged castigation reverberated in his ears.

Edric's back was bloody with welts by the tenth lash, and a mass of raw flesh by the last. Ranulf's own body was drenched with cold sweat by the time the punishment ended.

He had to credit Edric with courage. The man never once cried out, but showed only one concession to pain: when his bonds were cut and he was freed from the column, his knees sagged beneath his weight. But he glared with hate-filled eyes as he knelt in the rushes, just as Ranulf remembered glaring at his despised father.

His teeth clenched, Ranulf turned away, only to meet Ariane's troubled gaze across half the length of the hall. She had clasped a hand over her mouth to stifle a whimper.

"I trust you are satisfied, lady," she heard Payn say savagely beside her.

"No ..." she murmured. "I never wished him to challenge Ranulf—or to see anyone suffer so a harsh sentence."

"*Harsh?* Not half as harsh as the lout deserved. I vow it pained Ranulf more than the cursed culprit."

"What ... do you mean?"

"Ranulf knows the bite of the lash. His father taught him well."

"His father?"

"Aye, Yves ... the noble lord of Vernay." Payn's tone was a sneer as he looked directly at her. "You have seen Ranulf's back, have you not?"

"Those terrible scars," Ariane whispered, her voice faint with horror.

She met Ranulf's gaze across the way, through a crowd of vassals and retainers. He stood rigid, unmoving, his face a dark, expressionless mask. Yet he was not emotionally unattached, she would swear it. His eyes ... Was she imagining the tortured look in his amber eyes? Even across the distance, she could sense his pain ... a defenselessness she knew he would never wish her to observe. She was witness to a profoundly vulnerable moment, almost as if she could see into his soul. This proud, strong, vital man carried some kind of deep hurt. ...

She moved toward him as if drawn by an unseen force. Ranulf stood motionless, gathered into himself as if waiting for a blow. How vividly he reminded her of a starving houndpup she had once saved from the cruelty of some village youths. The piteous creature had been kicked and beaten almost to death, and flinched at even a simple touch of kindness. It had nearly broken her heart—as did the look on Ranulf's face now.

His expression was wary, guarded, yet there was a haunted emptiness in his eyes. His mouth was set in a rigid line, yet the deep brackets on either side were a mute testimony to his pain.

She did not know what to say to him. Instinctively she knew he would not want her comfort.

Her assumption proved true. Ranulf's shoulders abruptly squared and his haunted look faded, to be replaced by a cool remoteness.

"The responsibility for his crime lies on your head, demoiselle," he charged in a wooden tone.

Unable to refute the charge honestly, she did not reply to it. "May ... may I tend Edric's wounds?" she asked instead.

Ariane was faintly shocked when Ranulf nodded brusquely, giving her permission to tend the wounded man. She had not expected him to be so forgiving.

She bid several serfs carry Edric below to a small chamber off the kitchens, while she went to the herbal to fetch her supplies.

The oozing wounds of his flayed back were serious, yet a severed hand would have been more so. She washed the injuries with an aromatic oil to soothe the ravaged flesh and then applied a poultice to his back and made him drink an herbal tea she brewed.

He seemed in great pain, but he appeared to bear it stoically. Ariane expressed her remorse over his suffering, but gently made Edric understand that he must accept Ranulf as Lord of Claredon, as she had. It was a lie, perhaps, Ariane reflected silently, but she could not permit anyone else to suffer for her sake. In future, any defiance of Ranulf would come from her alone.

When she returned to the hall, the entertainment had resumed and the rafters resonated with the din of jovial song and laughter. It seemed as if the flogging had never occurred. She could not dismiss the incident so easily, though. She had not imagined the haunting pain in Ranulf's eyes, even though there was no trace of it now. The expression on his harsh, handsome features was cool, remote, detached.

Ariane did not know whether to be relieved or affronted when Ranulf ignored her presence entirely, but her heart skipped a sharp beat when after a few moments, he rose, and with a curt gesture of his head, ordered her to accompany him. Without protest, she followed him from the great hall, conscious of countless pairs of eyes watching them, aware they all suspected her of sharing the Black Dragon's bed.

To her surprise, Ranulf did not go directly to the solar on the floor above, but detoured to a small chamber nearby. The room was dim, lit by a candle and warmed by glowing coals in a copper brazier. A youth lay on a pallet, swathed with woolen blankets. Recognizing him as Ranulf's squire, Burc, Ariane could see the wounded young man was flushed and feverish but awake.

Ranulf went down on one knee beside his pallet and touched Burc's uninjured shoulder. "How fare you, lad?" Ariane had never heard his tone so soft or gentle. He cared deeply for this boy, she was certain.

The youth swallowed and answered in a weak voice, "Well enough, milord."

"I hear the arrow was removed cleanly."

"Aye, milord . . . 'twas fortunate."

Ranulf's jaw tightened, but he refrained from reply as he lifted Burc's head and held a cup to his lips. "Sleep now," he urged. "I shall look in on you on the morrow."

He said not another word, but his features had taken on the black scowl that she so dreaded, Ariane realized as she followed Ranulf along the stone corridor to the solar.

To her further dismay, they found the serving wench, Dena, awaiting him there, a wanton glint in her eye, a seductive smile wreathing her lips as she knelt beside the tub, obviously prepared to attend the lord at his bath—and more so if he wished.

When Ranulf returned her brazen regard assessingly, with frank masculine interest, Ariane was astonished by the fierce jealousy that surged through her. It shouldn't matter in the least whom Ranulf chose to bestow his attentions upon. He could rut with a dozen serving wenches for all she cared. She felt an inexplicable satisfaction, though, when he dismissed the wench.

A moment later, however, when the disappointed Dena had withdrawn, Ariane realized her triumph was premature. With both his squire incapacitated and the servants gone, it fell to her to attend Ranulf at his bath.

"I am waiting, demoiselle," he remarked in that dangerous, silken tone that said clearly he intended to make the experience one she would never forget.

Chapter 8

Comprehending that he intended for her to undress him, Ariane gritted her teeth and set down the pouch of medicines she had brought with her. Slowly she approached Ranulf, aware of the erratic thudding of her heart. Warily, silently, she unlaced his tunic and pulled it over his head, then did the same to his undertunic. The cuts on his side had ceased bleeding, she noted, and had crusted over with dried blood.

Trying unsuccessfully to ignore his bare, powerfully muscled torso, she knelt to untie his cross-garters. By the time she had unfastened the leather points that held his chausses to his braies, though, Ariane felt a shameful heat flooding her body.

"Everything, demoiselle," Ranulf said pointedly when she hesitated. "I cannot bathe half dressed."

Her cheeks flushed scarlet, but she untied the drawstring and pulled the short trousers down over his hips with more force than entirely necessary.

"Must I carry you to the bath as well?" she muttered.

A wicked smile curled Ranulf's mouth. "I would not like to see you attempt it. Your slender form could not bear my weight—not standing, at least. Lying down would be another matter, mayhap. Were you beneath me in bed, I wager you would find my heaviness stimulating."

His provocation was deliberate, she knew. He was determined to taunt her, to show her how powerless she was against him, to prove that he could command her complete submission. And it was effective, if her quickening pulse was any measure. To her chagrin, her mind filled with images of Ranulf covering a woman—covering *her*. Instinctively she knew he would make a magnificent lover— Ariane fiercely bit back a curse, determined that he would gain no response from her. When he turned to step into the tub, though, she was shocked anew by those terrible scars on his back.

A maze of unwanted emotions rose within her: compassion, tenderness, sorrow. Had Ranulf's father truly caused those savage scars on his back? How much more devastating would it be to bear marks created by one's own father? *Her* father had often ignored her, rarely showing her affection— a mere daughter. But never had he raised a hand to her in violence.

She watched as Ranulf settled himself in the steaming water, wondering how he had endured such suffering, wondering if his physical scars were matched by ones held inside. Firelight from the hearth created shadows across his face, casting the harsh angles and planes into softer lines, sketching gentleness where she knew there was only relentless resolve. And yet she could see his weariness in the way he let his head fall back.

To her dismay, it aroused in her an acute compulsion to touch him, to offer comfort. She moved toward him silently, drawn against her will.

Ranulf looked up abruptly when he heard her quiet footstep beside the tub. Ariane stood there, gazing down at him, a startling expression of sorrow softening her beautiful features.

Ruthlessly he steeled himself against the compassion he saw in her eyes. He did not want her pity, refused to accept it. He needed only to use this bewitching wench to forget the past hours of death and pain, the savage memories.

"Why do you tarry, lady?" he asked softly, his velvet tone a provocative taunt as he gazed up at her.

Ariane stiffened. The all-too-revealing pain had vanished from his eyes, to be replaced by a golden glimmer of challenge.

Unwillingly she knelt beside the tub, keenly conscious of Ranulf's nakedness. With trembling hands she took up a piece of soap in order to wash him.

She saw to his hair first, working the suds through his scalp with her fingers and then rinsing with fresh water from a ewer. Then came his magnificent body, beginning with his corded arms and powerful shoulders. No matter how she tried to pretend Ranulf was simply a well-born stranger deserving of this honor by the lady of the castle, she could not make herself believe it.

As she moved her hand reluctantly to his broad, muscular chest, she caught her lower lip with her teeth, her discomfort only made worse by the knowledge that he was watching her intently. When he raised his arm over his head to give her access to his ribs, she recollected the cuts in his side, acquired in the ambush, and gratefully latched on to them as an excuse to divert her attention.

"You should allow me to tend these wounds," Ariane said with concern as, with a gentle finger, she probed the raw, inflamed flesh encrusted with blood. "I brought my supplies."

Ranulf winced and drew back. "You delight overmuch in your inspection, wench."

Perhaps she did delight too much, yet it was not his injuries that fascinated her so. It was the feel of him beneath her fingertips: the granite muscle, the soft whorls of raven hair, the heat of his skin. Hardly daring to breathe, she drew the soap along his ribcage.

Ranulf held himself rigidly, wary of the way she fretted over his wounds. She was very gentle as she washed away the dried blood and cleansed the torn flesh, and she wore a faint look of distress, almost as if she cared for his hurt.

Her concern was pretense, he was certain; he could not trust her enough to believe otherwise. Most likely she was feigning solicitude in order to lower his defenses.

He forced himself to remain immobile while she washed him . . . until her careful strokes moved to his back and she began tracing the welts of raised scar tissue—

It startled her, how swiftly Ranulf moved. His fingers clamped around her wrist like iron manacles, thwarting her, while his frown deepened. "Do not touch me there."

Her eyes widened. "How can I wash your back if I am not allowed to touch you?"

Ranulf's heavy brows drew together. "You may wash, but don't linger."

"As you wish, my lord," she replied with forced meekness.

At her submissive response, he could feel his defenses swelling. He dared not accept the silent comfort she offered.

If he yielded to it, he would be leaving himself too open, too vulnerable, to her. Already he could feel himself softening, weakening at her tenderness. Her very nearness was soothing. The gentle curve of her cheek made Ranulf's hand clench as he fought the urge to reach up and touch her; it took all of his strength to resist.

"I am waiting, demoiselle," he chided deliberately.

She hurriedly finished his back, but when he propped one foot on the tub's rim so she could wash his leg, she moved more slowly. And when she came to the juncture of his thighs, Ariane faltered altogether.

Ranulf gave her his slow wolf's smile. "You gave me your oath to obey me," he reminded her. "Do you forswear it so soon?"

"No. My word is my honor."

"Honor?" The curve of his mouth turned dry. "I know few highborn ladies who can even conceive of the notion."

"You do not believe a woman can remain loyal to her liege?"

"I have witnessed more treachery in noblewomen than loyalty."

Ariane studied his face, wondering what had happened to make him so bitter against women of her class. "You are harsh to condemn us all," she said quietly.

He made a sound much like a grunt. "I have ample reason." Shaking himself then, he reminded her of her duty. "My loins, demoiselle. Your task is not finished."

She had hoped he had forgotten. Biting her lip, averting her gaze from his knowing expression, Ariane forced herself to attend to that masculine part of him that was so unlike herself.

Ranulf stiffened when she ran the soap over his swelling loins, suddenly recognizing the danger in his tactics. Not only had the wench aroused more painful memories of his past, but her innocent ministrations were arousing him physically, a state likely to remain painfully unfulfilled. He was fiercely aware of her nearness . . . her flushed skin, her white teeth catching her pink lower lip, her sweet scent . . . His nostrils flared with primal masculine arousal. He could almost feel her soft woman's body beneath him. . . .

Bewitched, aye, that was what Ariane had done to him,

and yet she was as defiant as ever. If he were wise, he would seriously attempt to change the situation. Not with force, though. Harshness was not the way to make her yield. Rather than show her the brunt of his temper, he would do better to follow the old adage about catching more flies with honey. To attempt the seduction Payn had counseled. To try and bewitch *her* in order to win her surrender.

Ranulf's gaze arrested as he stared at Ariane's beautiful mouth. If he applied his powers of persuasion, he would wager a year's tourney winnings she would not respond with the cool indifference and scorn that vexed him so. He would break down those haughty barriers and have her gasping and pleading for his touch. She would be eager enough to please him then. . . .

Ariane had finished her task with inordinate haste, he realized, feeling his loins throb. Schooling himself to patience, he took the soap from her nervous fingers and began making a lather in his own hands.

"Hand me my knife," he said, softening his tone to a husky murmur. When her eyes widened with apprehension, Ranulf added with a slow smile to reassure her, "I merely mean to shave. I would not wish to chafe your pretty skin."

He saw her quizzical frown with satisfaction. Let her wonder at his meaning.

When she had fetched his dagger, she stood looking down at him uncertainly. Ranulf held her gaze as casually, almost lazily, he soaped his jaw.

"Take down your hair," he ordered mildly.

"Why?"

"Because it pleases me for you to do so."

Ariane felt her stubbornness rising, and yet she could not refuse him. Her hair was fashioned in a braided coronet, and it took a few moments to remove the pins and unplait it. When finally she did, a cloud of pale copper tresses whirled around her shoulders and breasts.

Ranulf drew a sharp breath at the sight. The thought of having that bright, silken hair spread over his pillow as he plunged his male sword within her warm sheath made blood rush to swell him to his full, throbbing length.

A hot gleam entered his eyes as he surveyed her. "And now your clothing, demoiselle."

"You want me to disrobe?" Her voice was a breathless whisper.

"How can I enjoy your womanly charms otherwise?"

Her chin rose defiantly. "You will not 'enjoy' my charms, my lord."

"No?" The word was amused, indulgent. "Your duties are to serve me and to see to my comfort."

"True, but I will not play your leman. You lost that right when you renounced our betrothal."

With effort he kept his expression bland. Mentally he commended her spirit, though the scorn in her voice cut deep. "Mayhap I was mistaken when I dismissed that serving wench," he said with a soft, provocative laugh. "She has been hot for me, unlike the ice-cold reception you give me."

Ariane met his gaze with determined steadiness. "I would be more than happy to fetch her for you, so that you might slake your lust."

A slow smile played on his mouth. "No, demoiselle. You will not elude your pledge of obedience so easily. Your gown . . . or must I remove it for you?"

With a silent oath of frustration, Ariane turned away to undress, removing her bliaud and chainse and hose, until she wore naught but her shift. The thin linen offered little protection; it had long sleeves and the hem fell below the knees, yet the fine material showed her nipples and the triangle of curls at her womanhood—and did little to shield her from Ranulf's scrutiny when he ordered her to turn around. His gaze glided slowly over her body, as if measuring her breasts for the way they would fit in his hands, her legs for how they would wrap around his hips.

Blushing and furious, Ariane crossed her arms belligerently over her chest. "Must you ogle me like a prize ewe at market?"

"I see no harm in staring." His half-lidded gaze was appreciative, while a lazy smile lurked about his lips. "I confess I see much that I like."

More than liked, Ranulf amended to himself. She was a raving beauty who brought his keenly honed senses primitively alive. Her lissome young body was tall and long of limb, her bones fine and fragile, her lovely features haunting. Add to that breasts that were full and lush, a waist he could span with his hand, and hips made to succor a man, and he wanted her more than he could ever recall wanting a wench. He desired nothing more than to toss her on the bed and seat the burning shaft of him deep, deep inside her. . . .

God's teeth, but she provided a temptation that threatened his good judgment. He was mad to put himself through this. He had wanted to compel her submission, to seduce her into yielding, but he had forgotten that his games would leave him unsated and sexually frustrated and gnashing his teeth with lust. He had tied his own hands in that regard. He couldn't touch Ariane without paying the consequences, even if he broke down her resistance.

And yet . . . Why should he deny himself the pleasure of her flesh simply because he could not take her in the accepted fashion? The thought of having her ripe and eager, hot and writhing beneath him, made his loins ache and strengthened his resolve.

Finishing his task of shaving, Ranulf rinsed his face and then rose to his feet. When he had stepped dripping from the tub, he stood waiting with his legs spread, his arms held out.

"The towel, lady," he said blandly, flashing a careless, very male smile. "I am growing chilled."

Ariane's jaw snapped shut at that obvious falsehood. She had woken next to him this morning, and could honestly say she had never known a man with skin so hot as Ranulf's. It would take a winter's storm to chill his overheated blood—or reduce his swelling erection. His nude body was clearly aroused, she saw with a fierce blush.

"I see no harm in your growing chilled," she retorted in a dampening tone. "Mayhap it will cool your lust."

His smile widened provocatively, but she could tell by the hard gleam in his amber eyes he would not relent. He intended her to dry him and would not rest until she had obeyed his every command, down to the last detail.

Picking up a linen towel, Ariane approached him warily, trying desperately to maintain her composure. Ranulf was well over six feet of sheer power, all hard muscle and intensity, and he looked supremely dangerous with his raven hair wet and tousled, his golden, hawkish gaze focused solely on her, an unholy light dancing in their striking depths. Her acknowledged fascination for the man only added to her wrath, and she took her anger at herself out on him, using more force than necessary as she dried his beautiful, scarred body, her movements harsh and agitated.

"Have a care, demoiselle. I would keep my skin."

With effort, Ariane slowed her movements. She hated his reasonable tone, hated the helpless, powerless way he made her feel. And then he added insult to injury by saying in a voice soft with laughter, "And I should warn you, violence merely stirs my lust further."

She froze at that, unwilling to give him any excuse to force his unwanted attentions upon her. Then she caught sight of the fresh blood seeping from the cuts on his side and sucked in her breath in dismay. She had opened Ranulf's wounds with her harshness.

Immediately contrite, she gazed up at him. "You are bleeding anew."

"It is nothing."

Ariane shook her head, beset by guilt. She owed Ranulf at least a minimum of gratitude for his earlier restraint; he had spared the lives of his attackers, and he had reduced Edric's sentence to a more merciful one. Certainly Ranulf did not deserve to be *mauled* by her. "I must tend these gashes."

"I said it is nothing, demoiselle."

Her chin rose stubbornly. "I am acting in place of your squire, my lord—an assignment you yourself set for me. You will allow me to carry out my oath and serve you."

She spoke in a voice of authority, the regal command of a chatelaine accustomed to ruling a vast household staff. Ranulf stared at her a long moment, his look wary, as if he feared she might inflict him with bodily harm. "Very well," he said finally.

Ariane repressed the urge to respond with sarcasm. She had given him little reason to trust her, she reminded herself as she went to fetch her supplies.

Ranulf reluctantly allowed her to apply a poultice and bind his ribs with strips of linen, but he watched her closely. He told himself Ariane could do him no harm, and yet her ministrations seemed far too intimate for the simple task she performed. Or perhaps he simply felt too vulnerable. His former bride saw too much with those luminous gray eyes, making him feel as if his soul were stripped naked.

When Ariane paused momentarily to gaze up at him, some softer, gentler emotion slipped through him so surreptitiously that he could not quell it.

Ranulf cursed silently. The bewitching wench was weaving an irresistible spell over him. Despite his best efforts, he felt his blood begin to heat uncontrollably.

Against his will, he raised a hand to touch her cheek. When Ariane drew a sharp breath and tried unsuccessfully to draw away, Ranulf stilled. He did not want her flinching from him.

With a finger under her chin, he forced her to meet his gaze. "You need not fear me. I am not so harsh a master. I am gentle with horses, hawks . . . women."

"I am not afraid," Ariane lied, feeling her pulse race at the dark flame that lit his golden eyes. "But neither will I listen to you boast of your conquests."

That taunting smile returned to flicker across his lips. "I would not be so churlish," he replied innocently.

His utter calm was infuriating. When she tried to draw back, he caught her wrist. "Methinks I could win you, should I attempt it."

His audacity knew no bounds. Clenching her teeth, she wrenched her wrist from his grasp—yet she could not escape him. With deceptive speed, his arm wrapped around her waist and he pulled her upright, into the hot strength of his groin. Her body came instantly alive with tremors of excitement. Dismayed, Ariane pressed her palms against his broad chest, braced to fight, but it was like shoving against a wall of stone.

"Release me!" she exclaimed to no avail.

"Why should I?" His tone was husky, sensual, amused. "Earlier you were willing to exchange your body for the lives of your men."

"Not my body," Ariane replied through clenched teeth. "Only my services."

"Then service me."

The hot, hungry look in his golden eyes alarmed her. "You were the one," she said too breathlessly, "who refused to consummate the betrothal contract."

His voice dropped to a seductive murmur. "There are ways to enjoy carnal pleasure that do not involve losing your maidenhead, sweeting."

Her eyes went wide as she stared up at him. When slowly

he raised his hand, barely brushing the full aching globe of her breast with his palm, she gasped.

Noting her body's unwilling response, he smiled tenderly. "You want me, demoiselle, it is obvious. Your nipples are peaked ... your heart is beating too rapidly ... your breath has quickened ... your skin is flushed ..."

"I do not want you!"

"Your body wants me. It is clear you are a maiden languishing for a man."

Ariane shut her eyes, praying for deliverance. She should never have allowed him to know she resented her virgin state. "I am languishing for no one, most especially you!"

"You mean to say you have never wondered what it would be like to have a man between your thighs?"

"No ... I mean yes, I never ..."

"Permit me to show you," he murmured, his voice going even softer, deeper, stroking her senses like dark velvet. "Let us see if we can make your lovely body turn traitor...."

He cradled her against him with a gentleness that belied the dangerous determination in his eyes. Then, to her complete startlement and dismay, he bent and kissed her, his lips warm and incredibly soft. The shock sent a wave of heat streaking through Ariane, a shock so powerful it paralyzed her. She could do nothing to defend herself against the tender caress of his mouth as he coaxed hers open, the feel of his tongue, slow and hot and wet, as he leisurely explored her.

In truth, rather than fight him, she only wanted to cling to Ranulf. It seemed she had waited nearly half her life for this, to know the taste of his kiss. She had dreamed of it, of this man as lover, as husband. She could scarcely believe so powerful a warrior could be so incredibly gentle.

Of their own accord her arms lifted and twined around his neck. With a soft sound of triumph deep in his throat, he tightened his hold, enveloping her in the heat and smell of his body while his mouth ravished hers tenderly. He was a dark fire, slowly igniting her senses.

Long moments later Ranulf drew back, but only to whisper against her lips, "Let me show you pleasure, Ariane. Let me please you as I would have you please me...."

For one, mad moment she almost succumbed to his honeyed words. Ranulf knew about women, about passion, and she wanted desperately to experience what had been denied her for so many years.

So many years . . .

The remembrance jolted Ariane to awareness. She wanted to know about passion, but this black rogue would not be the one to show her!

With a sudden cry, she pushed hard against his chest. To her surprise, he released her at once. Freed, she fled across the room, her cool hands pressed against her burning cheek, her body trembling.

There was a taut silence while she stood there shaking. When he made no movement toward her, she at last risked a glance at Ranulf. He remained where she had left him, firelight outlining the sleek muscle and sinew of his nude body. He was watching her, an enigmatic expression on his harsh features.

His tone when he spoke, however, was calm, unheated. "You are stubborn indeed, but so am I, sweet vixen."

She was startled by the lazy smile that filled his eyes. There was a promise there in the golden depths, warning her that the battle was not over.

"It is time to retire," Ranulf said casually.

Ariane swallowed hard, realizing he had ordered her to bed, wondering if he meant to carry on the conflict there. She considered disobeying, but remembered how Ranulf had forcibly carried her there the last time. Had that been merely two nights ago?

Moving stiffly over to the bed, she climbed beneath the covers. Then she turned onto her side, giving him her back, and waited rigidly for Ranulf to join her.

She could scarcely keep from flinching when she felt his weight shift the mattress. For an interminable moment he leaned over her, while Ariane held her breath. She could feel his amber gaze caressing her, scrutinizing her, as if gauging the strength of her resistance.

Yet "Pleasant dreams, demoiselle," was all he said, before rolling over and settling his body for slumber.

Ariane willed her hammering heart to quieten. Once more she had escaped ravishment, but it was growing harder and harder to maintain her defenses.

*   *   *

The dream returned, this time far more erotic than any reality. She could feel the intense heat of Ranulf at her back, the hardness and detail of him as he pressed against her. Beneath the covers, her smooth bare legs entwined with his hair-roughened ones, his granite thigh wedged between her knees.

Through a dim haze she felt him slowly stroking her belly, gliding upward to cover her breast, to knead softly with his calloused palm. Ariane moaned softly in her sleep and arched her back against the sensuous pressure, straining closer to his caressing palm, wishing the thin barrier of linen between them would disappear. Her nipple tightened against his hand, and she shivered with delight. For such a large, rough hand, his touch was like silk. Her buttocks, nestled in the saddle of his hips, squirmed as pleasurable tremors coursed down the insides of her thighs.

Reveling in the naked heat and strength of him, she murmured in protest when his caressing fingers left off their erotic plundering. Yet his hand only moved lower beneath the bedclothes, to dip below the hem of her shift, drawing up the thin material. She felt her body quicken as his palm stroked along her thigh, her hip; the touch of his hand against her bare skin made her pulse race. When his fingers slipped intimately between her thighs, a hair's breadth from the heat of her womanhood, it excited her almost unbearably.

She should awaken, Ariane told herself. She should force her eyes to open and end this wanton dream, but then she might never know the completion of her fantasies, the elusive fulfillment of all her longings. And the wonderful, moist, aching weakness that pulsed to life in that secret shameful place between her thighs, the exquisite feelings radiating through her flesh, were not to be denied. Her woman's body craved his touch, craved the maleness of him. Her thighs fell apart, allowing him access.

His fingers splayed to clasp her woman's mound, pressing against the soft curls guarding her femininity. Ariane drew a sharp breath, her body stiffening.

Be easy, sweeting. You have naught to fear from me. His husky whisper soothed her, coaxing her restless, feverish limbs to relax. Blessed Saints, her dream was so real, so sinful. Almost as if Ranulf were truly here, lying with her, stroking her in wicked, forbidden ways.

She should push him away, and yet the clamoring in her blood prevented her from relinquishing her exquisite illusion. Her body was on fire, burning beneath his touch, her nipples aching points of flame. She mewed, her hips lifting in instinctive supplication as he found her soft, silky female cleft, parted the quivering folds of flesh. *Aye, open for me, cherie . . . let me in . . . let me savor your treasures. . . .* Dear Mary, she wanted this, wanted his incredible, magical touch.

The fingers were bolder now, exploring her with hot, slick strokes, sliding inside her, probing. *Jesu, so hot you are . . . so wet for me . . .* His heated words whispered into her ear an invitation to his own special paradise.

Ariane whimpered. Sweet Virgin, was it possible to die from so much pleasure? Her will was no longer her own. His lean, sinewy, stroking fingers had stolen it from her. Desire was like a taut bow inside her, drawn ever tighter by his brazen fingers. He was learning the moist secrets of her, every exquisite pleasure point, sending small convulsive reactions running through her.

Yes, show me your passion, my beauty. Let it go. . . .

Her breath came harshly, her senses reeling. Her mind had fled to a hot dark place filled with sensation, yet her body remained surrounded by fire, centered around the captivating caress of his hand. *Come for me, lover. Give in to the pleasure. Feel it. . . .*

Suddenly she was writhing with frantic need, straining toward a mounting, burning frenzy. She sobbed, clutching mindlessly at him as the world seemed to explode. With a cry she surged against his hand, enveloped in a fountain of flames. His arm came around her to hold her trembling body in the aftershocks of rapture.

For an endless moment, while the flames receded and her body cooled, Ariane lay there limply, not wanting to believe she had engaged in such a wanton act, twisting and straining with need so intense she'd been mindless with it. She could feel Ranulf at her back, his body hard against hers, throbbing with its own male need. Her heavy eyelids lifting, she gradually became aware of the candlelight, of the faint gray ribbons of dawn slipping through the shutters.

She blinked in confusion, while her cheeks flamed with mortification. This was real—no dream—her senses screamed in awareness. Ranulf had aroused her from sleep and stroked her to ecstasy, without her knowledge or permission. He had taken control of her body, displaying his power over her.

Ariane felt a wave of despair wash over her. Ranulf had vowed to compel her submission, and this was his proof. Perhaps he had stopped short of forcing her, but he had seduced her, shamed her—and shown her more pleasure than she had ever dreamed possible.

Sweet Jesu, what was she to do? She could feel the hunger in his big, powerful body, feel the throbbing heat of desire in the swollen shaft pressed against her buttocks.

With a gentle tug on her shoulder, Ranulf eased her onto her back. He saw how she kept her eyes shut, refusing to look at him, and a hard smile of primitive satisfaction curved his mouth. Her body had surrendered, overwhelmed by blind desire; he had won that victory at least.

His seduction had not been totally honorable, perhaps, for he had waited till she slept, till her defenses were lowered. Yet he had given Ariane precisely what she wanted, what her eager body had cried out for. What his own cried out for now.

Throbbing with the primal need to mount the hot, aroused woman in his arms, Ranulf slowly drew down the bedclothes, exposing that beautiful, slender form to his view, taking in her dishabille. Her chemise had ridden up over her hips and the thatch of red-gold curls at the juncture of her pale thighs drew his hot gaze. He bent over that sweet portal, his nostrils flaring slightly as he drank in the enticing scent of her. He wanted nothing more than to settle his body over hers and plunge into her, claiming the honeyed treasure there, but he would have to take his pleasure in less conventional ways.

"Beautiful . . ." he murmured hoarsely. "Open for me again, sweeting. Let me savor you . . . give you another taste of ecstasy. Let me fill you . . ."

Lowering his head, his mouth pursed, he gently kissed the dewy cleft between her thighs, his tongue flicking out to stroke the hidden bud.

Ariane had lain tense and rigid beneath his burning scrutiny, but at his scandalous action, she gave a startled yelp and clutched at his hair, gripping hard. When he lifted his head, their eyes locked, hers panicked, his hot and bright.

"No . . . you cannot. . . ."

"I can, demoiselle." The raw, husky sound stroked her sensitive nerve endings.

"No . . . please . . . I beg you. . . ."

He smiled indulgently as she caught the bold hand that had strayed to cover her thigh. "You may beg me all you like."

"No! *Ranulf!*"

Realizing her genuine shock, Ranulf abandoned his attempt to show Ariane another means of enjoying pleasure. His eyes smoldered as his hand turned to capture her wrist. "Then you touch me. Feel how hard, how aroused you make me."

Deliberately he drew her palm against his flat, hard-muscled belly, pressing her fingers against his throbbing member. She could feel him in her hand, hot and huge and pulsing. Ranulf grimaced in pure pleasure, while Ariane's eyes widened in alarm.

"No!" Again she tried unsuccessfully to pull from his grasp. " 'Tis sinful!" she exclaimed, clutching at any excuse that might save her.

His expression sobered. "You would deny me after I pleasured you?"

"Yes!" Oh, what would make him cease? "It is unholy, against Church law."

When she succeeded in wrenching her hand away, Ranulf's jaw hardened in sexual frustration. He wanted Ariane sweet and willing, not panicked and trembling like a frightened rabbit. He could not stroke himself, either, not without rousing her disgust. But his self-denial only left him aching carnally and his raw temper ready to explode—an explosion he resolved to control.

He had won a victory of sorts, he reminded himself. Ariane had found ecstasy in his touch. But while he felt a savage gratification knowing that he could affect her so, he would not rest until she surrendered fully.

"I doubt you fear opposing the Church as much as you fear the pleasure I make you feel," Ranulf murmured wryly, with a casualness he did not feel.

Ariane averted her face, realizing the truth of his accusation. She had proved an easy conquest. Ranulf had not boasted in the slightest when he warned her that women found pleasure in his arms, but his seduction had been effortless. She was mortified by her response to his wicked caresses, her wanton surrender. She had not put up the least resistance. She had *wanted* him to touch her, to make love to her. She wanted him as lover and husband and lord.

Her heart ached with the knowledge. She would not have protested even his most scandalous caresses had they been given in love, had Ranulf cared the slightest for her. But he considered her his enemy, and this was his method of punishment, of proving his power over her. Yet even more than the shame he had visited upon her, her own wantonness roused her despair. Ranulf might not have taken her maidenhead, but he had ruined her for any other man—and she had *enjoyed* her ruination.

Ariane closed her eyes, wishing she could disappear.

He had caught his fingers in her long tangled hair and was sifting it absently, as if testing a skein of silk for quality. When he raised an errant curl to his mouth, though, Ariane gasped and roughly drew it from his grasp.

"May I have leave to dress?" she snapped, still refusing to look at him.

"If you must. I would rather spend the next few hours teaching you a proper display of submission." His tone was soft, self-assured, ripe with satisfaction.

It earned him a baleful glare—which Ariane regretted immediately. He looked like a ruffian with his raven hair tousled, his hard, sculpted face darkened with a shadow of whiskers. Yet his flagrant masculinity called out to her as he lounged there on one elbow. Even at ease, he seemed so powerful, so very male, with his corded muscles and look of limitless strength.

It was his expression, though, that set her heart to pounding. His amber eyes gleamed sensually as he deliberately caught her hair again and slowly wrapped his fingers in her tresses, holding her prisoner.

"Do you think you can resist me for long, demoiselle?" he asked in a low, husky murmur that stroked her senses.

No. And that was the trouble. She could not resist this devastating man, not when he was looking at her thus, his eyes heated with a flame of desire and promise.

Summoning every ounce of willpower she possessed, Ariane raised her chin and invoked a look of scorn. "You flatter yourself, my lord, if you think I will ever submit to you willingly."

Ranulf's lips twisted in a male smile that was provocative, indulgent. "Unwillingly, then, it matters not, wench. In truth, I will enjoy taming your defiance . . . and devising a penance we can both enjoy."

Ariane quivered with the effort to keep her defenses in position. "I shall always despise you," she declared in a fervent, trembling voice.

His knowing smile never wavered he bent over her to kiss an impudent breast the way a lover might, making her flinch from the arousing warmth on her sensitive nipple. "Do not make rash statements, demoiselle, or I might be compelled to disprove them."

Untangling his hand from her hair, he threw off the covers and rose naked from the bed. Without another glance at Ariane, he found his braies and began to dress.

Chapter 9

"**D**id you pass a good night, my lord?" Payn queried when Ranulf joined him in the great hall to break the morning fast.

Answering with merely a grimace, Ranulf accepted a wooden cup filled with honey mead from a young page and settled into the lord's chair.

"I take that as a denial," his vassal said sympathetically. "The Lady Ariane was not accommodating?"

"If you have a care for your skin, you will refrain from mentioning that wench's name in my hearing." Irritably Ranulf glanced around the hall. The last of the straw pallets and blankets and hides were being rolled up to make way for the trestle tables, but the high table was bare. "Where is my cursed meal? Can a man not even be served a crust of bread in his own hall?"

Repressing a grin, Payn sent the trembling page to the kitchens for some victuals, before saying to Ranulf in a laughing undertone, "I thought you intended to give the lady a lesson in obedience, but it appears she remains as defiant as ever."

"The battle has only just begun, I assure you," Ranulf promised darkly. When Payn chuckled, Ranulf felt his vexation begin to dissipate. Against his will, he grinned ruefully. "Have you naught better to do than crow over my failure?"

"Indeed, my lord," Payn murmured amiably. "I know better than to linger with you in such a black mood. I shall leave you in peace to reexamine your strategy in taming the wench." Clapping Ranulf on the back as he rose, he left the high table to confer with two knights who had just entered the hall.

Relieved to be alone, Ranulf stared into his tankard of

mead and contemplated the unique experience he had just suffered. He was unaccustomed to being denied any wench he wanted, and unacquainted with regretting the deprivation so sorely. Never had he had a woman in his bed who did not leave it fully satisfied; never before had he permitted one to leave until *he* was fully satisfied. Yet that was precisely what had just transpired with Ariane. The ache still had not receded from his loins; his blood still simmered for her. He had never felt such desire as that wench roused in him.

By the rood, what hold did that beautiful witch have over him, that he should crave her so?

His planned seduction had gone awry, snaring him in his own trap. He had aroused the sensual woman beneath that cool, haunting demeanor of Ariane's, true, but afterward found himself burning with an unquenchable fire.

It had almost been worth the pain. For a few exquisite moments, he'd succeeded in compelling the defiant vixen to sheath her claws. The haughty maiden was not so regal, so disdainful, when she was panting and writhing with ecstasy in his arms. But the sight of her lustrous pearl-white skin flushed with passion, her glorious mane of silky hair tumbling wildly about her creamy breasts, her warm, sleep-scented form pressed fully against him, had increased his desire to a raging inferno. And then the wench had not only refused to succor him in return, she had looked at him with horror and loathing!

Shaking his head ruefully, Ranulf chided himself for behaving like a callow youth, allowing himself to be led around by his loins. He knew better. He had seen men so besotted by scheming noblewomen that they forgot to watch their backs. And he well knew the danger of underestimating his former bride even for a moment. She was a foe worthy of caution.

Yet he was more determined than ever to make Ariane yield. If he used his skills wisely, he could ultimately compel her cooperation, if not her loyalty. By employing passion as a weapon, by forcing her to experience ecstasy at his hands, he could destroy her will. . . .

A dangerous smile curved Ranulf's lips as he thought of the battles to come. They would see who was the victor.

With that mollifying thought, he drained the last of his

wine and called for more—at the same moment Ariane stepped up onto the dais on which the lord's table was erected.

"You come late to your work," Ranulf remarked mildly, vexed by the way his body responded merely to the sight of her. His loins throbbed nearly as much as the ribs that had been wounded in yesterday's ambush. "I did not give you leave to laze in bed the day long."

"I was *not* lazing about, my lord. I found it necessary to *wash*," Ariane retorted with studied haughtiness. In truth, she had scrubbed her skin till it tingled, yet she had not succeeded in erasing the memory of her shameful, wanton response to Ranulf's lovemaking, or the exquisite feel of his touch.

She felt his scrutiny now and raised her chin when his eyes narrowed at her appearance. She wore a rich bliaud of rose samite, with a deep blue chainse beneath. A square of patterned silk adorned her hair, held in place by a thin silver circlet around her forehead, while a jewelled girdle of silver links encircled her slender hips.

"You dress lavishly for a servant," he mused, his tone deliberately provocative.

"You said you wished me to address the field serfs this morning and repeat my pledge to you. I thought this appropriate attire."

If it was not quite the truth, Ariane felt justified in the lie. She had donned one of her better gowns, not to impress Claredon's serfs with her consequence, but to bolster her defenses and help her maintain some semblance of poise. The Black Dragon of Vernay might have shamed her with his wicked, mind-wrenching caresses, but she was still lady of this hall, still retained a measure of pride. If he expected her to surrender meekly, he had greatly miscalculated. She refused to fall swooning at his feet as Ranulf seemed to think was his due.

Lifting the pitcher of wine, Ariane refilled his cup, pleased that she could do so without shaking overmuch. As she leaned forward over the table, though, she felt a large, sinewed hand brazenly brush her buttocks.

With a gasp, Ariane jumped and whirled, her arm swinging instinctively. Grinning, Ranulf caught the hand that would have struck him an instant before her palm contacted his cheek.

"Do not touch me so!"

He gazed up at her with sensual challenge, his amber eyes dancing with teasing laughter. "Methinks you enjoyed my touch only moments ago."

"Methinks your much-vaunted prowess as a lover overrated," Ariane returned scornfully, glaring. "In truth, I found it sorely lacking."

For a score of heartbeats, amusement warred with Ranulf's pride . . . and won. Though wincing inwardly at the disparagement of his manhood, he could not help admiring the wench's courage. She dared taunt the dragon, apparently unafraid for her skin, while her gray eyes flashed sparks of fire.

He chuckled slowly, even as he gazed at Ariane in speculation. He had never seen her so angry, or so flustered. Gratified by the high flush of color on her cheeks, Ranulf wondered if he could provoke her into losing her temper altogether. Although it might be a childish desire, it would give him a small measure of satisfaction to make her feel a tenth of the frustration he'd experienced at being left unfulfilled after becoming so incredibly aroused.

Without giving himself time to debate, Ranulf scraped back his chair and drew her inexorably inside the cradle of his iron-muscled thighs.

Inhaling a sharp breath, Ariane braced her palms against his broad shoulders, feeling the chain mail links of his hauberk, which she had been required to help him don over his tunic a short while ago. She used all her might to resist, yet he refused to release her.

"You have not enough evidence to properly judge my prowess, demoiselle," Ranulf said silkily, laughter threading his tone. "My skill was not fully tested. Shall we return to the solar and resume the trial? I doubt not I could have you moaning in passion within moments, just as I did earlier."

Her cheeks flooded scarlet. The lout was enjoying himself far too much at her expense. "You arrogant braggart, release me! I may be your hostage, but I am no common villein that you may insult at your leisure."

His gaze raked her, his eyes gleaming with a dangerous sensuality. "No, that you are not, my lady. Were you any common wench I could take you as I willed. Here on this table even.''

Retaining Ariane's wrist, Ranulf reached out to wrap an arm about her waist and draw her down onto his lap. Her eyes widened in alarm as he held her tightly against him. Even through his armor, she could feel his desire grow against the back of her thigh, a pressure impossible to ignore. Holding her thus, he deliberately moved his hand to her hip, letting it roam over her curves in a bold caress.

With a gasp, Ariane glanced frantically around the hall, finding a dozen curious glances directed their way. ''Nay, cease!'' she hissed in a low undertone. ''They will think I am your whore.''

The protest might have won him, had he not been determined to prove his point. ''They will think I am disciplining you, demoiselle,'' he replied. ''You defy me at every turn, and I cannot allow it to continue.''

When Ranulf forcibly raised her hand to kiss the tender skin on the inside of her wrist, Ariane closed her eyes in mortification. That the Black Dragon would fondle her before the whole company, where her people would see how little respect he bore her, was the height of humiliation, but the havoc he caused her senses was worse. He could arouse her with merely a touch. ''I trust you are satisfied, shaming me before my people,'' she said through gritted teeth.

''They are my people now,'' Ranulf reminded her, refusing to let her see how her remark stung. ''They are my retainers. And mayhap they will heed the lesson.'' He smiled blandly at her. ''My servant needs chastising for her disobedience, and for daring to strike her lord and master.''

''You are not my master!''

''No? Do you forget the oath of obedience you swore me? And that the lives of your vassals are at stake?''

The color drained from Ariane's face. When he suddenly released her, she sprang to her feet and stood staring down at him resentfully, and perhaps a bit warily. ''You will not harm them,'' she said with less assurance than she wished.

Ranulf's look of amusement was pure provocation. ''Do not think to command me, demoiselle. You are answerable to me, not I to you. Or have you forgotten that as well?''

His words were goading her hard, but she bit back her scathing reply at the reminder. "No, I have not forgotten."

"No, what?"

"No, *my lord.*"

When a boy brought a bowl of oat porridge, Ariane took it from him and set it before Ranulf with restrained force, controlling the urge to dump it over his head.

He looked up at her challengingly, as if divining her thoughts. "I would not, were I you, or you will force me to take harsher measures. You would not care to be chained in the dungeon, I think."

"That will not be necessary, my lord," she replied stiffly. "You have me chained by my word just as effectively."

"Have I, demoiselle?" He gave a soft huff of laughter edged with doubt. "Then I suggest you show a proper docility. Go and eat, and then fetch your mantle. The morning air will be brisk, and I would not wish my hostage to catch a chill."

Her jaw clenched rigidly, Ariane turned away at once.

Still feeling the heat from her scorching gray eyes, Ranulf picked up his spoon to apply himself to his food, but his thoughts centered on his arousing, vexing former bride and his own frustrating impotence in dealing with her. Every encounter with the wench became a battle of wills, a battle he was hard-pressed to win. He had deliberately provoked her this time, true, but her reckless retorts were a provocation that demanded a response. Her public show of defiance in daring to strike him—

A sudden commotion beside him interrupted his thoughts—a clatter followed by a small cry of pain. Ranulf looked around, as did Ariane.

She had not seen what happened, but it was simple to guess. The young page, a boy of perhaps seven, had tripped and fallen beside Ranulf's chair, dropping a pewter pitcher and sending wine splashing over the rushes and onto his lord's boots.

Swiftly retracing her steps, Ariane bent to help the child rise. He scarcely seemed to notice her assistance. Trembling, the boy eyed Ranulf with terror, shrinking back as if fearful the lord might strike him with his powerful fist.

Instinctively Ariane stepped in front of the boy, sheltering him behind her skirts. "My lord . . . it was only a spill."

Ranulf went very still as he watched the child's white-faced expression. "Come here, lad," he said quietly. When the boy stood rooted to the floor, Ranulf added even more softly, "I will not harm you. I do not strike small boys."

Slowly the young page inched out from behind Ariane and approached Ranulf. "I b-beg pardon, m-my l-lord," he stammered in a high, frightened voice, while tears filled his eyes.

"What are you called, lad?"

"W-William."

"Your fall was an accident, was it not, William? You did not purposely drench me with wine."

"Aye, my l-lord. I m-mean, n-nay."

"Then I see no reason for punishment."

"B-But I was cl-clumsy, my l-lord."

"If you endeavor to serve me well in future, then I will think no more of this incident."

"Aye, my l-lord."

Ranulf's startling gentleness did not shock Ariane as it once might have although his kindness was sorely at odds with his renown as the feared Black Dragon.

"He is the son of Lord Aubert, a friend of my father's," she offered in explanation. "William fosters here as a page."

Ranulf smiled, that rare, dazzling smile that made it seem as if the sun had suddenly burst through a mass of storm clouds. The effect nearly took Ariane's breath away. "So you wish to be a knight?"

William's small face brightened, and he lost that petrified look. "Oh, aye, milord! My Lord Walter pledged to train me. . . ." The boy came to a faltering stop, as if remembering his lord was no longer in power.

"I see no reason your training cannot continue," Ranulf said mildly. "If you are diligent in learning your duties as page, then I will promote you to squire and teach you how to wield a sword."

"*You* will teach me? Oh, my lord. . ." The boy's tone held excitement and reverence, as if being trained by the Black Dragon was the height of his every ambition.

Ariane could see Ranulf had earned a devotee for life. And

she recognized the sentiment. She had once viewed Ranulf with that same adoration—hero worship for a powerful warlord who had been kind to a nervous young girl.

"I have a son about your age," she was surprised to hear Ranulf say, and more surprised by his look. His face had softened completely, his eyes filling with something warm, gentle. Ranulf dismissed the boy and sighed softly.

"I did not know you had a son."

He glanced at Ariane absently. "I have three, and three daughters as well."

She felt another jolt of surprise at his admission. Many lords had no notion of the number of children they had sired; generally they ignored their offspring as the regretful consequence of passion. But Ranulf not only knew, but had spoken of them with pride.

"They are bastards, all." His tone was pointed, almost challenging.

"So I would imagine," Ariane replied frankly, "since you have no wife."

She saw him bite back a smile, but there was little humor in his eyes; the amber depths were entirely serious. She was puzzled by Ranulf's expression. He watched her carefully, almost as if expecting her to respond with scorn and contempt.

"I would not expect a noble lady such as yourself," he said without inflection, "to hold an indulgent view of bastard children born to serfs."

"You have acknowledged them?"

"Yes. And provided for their welfare."

"Then there is no shame attached to their birth. As for indulgence, I have an example in my lady mother. She not only accepted my father's bastard, but brought him into the castle to train as a cleric."

"Would that all noblewomen could be so generous."

His bitterness confused her, disturbed her, but before she could quiz him about it, Ranulf stiffened suddenly, as if recalling to whom he was speaking.

"I believe I dismissed you, demoiselle," he said coolly.

His remote tone, coming on the heels of his warmth toward the young William, made Ariane flinch. With animosity bristling between them anew, she turned away with an abruptness that was almost flounce.

Alone, Ranulf ate his food without tasting it, his thoughts centered once more on how to deal with the disturbing wench. He could not quite believe her reasonable view of bastard children. He'd had too much painful experience with the scorn and derision of Ariane's noble class and station.

It could have been moments or hours before Ranulf heard a throat being cleared nervously. He looked around to find the aged, balding priest of Claredon standing beside his chair, gazing at him in trepidation.

"Might I beg a word with you, sire?"

Ranulf nodded courteously. "Father John, is it not?"

"Aye, milord."

"Should you not be saying Mass, Father?

"There was no one in the chapel." His gentle brown eyes looked faintly accusing. "You have imprisoned everyone of rank, and the villeins are afraid to risk your wrath, milord."

Ranulf frowned. "You may gather your flock without fear of retribution, Father. I would not deny the people of Claredon spiritual solace."

"I thank you, milord."

"Is that all?"

"Nay, milord." The priest stood for a moment, wringing his hands in agitation. "I fear I must speak. I can no longer be silent. I must make you see the wrong in what you do."

Ranulf's slashing eyebrows lifted. "Indeed?"

"It is the Lady Ariane, sire . . . and your . . . er . . . your treatment of her."

"What of my treatment?"

The elderly man hesitated to reply. "You have dishonored her . . ."

With effort, Ranulf kept his tone mild. "How have I done so, priest? I have required her to serve me at table and act as my squire, nothing more."

"You have held her prisoner in your chamber these three nights past."

"Merely to keep an eye on her. I cannot trust her to roam free, or she might aid another of her father's vassals to escape."

"But your . . . you . . . the disrespect you showed her just now ... It is not meet that you should embrace her in the hall, like a serf.''

"Did the lady ask you to entreat me on her behalf?''

"Nay, milord! She would never! But I have eyes to see ... and ears to hear. I have heard ... that you mean not to wed her.''

"We are no longer betrothed, 'tis true,'' Ranulf replied defensively. "She is my hostage for the nonce.''

"Will you not allow her to take refuge in a convent?''

"The lady claims she does not wish to enter a nunnery.''

"But what of her future? If she is not for the Church, then she must have a husband.''

"That is beyond your purview, priest,'' Ranulf observed. "King Henry will see to her future in due time, depending on the outcome of her father's treason.''

"But I have a duty—''

Abruptly Ranulf raised a commanding hand, making the old man fall silent. "Your duty is to minister to your flock, not to question my actions. The Lady Ariane is my prisoner, to deal with as I see fit. Now, this interview is concluded. I am certain you have business to attend to.''

"Aye, milord ...'' With an obsequious bow, the priest backed away.

The priest's rebuke was valid, Ranulf knew. A castle staff, like the larger feudal society, followed a stratified order that was believed ordained by God. He had upset that order by making Ariane serve in place of his squire. He'd thought forcing her to publicly acknowledge his authority the best way to compel her submission, and that of her loyal followers as well. But he never should have held her up to public ridicule.

He was willing to admit he had gone too far in that regard—but by the Cross, he should never have been forced to compel her obedience in the first place. And in his own defense, he had acted out of anger and carnal frustration. He had not considered that she would feel shamed, either. Few noblewomen of his acquaintance possessed the slightest sense of shame, and even less honor. They cuckolded their lords, abandoned their children, schemed and plotted and conspired to improve their own fortunes. ... Yet the Lady Ariane's former station as chatelaine at least merited a measure of respect.

Ranulf stared grimly at his bowl of porridge. Even before the priest's challenge, he'd begun having second thoughts about the wisdom of his plan to win her cooperation through seduction. Clearly, if he were to gain the respect of Claredon's people, he could not treat their lady like a common castle wench.

Very well, Ranulf concluded reluctantly, gritting his teeth. If she obeyed him, he would release Ariane from her pledge to serve him. If she was willing to admit her defeat, then he was prepared to show her lenience, even though it was entirely undeserved.

In the solar one floor above, Ariane was entertaining her own smoldering thoughts while she fetched her mantle at Ranulf's command.

As she fastened the clasp over one shoulder, she could not keep her gaze averted from the bed where Ranulf had brought her to pleasure. A flush stained her cheeks as she remembered the heat, the desire, he had aroused in her so effortlessly. Sweet Mary, she had found her first taste of passion incredible—and incredibly enjoyable, although white-hot irons could not have forced her to admit it to him.

For a moment her eyes clouded with sadness. God smite his gold eyes and black heart! Why could he not have honored the contract and wed her? She would have been a good wife to him, even under these trying circumstances. She would have endeavored to ensure his happiness. They could have shared a common purpose, to rule their land and serve their king. Perhaps they might even have found love, although she could not see how such a harsh, unfeeling warlord as the Black Dragon of Vernay could possibly have any room in his heart for so tender an emotion as love. He was a devil.

They would never find a common purpose now, not with the animosity and mistrust that raged between them. Ranulf would never honor her. She was naught but a possession to him, a pawn, a hostage he must needs prove his mastery over. He demanded her abject submission and would be satisfied with nothing less. She could expect no mercy from such a forceful, ruthless man.

Dragging her gaze from the bed, Ariane reluctantly turned to the door. Ranulf had not vanquished her yet, and yet it was becoming more difficult each passing day to hold out hope that she could win any victory over him.

When she left the solar, she was startled to find her half-brother Gilbert lurking in the shadows. Evidently he had been lying in wait for her, and from the heightened color of his fair complexion, he was bursting with fury.

"My lady! He has gone too far! It is beyond bearable! You must allow me to avenge your honor!"

Ariane sighed wearily. As much as she would like to see the Black Dragon defeated, Gilbert was not the one to do it. The boy would be crushed by so skilled and powerful a warrior as Ranulf—if my lord even deigned to accept such a challenge. As the son of a serf, Gilbert was proscribed from certain rights, such as challenging the nobility to combat. According to the rules of knightly conduct, only peers could fight one another. And Gilbert's youth was another strike against him. Boys were not allowed to use a knight's weapons. Even squires were permitted only wooden lances and swords with which to practice.

"I cannot bear to see the lady of Claredon so degraded and scorned!" the lad cried. "He treats you worse than a serf! He fondles you as if you were his leman."

She flushed in spite of herself. "That was not quite the way of it."

"It was! And I would avenge your honor!" Gilbert repeated fiercely. "I would challenge Lord Ranulf on the field of honor!"

Ariane shook her head. She would have to persuade the boy that his plan was not merely foolish, but suicidal. "Gilbert," she said gently, "you are untrained as a warrior, unskilled at arms. Lord Ranulf has vanquished even the most powerful of his foes. He would kill you in moments."

"It matters not. I cannot stand by and do nothing! I have the right, my lady. In our father's absence, I am your nearest male relative. It falls to me to protect you."

Ariane gave another sigh. "Gilbert, I thank you with all my heart for championing me, but I could not bear it if you came to harm. With my father under suspicion of treason, my mother gone, I have lost everyone I hold dear. I could not bear to lose you, too. I need you, Gilbert."

He clenched his fists, but the wildness seemed to leave his

blue eyes. "If you will not permit me to fight him, then we must seek redress in the courts."

"The courts?"

"Aye. I know something of the law, my lady. You have right on your side. We could sue the lord of Vernay in civil court for breaking the betrothal."

Ariane stared at Gilbert for a long moment. "Assuming we had a case, and assuming we could persuade the new king's courts to hear it, what would we gain by taking so bold an action?"

"Why, riches and land, my lady. Lord Ranulf has claimed the whole of your father's estates and reduced you to penury. Were you awarded a settlement, you would no longer be dependent on the new lord's generosity, nor would you be forced to serve him. And he would be made to pay for the ill he has done to you."

She nodded slowly. "Yet such a case might be difficult to win, especially since it is complicated by our father's situation. I am considered King Henry's political hostage."

"But we should try."

"I should like time to consider your proposal, Gilbert."

"But, my lady—"

"I shall think on it, I promise."

Her assurances evidently did not allay the lad's frustration, however. "If you will not challenge Lord Ranulf in the courts, then we must take some other course. At the very least, he should be made to honor the contract and wed you. It is only meet that he make restitution for casting you aside after so long, and for the dishonor he has brought you. In truth, you are already wed to him in the eyes of the church, but for the final vows and consummation. If you had proof he had violated you, then not even the wicked Dragon could repudiate the marriage."

Ariane frowned thoughtfully. It would solve many of her immediate problems if Ranulf were somehow required to honor the betrothal. Why had she never considered such a perspective before? Because for the past few days, she had been dazed by uncertainty and fear. She had not been thinking clearly or objectively. And in her despair at Ranulf's ruthless victory, her fury over his devious means of gaining possession of Claredon, and her humiliation at his repudiation, she had been *glad* to see an end to the betrothal, and thus acceded to his wishes without a fight.

But Gilbert was right on one score. Ranulf *should* have to make restitution for the lost years of her youth, and for ruining her chances of marrying honorably elsewhere. Did Gilbert but know it, Ranulf *had* effectively violated her. This morning he had stripped away her carnal innocence, had introduced her to passion, an intimacy which only a husband had the right to claim.

Yet her reasons for wanting to secure the marriage now went far beyond revenge. As the lord's wife she would be in a better position to protect Claredon and its dependents, as well as to safeguard the secret she had harbored for so long—a secret she would give her life to protect. Her own legal rights as a wife would be greater than those of a mere hostage, true, but more crucially, if her status of lady were restored, she could work on behalf of her father, to try and refute the charge of treason. He was not guilty, she knew in her heart, but only if she were in a position of power could she even begin to prove his innocence. As Ranulf's hostage, she could do naught, but as his wife . . .

For the first time since Ranulf had taken possession of Claredon four days ago, Ariane felt a fierce surge of hope. Her heart suddenly racing, she pressed a trembling hand to her mouth. Sweet Mary, she had little to lose and so much to gain. . . .

"What is it, my lady?" her brother asked anxiously.

"Hush, let me think!"

Even if she would rather be boiled in oil than take Ranulf de Vernay as her husband after all he had done to her, she had to attempt it. But attempt *what?* The betrothal contract was not binding so long as it remained unconsummated. And there had to be proof of consummation in order for the church to sanctify the marriage. So . . . was there a way to ensure its consummation?

How? Ranulf had sworn never to touch her—or at least, she amended, remembering his wicked advances this morning, that her maidenhead was safe from him. She could try to win his affections and pretend a fondness for him, yet if she showed the slightest softening toward him, he would see through her at once. She knew nothing of the arts that came so naturally to some women—of flirtation and simpering and flattery. She would make a wretched seductress.

Yet she had to do *something*. Gilbert was right. Simply ringing her hands and bewailing her plight would gain her naught. Somehow she had to persuade Ranulf to reconsider their marriage. At the very least she had to make it impossible for him to break the betrothal contract. If she could manage that, if she could win her rights as his wife, then she could use her power to aid the people who depended on her.

"My lady?" Gilbert asked worriedly.

Summoning her resolve, Ariane lifted her chin and squared her shoulders. She had been meek and acquiescent long enough. She had obeyed Ranulf's demands, suffered his demeaning retribution without protest, and he had given her only shame and humiliation in return. It was unfair that he be allowed to continue. And it was time he was brought to see reason.

"Calm yourself, Gilbert. All will yet be well, I swear it," she said with a confidence that was growing each successive moment.

"But what will you do?"

"I am not yet certain." She forced a smile as she gazed at her anxious half-brother. "But I assure you I will take your advice to heart. Somehow Lord Ranulf must be shown the injustice of repudiating our betrothal. And then . . . then he must be persuaded that he needs me for his wife."

Chapter 10

It was a subdued and thoughtful Ariane who accompanied Ranulf and his armed retinue to the fields. More than once he gave her a wary glance as she rode docilely beside him on her palfrey, until finally she bestirred herself to respond with her usual tartness in order to allay his suspicions.

When he compelled her time and again to address the serfs they found working the land, she did so with stoicism, telling them in gentle, sincere tones to bow to the new lord and they would find him a merciful master.

Ariane prayed her counsel was true. She did not want Claredon's serfs to suffer under the rule of the Black Dragon. Yet somehow she doubted they would. Ranulf might threaten and act the ogre with her, no doubt to frighten her into submission. And displaying her subservience was a cleverly calculated strategy to demoralize her people's efforts at resistance. But Ranulf was clearly not the brute his terrible reputation suggested. In truth, he had shown his rebellious enemies more mercy than she could rightfully expect. Perhaps there was softness beneath that harsh exterior, after all. A softness he kept hidden from the world.

Could she possibly use that to her advantage? Ariane wondered desperately. Could she somehow persuade him to wed her as he had promised years before?

It was imperative that she try. At this very moment, Ranulf's retinue of knights and men-at-arms was passing the eastern forest with its thick stands of oak and birch and tangled hedges of hawthorn—passing too close for Ariane's comfort. She was careful to keep her eyes averted, to show no special interest in this particular stretch of wood.

It had been merely four days since Ranulf had seized Claredon and taken her hostage, yet worry nagged at her conscience. How could she possibly escape the Black Dragon's scrutiny long enough to slip from the castle and pay a brief visit to these woods? It was a mission she could entrust to no one, a secret she could never share—although if the case grew desperate enough, she might have to consider it.

Furtively, Ariane stole a glance at Ranulf as he rode beside her. How would he react should he discover her secret? How would he feel about her aiding the wretched souls God had abandoned?

He looked supremely powerful and totally ruthless just now, arrayed in full armor, mounted on his prancing black war stallion. The nose guard of his steel helmet shielded much of his face from her view, yet his strong jaw suggested relentless determination, and he stared straight ahead, as if he were ruler of all he surveyed.

She was surprised, therefore, when he spoke quietly, almost reverently. "This land has heart."

He was gazing at the gently rolling countryside, the green pastures and planted fields and wooded groves, Ariane realized. His hushed, almost wistful tone held a possessiveness that made her stiffen. This demesne should still have belonged to her father.

"My lord father always thought so," she could not refrain from saying.

When Ranulf gave her a sharp glance, Ariane bit her tongue and vowed to remember her pledge to accept him as lord.

Yet some hours later, when he prepared to send her back to the castle under guard, Ranulf's parting command and maddening smile goaded her beyond bearing.

"I expect you to have a meal waiting for me upon my return, demoiselle," he said in that amused, mocking tone he employed specifically to provoke her. "I mean to hunt rebels for the rest of the morning and will no doubt work up a vast hunger."

"What a brave, fearless knight you are," Ariane observed scornfully, "to make war on peasants defending their homes and their true lord."

She regretted the reckless words even before she heard the collective murmur of shock from Ranulf's men behind them, or saw his blazing eyes. Appalled by her imprudence, Ariane drew a breath to retract the rash remark, but before she could even gasp, Ranulf had spurred his destrier close to her palfrey and swept her into his arms. Ariane found herself sprawled across his saddle, half lying in his lap, with one of his powerful mailed arms supporting her back.

Alarmed, she struggled in his embrace, with a terse order, Ranulf commanded his men to ride ahead.

"Shall we wait for you, my lord?" Payn asked mildly.

"Aye. I mean to teach this wench a lesson in obedience. It should not take long."

His insulting arrogance drew a muffled cry of outrage from Ariane, but though she tried to break free of his hold, he kept her pinned tightly against his body as his men rode away.

In the ominous silence that followed, Ariane felt her heart hammering wildly against her breast. She was alone with Ranulf, surrounded by woods. He could do whatever he pleased to her and there would be no one to save her or hear her cries. When she risked a glance at him, she found Ranulf staring down at her, his eyes glimmering with menace.

"I warned you, demoiselle," he said softly. With his teeth he drew off the leather gauntlet of his right hand.

Panic welled within her and she began to struggle in earnest, but she could not stop him from reaching beneath her skirts. Ranulf meant to punish her with his carnal attentions, perhaps even rape her.

"I could take you here on the ground like a field serf, my lady," he threatened.

"Nay!" she cried when his fingers found the mound of her womanhood. His deliberate stroking made a mockery of the magical caresses that had brought her to the heights of passion only that morning. Ariane writhed in humiliation, but she could not escape his probing fingers.

When she gasped a plea for mercy, though, Ranulf's hand stilled. "Will you cry truce, lady? Will you acknowledge me as true lord of this demesne?"

"Aye," she replied with a bitterness she could not hide.

"Say it!"

"You are the true lord here."

His smoldering gaze pinned her, but after another long moment, he removed his hand from beneath her skirts. Without another word, Ranulf set her on her palfrey and gathered her mount's reins in his own grasp.

Trembling with fury and something more, Ariane silently cursed him for a devil as he led her to join his men. Shamed, infuriated, she held her head proudly, looking neither right nor left, yet she vowed to make Ranulf regret every indignity she had ever suffered at his hands.

Growing fury spurred her on as she rode back to the castle under heavy guard. Her decision had been made. What she was planning might put her own life in danger, but the thought of the peril she might face was trivial compared to her desire to make that arrogant lout pay for his despicable treatment of her. He would wed her if it took her last dying breath.

It was critical, though, that she gain the blessing of the Church if she hoped to establish legal grounds for a marriage. And she would first have to offer proof to support her claim—which should not be too difficult. Father John could be counted on to take her side, Ariane thought, although she wasn't certain the gentle, elderly man of God would be able to withstand the storm she was about to create.

Ranulf would be outraged when he discovered that she had forced his hand, and mayhap even turn violent, but he had given her little choice, she reminded herself fiercely. And she could only pray that the end would justify the means.

When she arrived at the keep, Ariane was relieved that she had no need to summon Gilbert, for she encountered her half-brother in the great hall.

"Can I trust you to secrecy, Gilbert?" she asked in a trembling undertone while keeping one eye on Ranulf's vassals, who had returned with her.

"Aye, milady! You know you can."

"Then I ask for your help. Go to the kitchens and fetch me a piece of raw meat, calf's liver or fresh cut venison, I care not, as long as it is bloodied."

Gilbert nodded eagerly, his loyalty such that he did not even question her odd request.

"Good. Bring it to me in the solar, and then find Father John and send him to me. And Gilbert, not a word of this to anyone, especially Lord Ranulf. I rely on your discretion."

"Aye, my lady," the lad said with an eager glitter in

his eye. "Torture could not make me divulge aught to that
devil's spawn."

Ariane devoutly hoped it would not come to torture.

She was waiting in the hall with Ranulf's noonday meal,
precisely as he had ordered, when he strode in with his vassals. He had removed his helmet, and his hair was damp and
curling from being sluiced off at the well in the yard.

He was laughing with his men at some jest, so it was only
after he reached the lord's table that he noticed the unnatural
quiet in the hall. At nearly the same moment, he realized
Ariane sat in the carved chair belonging to the lady of the
castle.

His amusement fading, Ranulf frowned at the presumption.
"You forget yourself, demoiselle."

"I think not, my lord," she replied evenly, daring to meet
his eyes. "I believe I have the right to occupy this seat, since
as your wife, my place is at your side."

"My *wife?*" His brows snapped together. "You are hardly
my wife."

"Indeed I am, my lord. But . . . perhaps you would prefer
a smaller audience for our discussion."

With an impatient gesture, Ranulf dismissed his retainers
and squires, who scattered to other parts of the vast hall. His
vassals, except for Payn and Ivo, withdrew a polite distance.

"Now, what is this nonsense about my wife?" Ranulf
demanded.

"I believe this is all the proof I need." Ariane gestured at
the table. Before her lay a linen bedsheet whose clean surface
was marred by dark splotches. "The sheets of our marriage
bed have been exhibited before the castle household by the
priest, just as would have occurred in an official bedding
ceremony, had we formally wed. Since our betrothal contract
has not been legally voided, and since this is proof the union
was consummated, under both civil and church law, I am
now your wife."

Ranulf stared at the cloth for a score of heartbeats, before
his gaze sliced back to Ariane. "What knavery is this?" he
asked so softly that she wanted to flinch.

"No knavery, my lord. Father John has inspected the
sheets as is customary and testified that my virginal stains

were found. Surely you are familiar with the practice, even in Normandy? Bloodstains attest to a maid's purity and confirm her virginity.''

Swift, dark fury burned in Ranulf's eyes as he caught the sheet up in his fist. ''You expect anyone to be taken in by your lies?''

Ariane shook her head. She had not lied outright. She had been pure when Ranulf took her to his bed. Perhaps she had stretched the truth by staining the bedsheets with calf's blood and allowing Father John to draw his own conclusions, but she had only claimed her due, legally and morally.

''I did not lie, my lord. By permitting the priest to display the sheets, I merely ensure that you fulfill your obligations and your own long-standing promise to wed me.''

Ranulf flung the cloth away, his look scathing. ''You call this *proof*? This proves nothing!''

''No? Do you deny that I shared your bed last eve, and another night before that?''

A muscle throbbed in his clenched jaw. ''If you are no longer a maiden, it was none of my doing.''

''No? Would you care to describe to the good father how you ravished me this morn?''

''Ravished? I did not—'' Ranulf broke off, glancing around at the others in the hall, most of whom were pretending to be occupied with their duties. Not one of them would believe he hadn't taken the wench as she alleged, certainly not after his public fondling of her in the hall this morning. In truth he had come close to ravishing Ariane earlier, had gone to wicked lengths in his lovemaking, arousing her to climax in a way the Church considered sinful and depraved. But he had not claimed her maidenhead.

God's breath, he was well and truly ensnared by her outrageous deception—unless he could prove the falseness of her accusation.

Abruptly he beckoned to one of his men. ''Fetch a midwife to me at once!'' He shot a fierce glance at Ariane. ''Naturally you will not cavil at being examined to determine your maiden status.''

Ariane raised her chin, gazing at him steadily, though her hands trembled at his threat. ''As you wish, my lord . . . but if she finds my maidenhead breached, it will simply prove my case."

For the longest moment, he stared at her, his features savage with fury. Ariane held her breath as she awaited his reply, praying that her bluff would work. Ranulf could not be certain she was not a virgin; surely he would not risk a public discovery.

"This is how you keep your oath to me?" he said at last in a deadly voice. "With deceit and betrayal?"

She swallowed. "I have not betrayed my oath, my lord. I swore to serve you, and I will continue to do so—*as your wife*. I will keep your household and see to your comfort and honor you in all things—"

"Christ's holy blood!" Ranulf exclaimed viciously.

Ariane flinched. His cruel visage was almost frightening. The lord of Vernay resembled a wounded boar who had been cornered with no escape. But a cornered boar will often turn and charge. . . .

As if to underscore her thought, he took a step in her direction, his hand grasping the hilt of his sword.

It was his vassal, Payn, who came swiftly forward to lay a cautioning hand on his arm. "Have a care, my lord. You would not wish to kill the damsel."

"Would I not?" Ranulf's mien suggested differently. His eyes were nearly black with rage, his compressed mouth white with fury.

"You might come to regret it later," Payn cautioned. "She should be punished, aye, but mayhap it would be wiser to allow me to deal with her."

The quiet words penetrated his blind fury. His vassal was right, Ranulf knew. He was too angry to think clearly. And he had sworn a sacred oath never to act like his father, to sink to that brutish level.

"She tries my vows," Ranulf said through gritted teeth.

"Aye, but you are too astute to react with blind anger, my lord."

He knew he was being mollified, yet he forced himself to take a calming breath. His anger was indeed blind. The wench's lies had only justified his mistrust of her, but it was her professed lack of innocence that strangely infuriated him the most. Had some other man enjoyed that beautiful white body? Had some other lover taught her to respond with passion? Was she a virgin still? It should not matter to him if she had lain with other men, but it did, keenly. Ranulf's hands knotted with the sudden urge to shake the truth out of her—a truth he must now discover in private if he was to avoid risking public confirmation of her scheme.

God's teeth, but he had begun to hope she was different from the other manipulating schemers of her class, but he was wrong. He should never have trusted Ariane, never left himself vulnerable. The wench had exposed her true character, her grasping designs, her lack of honor; she was cunning, calculating, treacherous. He had let down his guard for a single moment, and this was the result. A wicked knife-thrust. A deceitful legal maneuver meant to entrap him.

"What do you hope to gain?" he demanded of Ariane.

Meeting his furious gaze, she clasped her fingers together to keep them from trembling. She had a great deal to gain, of course. She was fighting for her home, her loved ones, her father's life. As Ranulf's wife, she could better protect her castle and servants, but more critically, with her rights restored, she could petition the king and plead for her father. It was an additional irony that Ranulf would have to support her as a dependent. Yet she did not think the Black Dragon of Vernay would care to hear her reasoning just now.

"Justice, my lord," she said quietly. "I will not allow you to repudiate our betrothal with impunity."

Ranulf stared at her, rigid, nostrils flared. He understood well enough what she was attempting: to save herself from the wrath of the crown. As his wife, she would not be held accountable for her father's acts of treason; her husband would be responsible for her. But rather than fear the king, she should be more concerned about *his* wrath. That he was livid at her treachery was too tame a description. But she would not succeed in forcing his hand.

"Your ploy will not work," he declared, seething. "The marriage will not stand."

"I beg to differ, my lord. As you once pointed out to me, only the Pope can dissolve our marriage now."

"Then I will send a messenger to Rome at once to petition the Pope for an annulment." Ranulf's head whipped around as he searched the crowd that hovered nearby. "Father John!"

"Aye, milord?" The elderly priest stepped forward reluctantly.

"What are the grounds for dissolution of a marriage?"

"Consanguinity is the usual justification, milord, but your bloodlines are not closely related to the Lady Ariane's. Her father, Lord Walter, satisfied himself particularly on that score before arranging the betrothal."

"What else?"

"Why . . . deformity or disease—"

"Very well, I will claim all three."

"All three?"

"Consanguinity, deformity, disease. I have just discovered that the Lady Ariane is my cousin of the second degree."

"But . . . 'tis not true," Father John said in bewilderment.

"It is no more false than her claim of ravishment. As for deformity, the wench has grossly misshapen limbs that were never revealed to me when I agreed to the betrothal."

"But, sire! You can see that the Lady Ariane is perfectly formed!"

"Rome cannot know that," Ranulf retorted with grim satisfaction. In truth, such claims could easily be disproved, given the resources and political clout, but Ariane had neither—nor the freedom to wage a costly battle in ecclesiastical court. And perhaps the marriage would be dissolved before then. He was frustrated enough to try anything, including inventing evidence against her.

Yet the third justification for annulment would be easiest to establish—and the most difficult to refute. "It has been determined the lady is diseased," Ranulf added with relentless determination.

Ariane's heart sank like a stone. She had hoped to make it impossible for Ranulf to repudiate the marriage, but it seemed he would fight her every attempt at fairness.

"And just what disease am I supposed to have contracted, my lord?" she demanded dryly.

"The pox . . . leprosy . . . an illness of the mind, I care not. Naturally you will be confined to your quarters so you cannot inflict your malady on others." He smiled cruelly. "I suspected you would not care for such punishment. Meanwhile, you will enjoy none of the rank or privileges of my lady wife, only those of a slave."

His hard gaze searched the crowd, and lit on the serving wench, Dena. "You, girl, what is your name?" he demanded in heavily accented English.

The buxom young maid stepped forward hesitantly. "Dena, milord."

"What are your usual duties?"

"I serve in the kitchens, milord."

"No longer. Henceforth you are in charge of the hall. And you will assume your lady's place at meals."

Stepping up on the dais, he rounded the long table to Ariane's side. Grasping her arm, he pulled her roughly from the carved chair, then pointed a commanding finger at the vacant seat. A collective gasp shuddered through the company. It was a grave insult to raise a serf so high, particularly a trollop such as Dena—and unlawful, as well. Had Ranulf been thinking rationally, he would have admitted that, by law, he could not arbitrarily turn a noblewoman into a slave, or elevate a serf to the position of lady, but his thoughts were in no way rational.

Ignoring the reaction of the crowd, Ranulf turned to address them. "You will call this wench lady no more. She is my slave, nothing more. Until the marriage is annulled, she will serve me as any other menial. You will cease to honor her in any way."

Ariane closed her eyes in dismay. Ranulf not only had adroitly sidestepped her net, but he was intent on heaping shame upon her. She winced as he tightened his grasp on her arm.

"Come, slave," he ordered in a velvet-steel voice. "Let us retire abovestairs. I see no reason to make our dispute a public display."

Ariane gritted her teeth. She would much prefer to face Ranulf here, where there would be witnesses to his violence. "But, my lord, I thought you were *fond* of public displays," she retorted with mock innocence. "You insisted on Claredon's entire populace hearing my declarations of allegiance, and you openly insulted me in this very hall this morning."

"*Lady* . . ." he warned, his voice rumbling above her like thunder, "you press me too hard."

His grip was painful as Ranulf turned her toward the stair-well and forced her to march before him.

Payn followed, catching up to them as they reached the first step. "My lord . . . think carefully of what you do. Do not harm her overmuch."

"Have you ever known me to raise a hand to a woman?" Ranulf demanded, scowling.

"Nay, but I have never seen you in so murderous a rage—"

"Calm your fears, Payn. I will stop short of murder."

He would not slay her, Ranulf vowed as he urged Ariane before him, but neither would he countenance her defiance any longer. He would prove his mastery over her—if it took from now till the end of Christendom.

Forcing Ariane up two curving flights of stairs, he marched her past the woman's dormitory and thrust her within the bedchamber she had once called her own. Slamming the door behind them, Ranulf turned to face his bride . . . his enemy.

Ariane stood rubbing her arm, watching him warily. "I will not allow you to repudiate our betrothal," she repeated, her chin raised stubbornly.

"Allow?" His brows snapped together. "How many times must I remind you, slave, that you no longer have any author-ity, any rights, at all?"

She fell silent before his fierce scrutiny.

"Your plot was ill advised," he said finally, his tone pure ice. "You were foolish to think you could force me to wed against my will, or that you could save your skin with a lie."

"What lie is that my lord?"

"Our union was never consummated, as well you know. I never claimed your virginity."

"What you did to me this morning was close enough as to make no difference."

Ranulf gave a sharp bark of laughter. "You are greatly mistaken, wench. What I did to you was just a sample of what I mean to do in the future."

Alarm flickered in her eyes as he slowly began unbuckling his sword belt. "W-What do you intend to do?"

"Why, merely to prove your veracity." He did not need a midwife present to examine her and determine if she was a virgin still. He laid the sword and belt on a chest, before he moved purposefully toward her, stalking her. "Just two days ago you claimed you were still a maid who had never had a man. Either you were lying then, or you are lying now. I mean to discover which."

A sudden dryness welled in her throat as Ranulf came toward her. If he deflowered her now, as angry as he was, he would likely tear her asunder. "It will be rape."

"If it so suits you." His eyes fierce with fury, with passion, he reached out and caught her, pulling her inexorably into his arms.

"Nay!" she exclaimed, an instant before his mouth crushed down upon hers, smothering her angry words.

She writhed and fought to no avail; Ranulf simply closed his fist in her hair and held her still for his mouth, his tongue prying her lips apart in a fierce, hungry assault.

Ariane felt her heart hammering violently. Her head was forced back, her spine arching until her breasts were pressed full against his mailed chest. His embrace was hurtful, his kiss ravishing, a brutal act of aggression. Yet she would not plead or beg for mercy. He had none.

His tongue plundered, subduing her, robbing her of breath. She whimpered, but Ranulf paid no heed to her protests. His arms folded tightly about her in a merciless grip that would not permit her to move, his battle-clad thighs forged against hers.

He would not beat or maim or torture her, he vowed as he bent her to his will. He would merely frighten her into admitting the truth, force her to give up her scheme. He would merely punish her with his embrace and let her imagine the worst. . . .

The damning truth was, though, he had no desire to threaten her with physical violence. He wanted to punish her with pleasure instead. He wanted her mindless and gasping beneath him. He wanted to appease this relentless desire he had for her, to satisfy his fierce need to plunge hot and deep inside her, and perhaps to ease at last the raging ardor she awoke in him. God's breath, how he wanted her! Anger and arousal made his blood surge hot, his body harden and throb; he was driven by a force more powerful than his fury. Holding her hard against him, he anchored her head and devoured her mouth, a low, guttural noise sounding deep in his throat.

Unable to escape, Ariane opened helplessly to his plundering invasion. She tried to recall the countless reasons she should resist him, tried to remember the shaming memories of her recent surrender, and yet reason fled.

A strange warmth began to grow in the depths of her body, setting her pulse racing. Weak, dazed, Ariane found herself clasping Ranulf to her as she yielded to his flaming kisses, even as dismay licked at the edges of her consciousness. She would have to fight herself as much as him if this continued. She felt as if she were drowning in his possession. . . .

She heard Ranulf give a growl, raw and primitive, and almost cried out loud when he broke off his heated kiss. Her knees would have buckled had his large hands not been cupping her buttocks, but he supported her fully as his mouth moved hotly over her throat. Helplessly Ariane moaned, clutching at his powerful shoulders. "Ranulf . . . "

Ranulf froze at her hoarse plea for fulfillment. Suddenly he cursed, squeezing his eyes shut as desperately he fought for control, as he strove for sanity. How had he become so carried away when he had not even wanted to touch her? His rod was stiff and aching beneath his tunic, his body throbbing with forbidden need. He had been so hot to have her that he had forgotten his purpose in embracing her, forgotten this deceitful wench was his enemy. This was precisely what she wanted—for him to consummate their union.

"No, by the Saints! As God is my witness, you will not win. . . ."

His hands came up to grasp her shoulders as roughly he set her away from him. He would not allow her to work her wiles to gain his surrender.

He stood staring down at her, breathing hard as he fought the urge to drag her back into his embrace. In the contest of wills, he had lost this skirmish. His threat of physical violence had not been enough to frighten her. "You will pay fully for your treachery, wench. I will make your life a misery—I swear it! Henceforth all the meanest tasks in the castle will be yours. If you thought serving as my squire was humbling, you will find your new duties thrice as onerous."

No longer believing in his own self-discipline, Ranulf released her and forced himself to take a step back. His eyes swept her contemptuously. "I will leave you as untouched as I found you. If you have a care for your skin, you will keep out of my sight until an annulment is granted and I can be rid of you for good.''

His amber eyes fierce, Ranulf turned on his heel and stalked from the chamber, the door he had slammed reverberating in his wake.

Staring after him in dismay, Ariane raised a hand to her bruised lips, her thoughts a welter of confusion.

She had not wanted him to go. She had wanted him to remain with her. She had wanted his touch, his possession, wanted him to take her.

How was it possible? Ranulf was her enemy, the man she had sworn to hate. Yet she had melted instantly at his touch. His fierce kisses had turned her blood to fire; the scent and taste of him still burned in her memory. *Sweet Virgin, what was she to do?* He had left her aching with longing, her body trembling with need and regret.

Daunted, she touched her fingers to her aching lips, still hot and tender from his assault. She had survived his fury for the time being, yet she had lost this battle, just as she feared she would lose all the ones in the future.

Ranulf had thwarted her attempt at justice, vowing to annul their marriage and force her to serve as his slave. Yet his method of revenge was not what alarmed her. What frightened her most was how he could command her body at will.

Chapter 11

Ranulf had a revolt on his hands.

It began so subtly that at first he was not even aware of it, but as frequent, inexplicable accidents and incidents of subversion occurred all over the keep, he realized the Claredon castlefolk were up in arms against him, on behalf of their lady.

The first incident befell him two days after he had relegated Ariane to the life of a castle drudge. The dishes of his midday meal were so salted as to render them inedible, the wine so foul, he suspected it of being poisoned. Gagging, Ranulf spat it out and bellowed for the castle cook.

The large-bellied man who came hurrying up from the kitchens put on a humble show and professed his abject apologies to the lord, lamenting that he had been too liberal with the salt, vowing that his hand had slipped over the wine barrel.

When, disbelieving, Ranulf tersely suggested the former lady of Claredon might have been involved in a bungled attempt to poison him, the accusation was vehemently denied. Unable to prove otherwise, Ranulf repressed the urge to clout the oaf, but as punishment, forced him to drink the entire flagon of wine, smiling in grim satisfaction when the man raced for the garderobe to empty his stomach.

His satisfaction faded that afternoon when he discovered that a dozen saddle girths had been cut, not clear through, but enough to avoid obvious detection and cause injury if they gave way while in use. Roaring his displeasure, Ranulf had every groom and lackey in the stables dragged before him for questioning, but no one admitted to the deed.

The incidents continued during the following week, none fatal, all highly annoying and a direct challenge to his authority. First there was the foul-smelling soap that found its way into the garrison barracks, whose unfortunate use stank up the hall for two days. Next, an epidemic of skin rash broke out among his men, caused by nettles sprinkled over the sleeping pallets. Then Ranulf's favorite tunic was ripped beyond repair while being laundered. And while the lord was away overnight securing yet another of Claredon's distant properties, someone sneaked into the mews and freed the prize falcons and hawks from their jesses.

The petty rebellion incited Ranulf's fury, inflaming the raw wound that festered inside him after a lifetime of repudiation. Frustratingly, he could never discover the culprits responsible. The castle servants toiled as usual, and had ready excuses for their slipshod work, but their hostile glances and sulky, accusing expressions told him clearly they were in collusion against him.

For that he placed the blame squarely on Ariane. He had no proof, yet he felt certain she was encouraging her people to insurrection and inciting them to mayhem. Almost daily Ranulf found a new problem to rouse his temper. And if ever he regretted his method of punishing Ariane, or felt the slightest sympathy for her plight, he crushed it mercilessly. He would not allow her to make a fool of him.

In truth, Ariane was not entirely innocent of the charges, though at first she was far too weary toiling at the menial duties Ranulf had devised for her to contribute to the revolt: slaving in the scullery, turning the spits over the great hearth in the kitchens, shoveling flat manchet bread loaves into the ovens to bake, sweltering over boiling tubs of laundry, carting offal and refuse to the midden . . . the least pleasant chores of any castle. And Ranulf had set two guards to control her every move and to prevent her people from coming to her aid and performing those loathsome tasks for her as they initially tried to do.

When she first learned of the frequent episodes of defiance, Ariane wanted to laugh and weep at the same time. She could not help but be pleased that the servants of Claredon remained loyal to her, yet she was horrified to contemplate Ranulf's revenge for their efforts on her behalf. She had no desire to see anyone else punished for her sake. And yet she did not truly fear Ranulf would repay her desperate bid to become his wife by taking vengeance out on her people. She had seen his leniency, had seen him act with restraint toward his dependents, so unless they were actually caught outright, he would not penalize them unjustly. If so, she meant to take blame. If not, she suspected that she would bear the brunt of his fury in any case.

Thus she began quietly encouraging and abetting their small acts of subversion, reminding herself that Ranulf had given her no choice but to defy him covertly. And in truth, it was gratifying to watch the Black Dragon's frustration and helplessness, which actually were minor compared to her own.

He had kept his vow to make her life an utter misery. Each night when Ariane at last climbed the stairs to her solitary chamber, she crawled into her bed, clenching her teeth in pain and weariness, groaning at aching muscles strained by unaccustomed physical labor, wincing at the fresh blisters and raw welts on her hands and feet and knees. Each morning when she dragged her aching body awake, she silently cursed the cause of her torment, wondering why she had ever felt pity for Ranulf's suffering or spared a moment's grief for the terrible scars on his back.

The humility of her position was harder to bear than the physical exhaustion. Her guards watched over her every moment, as if she were a common criminal, and treated her with cold contempt—no doubt, Ariane suspected, because Ranulf had threatened their very lives if they failed in their duty.

She was not allowed to speak with any of her people and was dressed as a slave. Ranulf had ordered all of her gowns of finest linen and silk confiscated, requiring her to wear the most inferior homespun—rough wool that itched and scratched her tender skin. One of her best tunics he gave to Dena, who clearly took great enjoyment in being so favored by the new lord and in flaunting her new position.

That Dena shared Ranulf's bed was assumed—although she was never known to spend the entire night in his solar. At meals, she sat beside him at the high table, occupying the place of honor, the lady's chair. Even gowned in the richest cendal, Dena still looked like a harlot, and it hurt Ariane to see such a creature assume her blessed mother's place. It hurt also to see Ranulf laughing with the common wench, smiling his rare, beautiful smiles and treating her with the affection of a lord toward his favorite leman, or a suitor toward his chosen bride—although wild horses could not have dragged the admission from Ariane.

She was determined to endure her servile position with fortitude. He would not defeat her, Ariane vowed. She would not break. She would bend like the willow and remain standing long after the storm passed.

Thinking it wiser, she took pains to keep out of his way. When she was unfortunate enough to attract his notice, his mask of icy coldness told her clearly that his fury at her had not abated in the least.

The worst times occurred when she was allowed to retire each night, for she had to cross the hall to reach the stairwell behind the dais, accompanied by her guards. Ranulf would level a penetrating stare at her, his face rigidly aloof, yet she could feel his golden hawk's eyes following every step of her progress, could feel her heart racing at his scrutiny. It was always a relief to reach her chamber unscathed, her sole place of refuge, although often the echo of Dena's grating laughter followed her there.

On one particular evening, when the serving wench's raucous sound seemed especially coarse and unrefined, Ariane would have been gratified to know Ranulf shared her opinion. Below in the hall, Dena wet her lips and tossed her head at the lord seductively.

"That one always did think too high of herself," the serving maid said coyly of Ariane.

Ranulf sent the girl a quelling glance. "You forget yourself, wench. It is not your place to criticize your former lady."

She looked startled at the rebuke. "Milord, forgive me," Dena murmured plaintively. "I meant no offense." Leaning near to clutch his arm, she pressed her full breasts against him in lewd suggestion. "It is said the former lady of Claredon avoids the tasks you set for her at every opportunity."

His frown deepened as he drew his arm from Dena's possessive grasp. "I have no desire to listen to castle gossip."

Apparently unconvinced, Dena trilled another strident laugh. " 'Tis not only gossip, milord. Why, I could tell you things I've seen. . . . My Lady Ariane is not so pure. Know

you that in the past she oftentimes left the castle unattended
and went to the wood to meet her lover?''

The maid's malicious tale struck Ranulf like a blow to his
vitals, arousing savage memories and sending his thoughts
spinning backward in time. In mind's eye, he saw not Ariane,
but the noblewoman who had borne him, the mother he had
never known, slipping from the castle to consort with her
peasant lover, to carry on her adulterous affair. With vivid
intensity he remembered the pain and fear her betrayal had
caused him his life long, how she had destroyed any possibility of hopes or dreams. . . .

Reacting blindly, Ranulf struck his fist on the table.
''Enough!''

The sharp command silenced Dena's coarse chatter.

Scarcely seeing her, Ranulf turned a dark look on the serving maid. ''I give you leave to go. I no longer require your
presence this evening. And in future, I suggest you refrain
from discussing matters that are not your concern.''

Alarm glinting in her eyes, Dena hastily rose from the table
and bobbed a fearful curtsey. When she had gone, Ranulf sat
toying moodily with his eating dagger, carving patterns in
the remnants of a meat pie.

At his other side, Payn watched him with a barely concealed frown. The two of them sat alone, as most of Ranulf's
men were playing at dice near the great hearth, while the
serfs cleared the trestle tables.

''That lazy wench doubtless knows sloth intimately,'' Payn
observed quietly, ''but she lies when she suggests her former
lady has been slack in her duties.''

Ranulf grunted in agreement. The reports he had been
given concerning Ariane's toils suggested that she had obeyed
his every command without complaint. And to his knowledge,
she had not repeated her outrageous claim of being his wife.
He had nothing to rebuke her for—which perversely only
served to increase his fury. The uncertainty Dena had just
raised in his mind did naught to calm him, either. Had the
wench spoken the truth? Did the Lady Ariane often leave the
castle unattended to sojourn in the wood with a lover?

''Dena grows overbold, methinks,'' Payn murmured,
''since you granted her respite from her duties. She considers

herself your favorite, but I wonder that you permit her presumption. Her buxom charms are not *that* spectacular.''

Ranulf nodded absently. From the start he'd regretted the rash impulse that had led him to raise Dena to her lady's place, but he stubbornly refused to countermand the order. He had acted irrationally, out of rage at Ariane's maneuver with the bedsheets, but he could not back down now, not and hold a shred of hope for respect from the people of Claredon. In this instance particularly, it was imperative he prove that he meant what he said, and that his wrath was not to be taken lightly. Soon enough he would have to consider how to make a tactical retreat. King Henry would doubtless raise objections to one of his noble subjects—even a traitor's daughter—being forced into servitude as a slave.

Meanwhile, Dena grew overly bold, Ranulf admitted. In truth, Payn would have been astounded to learn he had not availed himself of Dena's obviously eager desire to share his bed. But the coarse, lushly endowed wench held little appeal for him. He had wearied of her charms within a day.

All too often he found himself remembering the infuriating, defiant, highborn lady who had once been his bride. No peasant, however winsome, could compare favorably to Ariane. Her elegance, her regal grace, her sweet woman's scent, even her tart tongue, held an allure for him that, absurdly, he could not shake. The Saints knew he had tried. Yet he could not dismiss her from his mind ... or his body. Every time he saw her, he felt a stirring in his groin. Merely looking at her made him hungry.

And his masculine instincts made him keenly aware that others of his men felt as he did, harboring the same desire to bed her. She possessed a cool sensuality that any warm-blooded male would find challenging.

Her own men no doubt felt it as well. Especially that fair-haired lad called Gilbert who followed her around like a drooling pup. Even now Gilbert was glaring daggers at him from the length of the hall. *Was this one of the lovers Dena had spoken of? The lover Ariane met in the forest?*

Beside the young clerk sat the elderly priest and the Claredon steward—which reminded Ranulf of another incident that had inflamed his temper.

"Did you know," he demanded resentfully, "that cursed

steward tried to pass off a dozen miscalculations in the accounts as my own error this morning?''

"No doubt he thought you could not tally," Payn said sympathetically. "You will have to appoint your own steward, my lord."

Ranulf nodded and drank deeply of his wine, which had the benefit of being unsalted. He could cipher and read well enough to know when he was being deceived. "Do all the folk here think me a lackwit?"

Not answering at once, Payn picked up a lute and lazily began plucking a tune. The knight was an adequate musician, and possessed a clear, melodious voice. "I fancy they consider you to have ill used their lady," he said finally, at the end of a verse.

"Ill used?" Ranulf's expression darkened as he muttered, "I have not used her half as ill as I should have. She is fortunate I did not clap her in chains for her treachery."

"We have all suffered a woman's deceit at one time or another. At least the Lady Ariane felt she had sufficient claim to declare herself your wife."

Ranulf narrowed his gaze dangerously. "Do you defend the wench?"

"Not I, my lord," Payn asserted blandly. "But I fear you are not winning the battle. Perhaps you would be wise to change your strategy."

"Beseech me not on her behalf," Ranulf snapped.

"Not on *her* behalf, my lord, but your own. You know I serve only your interests. The Lady Ariane claims an uncommon support among her people, wherein lies her strength—"

"Lady? I told you not to call her that."

Payn shrugged. "I fear the title of 'lady' is not something you can take from her merely by decree."

Morosely, Ranulf stared into his wine, aware his vassal was right. The woman he had unlawfully deemed a slave was every inch a noble lady. Despite the rags she now wore, her blood and breeding showed. Ariane held herself regally as a queen . . . proud, indomitable, beautiful. With all his show of might, he had been unable to cower her.

Doubtless it had hurt him more to be forced to use such methods with a female, against his vows. Yet she deserved punishment for her crimes.

If he felt more than a twinge of guilt to see Ariane labor as a slave, he quelled it. He had always maintained a fierce control over himself, one that tolerated no emotion, no softness. He was a man of discipline, with the ability to exercise an iron restraint over his will and his passions.

The trouble was that Ariane tested even his limits. More than once he'd had to stop himself from giving in to his protective urges and calling a halt to the strict execution of her sentence. Twice in the four days since her brazen, public declaration, he'd found himself assaulted by tender feelings.

The struggle to suppress his attraction for her was even less successful, Ranulf conceded. Often he found himself listening for Ariane's quiet footstep, or scenting the air for a hint of her perfume, or searching for her among the crowd gathered in the hall for meals.

It disgusted and infuriated him, his foolish desire to be with her. Remarkably, he had even enjoyed having her next to him in sleep during the few nights he had forced her to share his bed. Perhaps he had played into her hands by banishing her to her own chamber, but he knew he could not be around the wench and keep his lusts under control.

"What do you advise, then?" he asked his vassal. "The wench must learn she is subject to my will. I have no proof, yet I know she has been urging her serfs to mischief."

"I am not so certain she is the culprit—although undeniably she is the cause. I suspect her people's rebellion is fueled by what they see as injustice to her. Doubtless they consider her to have been cheated of her rights, denied both her castle and her place as your lady wife, and now stripped of her rank and forced to serve as a slave. Perhaps her punishment is too visible, Ranulf. Could you not devise a more . . . private sentence? One that would not render her a martyr?"

Just then, the huge oaken door to the hall swung open to admit two sentries. They came hurrying up the aisles between the trestle tables.

"My lord," one man said urgently. "I fear I bear bad tidings. There has been another occurrence of willful destruction."

Ranulf shot Payn a grim look before asking, "What is it this time?"

"It is the armory.... But mayhap you should see for yourself."

Smoldering silently, the new lord of Claredon and his vassal accompanied the sentries outside and down the tower entrance steps to the armory below, whose door now stood open. Within lay the store of weapons and armor used by the garrison. By the light of a torch, they could see the gleam of a thick, shiny matter covering nearly every surface.

With a finger, Ranulf tasted the sticky substance. "Honey! By the Chalice! ..."

Someone had dripped honey over the chain mail hauberks and steel helmets, the swords and lances and shields. It would require every squire and page in the garrison to labor for countless hours, cleaning the metal with sand and vinegar to remove the gluelike coating.

"Injustice, you say?" Ranulf asked Payn in a dangerous tone, before he spun on his heel and stalked from the building.

He went directly to the fourth floor of the tower, to Ariane's chamber. The guards on duty before her door snapped to attention when they spied their lord, and hastened to produce a key.

Unlocking the door and shoving it open, Ranulf entered and slammed it closed behind him.

He stopped abruptly in realization. He had startled Ariane in the act of preparing for bed. He caught a tantalizing glimpse of pale buttocks and long, slender legs before, with a gasp, she grabbed up the first thing to hand—her woolen tunic—and whirled to face him, clutching the garment to her breasts in an attempt to cover her nakedness.

"My lord ... what do you want?" she demanded breathlessly.

His amber eyes, glittering with fury, darkened with another emotion as he stared intently. "I wished to speak with you, wench."

"I was washing away the day's grime. Will you permit me a moment of privacy? I should like to dress."

"No."

Her eyes widened. "No?"

"A slave has no need for privacy."

His taunt made Ariane stiffen her spine. "I am not a slave, my lord, as I have told you before. I am your *wife*."

The outrage returned abruptly to Ranulf's amber eyes. "You are my possession, nothing more. I will never acknowledge you as my wife—a mercenary, deceitful jade. Nor will you ever profit from my wealth and position."

"I care naught for your wealth or position," she retorted, her own eyes flashing defiance.

Ranulf stared at her, fury and admiration warring with each other. Fury won. His mouth curled. "More lies, slave?" When she stood regarding him with regal haughtiness, he gritted his teeth. "It matters not. The marriage will soon be annulled. I have sent a petition to Rome with a heavy bribe, applying for a swift hearing. But I did not come to argue a moot point. I mean to discuss the accidents and wanton destruction that have been plaguing the keep. I want them to cease at once."

"Why come to me, my lord? I had naught to do with them. I have done precisely as you bade me."

"I hold you responsible."

Ariane's eyebrows lifted. "How so? I no longer run this household. I can hardly be held to blame if things go awry. You are lord here now, as you have told me countless times."

"And you have pitted your people against me, do not deny it!"

"I shall not attempt to, my lord. You would not believe me, in any case."

"No, I would not." His gaze, cold and vividly gold, held hers. "It will fall to you to clean the armor that your accomplices sought to ruin. And you will speak to your former people once more to demand that they cease their tricks."

"Or what, my lord?"

Her contemptuous calm was infuriating. Ranulf clenched his fists to repress the urge to shake her. "I warn you, wench, I am at the end of my patience. One more incident of subversion and I will punish the lot of them, without regard to justice! The officers of the household will be thrown in the dungeon. The freemen, I will cast out to starve. The serfs will be sent to the fields, where they may apply their backs to pulling a plow in place of oxen. The guilty will suffer with the innocent."

Ariane winced inwardly at his threat, yet she met his furious gaze with an innocent look of serenity.

"I will speak to them, my lord. But I cannot promise complete success. The people of Claredon are not sheep, to blindly offer loyalty to a new lord. It must be earned." She smiled archly. "And waging war against *me* is not the way to go about it. Doubtless they would accept you more readily if you allowed me to run the household once more."

His heavy brows snapped together. "God's splendor! Do you think I am fool enough to trust you with such authority?"

"I think you would be a fool *not* to trust me."

Ranulf seared her with a blazing look. Their eyes locked in a silent battle of wills. She could see the rigid muscles flex in Ranulf's jaw.

Slowly, without speaking, he moved toward her, closing the distance between them, till he stood directly in front of her, his nearness intimidating.

Ariane raised her chin, defiantly meeting his smoldering gaze. She refused to cower before him, although her heart had begun hammering like a drum. His next command startled her entirely.

"I would see you without your clothing. Remove it."

"What?" She stared at him in disbelief, her composure suddenly shaken.

"Are you deaf, sweeting? I said I wish to see you. Take the garment away."

When she remained frozen, Ranulf smiled tauntingly. "A slave has no need for modesty. And"—his gaze raked her boldly—"I much doubt you possess any charms I have not viewed before. I've seen any number of naked females . . . including you."

"Then why must you see me again?" Ariane demanded breathlessly.

"Simply because I desire it." His slow smile was wicked, deliberately taunting, while the devil's own gleam shone in his eyes.

He meant to prove his power over her, Ariane realized, grinding her teeth. And there was little she could do to prevent him.

With stubborn determination, she lifted her chin regally,

feigning indifference. She would not let him see her mortification.

Proudly, quivering, Ariane did as she was bid and let the tunic fall away. To her acute dismay, she felt Ranulf's heated gaze scrutinizing her body, measuring, touching her intimately. Moving slowly over every inch of her, studying her as he would a slave. It was strangely, inexplicably arousing.

It was even more arousing to Ranulf. He sucked in his breath at the sight of Ariane naked and vulnerable before him, letting his gaze caress the high, sweet mounds of her breasts ... the narrow waist and flaring hips ... lingering on the thatch of red-gold curls between her thighs ... her long, slim legs ... He knew he should leave at once, before his iron control slipped irrevocably, and yet he could not bring himself to take the first step.

He looked his fill, studying her openly, drinking in every nuance and detail of her exquisite form. She was a woman made for a man, her breasts tipped by delicate, rosebud nipples, her hips deliciously rounded, her thighs long and smooth. His own body tautened with hunger. He wanted to touch her ivory marble skin, to revel in her silky softness, to suckle those inviting nipples, to taste her woman's essence. He yearned to have her naked beneath him, the slick heat of her sheath enveloping him as he rode her, her legs wrapped around his waist while she writhed in ecstasy....

Realizing where his urges were leading him, Ranulf cursed silently at himself. It enraged him that the deceitful wench could make him want her so powerfully.

Ariane shivered as the tense silence drew out. Ranulf's regard was always like scorching embers, but now it seemed to burn everywhere it touched.

"My lord? ..." she said breathlessly, ashamed at the weakness in her voice.

Ranulf's voice, when he replied, was low and husky and intense. "Your form is pleasing to look upon. I wonder that you do not use it to court my favor."

She stiffened at his insulting implication, and abruptly drew the woolen tunic back up to cover herself. "I am not a strumpet, any more than I am your slave."

"No?"

Even as she steeled herself for an assault, Ranulf reached

up and slid his hand beneath the crumpled tunic she held, the flesh of his palm deliberately grazing her erect, swollen nipple. Her breasts engorged painfully under that light touch.

She gasped and took a step back, yet there was nowhere to run. Her buttocks came up against the oaken table that contained the washbasin.

His teeth flashed in a wolfish smile. With thumb and forefinger, he captured her left nipple. The resultant shock of fire that streaked though Ariane weakened her knees, yet she clenched her teeth, refusing to surrender.

"Do you recall the pleasure I gave you when I stroked your nipples?" Ranulf asked, his husky murmur caressing her senses the way his fingers did her breasts.

"No ... please ... do not ..."

Her plea was ignored entirely. He stood over her, crowding her with his powerful body, and tugged the tunic from her nerveless grasp. "Do you remember how I plied the wet rosebud between your thighs?" Holding her gaze, he traced a finger between her breasts, downward to her narrow waist, drawing his hand slowly, lingeringly, over her skin. "I could show you such pleasure again, sweeting...."

Unable to bear the taunting gleam in his eyes, the hard sensuality of his expression, Ariane averted her face. Yet she could not move. She stood helplessly as he threaded his fingers through the dense curls guarding her femininity. Her body went rigid at his expert touch; her cheeks flushed scarlet. But she could no more have resisted him than she could have overpowered him.

Insinuating his hand between her thighs, he stroked her moist cleft, his finger toying with her. "Do you not find this arousing?"

Her gasp became a moan as a spasm of longing went through her. Her hips arched instinctively, her quivering thighs opening to him.

"I thought so." Ranulf laughed softly. "I would win a reckoning between us," he said evenly, even as he wondered if it were true. "I could take you here and make you beg for me."

"Could you ... my lord?" Trembling, she raised her gaze to his.

Ranulf hesitated. His narrowed look had followed every

flicker of shock, every startled reaction, on her face. Now he saw the triumph in Ariane's gray eyes and froze, fighting the battle between desire and self-control that raged within him. She would prey on his weakness if he gave in. . . .

His laughter turned harsh. "Ah, no, slave. You will not prevail so easily. Our union will never be consummated. Rather than enjoy you myself, I will throw you to my men and watch as they have you."

It was an idle threat, in truth. He would break his vows and lock her in the dungeon long before he let another man mount her. Ariane was *his*. He would never permit another man to touch her.

His hand fell away, his mouth curling in contempt as he stepped back, needing the distance.

Their eyes clashed wordlessly.

"I *will* win," he repeated with ominous softness, before he turned abruptly and let himself from the chamber.

Wanting to scream with vexation, Ariane dug her nails into the wool tunic she still clutched to her breast. Her heart was thrumming from the dangerous encounter, her breath coming too rapidly.

Shaken, dazed, she closed her eyes and drew a shuddering breath. Only now, after he was gone, was she even aware how badly she had wanted Ranulf to stay. Only now, after her near escape, could she think clearly enough to frame into words the vague notion that had come to her as he'd tormented her with his sensual caresses: Somehow she had to turn his lusty passions to her advantage. She was no temptress, but somehow she had to learn to tame the dragon. For if Ranulf could be persuaded to bed her, it would greatly strengthen her claim to being his wife.

Remembering the intense heat she'd seen in his golden eyes moments ago, Ariane chided herself for a fool. She had been close to victory without knowing it—and then she had senselessly reminded him of their controversy by challenging him openly. If only she had curbed her tongue, Ranulf might even now be claiming her maidenhead and spilling his seed within her. Lashing out at him in defiance was not the way to win a man's regard, or to consummate a betrothal. She should have feigned meekness at least, even if she could not have managed the grace and equanimity her lady mother would have counseled.

Throwing the despised woolen tunic on the floor in disgust, Ariane glared at the oaken door with its heavy iron bands.

"I would not wager on victory yet, my arrogant lord," she muttered. "You are not so ruthless as your legend suggests, nor as invincible as you pretend."

Chapter 12

How did one tame a dragon? Especially one as ruthless and unyielding as the Black Dragon of Vernay?

Ariane began by assuming the consummate appearance of obedience and complying with Ranulf's demands: She pleaded once again with Claredon's serfs and freemen and household officials to desist in their defiance and to serve their new lord willingly. She took great pride in their loyal support of her, she told them earnestly, but did not wish to see them crushed in the fist of the Black Dragon. Nor did she wish to see Lord Ranulf carry out his threat to punish the innocent with the guilty. Until now, she declared, he had dealt justly with transgressors; indeed, he had shown great restraint. He was their conqueror, yet they had not suffered unduly.

Nor had he harmed *her*, even if he had repudiated their betrothal. Their quarrel was personal, Ariane admitted, and would not be swiftly settled. Certainly rebellion would not aid her cause. Rather it would only work against her. If they wished to support her, then they would obey their new overlord without question and accept his authority. She was satisfied Lord Ranulf would make a good ruler of Claredon.

This last assertion of Ariane's surprised Ranulf and roused his suspicion. That the former lady of Claredon should praise his rule made him wonder if she were not enacting some scheme to further her own ends.

Once the incidents of subversion ceased, however, the path was clear for him to assume the lord's duties. Ranulf began holding court in the great hall each morning, granting interviews and dispensing justice and settling disputes.

Ariane, whose work station had been relocated to the hall so that he could keep a closer eye on her as she performed her task of cleaning armor, was taken aback by this new tactic of Ranulf's. She could not imagine so powerful a lord taking an interest in the affairs of the peasants. Even her father had left such matters to his seneschal and bailiff.

Yet the Black Dragon listened seriously to the most minor concerns of Claredon's serfs and freemen, and though Ariane was loath to admit it, often impressed her with his verdicts.

When a yeoman wantonly killed another man's ox and would not pay reparations, Ranulf sentenced him to pull the plow himself. When a swineherd who grazed his pigs in the forest enticed another man's sow to join his herd, Ranulf awarded the victim three of the perpetrator's piglets but required him to pay for grazing rights.

That both men saw the fairness of this verdict was evident when they thumped each other on the back in friendship and left grinning.

"Henceforth, you shall be known as Lord of Swine, Ranulf," Payn declared, laughing.

From her position at one side of the hall, Ariane saw the answering humor that glinted in Ranulf's eyes, heard his rough chuckle as his teeth flashed white in his harsh-featured face. She was surprised that he made no objection to his vassal's gibe, yet he clearly bore an affection for Payn. It was just as obvious that he enjoyed his role as chief arbitrator, and that he was making an effort to be a just lord.

The ruling that surprised Ariane most, however, was when, for his own unstated reasons, Ranulf assisted two young lovers in gaining their heart's desires. They were seeking permission from the lord to wed, over the objections of their parents—freemen who had arranged betrothals for their children to persons with an acre of land each, a prize of no mean worth.

When the young people professed their love for each other and declared their willingness to live in poverty, Ranulf not only allowed them to wed, he dowered the bride, giving the couple a hut to live in and a cow to begin their life together. Their joy was evident on their beaming faces, their gratitude obvious in the way they fell to their knees and kissed the lord's hand.

Payn seemed to see nothing odd in the ruling, but Ariane

stared at Ranulf in disbelief, bewildered by his uncharacteristic action.

For a fleeting moment, she caught his gaze across the hall, and from the way his expression suddenly darkened at the sight of her, she could tell he was recalling their own broken betrothal. Then, to her dismay, Ranulf's mouth curved in a slow, taunting smile. It was a silent challenge to her, Ariane knew, a private acknowledgement of the battle between them and his determination to win.

Ariane repressed the urge to toss her head in a reckless show of defiance. Thinking it also unwise to draw Ranulf's attention further, she reined in her curiosity just then, but at the next opportunity, when she served him at the midday meal, she abandoned her pretense of subservience long enough to question him about his decision.

"I confess to surprise, my lord," she said in a voice too low to be overheard by his vassals, "that you should part with good coin for the sake of true love."

Ranulf gave her a guarded glance, as if mistrusting the intent of her remark. "I saw no reason to force them into a marriage merely to satisfy their parents' mercenary desires."

"Your compassion is commendable. And to think," Ariane could not resist adding archly, "the world believes your heart wears a sheet of iron."

For a moment Ranulf was caught between anger and amusement at her comment, but he merely responded with a mocking smile. "You are mistaken, demoiselle. I have no heart."

Perhaps that was so, Ariane reflected thoughtfully as she gazed down at him. And yet she had seen with her own eyes Ranulf's momentary lapses into kindness, actions that suggested he was more vulnerable than he wanted to acknowledge.

Ranulf, suddenly uncomfortable with her clear-seeing gaze, averted his own, but made the mistake of glancing down at her hands. Their condition appalled him; the flesh was nearly as red and raw as fresh meat.

A surge of remorse rose up in him so quickly that he could not check it. Forgetting the retort he had been about to give, Ranulf reached out and gently took Ariane's hand. Turning the delicate appendage palm up, he stared down in dismay at the oozing blisters.

"God's blood, how came you by these?" he asked, although he feared he knew.

"Cleaning your armor, my lord. Scrubbing chain mail with sand and vinegar is not renowned for its salubrious effect."

"Why did you say nothing?" Ranulf demanded, his tone brusque with anger at his own thoughtlessness.

"I did not think you would care to hear my opinion, my lord," she replied dryly, unable to refrain from the gibe.

Ignoring her sarcasm, Ranulf frowned as his thumbs traced the blistered flesh, careful not to touch the tender areas. Against his will, he felt a grudging respect and admiration for her fortitude. Not once had Ariane complained about the savage treatment he had accorded her. "I have seen battle wounds as severe as these."

"But I thought you wished to see me suffer," Ariane reminded him.

"I had no desire to see you injured," he answered, vaguely aware of the inconsistencies in his logic. "Do you not have a potion you can apply to your hands?"

"Yes." The word came out more breathless than she intended. Ranulf was stroking her palm almost absently, arousing an unbidden sensual response within her merely with a featherlight pressure on her skin.

"Then do so."

He released her hand, yet his features remained disturbed as he studied her. If Ariane had not known better, she would actually have thought him concerned for her welfare.

"And you may turn the task of cleaning armor over to my squires." He hesitated. "Your work leaves much to be desired, in any case."

Though realizing from the sudden dry note in his voice that Ranulf was deliberately provoking her, Ariane gave him an indignant glance, annoyed by that untruth. She had done as good a job as any squire, for she refused to give Ranulf any cause to find fault with her. Yet she would be grateful to be relieved of the responsibility of caring for his armor. Cleaning chain mail was physically easier than other menial tasks Ranulf had assigned her, but the chore tortured her hands.

She might have expressed her thoughts on the matter, except that Ranulf startled her by suddenly rising from his chair. The gentle brush of his finger on her cheek unsettled her even more. Lifting her head sharply, she stared at him, unable to look away. Was he purposefully using his compelling touch to discompose her, conducting a bold seduction right here in the hall?

She was certain of it when Ranulf's mouth curved in a tantalizing half-smile, one that held a devastating appeal and set her heart to thudding. He was well aware of his power over the female sex, Ariane knew.

"Go now, and see to your wounds."

"B-But . . . what of my duties?" she stammered, nervous at his proximity and the sudden softness of his tone, as well as suspicious of his motives.

"On the morrow you can return to working in the kitchens and serving tables, so long as you remain where I may keep an eye on you."

Weighing the advantages, Ariane nodded slowly. If she remained near him, she would be vulnerable to his vexing tactics, yet she would have better opportunities to pursue her own plan to tame the Dragon. And she could keep a close eye on Ranulf as well, and be there to intervene should he deal harshly with any of her people.

She watched him more closely after that. Not only did Ranulf make progress on the domestic front, he also succeeded outside the castle walls. Militarily he tightened his hold of the demesne, flexing his might in countless ways. His patrols made endless forays about the countryside searching for rebels, and Ranulf himself seized the other two manor houses within a day's ride of the castle. By the end of his second full week at Claredon, the garrison began to follow a predictable routine, alternating between patrolling the countryside and practicing arms daily in the exercise yard in the lower bailey.

It was a familiar sight for Ariane, seeing seasoned knights hacking at each other as they trained in warfare—except that these were the wrong knights. Her father, Walter, should be lord here. Seeing Ranulf settle into his role with such ease disheartened her greatly, and an ache caught at her throat whenever she remembered her father's uncertain plight. She could only pray that his vassal, Simon, had by now reached him, and that, by some miracle, Walter would be cleared of the charge of treason. Perhaps they would even discover the means to deliver Claredon from the Black Dragon.

She prayed also for the inhabitants of the eastern forest. Guarded so closely, she had found no opportunity to slip out of the castle to visit them, and time was growing short.

Her own plight seemed just as uncertain, although her circumstances improved minimally after her encounter with Ranulf when he saw the consequence of his punishment. He lightened her workload to a degree, allowing her to perform the less physical chores, and her hands were healing. Yet he had not forgiven her in the least for her claim of ravishment. A storm was brewing between them, she could sense it. And she suspected that one day soon, it would break over her head.

When trouble next came, however, it was from a direction Ariane had not foreseen—one of Ranulf's own high-ranking vassals.

She had just climbed the stairs from the kitchens with a wooden platter of honeyed cakes for the last course of the evening meal when she found her path blocked by a tall, dark-haired knight whom she recognized as Bertran de Ridefort, a cousin of Ivo's and one of the knights who regularly sat at the lord's high table. When she gave him a quizzical glance, he responded with a friendly leer.

"Well met ... my beauteoush lady." His words were slurred, and he swayed on his feet, obviously the worse for drink.

Ariane lowered her gaze to hide her scorn. "Please, my lord ... allow me to pass."

"What if I do not, little wi-sh ... witch?"

"Lord Ranulf would not be pleased if I tarried."

Bertran flashed her a charming grin that was not unappealing; he was rather handsome when he smiled, despite his drunken state. "Methinks Lord Ranulf would not care if you tarried with *me*."

Ariane grew uneasy with his lascivious scrutiny, her fingers tightening involuntarily on the wooden platter. She was not afraid for her virtue. There were twoscore men within shouting distance who would doubtless come to her rescue if needed. And yet she did not want to make an enemy of Ivo's cousin. Next to Payn FitzOsbern, Ivo de Ridefort was Ranulf's most trusted vassal, the knight left in charge of Claredon when the lord was away. His cousin Bertran, while not as high in station, was frequently in Ranulf's company and obviously valued for his counsel. It would be better if she could handle this overamorous knight on her own, without appearing to spurn his advances. Indeed, her best course might be to claim Ranulf's protection, she decided.

Ariane forced herself to smile. "I fear *I* would care, sir. In the eyes of God, I am Lord Ranulf's wife, and I would remain faithful to him."

Bertran frowned, as if having difficulty following her reasoning. "Not his wife . . . Fear Ranulf is engaged with . . . that slut, Dena. He will not missh you, schweeting. He has wearied of your charms . . . but I vow I will not."

Ariane stiffened at the mention of that strumpet's name, astonished at how fierce and hurtful the pang of jealousy that coursed through her.

Giving a cheerful leer, Bertran leaned closer, his breath heavy with wine fumes. "I can ease your labor, sweeting. A beauty such as your-sshelf should not be slaving like a peasant. I have a *mussh* more pleasant occupation in mind."

To her startlement, he reached out and gave a tug on the drawstring at the neckline of her woolen bodice. Ariane gasped in alarm. She tried to draw back, but his hand caught her wrist, nearly causing her to drop her platter. His strong fingers dug into her flesh almost painfully, as if he was unaware of his strength.

A frisson of fear danced down her spine. A knight could take a field wench without a thought, and although an honorable man would not abuse his lord's unwilling servants within the keep, in his befuddled state Bertran could easily have forgotten her rank—and more easily overpower her, if he wished.

With a desperate jerk of her arm, Ariane managed to free her wrist from Bertran's grasp. Clutching her platter, she slipped past him, intending to flee—and collided directly with a broad, unyielding chest. The force knocked her platter of cakes from her grasp, and sent it spilling to the rush-covered floor with a thud.

She recognized that familiar chest, that hard, powerful body. Horrified, Ariane looked up into hard eyes of amber gold. "M-My lord . . . " she stammered. "I beg pardon. . . ."

Ranulf's gaze went from her flushed face to his vassal's. "It seems you have lost your way, Bertran. You sought the garderobe to relieve yourself, I believe."

He shook his dark head. "Rather relieve myself with this wensh, Ranulf."

Ranulf leveled an arctic stare at the knight. To Ariane's shock, he slipped his arm around her waist and drew her hard against him. "Not yours. *Mine*. And I guard well what is mine."

She sucked in her breath sharply as she felt Ranulf's hand brazenly brush her breast. She wanted to slap his hand away, yet considered it wiser not to protest when his display of male possessiveness offered her protection.

Bertran blinked at the action, while his expression grew sulky. "Aye, milord. I knew not how it was between you. I shall find me another wench-sh." With a vapid smile, Bertran turned and strolled off in search of more willing female companionship.

To Ariane's relief, Ranulf released her at once.

"Were you harmed?" he asked sharply.

"No," she replied, rubbing her sore wrist. Her relief faded as Ranulf's hot gaze shifted to hers, hard and accusing.

"I will not have you seducing my men to win their sympathy," he said in a voice tight with anger.

"Seduce—?" Ariane gaped at him. " 'Tis not true. I did nothing to encourage his interest."

Ranulf's mouth curled as his gaze dropped to her bosom, where the bodice of her rough woolen gown gaped open, exposing the upper swells of her breasts. "Indeed? You merely allowed him to ogle your charms and taunted him with the promise of your body? Cover yourself," Ranulf ordered as she opened her mouth in denial.

Ariane ground her teeth in indignation, but she obediently retied the drawstring to her bodice. Ranulf would not believe her protestations of innocence. He was stubbornly determined to think the worst of her—

A plaintive whine at her feet momentarily distracted her attention. The castle dogs had gathered around to sniff the rushes. With a grimace, Ariane bent to pick up the platter she had dropped. Most of the cakes had fallen on the floor, and she left them there for the dogs to devour.

When she stood once more, Ranulf was still eyeing her sternly. "Be warned, wench. You think to ease your plight by winning over my vassals, but I am well acquainted with the ploys of your kind. I will not countenance such trickery in my keep, do you comprehend? I will not have my men sniffing at your honey the way these hounds pant after sweets."

At the unfairness of the accusation, Ariane was almost too incensed to speak. Almost. She understood why Ranulf would side with his knight against her, but *he* was to blame for the indignity she had just suffered. Her reduction in status to menial laborer had earned the disrespect of his vassals, while Ranulf's own contemptuous treatment of her for the past two weeks had encouraged others to treat her similarly.

"Then I suggest, my lord," she retorted, her eyes flashing silver sparks, "that you lock your men in the kennels where they may be safe from my evil influence!"

Not giving him a chance to reply or to reprimand her for her insolence, she whirled, her head held high, and marched back to the stairwell leading to the kitchens, feeling Ranulf's piercing gaze boring into her all the while.

He seemed to watch her more intently after that. Each time Ranulf spied Ariane with another man, be it his own or one of Claredon's, she felt the impact of his smoldering scrutiny. Had she not known better, she would have thought him jealous. But Ranulf cared nothing for her, Ariane was certain. He watched her only to see if she would make a false move.

His caution annoyed her, until she remembered his admitted contempt for highborn damsels. For some reason, Ranulf did not trust noblewomen—and after her attempt to cement their betrothal, he trusted *her* least of all.

Still, his vigilance was not due solely to mistrust, Ariane suspected, or a desire for revenge, or the possessiveness of a lord toward his property. The savage heat in his eyes was not mere suspicion, or hostility, or even a determination to conquer.

Desire was there as well.

Each time she came near Ranulf, the air crackled with a tension that was two parts sexual. And he resented her for rousing his lust, Ariane was certain. She could almost feel the conflict within him, a strong man battling for control over his own will. Certainly she could sense the pressure building behind his temper.

An explosion between them seemed imminent. Yet Ariane found herself anticipating it with a strange mingling of apprehension and excitement.

The explosion nearly came the day after the incident with Bertran, when Gilbert waylaid her on her way to early mass. Ranulf had relented enough in his punishment to allow her to seek comfort for her soul. As she prepared to enter the chapel in the inner bailey, Gilbert drew her aside on the pretext of offering her a cool drink of water from the well.

At first she listened to him with only half an ear, her thoughts distracted as she mentally debated the wisdom of asking Gilbert to pay a visit to the east woods in her stead. But his ranting soon alarmed her.

Ranulf, returning from exercising his destrier in the outer bailey, felt his heart lurch when he spied the two of them standing so close together. The boy's fair hair was a shade lighter than Ariane's, and their heads glinted pale red-gold in the early morning sunlight.

The sight seared Ranulf with jealousy. He put little trust in the faithfulness of women, noble ones most of all. And since hearing the rumor of Ariane's wanton activities from the serving wench Dena, he had been haunted by images of his former bride sneaking out of the castle to consort with her lover, this lad in particular.

His first primal instinct was to thrash the young whelp to a pulp, and yet he clamped it down. Rather than trysting, they were more likely conspiring to rebel against his rule. The boy seemed to be arguing with Ariane, about what Ranulf could not hear at this distance. The lad was holding forth intently while Ariane shook her head.

Urging his powerful warhorse closer, Ranulf caught a snatch of their conversation: ". . . that devil-lord."

Ranulf concluded that *he* was the subject under discussion, but he could barely make out Ariane's reply: "If you continue to fight him, you will only suffer for it."

"Were I to challenge him—"

"Nay, you cannot. You would be killed—"

She must have heard his horse's hooves, for she broke off suddenly and turned with a start. There were secrets in her eyes, he noted with a tightness squeezing his chest. Secrets that only strengthened the suspicion they were intriguing against him.

"Where are your guards?" Ranulf demanded as he reined the destrier to halt.

Ariane eyed him warily. "In the ch-chapel, my lord," she stammered in reply.

But Ranulf was no longer listening. His attention was fixed entirely on Gilbert, his expression hard and unsmiling. He kept his voice soft in an attempt to hide from himself how fierce was the jealousy he felt. "Do I know you, boy?"

"I am called Gilbert, milord," the youth replied sullenly. "I serve as clerk to Baldwin, the castle steward."

"Ah, the steward who thought to cheat me with the erroneous accounts."

Gilbert flushed, looking uncomfortable, but remained silent, the set of his jaw belligerent.

"Have you no duties to attend to?"

"My duty is to serve my lady, sire."

Ariane gasped at her brother's insolent reply, while Ranulf reached for the hilt of his sword. He no longer desired merely to flog the impudent whelp; he wanted to skewer him to a wall. He'd had his fill of such defiance—this continual contempt for his authority and his right to rule.

Alarmed, Ariane stepped between them, in the path of the massive destrier. "My lord, he did not mean it!"

"Did he not? Obviously he forgets your changed status."

"Yes, I am certain he forgot." She gazed at Ranulf in consternation, while holding her hands up as if to ward off a blow.

Ranulf gritted his teeth, furious that Ariane would defend the boy so urgently, and that he himself would care so keenly. He had never before been struck by such an irrational jealousy over a female; it amazed and disturbed him, the violent urge that bored into him like the point of a lance. But then he had never before been plagued by such a vexing, defiant wench as his former betrothed, or her ardent supporters.

Ranulf clenched his jaw to control the unreasoning suspicions welling inside him. His anger was directed not only at the two conspirators staring up at him, though; he felt a surge of anger at himself for not mastering the violence that lived within him.

"I beg you, my lord . . . do not pay him any heed. He is but a boy. A *foolish* boy," Ariane added with a repressive glance at Gilbert.

Ranulf's eyes coldly swept the lad, who fairly bristled. "Apparently he is old enough to hide behind a woman's skirts. At his age I had nearly earned my spurs."

Gilbert stiffened and stepped forward, squaring his shoulders. "I hide behind no one, sire. If you wish me to prove my mettle, I will gladly oblige."

His jealousy goading him, Ranulf flashed a contemptuous smile. "You look soft, boy. Methinks you would need some training before challenging a knight to combat."

"Gilbert is not a soldier, my lord," Ariane intervened hastily. "He is a scholar."

"Then I suggest he go about his scholarly duties," Ranulf advised, his voice dangerously soft.

With a frustrated glance at Ariane, Gilbert tugged belligerently on his forelock and bowed to the lord with a pretense of respect, although he looked as if he would have preferred to swallow poison.

When the lad had left them to enter the chapel, Ranulf sat staring down at Ariane. He looked supremely powerful, mounted on his huge warhorse, despite his lack of armor or helmet. His waving raven hair gleamed with blue highlights in the sun, while his eyes glittered chill gold.

"I beg forgiveness for his impertinence, my lord," she said quickly, knowing Gilbert had gone too far. No lord would tolerate such insolence from a serf, or such a flagrant challenge to his authority.

"I have flogged men for lesser offenses."

"Please . . . let him be. He only thought to protect me."

"You have too many protectors, to my mind," Ranulf muttered in reply.

"Please . . ." she repeated.

"You ask again for leniency, slave?"

"Yes, I ask it."

"What have you left to bargain with?"

Ariane lowered her gaze at the challenge in his amber eyes, remembering her plan to win Ranulf through cooperation. "I have nothing to offer you."

"So meek. So humble." His tone was taunting. "I vow your humility is as false as your claim of ravishment."

Ariane bit her tongue hard. Her humility *was* false, but she would not allow herself to respond to Ranulf's provocation, or let him know how much it stung, though his mockery cut deep.

"What? No rejoinder, wench? Have you suddenly gone dumb?" He made a scoffing sound. "You would be wiser to change your tactics. Docility does not become you."

He watched as her head snapped up, and felt a sense of satisfaction. She was not cowed as he had thought, but had been trying to hide her fury. Ranulf smiled in grim triumph. He had wanted to provoke Ariane, in truth, but he wanted her to fight back with the same spirit she had shown in their earlier confrontations. He found he enjoyed her anger far more than her apprehension or humility.

Just now her beautiful eyes were flashing sparks as she retorted through clenched teeth, "I understood you to say that you desired docility in your hostages, my lord."

His smile widened sardonically. "I did not know you were so eager to fulfill my desires, wench."

Before she could reply to that provocation, he went on the offensive. "I thought you had been given ample work to occupy you and keep you out of mischief. Yet you seem to find time to conduct trysts with my rebellious retainers."

"Trysts?" Ariane's wary gaze narrowed. "Just what do you accuse me of this time, my lord?"

"Judging from the discussion I interrupted, the two of you were plotting my overthrow. Do you deny you were conspiring against me with your lover?"

Her gray eyes widened at that last word. "*Lover?* Are you jesting?"

"Do you deny it, wench?" Ranulf persisted.

"Of course I deny it!" Ariane defended hotly. "Gilbert is my brother!"

Ranulf stared at her. "*Brother?*"

"Half-brother, actually. The baseborn son of my father's

leman. I told you of him.... Oh, you ... you ..." She sputtered in outrage at his insinuation. "Incest is a mortal sin!"

Ranulf stared down into her flashing silver eyes with a vast, overwhelming sense of relief. The lad was her *sibling*. A close kinsman. Which explained the slight resemblance he bore to Ariane, as well as the obvious warmth between them. It also explained his bristling hostility. Gilbert had good reason to resent the lord who had taken his sister prisoner, claimed her inheritance for the crown, and repudiated their betrothal. Ranulf threw back his head and laughed aloud at his mistake.

Ariane gave him a startled glance, as if wondering if he had lost his wits, but Ranulf merely shook his head. He was still angered by the boy's foolish defiance, but at least it was now understandable. He could even feel a measure of kinship to the lad, a bastard who doubtless had been made to pay throughout his life for the circumstances of his birth.

He would not countenance the boy's flagrant disrespect, or allow his conspiracies to continue, but in truth, he could admire the lad for showing such loyalty to his sister. He prized loyalty in a man—just as he prized spirit in a woman.

He much preferred the tart-tongued, hot-eyed wench standing before him now to the retiring, spineless maid Ariane had played for the past week and more after earning his wrath by falsely staining the bedsheets and declaring herself his wife. Her tempestuous defense of her brother just now made Ranulf realize how much her recent meekness had worn on his nerves. He would rather have her spitting at him honestly than pretending to be a mouse.

In truth, he would rather see honesty from her than pretense under *any* circumstances. He studied her with careful neutrality, trying to gauge the sincerity of her present performance. Perhaps there was perfidy behind those bright eyes with their look of wounded virtue, but he found himself wanting to believe in the innocence.

He would be a fool to absolve Ariane of guilt entirely, though. With his own ears he had heard the heated discussion terming him a devil-lord. Doubtless she and her brother were still plotting his downfall, along with all the rest of her former retainers. He could not afford to believe Ariane's motives

pure; to trust her like that was asking for a kick in the gut—
or a dagger in the back.

"The boy is fortunate to have you as defender," Ranulf
said finally, his voice softening, "but he must be witless to
consider challenging me."

"Gilbert is extremely clever," Ariane retorted staunchly,
"and a good clerk, which you would have known, had you
bothered to learn about the people who now serve you. A
lord should familiarize himself with the character and merits
of his retainers if he is to be a fair judge."

"A pretty speech," Ranulf said dryly, feeling the sting of
her insult that questioned his fitness as lord, but determined
not to reveal it. "But my management is not at issue—nor
is it even your concern."

"Claredon *is* my concern, as are its people."

"No longer, slave." His mocking grin was a deliberate
taunt. "You have no rights but those I permit you. I suggest
you get yourself to Mass before I revoke those privileges."

Ariane watched impotently as Ranulf turned his destrier
and rode for the stables, rage simmering along her veins. She
had sworn to show him only cooperation and sweetness in
order to tame the savage dragon, but it was all she could do
to control her temper and prevent herself from hurling invec-
tives after him.

How she wished she were a man who could defend his
honor by might of arms! But she could only battle Ranulf
with words and wit—pitiful weapons indeed against a ruthless, seasoned warrior with no heart.

Chapter 13

The storm broke the following eve. The hour was late, but Claredon's great hall echoed with sporadic bursts of ribald laughter and the bawdy music of a wandering minstrel.

Rather than retiring to the solar, Ranulf had stayed to dice with his men, and wound up singing songs and watching them dance with the castle wenches. By now most of his knights were befuddled with drink. For some time they had been passing around a wineskin and the strumpets who entertained them, with Bertran de Ridefort leading the frolic.

The revelry had gotten somewhat out of hand, yet Ranulf was reluctant to end their harmless pleasure. His men needed release after the months of service they had given him. Unaccountably, the merrymaking lowered his spirits rather than raising them. Yet it was difficult to ignore the clamor.

When a brown-haired, disheveled wench with huge, jiggling bare breasts lifted her skirts to expose her cunny and challenged Bertran's manhood, the knight threw back his dark head and roared with good-natured drunkenness. Amid shrieks of laughter, he tossed the whore flat on her back upon one of the long trestle tables. Shoving her tunic up to her waist, he loosened his braies and plunged his organ between her fleshy white thighs, grunting with pleasure as she squealed. Each of his big hands gripped a thrusting breast while his hips pumped rhythmically, his lust incited by the obscene jests and cheers and shouts of encouragement of the rowdy onlookers.

Sitting at the lord's table on the dais, Ranulf stared broodingly at the hearth fire. Occasionally in the past he had been known to whore with his men, but tonight he was in no mood to enjoy the sport, or to appreciate the attentions of the serving wench, Dena. When she sauntered up to him and lowered

199

her bodice to press her naked breasts against his face, he
drew back without interest.

He had no particular desire to mount her. Dena had doubtless been enjoyed by half the garrison since the occupation
of Clarèdon, and she stank with the musky odor of stale
sweat and sex and ale, a scent utterly unlike the clean, sweet
fragrance of her former mistress—who was no doubt slumbering upstairs in her chaste bed.

"I can show you pleasure as sweet as the honeyed wine
you drink, lord," Dena purred in his ear.

Distracted from his thoughts, Ranulf glanced at the couple
mating on the lower table, panting and heaving to the cheers
of the crowd. "Not this eve, sweeting. I fear I would not
do you justice tonight. Doubtless Bertran would provide you
livelier sport."

Dena pouted prettily. "That Bertran is a clumsy lout, with
no notion how to please a woman."

Beside her, Payn chuckled and reached out to fondle her
shapely buttocks. "Take care Bertran does not hear you disparage his skill, wench, or his pride will be offended."

With a saucy grin at Ranulf's chief vassal, Dena turned
her attention back to the lord. Clasping Ranulf's hand, she
drew it up under her skirts, pressing his fingers against her
cleft that was wet and slick and hot.

The arousing feel of her made Ranulf set his teeth. After
the night's revelry, culminated by Bertran's exhibition, he
was stiff and aching for a woman. And release was at hand.
He needed only to free his swollen manhood and draw the
eager wench down onto his lap in order to ease his ache.

He was half sorry when Payn reached over to grasp Dena
by the arm and draw her off him. With a flirtatious toss of
her head, though, she refused to leave. To the surprise of
both men, she settled her hips on the table between them and
boldly lay back with her elbows braced behind her. Hiking
up her skirts to show the dark bush between her naked thighs,
she spread her legs wide, one hand clasping her woman's
mound in carnal invitation.

The sight of that hot pink flesh tempted Ranulf, in truth.
Already his shaft was swollen and thick, straining at his
braies. He was actually thinking of covering her when the

hall suddenly grew deathly quiet, except for Bertran's gasping breaths.

When Ranulf realized all his men were staring behind him, he glanced over his shoulder. His eyes widened to see Ariane standing at the foot of the stone stairwell, gazing in stunned dismay at the company.

For a score of heartbeats, she remained rigid with shock at finding Ranulf and his knights fornicating on the tables in her father's hall, but anger burst on her swiftly.

"Mother Mary, have you no *shame*?"

Not a single man responded, not even the two guards who were escorting her from the kitchens to her chamber at the end of her day's labor.

"Not in my father's hall," she avowed, her voice trembling with rage and scorn. "And not on the tables. You will *not* dishonor Claredon this way!"

Before anyone could respond, she marched determinedly to the lord's table, where she snatched up the first weapon in sight, an eating dagger. Both Ranulf and Payn stiffened in their seats, their instinct for danger on full alert, but Ariane ignored them as she brandished the knife in Dena's face.

"Get out! Go and carry on your debauchery in the stables with the beasts—and do not *dare* show yourself here again."

Dena whimpered in fear and slid from the table to her knees. With Payn's aid, she struggled to her feet. Edging past Ariane, she fled, almost tripping in her haste to reach the great door.

When the frightened Dena had gone, Ariane turned her outrage on the company. In a state fit to poison the lot of them, she lashed out blindly, pointing at the door with the knife. "Out! All of you, out, now! Be gone with you."

The startled knights looked to Ranulf, whose face had darkened to an enigmatic mask. When their lord made no move to countermand her order, though, a few began backing toward the entrance, away from the knife-wielding fury.

"Out, I say!"

Several of the soldiers stood their ground, until Ranulf gave an almost imperceptible nod, endorsing her command. Then even Bertran hurried to obey, tugging up his braies and marshalling his wench from the keep after the others, leaving the hall in sole possession of the lord and his household

minions, who had been vainly attempting to sleep on the
pallets arrayed along the walls.

"By the Virgin's milk," Payn said with a chuckle of admiration. "They did not even draw their swords. My compliments, demoiselle. Never have I seen them move their lazy
arses so swiftly. What a Valkyrie she is, Ranulf."

She did indeed resemble the legendary Norse maidens,
with her knife drawn and fair hair swirling in a cloud about
her shoulders, Ranulf reflected. She looked magnificent, a
warrior woman staking a claim to her throne.

Except that she was supposed to be his slave. He had been
fascinated, perhaps even amused, to see her drive his valiant
knights and men-at-arms from the hall—and somewhat chastened as well. He had violated his own rigid code by allowing
such debauchery in his hall. In his own defense, he had never
expected Ariane to see it. And while her outrage might be
entirely justified, it was not her place to order his men about.

Ariane must have realized the extent of her infraction, for
she stiffened suddenly, and looked down at Ranulf as he
lounged in his high-backed chair.

Gray eyes clashed with amber. She was still trembling with
rage, but when he caught her wrist and gently pried the knife
from her clenched fingers, she made no protest.

"I could not countenance such a disgusting display," she
said defensively, justifying her rash temper.

"It was in poor taste," Ranulf agreed mildly, to her bewilderment. She had never expected him to support her against
his men.

"Such obscene affairs should be conducted in private,"
Ariane insisted stubbornly.

He startled her with a rueful smile. "In future I shall see
they are."

Still holding her wrist, he rose slowly to his feet. He had
been fascinated by her explosion, yet he could not permit her
outburst to go unchallenged.

"Sleep well, Payn," Ranulf threw carelessly over his
shoulder as he drew the suddenly resisting Ariane toward
the stairwell.

Payn chuckled. "I would wish you the same, my lord, but
I much doubt sleep will be on your mind tonight."

Ariane's heart began hammering at the knight's supposi-

tion. Ranulf's hard features were set in an enigmatic mask
that was impossible to read. His amber eyes glittered—but
not with anger, she thought hopefully. The light of battle was
in his eyes, but the heat seemed due more to determination
than fury.

To her dismay, Ranulf dismissed her guards and led her
directly to his solar. When he had ushered her inside, he shut
the door with studied care. Ariane watched him warily as he
turned to face her. A fire burned low in the hearth, and the
bedside taper had been lit for the night, faintly illuminating
the chamber. In the golden light, his eyes gleamed
dangerously.

Ranulf leaned his broad shoulders against the iron-banded
door and crossed his arms over his powerful chest, yet even
his relaxed stance unsettled her.

"What . . . do you intend, my lord?"

His slow, wolfish smile made her heartbeat quicken. "You
agree you have earned a punishment for your willfulness,
vixen?"

Ariane stiffened. "Nay, I do not. I could not stand by while
you engaged in such licentious deportment with your leman."

"Indignation is misplaced in a slave."

She could feel her temper rising again, though she sought
to control it. "Sweet Mary, you were preparing to fornicate
on the lord's table with that . . . that slattern!"

Ranulf's eyes narrowed thoughtfully. "Could it be that you
are jealous, sweeting?"

"*Jealous?* You flatter yourself, my lord. I simply do not
care to have Claredon's hall disgraced with such shameless
debauchery."

"Come here," he said silkily.

"Do you . . . mean to beat me?"

"I do not beat women. Besides, I like your skin just as it
is. Why would I wish to mar it? Now come here."

Knowing he would force her compliance if she refused to
obey, Ariane moved slowly to stand before him. The gold
glitter in his eyes seemed to soften.

"I never had the wench."

Ariane eyed Ranulf skeptically, unwilling to believe his
claim. "You would have if not for my intervention."

"But you did intervene. Thus . . ."—he smiled down at her blandly—"it is up to you to make amends."

When she stared up at him in puzzlement, Ranulf's eyebrow lifted. "I wanted a wench tonight, yet you drove her away. But you will serve as well as Dena."

"*Serve,* my lord?" Her breath seemed to shallow.

"If you do not wish the castle wenches pleasuring and entertaining me, then you must needs provide such service yourself."

Ariane took a step back, her nails digging into her palms. "You have no right to require I serve you that way."

A cool smile touched his lips. "You forget, it is my right as lord to take any serf in my demesne."

Their gazes locked, warred. Ariane felt her temper rise, along with her resentment. In her shock at Ranulf's abrupt reversal, she had momentarily forgotten her goal to consummate their betrothal. Now that Ranulf seemed willing, however, she was no longer quite so eager for the union. She had dreamed of this man making her his own, yearned for it, but not in anger, not in vengeance or as punishment for minor misdeeds. She wanted Ranulf to take her in love.

There was no sign of love or even tenderness in his expression now. Only a dangerous, seductive male arrogance that clearly said he intended to have his way, whatever her desires.

Her chin lifted. "I forget nothing, my lord. Indeed, I recall clearly your promise to wed me. I also remember that the Church considers me your *wife,* not your serf."

Ranulf did not rise to the bait. "The marriage will soon be annulled."

"Perhaps. Then again, perhaps not. There is a chance the Church will side with me."

He smiled, almost lazily. "The issue is in the hands of the Pope now."

"So it seems."

"However . . ." He reached out to finger a lock of her silken hair. "As long as you have falsely declared yourself my wife, I see no reason I should not enjoy the entitlements of a husband. No one will gainsay me."

"What . . . do you mean?"

"You are my possession. Why should I not avail myself of your lovely body?"

His voice had dropped to a sensual caress, making the insult sound like a promise of pleasure. Ariane felt herself go rigid as she tried to repress the thrill that quivered through her. "You would make me your whore?"

Unperturbed, Ranulf shook his head. "You speak in contradictions, demoiselle. You cannot be both whore and wife."

"I can, if you refuse to acknowledge me as your wife."

"I will never acknowledge you as such," he replied casually.

"I will not whore for you!"

"And yet you will for other men."

"What are you saying?"

"You lied about my ravishing you, so it is not unreasonable to assume you lied about other circumstances. For all I know, you may have shared your charms with half the men of your father's garrison."

She struck him then, drew her arm back and slapped his face with her open palm.

Ariane stared in horror at the livid imprint of her hand on his cheek. To her astonishment, Ranulf's mouth curved in a slow grin as he rubbed the offended flesh. "I like you better fighting me. A spirited wench provides far better sport than a docile one."

"*Sport!*" Her eyes flashed with fury. "Oh, you . . . you . . . arrogant oaf! If you want sport, you should go back to your leman!"

His arm shot out to wrap around Ariane's waist. With inexorable insistence, Ranulf drew her to him, making her feel the desire that was so compellingly clear in the bulging contours beneath his tunic. "I want no other wench," he murmured. "I want you."

She started to struggle, but his hold was unbreakable. "You mean to rape me?" she demanded breathlessly.

"Rape or seduction . . . you may choose." The amused light in his eyes clearly said he knew which one she would eventually choose.

He bent his head then. With unwavering determination, Ranulf captured her mouth, intent on sensual mastery.

He had waited long enough for her surrender. For too long

he had tolerated her defiance, had maintained his rigid self-control, when there was no need. She was not his lady wife, merely his rebellious hostage. She should be sharing his bed instead of driving him to madness. The marriage would be annulled or not, regardless of whether he had her now, whether he satisfied his fierce craving for her, and he could contain his need no longer.

He was a fool to have denied himself all this time. Why should he not enjoy what was his for as long as he wanted her? Or until the annulment was granted? He had resisted the moment of surrender for fear of exposing his weakness, his vulnerability to her, defying the power she had to bewitch his mind and control his body. But he was done fighting himself.

At her soft sound of protest, Ranulf gentled his mouth the slightest measure, but he refused to release her. He could feel his loins tighten in a fiery ache of anticipation. In moments he would have her beneath him, mounted and penetrated. If she was not a virgin, if she had played him false with other lovers, there would be no question as to whom she now belonged.

Then, God willing, his feverish desire for her would end. Once he had her, he would at last be delivered from the insane yearning that had tormented him for days. He could be rid of his wild obsession for her.

The tumult of his feelings showed in the fierce passion he showered on her. He kissed her as if taking what belonged to him, his tongue driving deep, plumbing the depths of her honeyed sweetness. She fought the domination of his mouth at first, wedging her palms against his chest, but he thwarted her resistance by catching her wrists and forcibly twining her arms around his neck. Before she could escape, one of his hands swept downward to cup her buttocks, the other arm tightening at her waist, making her back arch against the powerful pressure.

Moments later, he felt a tiny shudder run through Ariane, heard the soft moan dredged from deep in her throat, a bewitching sound of surrender. His own passions spurred and heightened by her submission, Ranulf deepened his kiss, marking her as his, demanding, possessing . . . exulting when her arms closed around him of their own accord.

When finally he released her mouth and raised his head,

Ariane stared wildly into his bright, triumphant eyes. She could read the truth there: the time for waiting was over.

She closed her own eyes and swayed against him, feeling the hard bulge of his sex throb against the soft yielding of her loins. He had won. She would not fight Ranulf, even though he desired her merely to appease his lustful appetites. He still refused to acknowledge her as his wife, still intended to annul their marriage, but she would not dwell on the sinfulness of a carnal relationship without the sanction of the marriage vows. She *wanted* to consummate their union, and not simply to strengthen her legal position as his wife. She wanted Ranulf, wanted his kisses, his caresses, his possession. And she wanted to try to conquer his hostility. Perhaps if she surrendered fully to him, she could persuade him to change his mind about her, could make him see that she was not the treasonous jade he thought her.

She could only pray he would not hurt her overmuch. She had known no man intimately. Ranulf was so powerful, so strong, that he could crush her with one hand, or split her apart if he took her roughly. Some primal instinct assured her that he would not harm her, yet she had never been able to trust her senses where this man was concerned.

"Ranulf," she whispered, her eyes imploring him to be gentle. "I have no desire to fight you. Show me what you want of me . . . how to please you."

Ranulf's own eyes darkened at her surrender. He took a deep breath, trying to slow the hammering of his blood, grateful that she was willing to yield. He had never forced a woman to his will. He had no taste for rape, especially not with this woman, whose cool, regal beauty and defiant spirit had bewitched him from the first. If she ever knew the power she held over him . . . God help him. . . .

His real need was to conquer her with pleasure; he would be truly satisfied with nothing less. Experience told him he need not worry. The persuasive passion that was appreciated by his own castle wenches would stand him in good stead now. And yet Ariane was like no woman he had ever known. This tumult he felt inside—this warm burgeoning in his chest—was like no other feeling he had ever experienced. It shocked him to realize his hands trembled.

"Seduction, then," he murmured, the words a husky,

heated rasp against her lips as he gently drew her close in another devastating kiss, this one to seal their pact.

Almost reverently then, he loosened the drawstring at her gown's neckline, and drew down the bodice, baring her beautiful breasts that loomed eager for a man's caress. Her rose-hued nipples were already taut with arousal, he saw with primitive satisfaction. Bending his head, he captured one in his mouth.

In shock, Ariane drew a sharp breath as she felt the strong pull on the distended bud. Incredible heat washed over her, made more intense by the gentle lashing of his tongue. *What was he doing to her?* 'Twas indecent that he should suckle her like a babe. And yet she could not find the strength to push him away. Her fingers clutched at his shoulders, even while her knees grew weak.

He subjected her other nipple to the same light, exquisitely gentle washing by his tongue, the same searing, wet heat. To her dismay then, he left off his attentions and began to undress her. In a few moments Ranulf had removed her clothing and she stood naked before him, her skin flushed with embarrassment and desire.

After a slow, rapt scrutiny of her body, however, he no longer seemed engrossed by her nudity. He was staring at the abraded skin on her shoulders and neck made by the rough wool of her tunic.

"Your garments did this?" he asked, reaching out to trace the rash with his fingertips.

Ariane winced and nodded warily.

The concern he felt mellowed the sharp desire to a softer longing. Needing to touch her, to assuage her pain, he stepped closer and bent to place a soft kiss on the line of her collarbone. The delicate contact was incredibly light, and yet she felt it intensely, as if his lips were smoldering coals.

Ariane gazed up at him in confusion. She couldn't understand why Ranulf was being so gentle with her. When was her punishment to begin? He acted not as if he meant to wreak vengeance on her; in truth, he treated her as if she were something precious.

Without a word, he lifted her in his arms as though she were nearly weightless, and carried her to the bed. Lowering her to the soft marten fur, Ranulf gave her a kiss that was ravishing in its tenderness, then stood back to undress.

Suddenly breathless, Ariane watched him, unable to look away.

Loosening the underarm laces of his tunic, he drew it over his head and tossed it aside. His shirt followed, exposing the corded muscles bulging in his arms and shoulders and powerful chest. Her eyes darkened at seeing the healing gouges on Ranulf's side, the fresh scars reminding her of how he had been assaulted by his enemies . . . her people.

His shoes and chainse came next, baring iron-hewn thighs and strong calves. Ranulf's bold gaze met hers as his hands went to the waist tie of his braies. When he tugged them down over his hips and stood, Ariane's breath caught in her throat. He was fully aroused, his blatant erection rock-hard and straining to his navel, rising proudly from the crisp, black hair at his groin.

She trembled at the enormous, pulsing size of him, and yet a shiver of excitement ran up her spine at the sight of the shameless, compelling man standing boldly before her. There was beauty in such stark masculinity, the incredible power of his body, the sculpted perfection. He was potent and vital, the epitome of every feminine fantasy. And she wanted him.

He was watching her, his eyes hot with thinly veiled desire. His smoldering gaze sent a responsive desire coursing through Ariane, despite her innocence.

"Do you fear me?" he asked, his voice a rough whisper of sound.

Ariane swallowed and forced herself to shake her head in denial. She would not think of how Ranulf might hurt her with his remarkable size and strength. She would think only of the incredible pleasure his caresses had once made her feel.

"Good." His slow smile held the quiet brilliance of a rare jewel, while his eyes glimmered with pure male sensuality. "I would not wish you to be afraid."

How could she possibly be afraid when he was looking at her as if she were the most beautiful woman in all Christendom?

He joined her in the bed, then. Still holding her gaze, Ranulf sat down beside her and ran his hand slowly over her body with a practiced touch. She tensed, trembling at the featherlight caress. When his stroking reached her flat belly, she drew a sharp breath. And when he splayed his long fingers at the rise of her woman's mound, her breath arrested entirely.

Ranulf smiled in grim satisfaction at her response. He was aching with need, the pulsing of his blood, the swelling of his erection causing a longing so fierce it was near pain. And yet he could not sate his primitive hunger just yet. First he must fulfill the exquisite task of bringing her to pleasure.

She gave a start when he reached above her head for a pillow and carefully placed it beneath her hips. Her cheeks flamed scarlet. "M-My lord Ranulf . . . what are you doing?"

Without replying, he shifted his position and moved over her, to kneel between her parted legs. She felt the soft rush of his breath as he bent to kiss her belly.

"Be still," he commanded when her hips shifted nervously.

His heated eyes roaming her body, he ran his hands slowly up her quivering inner thighs, making her open wide for him. Ariane trembled in mortification and anticipation. He seemed to be studying the triangle of red-gold curls between her thighs.

With sensual determination, his hands slid beneath her body to separately cup the pale spheres of her buttocks. Ariane bit her lower lip to keep from whimpering as he slowly squeezed and kneaded, as his fingers stroked the dark crevice between.

"Ranulf . . ." she murmured in protest. "You should not . . . 'tis sinful . . ."

"Hush," he ordered in a harsh, deep tone that vibrated with urgency, resonating in her blood and the throbbing between her legs.

To her shame, he turned his attention to that aching part of her. Parting the sleek folds of her cleft with his thumbs, he traced a probing pad over the small, hidden nub of her sex, slowly circling.

Ariane whimpered.

To her infinite shock, Ranulf bent and brazenly pressed his mouth against her there. She went rigid from an unbearable surge of pleasure.

"Nay!" she gasped, trying to pull away.

Ranulf laughed softly at her reaction, even as he captured her wrists and pressed her hands against her sides, preventing her from moving. Bending to her again, he found her essence with his mouth. He licked the heated flesh, making her feel the soft slither of his tongue . . . his warm lips sucking softly in a kiss.

Ariane trembled under his erotic assault. His scandalous attentions stunned her. What wicked madness was this?

And yet she could not summon the will to protest as his tongue lapped at her, plying the swollen, aching folds of her flesh. His probing kiss inflamed her with sensation, robbing her of breath. Her skin grew hot as he ravished her senses; an exquisite pleasure, so intense it was almost painful, shot through her body.

He gave her no opportunity to evade his burning mouth or the fierce lash of his tongue. He held her captive, as though she were his prisoner, meant solely for his heathen pleasure. His tongue swirled and licked and stabbed her with fire.

Ariane clenched her teeth to stifle the moan building in her throat at his wicked assault, but Ranulf went on tasting her to his ruthless satisfaction. The musky, primitive scent of her made his loins grind with need. Her taste was intoxicating, hot and sweet as wild honey. Mercilessly he stroked her, savoring her taste, nibbling on her succulent sweetness, until her soft whimpers told him she was hot and throbbing for him.

Then deliberately, with exquisite care, he thrust his tongue within her, a tantalizing act of primitive possession. The brazen invasion forced a shuddering moan from her. She arched and cried out in denial, her hips surging up to meet his feasting mouth.

"Ranulf . . . sweet God . . ."

A spiking surge of lust ripped through Ranulf's senses. She was hot and excited and oblivious to everything but what he was doing to her. Her low, rapturous cry thrilled him. His grip on her buttocks tightened as she twisted against him, writhing. He held her surging body down, his mouth pressed hard against her as she shook with convulsions of pleasure.

When the last aftershock had passed, his mouth tenderly grazed her heated flesh, now slick with her own dew, then swiftly moved up her sweat-dampened body. Without giving her time to recover, Ranulf stretched above Ariane and settled his hips in the cradle of her thighs. He could wait no longer. Never had he been so hard, so near to bursting.

Holding himself above her, he kneed her thighs wide apart. With the searing tip of his shaft poised at the very heart of her, though, he hesitated. Had she lain with another man like this? Driven other foolish swains into a frenzy of desire for her with her bewitching, responsive body? Or was she truly the innocent she seemed?

Trying to dismiss his irrational jealousy, he concentrated on the beautiful woman beneath him. He needed this, needed her, craved the fierce release only she could give him.

Dazed from the fiery explosion that had shattered her senses and set her pulse pounding, Ariane reached for him eagerly, never wavering though her lover prepared to invade her body with his huge shaft.

"Ranulf . . . please," she breathed, her voice holding a plea, for what she knew not.

"Hush, sweeting," he murmured hoarsely in return. "Open yourself to me."

All of his natural instincts screamed at Ranulf to take her swiftly, to ease the fierce, almost desperate ache in his loins, but he sank slowly into her, with teeth-gritting caution. Despite his care, her thighs clenched around him in a futile effort to halt the spearing, alien intrusion. When he felt the fragile barrier denying him entrance, Ranulf almost drew back, afraid he could not control himself, afraid he would cause her pain, yet he could not stop now . . . could not stop . . . could not . . .

Ariane winced in pain as her tender, virgin flesh stretched and split, and cried out when he pressed more fully within her. The pressure was almost too great to bear. His rigid length was a huge lance thrusting within her, a mighty weapon that was tearing her asunder.

She heard herself sob, felt the gentle brush of his mouth as he tenderly kissed her lips in an effort to soothe the ache.

Helpless to do more, Ranulf held himself completely still as she shuddered around him, wanting to curse and shout in triumph at the same time. A virgin! A chaste innocent untouched by any other man. She had lied to him! He was her first lover; she was his now. They were joined together intimately, his hard flesh buried in the heated, sweet center of her body.

He clenched his teeth, holding back the raging desire he felt for her, forcing himself to wait until she could accept the pleasure of a man's fullness stretching her and probing deep. His powerful thighs kept her slender ones parted wide, his broad chest barely touching her breasts. Her breath was coming in shallow pants, her eyes tightly closed.

"Ariane ... look at me."

She obeyed reluctantly, her lids fluttering open to reveal luminous gray eyes misty with tears.

His own eyes smoldered with fire. "Is it better?"

"Y-Yes ..." she answered honestly, although her breathless reply held little confidence.

"Can you take me deeper, sweeting?"

She frowned thoughtfully, staring at him with skepticism. "There is more of you?"

His smile, slow and sensual, was as tender as it was amused. "I fear so. But I can refrain from seating my shaft fully."

"No ... please ... I want you ... fully."

Even as she spoke, her hips moved tentatively, tilting a little to give him better access.

Ranulf drew a sharp breath. Her slightest movement made him wild to go deeper, but with a fierce effort, he forced himself to rein in his impatience. Slowly he shifted his weight above her, purposefully grazing her breasts with his furred chest.

Her sensitive nipples tightened at the arousing contact, the throbbing ache echoing between her thighs, yet he could not make her forget entirely what the rest of his body was doing as he penetrated her, submerging himself fully, imbedding himself deep inside.

Ariane tensed, holding her breath. . . . It was odd, but the hurt had faded, leaving behind a burgeoning ache that was not entirely painful. In truth, she felt a traitorous warmth stir within her, blurring the edges of her pain and apprehension.

Then Ranulf's lips settled over hers, and she tasted her scent on his mouth—a taste that was both shocking and erotic. Ariane quivered as his warm tongue thrust into her mouth with surprising softness; of their own accord her hips rocked against his.

She almost moaned in protest when she felt his rigid length withdrawing from her.

But Ranulf had no intention of leaving her entirely. Instead, his hand slipped between their bodies, his fingers finding the hot, sleek bud that was the center of her desire.

Stunned by the spasm of pleasure that rippled through her, Ariane whimpered and reached for him, her arms twining tightly around his neck. Blindly she murmured his name in a plea for mercy, but he ruthlessly went on stroking her, his back arched, his eyes half shut. She felt the shudder that quivered through him moments before her body caught fire again.

The world disappeared for her, leaving only flame-hot desire. Her hands clutched at the broad, straining shoulders of the man above her, her hips writhing.

"Yes, sweeting," Ranulf rasped in hoarse approval, encouraging her wild abandon.

She was only dimly aware of his husky voice murmuring in her ear, barely conscious of the ridges of scarred flesh beneath her fingertips as she clawed at his back. Reduced to pagan need, she clung to him, frantic for release from the incredible tension in her body. In mere moments she arched in the next convulsive climax, her gasping cry of pleasure rocking Ranulf to his very core.

"Sweet Jesu!" He stiffened for an instant, his eyes closing in sensual pain. Then no longer able to help himself, he began to move, his hips thrusting in and out in a hot, urgent rhythm. His restraint shattering, he drove into her fiercely while Ariane clung to him and trembled and quaked.

The raw, primitive explosion that ripped through Ranulf held such a violent intensity that it clamped his teeth shut. And then he could no longer control even that. He cried out in his own savage release as he poured into her with pent-up wildness, his body clenching and shuddering.

For long moments afterward, they lay fused together, unmoving except for the ragged tempo of their breathing. Desperately Ranulf drew air into his heaving lungs as he tried to focus his thoughts. His skin was drenched with sweat, his body hot with need, his rage of desire dulled but not sated.

He wanted her still.

His body felt heavy and languorous, yet he was half hard already. He didn't want to leave the hot haven between her thighs, but he knew for Ariane's sake he must. Slowly, with effort, Ranulf eased from her body, shifting his weight to one side, and raised his head.

He had been far too rough with her when he meant to be gentle and considerate of her inexperience.

"Forgive me . . ." he murmured, looking down at her exquisite, flushed face framed by the wild tangle of her hair. Her breathing had quieted; her eyes were closed.

She made a soft sound that might have been agreement, yet Ranulf could not excuse his conduct so easily.

It stunned him that she could have made him lose control that way. He had not been so inflamed by a wench since he was a stripling lad. True, he had been celibate for some weeks now, but even that did not explain his violence, or his fierce desire for Ariane. He had experienced orgasm too frequently to dismiss the savage ferocity of his release, or the shattering satisfaction afterward. Or his continued state of arousal now. He felt the same alertness he experienced after battle, nerve endings tingling, blood pounding. There was an urgency still within him, a fierce need for this woman that could not be sated by a single possession.

Such a response was unique in his experience. Once he had possessed her body, his lust should have dimmed. And yet his attraction for Ariane was as fierce as ever. . . .

Ranulf's lips twisted in a wry, indulgent smile as he gazed down at the sleeping woman in his bed. Evidently Ariane felt none of the same urgency he felt. She had fallen into an exhausted slumber in the aftermath of passion.

His gaze traveled over her slender, sweet-breasted body, pausing when it reached her legs. Ranulf's smile faded. Pale pink blood, mingled with his pearly seed, streaked her thighs and splotched the sheets.

His eyes darkened in triumph. His claiming of her maidenhead had been a victory for him. He had been the first man to possess her. The only one.

"You are mine," he declared in a low, controlled whisper as he brushed a fair, tumbled lock back from her face.

Reaching down, he covered them both with the bedclothes.

Then, with a tenderness that was almost foreign to him, Ranulf drew Ariane into his arms, pressing her head into his shoulder, and closed his eyes.

Roused briefly from slumber, she sighed and nuzzled her face more deeply into his warm skin. She had feared Ranulf would take her in anger, but instead of forcing her, he had turned seducer . . . a sensual, considerate lover. The change in him had bewildered her. . . .

Suddenly awake, Ariane felt the sudden prick of tears behind her eyes. Ranulf's tenderness moments ago, when he had taken her body and taught her the wonder of being a woman, made her want to weep. If events had not intervened, this forceful, charismatic man would have been her husband. This would have been her marriage bed, her wedding night.

Instead, he had claimed her body as he would any serf's, merely to prove his dominance. He had treated her as a possession, an object upon which to slake his lust. He had given her devastating pleasure, true, but only as a means to force her surrender.

Their coupling had meant far, far more to her, though. Their consummation had been more than a passionate union of the flesh. In her heart, they had truly mated. Ranulf had adamantly refused to acknowledge her as his wife, but she felt joined to him now. She belonged solely to him.

Swallowing the ache in her throat, Ariane closed her eyes, breathing his clean, musky scent. And as she willed herself to sleep, she clung to the hope that someday Ranulf would come to feel more for her than simply carnal desire.

Chapter 14

"**G**reetings, my sweet."

Ariane stirred beneath the covers at the husky masculine voice murmuring in her ear. When she felt warm lips nuzzling her neck, accompanied by the sensual rasp of a stubbled jaw against her skin, she forced her eyes open and blinked to find Ranulf leaning over her, his weight braced on one elbow. He was smiling, the transformation of his dark visage startling. In the dawn light, he looked endearingly boyish and incredibly seductive, with his hair tousled and his jaw roughened by a night's growth of black bristle.

"Have you no proper greeting for your lover?"

Still befuddled with sleep, she dragged her gaze from him and tried to focus her thoughts. The rays of sunlight filtering through the shutters made her realize the lateness of the hour. "Why did you not wake me earlier?"

"You were weary from your exertions last night."

Ariane flushed as sensual memories of those exertions suddenly flooded her: the hot image of this man straining between her thighs, his lean, thrusting body shuddering as he moved over her, within her, his power immense, yet restrained. He had shown her an ecstasy she had never dreamed possible.

Unaware of the tumult of emotions rioting through her, Ranulf bent to cover her passion-bruised mouth with a fleeting kiss. "You pleased me well last night, wench."

His sunny mood grated on Ariane's raw sensibilities. Not only did it shock her to be awakened by a naked man's brazen, carnal attentions, it stung to be reminded so vividly of her surrender—and of her wanton conduct.

"Should I be honored by your praise, my lord?" she responded sourly in a voice still raspy with sleep.

To her surprise, Ranulf laughed, a sound that stunned her with its richness and warmth. "Verily, you should. I do not bestow such praise lightly." He gazed down at her with heated eyes. "I wonder if the pleasure will be as great, now that the novelty of your virginal state has passed." With one finger, he traced her lower lip. "I wonder how much greater *your* pleasure will be. . . . I vow you tempt me sorely to examine the question, but you will doubtless be tender after having your body used so roughly."

Her eyes had widened in dismay at his suggestion that they repeat their wicked coupling in broad daylight, but at Ranulf's consideration, she relaxed to a degree. Testing his theory, Ariane moved her hips gingerly and winced at the twinge she felt between her thighs.

"Does it pain you?"

Grudgingly she shook her head. Her physical symptoms pained her far less than her conscience did. "Not much."

"Good." Ranulf smiled indulgently. "You may sleep for the remainder of the morning, but I had best rise. My men will not wonder to find me still abed with a winsome wench, yet I have matters that need my attention."

Ariane shut her eyes in mortification. After the scene she had made last eve in the hall, his men would know precisely what had passed between them during the night. She had lain with Ranulf, if not eagerly, then without protesting overmuch. "I have no desire to be found here in your chamber," she muttered, "much less in your bed. Nor do I intend to laze about all day."

"Suit yourself. But I intend to amend your sentence. You will no longer be required to labor in the scullery."

"Your generosity is overwhelming."

Ignoring her sarcasm Ranulf reached for an object he had tucked among the pillows and held it up for her inspection. "Perhaps you will find this more to your liking."

He was holding a gold necklace of some sort, Ariane realized with a warm jolt of surprise. A collar torque whose ornamented ends bore Norse figures of dragons with jeweled eyes. The length of heavy gold tubing twisted on and off and opened in front.

Slipping his hand beneath her neck, Ranulf carefully

wound it around her throat, while Ariane stared at him in shock.

"F-For me, my lord?"

"It was meant to be my wedding gift to you," he murmured, "but although there is to be no marriage, I see no reason you may not have it. Consider it payment for the gift you gave me last night."

Her maidenhead, Ariane thought with a savage pang of dismay, feeling the cool metal press against her skin like ice. She could have loved Ranulf, but she meant no more to him than any of the castle strumpets; he slaked his lust on her and paid for the pleasure with pretty baubles, and considered it a fair exchange.

"Forgive me if I fail to express proper gratitude, my lord," she declared with asperity ringing in her tone.

Her stinging reply took Ranulf aback, as did the sudden flash of hurt in her eyes. He had never bestowed such an expensive gift on a wench, but he had thought she would be pleased by his costly gesture. The ladies he knew at court all craved expensive presents, but Ariane's eyes had first lit with suspicion rather than greed, and now she was staring at him with haughty disdain, as if he had committed a grave offense.

"I had thought it might serve to sweeten your temper," he said uncertainly.

"There is naught wrong with my temper, save perhaps a surfeit of your lascivious attention."

Shrugging off what he did not understand, Ranulf chose to fight her incomprehensible anger with persuasion. Lazily he drew down the covers to expose a rosy-nippled breast, then dismayed her further by reaching his hand up to cup the pale globe. Despite her sudden squirming, he bent and pressed his lips against her abraded collarbone. "You may have your own garments back as well, sweeting. I will not have those rough peasant gowns marring your tender skin."

Trying to repress the surge of tension and excitement his mere touch awakened in her, Ariane raised a scornful eyebrow. "Do I detect a pang of guilt, my lord, for your despicable treatment of me?"

He grinned. "Guilt is not what I feel for you, wench. As for treatment ..." Some of his amusement faded. "After your deception, you deserve much worse than a simple rash."

"I do not call it deception to claim what is my legal due."

Ranulf shook his head, refusing to be drawn into an argument. "I will not debate the point with you again, my sweet." His hand slowly, deliberately, swept down her body to delve beneath the covers.

Ariane drew a sharp breath when his fingers tangled in the warm thatch between her thighs. "Nay ... do not! 'Tis indecent!"

"Is it?"

"You know it is," she gasped as she tried to evade his probing fingers, though knowing she would use almost any excuse that might keep her from repeating last night's wanton surrender. "The Church has proscribed such heathen acts."

Ranulf grunted, although he removed his hand from her thigh and let it rest possessively on her stomach. "I doubt one more sin will render my soul any blacker. I have it on good authority that I am possessed by demons."

Ariane was too genuinely shocked by his blasphemy to probe the bitterness that edged his tone. "Your soul may be beyond redemption, but what of mine?"

His gaze searched her face intently. "Are you so pure and innocent then, demoiselle?" When she had no answer for that, Ranulf shrugged. "The debauchery of the Church is well known. Half the clergy break their own laws regularly, holding orgies that make our revelry in the hall last night seem tame."

"Even so ... I do not wish you to ... touch me like that ..."

"You mean to pretend I do not arouse you?" he asked with a smile of amused mockery.

It vexed Ariane sorely that he should comprehend the real source of her discomfiture: his ability to stir her passions so effortlessly and turn her into a wanton. "You do not arouse me half so much as your impossible conceit would lead you to believe," she retorted.

"*Conceit?*" His eyebrow shot up. "No wench has yet had cause to complain of my prowess."

Ariane raised her eyes to the beamed ceiling, praying for patience. Ranulf de Vernay was an arrogant, coddled male, so secure in his practiced power with women that she yearned to box his ears. "Mayhap you never heard a complaint because you never *wished* to hear one."

His teeth flashed in a slow grin that was both intimate and sexual—and totally infuriating in its brazen disregard for her calculated insult. In lazy response, his hand swept slowly up her body to her breast again. With thumb and forefinger, he gently pinched the sensitive nipple, making it tighten instantly, and causing Ariane to draw another sharp breath. "Mayhap you protest because you fear what I make you feel."

"I do *not* fear you," Ariane gritted, wishing she could wipe that superior grin off his handsome face. "I simply have no desire to listen to you boast of your conquests."

Before she could say anything further, though, Ranulf suddenly suspended his teasing and rose to dress. Unconcerned by his nudity, he strode across the chamber and bent to retrieve his clothing from a leather-covered coffer, giving her a view of his taut buttocks and long bare flanks, sleek and thickly muscled.

Ariane found herself staring at him in helpless admiration. There was strength and power in every hard line of his body, a masculine beauty that called to everything feminine within her. A beauty that made the savage scars on his back stand out even more incongruously. She remembered feeling those rough ridges beneath her fingertips last night as she clung to him in the throes of passion. Dismayed by the pity—as well as the hot feelings—the memory stirred in her, Ariane averted her gaze while Ranulf washed.

She was surprised that he did not require her to act as his squire when he began to dress, but when she grudgingly offered her assistance, Ranulf replied enigmatically, "No, I have a better use for you."

"And what might that be?" Ariane asked warily.

"You will serve as my leman."

Ariane sat up abruptly in bed, clutching the covers to her chest. Leman was but a polite name for mistress. "Nay, I will not!"

His suddenly cool gaze found her. "You will, demoiselle. Your new duties will include servicing me in bed, as a leman would. I indulged your anger last night because it suited me, but you will know your place."

"As long as you refuse to acknowledge me as your lady, my place is not in your bed!"

"It is," he replied tersely. "You are mine, to use as I will. When I crave pleasure from you I will take it. I will have you at my leisure, when and where I choose."

Ariane stared at him in dismay. The hurt his assertion inflicted upon her was due to more than just outrage or humiliation. She simply couldn't face being used by him as casually as a knight would take a strumpet, or a stallion would service a mare.

When Ranulf noticed the look in her eyes, his expression softened. "You will not find the position so onerous. I daresay you will even come to enjoy it."

"I would rather scrub pigsties."

He sent her a wicked grin—that potent, roguish male smile he gave so rarely. "Perhaps, but I am no longer angry enough to require you to do so. And it would be a waste of your beauty and talents besides."

Her hands fisted around the covers in impotent rage and despair. "Why?" she cried in a low voice. "Why must you shame me so when there are doubtless other women who would be pleased to share your bed?"

Surprised by the question, Ranulf regarded her skeptically. It was no shame to secure the attentions of a powerful lord. In truth, Ariane should be honored by his favor. He could name a hundred wenches who would have eagerly taken her place. If she did feel resentment because she no longer held the position of chatelaine, she would get over it soon enough with the pleasure he intended to shower on her. But if she was attempting to arouse his guilt for not wedding her . . . she would not succeed.

Nor would she learn his true reason for taking her as leman. He would never admit to Ariane that having her in his bed was the only way he knew to conquer his obsession with her. "You are a desirable wench, and I desire you. I need no other reason."

He turned away to pull on his undertunic, vexed that she would object so strenuously to his plan. She should be grateful to be relieved of her crushing duties in the scullery—and triumphant in her victory, if she only knew it. He had lost the battle with his iron will last night, surrendered at last to

his obsessive desire for her. He had even changed his long-
standing policies because of her. Rarely before had he allowed his women to sleep with him. And yet he was willing
to make exceptions for Ariane.

In truth, he liked the thought of her waking in his bed,
rosily naked, seeing her cheeks sleep-flushed and pink, smell-
ing his scent on her. He could have her first thing upon
waking, when his appetites were strong and immediate. He
liked having her near, just for the pleasure of touching her,
although he had never been a man to touch anyone without
reason. He liked kissing her, as well. He rarely kissed his
women on the lips, but the heat of that sweetly curved mouth
bewitched him. *She* bewitched him.

He wanted nothing more than to return to that bed just
now and savor her delicious heat, to bury himself deeply
within her and explore the depths of her passion. He wanted
to spend the entire day with her, teaching her how to enjoy
her body and showing her how to please him. But he remembered Ariane's virginal state and crushed the notion.

A feeling of tenderness swept through Ranulf as he recalled
her pain. How fragile and delicate she had felt in his arms.
How innocent. How hot and wild she had become, writhing
in ecstasy beneath him. He would give her time to recover
from his attentions, but tonight. . . . The thought of what he
would do to her then made Ranulf harden abruptly.

He should be furious with himself—and her—for his surrender last night, Ranulf knew. By his own actions he had
sealed their betrothal contract. But it made no matter. He
would not withdraw his petition from Rome. The annulment
would still go forward as planned. He would not allow himself to feel guilt, either. Ariane had no one to blame but
herself for the consequences of her deception.

Meanwhile he would make use of her body. Just until he
satisfied his fierce craving for her. Only until she surrendered
fully to him. He intended to keep her warm and weak and
pliant from his lovemaking, until she became used to his
possession. Ariane was stubborn and strong willed, more than
a challenge for any warrior, even him. He would need every
advantage at his command in order to defeat her, to make
her yield.

Ignoring the bristling woman who was glaring daggers at

him, Ranulf finished dressing in a tunic of forest green velvet. Then he slung his mantle carelessly over his shoulders and turned to her.

"Reconcile yourself to your fate, chérie. I want to find you here in this chamber each night, beginning tonight. I expect you to be awaiting my pleasure when I return."

With that, Ranulf stalked from the room, ending the argument abruptly as he had so many times before when they had disagreed.

A curse rode Ariane's tongue as she stared at the door. He had taken her body as casually as he had taken her father's castle, and now he meant to formalize their sinful relationship by making her his mistress, without the blessing of the Church. In a matter of weeks, she had gone from betrothed to serf, to slave, and now to leman. She wanted to scream at the unfairness of it all.

What would she do as Ranulf's mistress? Notwithstanding the mortification, she would go mad sitting idle the day long, awaiting her lord's pleasure. She was accustomed to keeping busy with the duties of chatelaine. For four years she had commanded the vast household staff at Claredon, as well as overseen the domestic staff of several manor houses and minor fiefs. The menial tasks at which she had been forced to toil for the past week at least had the benefit of making her too weary to think when she fell exhausted into bed each night, too drained to dwell on her myriad troubles. Were she to laze about the entire day with naught to distract her, the boredom would drive her to despair, while her worries drove her to desperation.

And then there was the shame of being forced to serve Ranulf in such a debasing role. She was a highborn lady, one who should have been his honored wife. Perhaps she deserved punishment for trying to force him to honor the betrothal, and even for her outburst in the hall last night, but she did not deserve such ignominy as he intended to heap on her. Ranulf was a cruel, heartless brute—

No, that was the trouble. Ranulf was *not* a brute. He had never harmed her physically, or ever raised a hand to her, even if he had trampled ruthlessly on her heart. For all his savage reputation and fierce bluster, the Black Dragon of Vernay was restrained and gentle with women—even her, though she had given him ample cause for fury. Even his punishment of her had been measured. And his lovemaking . . .

Ariane closed her eyes as she remembered Ranulf's tender assault on her senses last night. She wished he had ranted and railed at her instead, for she could rally her defenses against his anger. How could she possibly resist him when he was being tender and considerate?

She heard her own sigh. She had lied to Ranulf earlier. She did fear him. . . . She feared the cold, merciless warlord known as the Black Dragon, yet she feared even more the tender, seductive lover he had become last night.

It dismayed her to realize how vulnerable she was to him, to his potent masculinity. The danger Ranulf presented was very real. Last night he had laid claim to some secret part of her . . . and then dismissed their mating as no more than a pleasurable whim to be paid for in coin.

Bitterly she fingered the gold collar at her throat, whose dragons branded her as Ranulf's possession. She wanted to tear it off, yet she carefully unwound the precious metal from around her neck. She could not bear to be rid of it. Ranulf had once thought enough of her to bring her a costly gift fit for a nobleman's bride. She would keep it, but carefully put it away, determined never to wear it unless and until Ranulf claimed her as his bride.

An event unlikely ever to happen, Ariane admitted despondently.

She wished she could hate him, but she greatly feared it was too late. After all the years of torment and neglect he had subjected her to, despite his current cruelty, Ranulf was still the dazzling warrior who had captured her young heart so long ago.

He would not want her heart, Ariane knew. He would use her until he no longer found his newest possession amusing, and then he would cast her aside in favor of some other wench who caught his fancy—unless he indulged in his lust with other women even while forcing her to service him.

The thought made Ariane want to weep. Sweet Mary, how could she possibly protect herself from such hurt? She would be safe only so long as she could keep her distance. Yet now she would be required to share Ranulf's bed. She would be forced to endure his passion, to submit to his carnal attentions each night, and perhaps each day as well.

And, God help her, she could not in all honesty deny that was what she wanted.

Chapter 15

Ranulf was gone from the hall by the time Ariane dared
steal downstairs to assuage her hunger. To her surprise,
the sentries who usually watched over her were nowhere in
sight.

A realization struck her then that filled her with hope.
Being the lord's mistress might offer an unexpected advantage she had not considered: Ranulf might eventually lower
his guard around her. If she was not watched so closely, she
could perhaps slip out of the keep and perform her desperate errand.

To her further surprise, she found Payn FitzOsbern seated
alone at the lord's high table. To her complete astonishment,
he hailed her at once, as if he had been watching for her.

"Will you join me at table to break your fast, demoiselle?"

Ariane eyed him warily, wondering if he meant to chastise
her for her explosion last night.

The knight smiled, a friendly, persuasive greeting that
strangely set her at ease. "I would be honored, lady, if you
would join me. Come, I will not bite," he added in a laughing
undertone as he stood to pull out the chair next to him—the
lord's chair. "And should I be so bold as to attempt it"—
he chuckled under his breath—"I am certain you would
bite back."

Ariane could not help but respond to his teasing with her
own tentative smile.

"I wish to tender an apology for our lewd behavior last
eve," he said as soon as she was seated. "You had the right
of it. It was inexcusable to dishonor Claredon's hall in such
a manner."

Before she could reply, Payn raised a hand and summoned
a serf. "Bring your lady some food at once."

"Lady?" Ariane replied bitterly when they were alone. "I see Lord Ranulf neglected to inform you of my new role."

"Nay, he told me. And I must say, I am grateful to you."

"Grateful?"

"Aye, for soothing his vile temper. As his first in command, I am the one who bears the brunt of his ill humor. His mood was far sweeter this morn than it has been in months." Ariane stiffened, but Payn went on cheerfully as he poured her a goblet of wine. "It was only a matter of time before the explosion came, and better sooner than late."

The servant returned with a platter of cold mutton and bread and set it before Ariane. Dismissing the man, Payn eyed her thoughtfully. "What do you know about Ranulf, demoiselle?"

She thrust her eating dagger into the mutton in answer. "I know he is a ruthless, coldhearted, domineering, arrogant, *tyrant* who does not honor his promises."

Payn flashed her a sympathetic grin. "Nay, I meant, what do you know of his past?"

Ariane frowned. "Merely what my father told me. And of course, I have heard rumors. The Black Dragon is said to be invincible in battle and merciless toward his enemies. And they say ... he fought and defeated his own father, and claimed his inheritance at the point of a sword."

"The rumors do not exaggerate. Ranulf was forced to win back the Vernay lands lost to him when his father doubted his paternity and disinherited him."

"Then it is true? About his mother's ..." She faltered, uncertain how to put the question delicately.

"Her adultery? Aye, it's true. Before his birth, his mother indulged in an illicit affair with a lowborn freeman—the castle huntsman. To this day, it is not known whose offspring Ranulf is, although I have my opinion. Ranulf resembles Yves de Vernay too closely in appearance and character to be anyone else's son."

"You seem to know Ranulf well."

"Better than most. We fostered together as boys in the same Norman lord's household."

Ariane nodded absently. It was common for a son born into nobility to serve his knightly apprenticeship in another lord's household.

"From the first," Payn remarked, "Ranulf excelled at the rigorous training given us. He regularly defeated the other squires, even me, and we all deferred to him. He was large for his age, and his bearing lent him stature, yet his success was due to more than physical advantage. It was as if he were driven to prove himself better than anyone else. Not that he acted the bully, demoiselle." Payn smiled thoughtfully, as if in remembrance. "Indeed, Ranulf was first to defend the least powerful among us, and more than once championed weaklings against a brutal fist. But none of us knew him well. He had few friends, for he kept to himself. Years passed before he told me the story of his parentage, and then solely because he considered me his friend and too much wine had loosened his tongue. It was not a pretty tale."

His expression pensive, Payn sipped his wine, while Ariane waited impatiently for him to continue, her sympathy aroused.

"Yves de Vernay was ... shall we say ... a bitter man? He slew his wife's lover and nearly slew *her*. For her transgression, he locked her away in a tower cell for the remainder of her life. The Church, as you may know, no longer considers adultery sufficient cause to terminate a marriage. As for her babe, Lord Yves could never look upon him with other than loathing, which was doubtless a blessing for Ranulf. He escaped notice till he was a boy of four, when he had the misfortune to be brought to the lord's attention. Yves ... resolved to punish the despised son for the mother's sins. His method—to flay the body in order to purify the soul." Payn looked directly at Ariane. "Ranulf's back bore the brunt of his rage."

"Mother of God, those terrible scars," Ariane whispered, her voice faint with horror. "What manner of man would do that to a child?"

"Monstrous, was it not? His noble father sought to drive the devil from him, to purge the demons from his soul."

"Demons—but he was just a boy! A babe! Entirely innocent of his mother's misconduct."

"Aye, a boy—but endowed with a man-sized vengeance. For two years Ranulf endured the torment, until he was sent away to foster. He was liberated from his father's cruelty then, but he never, never forgot. His scars run far deeper than those on his back."

Ariane gazed at him in despair, as well as bewilderment. "Sir Payn . . . you spoke true—it is a dreadful tale. But why do you tell me?"

"I wished you to know what manner of man Ranulf is, the factors that have forged him into the man he is now." Payn's answer explained little, and even less when he added, "I wished you to understand why he has good reason to be wary of noblewomen."

Frowning in puzzlement, she nodded. "I am listening."

"It is my belief . . . Ranulf's reluctance to wed you stems from his deep mistrust of ladies of your class. He never said it in so many words, but I felt sure he feared you."

"Feared . . . ? *Me?* Whyever would he fear me?"

"I am coming to that, my lady." Payn smiled faintly at her expression. "You see, Ranulf learned long ago to put no faith in women. He considers most to be without honor. First his mother's adultery, which rendered his life a living hell. Then his later experiences . . . Well, I suppose I should elucidate. You have seen Ranulf's charm. He can—"

"I beg to differ," Ariane interrupted stiffly. "I have not seen the slightest evidence of *charm* in Lord Ranulf."

"Well, perhaps he would not attempt to charm *you*, demoiselle, under the present circumstances."

No, he would attempt it with any woman *but* her, she thought with a twinge of jealousy, remembering how Ranulf always had a ready smile for the castle wenches.

"His flair with females, then. Women seem to flock to him like bees to honey, despite his harsh countenance. I have never quite understood his appeal, I admit," Payn added with a wry, self-deprecating smile. "Ranulf does not have what you ladies would consider masculine beauty."

Not beauty in the common way, Ariane reflected. It was his raw, magnetic masculinity that was beautiful. That virile, dynamic, charismatic personality was a potent force, impossible to ignore. That, as well as the bleakness in his eyes that until now she had never understood, prompted much of his allure. Every woman would want to be the one to tame him, to soothe the beast within him—and to offer him comfort. She had felt the primal, instinctive yearning herself, beneath her fear and fury.

"Pray continue, my lord," Ariane murmured noncommittally.

"Very well. As I said, Ranulf excelled at military training. He was knighted at seventeen for courage in battle, but after he earned his spurs, he stayed on to serve his foster lord. He was a third son, with no expectation of inheriting the vast estates of Vernay. And as you know, a landless, penniless, unproven knight has few choices. But then ... a scandal ensued. In short, his foster lord's wife attempted to seduce him."

"The lord's *wife?*" Ariane stared in shock. "The lady of the keep?"

"Yes. Ranulf was entirely innocent of the charges, I am certain. After his past, he refused to cuckold any man, especially his own lord. Nor would he fight his overlord, even though he was called a coward for refusing. He left the lord's service in disgrace rather than accept a challenge at arms. In truth, he did the man a service, for Ranulf would have won with ease. At any rate, I gave up my position to follow him."

"You must have thought highly of him."

"There is no other lord I would serve," Payn said simply. "As it turned out, the decision was a boon for us both. We spent two years on the tourney circuits in Normandy and France, growing rich from the ransoms we won, and the years afterward fighting as mercenaries for Count Geoffrey of Anjou. We helped Geoffrey wrest Normandy from France, and helped make his son Henry duke."

Ariane had heard much of Geoffrey Plantagenet, a wise and forceful ruler who had conquered Normandy and built it into a power to be reckoned with. He eventually had bestowed the dukedom on his young son Henry, who was now the new king of England.

"Ranulf's tremendous skill came to young Henry's attention, and when the next scandal broke, Ranulf entered Henry's service."

"The next scandal?"

Payn's smile held no amusement. "The noblewomen of Geoffrey's court proved no more honorable than any others Ranulf had known. While there, a married *lady*—and I use the term with reservation—pursued him flagrantly. When he would not return her ardor, she falsely claimed that Ranulf had ravished her."

Payn waited while that sank in. Not unexpectedly, Ariane

felt like squirming beneath his gentle gaze. *She* also had falsely claimed ravishment at Ranulf's hands. But the circumstances were not at all the same, she thought defensively. Ranulf had promised to wed her and then reneged after five *years*.

"So you see," Payn said gently, "Ranulf's belief in the faithlessness of highborn women is not without justification."

"I do see why he would mistrust my sex," Ariane replied guardedly. "But your assertion begs a question. If he held me in such low esteem, why did he agree to our betrothal?"

"The usual reasons. Heirs and land. It is my belief that the latter was most important to him."

"But by then Ranulf already possessed vast holdings, did he not?"

"Aye, he was awarded several wealthy fiefs for his services to Geoffrey, and then rewarded handsomely for his loyalty to young Henry—primarily for helping Henry consolidate his rule of Normandy and later, to pursue the English throne. And by then Ranulf had won back the Vernay demesne. But you must remember the hatred he bore his father. It has influenced his every action, shadowed his every thought his entire life long."

"I imagine he wanted vengeance on his father?"

"After seeing his back, can you blame him?"

Ariane shook her head sadly. She could understand why a man would be driven to seek revenge for those terrible scars, even if she could not fathom how someone could hurt a child so savagely as Lord Yves had hurt the young boy who very likely was his son.

"But the beatings were not the catalyst," Payn said quietly. "Even then, Ranulf might have accepted his lot. But shortly after becoming Henry's vassal, Ranulf's two older brothers died within months of each other—one of a putrid wound acquired in battle, the other of the bloody flux. Even after their deaths, Lord Yves refused to acknowledge Ranulf as his son or to name him as heir. That was when Ranulf's tolerance ended. In Henry's name, he besieged Vernay and challenged his father to mortal combat."

"What happened?" she asked earnestly.

"Ranulf won, naturally, but he stopped short of killing his tormentor, even though it would have been justified. His father fled to France, taking refuge with King Louis—where he lives to this day. Ultimately, I understand, Yves turned to God, although how so ungodly a man could hope to save his black soul, I vow I cannot fathom. As penance he went on pilgrimage to the Holy Land, and came back a changed man. Ranulf refused to forgive him, though.''

Ariane understood Ranulf's sentiments completely.

''In gratitude for winning such a vast holding, Duke Henry made Ranulf castellan of Vernay and signed a charter of nobility, giving Ranulf the right to call himself his father's son. Eventually he was awarded the entire Vernay demesne. Not satisfied with his holdings, though, Ranulf continued his drive to become one of the most powerful barons in Normandy.'' Payn paused to look at her directly. ''He knew that you, as an heiress, could help him attain that goal.''

''So he agreed to wed me.''

''Aye, but he regretted the action almost at once, I could tell. When you have served a man as long as I have served Ranulf, you come to sense even his deepest feelings.''

Ariane lowered her gaze to hide the hurt in her eyes. ''I have feelings, also, Sir Payn. I once pledged him my loyalty, to honor and serve him as wife. I would have given him my heart, and yet he repudiated me.''

''I do not *justify* his actions, my lady,'' Payn said quietly. ''I only seek to make you understand them. Ranulf is a brave man; his valor and his dauntless deeds have proven that. The dreaded name of Black Dragon is well deserved, I assure you. Yet for all his courage, he fears being hurt again. And when you refused to yield Claredon to him, as his father refused to yield Vernay, you roused feelings of rage and hatred in Ranulf that he has held his life long.''

''I understand that—now. But again . . . why do you tell me this?''

''Because I love him like a brother. He deserves far better than what fate has hitherto seen fit to give him.''

''Your loyalty to him is admirable,'' Ariane murmured truthfully. ''Few men would serve a landless, dispossessed knight with such devotion as you have shown.''

''He has earned my loyalty tenfold, demoiselle. His skill at arms is unquestioned, as is his prowess as a military commander. He is a leader of men. But he is a good lord as well, one who has proven himself careful in administration. Ranulf has ruled his fiefs with justice and compassion.''

Ariane nodded slowly. She had seen for herself his efforts to rule Claredon justly. He had commuted the sentences of his transgressors when it served him better, and shown a degree of leniency that was unheard of for a warlord, especially one who had reason to be so vengeful. He was not the ogre she had feared. The Black Dragon, she had begun to realize, was not so terrible as his name implied.

"So my father thought," she said quietly. "It was why he chose Ranulf as my future husband."

"It is still a wise choice. Ranulf is not without heart, demoiselle. It is just that he has hidden it behind a shield of armor. Ranulf is a soldier. Killing is his trade—he was born to it. He knows naught of love or tenderness, only of fighting. Violence and combat have been his whole life. Well, wenching, too, but what knight has not sown a few wild oats?"

Her mouth curved wryly. "What indeed?"

Payn cleared his throat. "The right woman could change him."

"Think you . . . I might be that woman?" she asked in a small voice.

"I trust so. But you will not have an easy time of it. Ranulf never forgets an ill, and you already have numerous marks against you: refusing to surrender Claredon, setting your father's vassal free to lead a rebellion, falsely declaring your betrothal consummated . . ."

"It *is* consummated now," Ariane declared, even as she flushed to admit it.

"Perhaps so, but the manner of it will hardly serve as the basis for a congenial marriage. And then there is your father's treason against the crown. By association, you are a suspected traitor."

Her chin came up abruptly, her entire body stiffening. "My father is *not* a traitor, my lord, nor am I. When King Stephen died, my father immediately declared for Henry—and nothing occurred in the interim to change his mind. When he left for Bridgenorth, he was Henry's man. His innocence has yet to be proven, but it will be."

Payn looked at her a long moment. "I think I could believe

you, demoiselle, but my opinion is not the key one. It is Ranulf who must be convinced.''

"What . . . do you suggest I do?"

"Step carefully with him, demoiselle. Somehow you must win his trust. Without trust, Ranulf will never overcome his deep-rooted fears.''

She looked down at her hands. "I am honored by your faith in me, Sir Payn. I only hope I my prove myself worthy of it. As you said, it will not be easy. Often it is all I can do simply to hold my own with Ranulf.''

Payn flashed her a grin that held respect and sympathy. "Methinks if any lady could, 'twould be you."

Rising from the table, he gave Ariane a deep bow. "I look forward to the day when you resume your rightful place as lady of Claredon, demoiselle.'' Turning then, he made his way from the hall.

Ariane watched him go in bemused silence, feeling more hopeful than she had in weeks. In Payn FitzOsbern, she had discovered an entirely unexpected ally. She had listened to him, primarily because she was greedy to learn more about Ranulf, but also because she knew it would not hurt to culti- vate his chief vassal's goodwill. She was surprised to feel a genuine liking for the handsome knight. He had been a loyal and trusted friend to Ranulf, and she would truly be honored to call him friend as well.

Her meal virtually uneaten, Ariane sat there, thinking over all that Payn had told her about Ranulf's terrible past, her heart aching for what he had endured. She could only begin to imagine his suffering.

His noble father had sought to purge the demons from him. So that was what Ranulf had meant when he claimed demons possessed his soul. He had been punished for his mother's sins, and then denied his rightful heritage because of his questionable paternity.

Ariane shook her head, fighting a wave of fierce tenderness for him. Even though now she better understood the reasons he did not trust her, the realization still *hurt.* And yet she had never once considered their betrothal from *his* perspec- tive. Ranulf actually *feared* the hurt she might do him.

He was wrong about that, just as he was overly harsh to judge her a traitor. Yet it would be difficult to prove herself worthy of his trust. He already thought her a scheming jade. Staining the bedsheets had been a critical mistake, she realized now. Trying to force Ranulf to acknowledge their marriage had only hardened his heart further against her.

Worse, she might never be able to deal with him in complete honesty. She harbored a secret that she dared not reveal to anyone, particularly the new lord of Claredon, who held the power of life and death over those in his demesne. She had not lied to Ranulf yet about it, but she would, if necessary.

Dispirited by the thought, Ariane gave a weary sigh.

The challenge before her was daunting. She no longer simply wanted to win her rights as Ranulf's wife. She wanted to win his heart as well. And that task would be more difficult than anything she had ever imagined.

Chapter 16

Ranulf returned to the tower for the midday meal earlier than planned. He had spent the morning inspecting the castle grounds with Baldwin, the estate steward, and was satisfied with the progress he had seen. There had been no more pranks or acts of subversion—or if so, the castlefolk had been wise enough to keep it from the lord's attention.

He had been mistaken, though, to believe himself free of Ariane. He had thought that after bedding her at last, he could put her from his mind long enough to devote his thoughts to dull administrative duties. Yet as Ranulf toured the stables and smithy, and spoke to the keepers of the kennels and mews and granaries, his thoughts continually strayed. He kept remembering the exquisite pleasure Ariane had brought him last night, and his fierce desire to have her again surged. Fire raged in his loins, unquenched by the single, enthralling taste he had been afforded. He was hungry for her still, his obsession as strong—stronger, perhaps—than before.

His pride, however, demanded that he control his lusts. He had ordered Ariane to await him in the solar at the day's end, and he would adhere to his plan if it killed him. He did not want to give the wench any hint of how thoroughly she had bewitched him, or that her feminine arts wielded any undue power over him.

Moreover, he had promised his men an afternoon of sport on the hunting field, a well-deserved respite from the grind of military duty. And he wished to see for himself what game his forests held.

Telling himself he would have to be satisfied with a mere glimpse of her, Ranulf felt a keen disappointment when Ariane made no appearance in the hall for the noon meal.

The meal seemed interminable, and Ranulf was hard-

237

pressed to maintain a semblance of good humor, or to keep his gaze from roaming the hall in search of her. Payn, strangely, was more jovial than even his usual sunny disposition warranted. The knight agreed easily when Ranulf directed him to gather the huntsmen in the bailey and await him there. Payn even refrained from commenting about the lord's odd excuse for delay when Ranulf said he wished to fetch his gauntlets from the solar, although any number of pages and squires would have willingly accomplished the errand.

She was not in the solar, Ranulf discovered to his growing irritation, before his search led him to the adjacent weaving room. To his surprise and misgiving, he found Ariane there, surrounded by her ladies, embroidering tapestries, while nearby, skilled craftswomen plied their trade, winding wool into long skeins, spooling thread, and weaving cloth.

The clacking looms and female chatter came to an abrupt halt when his presence was detected. At the sudden silence, Ariane looked up in startlement to find Ranulf looming in the doorway. His powerful, commanding form seemed out of place in a chamber meant solely for women.

She was dismayed that Ranulf would seek her out here, dismayed still further by his intent scrutiny. His burning eyes were bright and hot, his lust bold for anyone to see.

Flushing, Ariane set aside her embroidery and rose, then followed him from the weaving room to the antechamber. "My lord? How may I serve you?"

Her choice of words was unfortunate, for his amber eyes darkened. His hands closed over her arms, as if he might draw her against him—but then Ranulf made himself halt. It took all of his strength to pull back. His manhood had warmed and swelled at sight of her, and the feel of her was tantalizing, and yet he refused to be distracted by her allure.

"What do you do here, wench?" he demanded, his tone more curt than he intended.

Ariane gazed up at him warily. "Why, I was seeing to the clothmaking. The spinning and weaving and needlework have suffered neglect since your . . . seizure of Claredon."

"I disremember granting you leave to spend your time in such pursuits."

"You did say I no longer had to serve in the kitchens."

"You no longer need work at all, except to fulfill your duties as leman—and those entail sharing my bed and being at my beck and call."

Hot color rose to her face, but she managed to say evenly, "I am not accustomed to being idle, my lord."

"You will not be idle," Ranulf replied, his voice dipping to huskiness. "I intend to keep you too busy to think of labor."

Ariane set her jaw, wanting to argue with him. Even if he kept her sprawled on her back each night and much of each day, there would still be too many empty hours to fill, as well as tasks that demanded a woman's attention. She did not wish to see her former home fall to ruin for lack of a chatelaine. Indeed, her lady mother would be offended to see what deplorable condition the keep had fallen into so shortly after being occupied by Ranulf's forces.

Remembering, though, her newly formed pledge to conquer Ranulf's heart, she lowered her gaze and murmured, "As you wish, my lord."

Her docile reply roused Ranulf's wariness further, and yet he could find nothing in her answer or attitude to take umbrage with.

"In future you will be present at meals," he said coolly. "Beginning tonight. I expect a large repast this evening. I always work up an appetite while hunting."

"You mean to hunt?" she was dismayed into asking.

"Yes. You find that surprising?"

Her gaze flickered uneasily to the arrow loop in the outer wall. She had not previously noted the sounds that floated through the opening—riders, huntsmen, and hounds gathering in the yard in preparation for a hunt. The realization struck her with foreboding.

"No, not surprising," Ariane prevaricated. "Where do you hunt, my lord?"

"What does it matter?"

"The south wood is known to be full of game."

"Is it, indeed? I find it curious that you should think to advise me on the chase."

Seeing the penetrating interest in Ranulf's hard eyes, Ariane carefully schooled her features to show no expression. "I merely wish your sport to be successful. We all would enjoy fresh game for supper—and your mood is sweeter when your desires are not thwarted,'' she could not resist adding tartly.

His mouth curved up at the corner, yet his countenance held little amusement. ''I have never noted your particular eagerness to satisfy my desires before now, demoiselle. Could there be another cause for your concern?'' he said slowly, searching her face. ''Rebels you wish to aid, perchance? Your supporters could easily set up a base from which to conduct their assaults on my patrols, like the one that killed my archer and wounded my squire. Perhaps they hide in the north wood, which is why you seek to direct me south.''

She tried to remain calm as she replied airily, ''If there are rebels on Claredon land, I know naught of them.''

''The eastern forest, then?'' Ranulf persisted, watching her closely. He saw the flicker of alarm in her eyes, but could not determine the cause. *Was* she seeking to conceal the presence of rebel forces?

A chill swept Ariane at the mention of that section. Hastily she lowered her lashes over the secrets she knew must lie in her eyes. She should never have mentioned any of the forests, but now that she had, there was nothing to do but brazen it out.

''The eastern wood is said to be haunted by evil spirits, my lord. The serfs and villagers avoid it resolutely, and the hounds will not hunt there willingly.''

''Evil spirits?'' The hard voice turned softly menacing. ''It is fortunate then that I hold no belief in such superstition.''

Sensing Ranulf's growing suspicion, Ariane retreated from that obviously false explanation. ''Of course I put no faith in those old wives' tales,'' she assured him, keeping her eyes downcast, ''but it is true that vicious wolves roam those woods.''

''All the more reason to hunt there. I should think you would consider it laudable to rid the forest of wolves.''

''Yes . . . but . . .'' Ariane faltered, knowing she was sinking deeper into a morass, yet not knowing how to extricate herself.

''Mayhap,'' Ranulf said dangerously, ''you seek to shield someone else. Is that, perchance, where you go to sport with your lover?''

She glance up in startlement, her eyes wide. "You well know I have never had a lover until you."

"Castle gossip says otherwise."

She went rigid. "You yourself saw the proof of my innocence, my lord."

"There are ways to enjoy passion without breaching a maidenhead, as I have shown you."

"I have never had a lover," Ariane repeated with rising indignation.

Ranulf's look turned grim as with one hand, he caught her chin, forcing her to meet his gaze. "Not even your father's vassal? The prisoner you freed, Simon?"

Ariane winced at the pressure of Ranulf's fingers on her chin and on her arm. "Not Simon, nor any other man."

"And it shall remain that way," Ranulf said, his voice low and taut. "Henceforth, I will be your only lover. I will kill any man who touches you. Do you comprehend me?"

"Yes ... Please, Ranulf ... you are hurting me."

He released her abruptly, as if he had held smoldering coals, although his gaze remained fierce. Gingerly Ariane rubbed the tender flesh of her arm as she watched him warily. She could not understand his jealous fury—until she recalled the experiences he had endured at the hands of other women of her class. Ranulf thought her no better than any of the adulterous noblewomen who had filled his life with pain and scandal.

"I have no lover," she said quietly, "in a forest or elsewhere. I only sought to advise you."

He could not quite believe her. He had seen the guilt in those luminous gray eyes, seen Ariane's reluctance to meet his gaze. She was not telling the complete truth, he would swear it. That she would think to deceive him filled him with bitter anguish, but her championship of his enemies would make no difference in the end. He was well accustomed at flushing out insurgents who would foment rebellion. If she was protecting Simon Crecy or any other traitor, he would find and deal with them swiftly.

Ranulf tore his gaze from Ariane. He did not want to hear any more lies coming from those sweet lips. "You take too much upon yourself," he retorted stiffly, before turning to-

ward the stairway. "You had best pray I find no trace of
your traitorous cohorts."

As she listened to the retreat of his jingling spurs, Ariane
pressed a hand to her mouth in dismay. God's mercy, what
had she done? Arousing Ranulf's suspicions had been inex-
cusably stupid. Ranulf was no fool, but a seasoned knight,
experienced in dealing with enemy resistance. He would
search the east wood for rebels and perhaps stumble upon
the secret she would give her life to keep hidden.

Dread curled in the pit of her stomach as she thought of
what he could find. Despite his past leniency, in this instance
he would not be so eager to show mercy and compassion,
she was certain.

"No," Ariane whispered to herself, trying to calm her
agitation, as well as bolster her courage. All was not lost.
Perhaps it was even a blessing that Ranulf's suspicions centered on fantasy rebels. As long as he was searching for
miscreants, he might overlook the dire dilemma she had spent
the past four years endeavoring to conceal.

She forced herself to release the breath she had been holding. She would not give up hope. Very soon she would have
to discover the means to attend the wood's inhabitants, before
their plight grew desperate, but she had time yet to plan how
to escape Ranulf's vigilance.

She *would* pray, as he had suggested, though. She would
pray that the secret of Claredon forest would be safe for a
great while longer.

Ranulf found no trace of wolves or rebels, or any other
sign of revolt in the expanse of forest some quarter league
east of the castle walls, although, much to the disgust of the
keepers, the hounds did seem to fear the area. They whined
and snuffled and started at shadows, until finally they picked
up the spoor of a wild boar which led off to the north.

The sport was good, the hunt highly successful—the party
killed two boar and five hinds—but Ranulf was more relieved
to find his suspicions apparently unfounded. Had he found
Simon Crecy hiding in the wood, he would have run the man
through with his sword without a qualm.

Such jealousy was wholly unreasonable, Ranulf knew, yet
he could not contain it. He became irrational whenever he

merely thought of Ariane with another man. In truth, his
savage feeling of possessiveness toward her startled and disturbed Ranulf. No wench had ever had the power to move
him to jealousy; he had never allowed one close enough. For
all his enjoyment of their bodies, he purposefully kept his
women at a distance, his heart hardened and detached.

Ariane would be no different, Ranulf tried to tell himself.
She was a female body, just like the scores of others he had
possessed. No, not *just* like the others. Her cool, haunting
beauty and feminine softness, combined with a sharp tongue
and defiant wit, gave her a bewitching allure that he had
never before encountered—and made the sport far more gratifying than any he had experienced before now.

It was that allure that made him ride eagerly back to the
keep at the day's end. That allure that caused the singing in
his blood as he turned his destrier over to a page and bounded
up the tower stairs. His pulse was racing when he spied
Ariane in the hall, supervising the serfs who were lighting
the torches along the walls and arranging the trestle tables in
the center.

She wore a flowing bliaud of jonquil silk over a long-
sleeved crimson chainse. The golden band that encircled her
forehead caught the gleam of torchlight, as did her pale, un-
bound hair, which rippled with copper and gold and flaxen
highlights.

She was not wearing his gift, he noted with a sharp sense
of disappointment, and yet she was beautiful enough without
it. The sight of her took Ranulf's breath away.

He crushed the urge to sweep her up in his arms right
then, and merely acknowledged her with a lordly nod. Yet
like a callow youth eager to impress a lass, Ranulf hastened
upstairs to wash the worst of the dirt and blood of the hunt
away, and then hastened back down again.

Ariane stood hesitantly beside the dais, awaiting his arrival.
Payn, who had been laughing jovially with some of their
men, strode to the table just then, and reached her first. The
knight bowed over her hand and gave her a smile of masculine approval that made Ranulf set his teeth.

"You grace us with your presence, lady," Payn said ad-
miringly as he held out the chatelaine's chair. "Does she
not, Ranulf?"

Ranulf, irritated that his vassal's chivalry had prevented his own, grunted in agreement. "That gown does you credit," he added in a softer voice.

Ariane lowered her eyes modestly. "Thank you, my lord. It was good of you to return my clothing to me."

Her gentle barb stung, and vexed Ranulf all the more.

At least the food, while perhaps not a feast, was the best meal he had enjoyed since taking possession of Claredon. The game they had just killed would not be butchered till the morrow, but there was pheasant and roast suckling pig and smoked herring, prepared with spices and mouthwatering sauces. During the first course, Ranulf discovered from Payn's leading questions that Ariane herself had ordered the preparations. He was not certain he liked her taking so much upon herself, and yet he could find no fault in the result.

Payn's effusive compliments began to wear on his temper, though, especially since for the second and third courses, Ranulf scarcely tasted what he ate. The conversation flowed around him while he remained silent, acutely aware of the beautiful woman sitting so cool and regal beside him, and his own ache to possess her. He wanted the interminable meal to end so that he could have her alone, beneath him.

His plan to take Ariane as his leman was foolish, perhaps. He needed to resist the temptation of her body, if only to prove that he was not reduced to submission by the gentleness in her gray eyes, by the warmth of her touch, to prove that he cared nothing for her. But he could not have denied himself tonight had his very life been at stake.

The evening's planned entertainment was to be a troupe of jugglers, but Ranulf had no intention of remaining to watch. And when he caught her eye, Ariane knew it as well.

She felt her pulse quicken at the dark light in his eyes. She, too, had scarcely tasted the dishes, her mind on the night ahead. Her skin felt hot, and there was a curling sense of anticipation within her, a sensual arousal brought on by excitement and apprehension and the knowledge of what would happen between them.

"Go and order me a bath," Ranulf murmured in her ear the moment the music began. When Ariane nodded and made to rise, he forestalled her with a hand on her arm. "You will remain there to attend me," he added in a low voice, his intent clear. She would provide a service that entailed far more than merely washing his back.

The serfs Ariane called upon hastened to do her bidding, and in short order a steaming, perfumed bath stood in the solar, awaiting the lord. The last of the servants had just withdrawn when he arrived.

His eyes hot and lust-bright, Ranulf drew her into his arms the moment the door had shut. His mouth covered hers in a fierce possession, tasting with the full measure of his need. Fire, hot and sweet, surged from him and through her, stealing both their breaths away. She could feel him thickening, swelling against her, and when at last he raised his head, she was trembling.

His smile was a trifle wolfish as his hand trespassed boldly beneath her skirts. "I have wanted to do that since this morning."

To her surprise—and somewhat to her embarrassment—Ranulf undressed her first, showing as much deliberate care as any tirewoman. The difference was his use of mouth and hands—nuzzling the bare skin he exposed . . . stroking her body . . . smoothing her hair to a profusion of silken waves. By the time she stood naked before him, she was quivering with need.

"You tempt me unmercifully, witch," he murmured in a rough voice as he bent to taste her budded nipple. "Your coolness makes a man burn for you, makes him hot to seek the hidden fire beneath."

Coolness? How could she be cool with the scorching heat spiraling within her?

Choking back a whimper, Ariane nearly melted against him. It dismayed her, how little resistance she could summon against him. If she responded to Ranulf's passion as she had all the times before, if she surrendered this easily, she would have no hope whatsoever of maintaining her defenses. Making a last desperate effort to stiffen her resolve, she pushed against his broad shoulders, trying to make him raise his head from her breast. "My lord . . . no . . ."

"Yes," Ranulf insisted as his hand slid between her bare legs. He brushed his finger against her sweet, hot cleft, rimming the lips. "You want me, wench. See, your honey flows for me."

She did want him, Mary help her. She was his unwilling leman, and yet he possessed the power to make her forget everything except his sensual touch. His fingers were slowly opening her, seeking entrance, finding it. Ariane's breath caught in her throat and she shuddered as his finger thrust slowly inside her.

Ranulf's eyes blazed in triumph as he felt her surrender. Catching her hand, he forced it beneath his tunic, covering the braies cupping his sex. "See how I want you, too? Undress me," he commanded hoarsely.

With shaking hands, she obeyed. Ranulf aided her, too impatient to wait. In the time it took her to remove and fold both his tunics, he had stripped off his boots and chausses and braies. When she turned back to him, he stood magnificent before her, his nude, powerful body bulging with muscle.

Ariane could not take her eyes away, or keep her gaze from moving lower . . . over the thick pelt covering his wide chest, along the ebony trail that narrowed over his abdomen. His huge member thrust up from the curling black hair between his thighs, long and flushed and engorged with lust. It no longer frightened her, though, for she knew now what pleasure it could give her.

Ranulf was watching her, as well, Ariane realized dazedly. His eyes were fixed hungrily on the pale globes of her breasts.

Without a word, he stepped toward her and cupped them in his hands, whisking her nipples with the rough pads of his thumbs. She inhaled sharply as a tremulous wave of longing racked her body.

He smiled, a sexual, carnal, arrogant male smile.

"Come, attend me." Taking her hand, he led her to the bath. Alone, he stepped within the tub and sank to his knees in the steaming depths.

She would have knelt beside him, but Ranulf forestalled her by reaching out to grasp her bare hips. His amber eyes glittered as he gazed up at her, along the naked length of her body. Leaning forward, then, he pressed a hard, hot kiss to the soft mound between her thighs.

Ariane gasped in shock, her hands reaching out to grasp his shoulders for balance. "No . . . Ranulf . . . 'tis heathen . . ."

Ignoring her plea, he urged her legs to part for him, savoring the sweet scent of woman rising to his nostrils. The sight of her flushed sex drove him to the edge.

"I crave a sampling," he muttered hoarsely as his tongue lapped her pink woman's flesh.

She drew back with a jerk yet could not escape completely; Ranulf caught her wrist in a grasp of velvet steel and drew her down beside the tub. Weak-limbed and dazed, she sank to her knees.

"Show me how you can please me, vixen," he ordered, pressing her palm to his breast so that she could feel his thundering heart.

He compelled her to wash him. Lathering her palm with soap, he guided it over his body, until her own primitive need to touch him took over. Her trembling fingers slid down over his hair-roughened chest, stroking lower, dipping below the warm water, gliding over the hard ridges of his stomach.

When she hesitated at his flat, hard-muscled belly, Ranulf leaned forward to brush his lips against her flushed face, her jutting breasts.

"All of me. My rod is stiff and aching. Hold me in your hand."

Ariane obliged, finding his granite member slick and throbbing with heat that had nothing to do with the temperature of the water.

"Harder, tighter ... you cannot hurt me."

She squeezed gently, and the passion that blazed in his eyes shook her to the core.

"Ah ... yes ... please me, wench. ..." With a low groan, Ranulf closed his eyes and let the male ache wash over him in ripples of pleasure-pain. His hips thrust upward into her hand, once, twice ... and then suddenly he drew back, refusing to seek his ecstasy alone.

Rising half out of the water, Ranulf snaked his powerful arms around her and lifted her into the tub to sit astride him, her knees on either side of his hips, her thighs open wide.

Ariane gasped in protest and struggled in his grasp, but Ranulf's arms closed around her to hold her still. "Hush," he rasped. "You have never ridden a man."

" 'Tis not natural ..."

"Oh ... but it is, sweeting." His eyes smoldered with gold flame. "The most natural thing in the world."

His hands closed over her buttocks and lifted her slightly, only to lower her deliberately onto his shaft. The rigid length of him filled her with tantalizing slowness, impaling her. Whimpering at the shocking fullness of him, Ariane arched her back and rocked against him, her ripe, wet breasts pressing against the hardness of his chest.

His response was a guttural sound and a deeper thrust. He could scarcely bear the delicious thrill such deep penetration sent through him. He shuddered convulsively, grinding his teeth to hold back the primal sound rumbling in his chest. The slow, instinctive undulation of her hips was driving him mad, as was the spasmic clasping of her inner muscles around him.

His neck corded with the force of his denial, Ranulf pressed deeper, burying his shaft to the hilt.

She gave an incoherent cry of pleasure, even as her slender body clenched, and then she startled him by sinking her teeth in his shoulder.

He laughed, a low, male sound of triumph, and gripped her buttocks harder, working her up and down in rhythm with his thrusts, until Ariane's body caught fire, blazing out of control. Her gasping breaths sounded loud in his ears as she pumped her hips wildly and sent bathwater splashing over the tub's edge. A dozen heartbeats later, she erupted, arching against him, her head thrown back in helpless surrender, her nails digging into his flesh.

At her low, keening, helpless cry, Ranulf abandoned his own rigid control and hauled her closer, his rough excitement matching her own frenzy as he surged deep inside her.

"Sweet God! . . ."

Through a heated haze of awareness, Ariane felt his lean, powerful body clench, heard the hoarse unintelligible groan Ranulf gave as the convulsions of passion claimed his control and he began the shuddering fall into ecstasy after her.

They clung to each other when it was over, breathing hard as the waves of savage, unrestrained pleasure washed over them and receded.

At last recovering her dazed senses, Ariane realized she was lying limply in Ranulf's arms, her face buried in the wet curve of his shoulder. He was stroking her naked back, stroking her hair, his hands gentle and soothing. With a soft sigh of repletion, she nestled against him, never wanting to move again.

Thus it startled her when she felt Ranulf swelling and growing rigid inside her. Her sleepy eyes opened wide as he gathered her in his arms and stood up, water cascading from their bodies.

"The bath can wait," he murmured. "I cannot."

Stepping from the tub, he carried her to the bed and laid her upon the mattress in a single, sure motion, never breaking contact. Sinking deeper between her legs, he covered her wet, naked body, pressing her thighs wide apart with his. His urgent need to have her was like an unquenchable fever. His rod was engorged and aching again, even though it had only been moments since he had experienced the most exquisite pleasure of his life.

He gritted his teeth as he thrust upward into her hot, silky sweetness. She shuddered and arched her back in sensual response.

"No, open your eyes, sweeting," Ranulf commanded. "Watch me when I take you."

Ariane opened her eyes to stare at him. His own eyes were hot, his damp raven hair falling over his broad forehead, his dark-complected skin stretched taut over prominent cheekbones.

"Watch as I enter you." Withdrawing his shaft most of the way, he raised up on his hands, forming a wide space between their bodies.

Her cheeks flushing, she let her gaze drift lower. Water glistened in the dark hair on his chest, but there her courage faltered.

"Ariane . . ." he said softly, coaxingly.

Forcing her gaze downward, she did as she was bid, looking at the sight of their joining. His organ was huge and red and slick as it poised at the threshold of her womanhood. The sight was erotic and incredibly arousing—yet not as arousing as the fiery feel of him as he slowly thrust inside her, penetrating deep.

She groaned, and clutched at his shoulders, ignoring his command to keep her eyes open as she gasped out his name. He was throbbing within her, demanding her sensual response. She heard herself whimpering and knew she was undulating her hips shamelessly.

"This is how I want you," Ranulf muttered, raw desire darkening his husky voice. "Hot and wild beneath me."

This was how *she* wanted to be, Ariane though dazedly: Ranulf claiming her, making her feel totally possessed, each slow plunge making her crave the next as she quivered beneath his sensual domination.

This was how she wanted *him,* she realized as she felt Ranulf's body shudder. He was losing control, trembling with hunger. She had a blurred glimpse of his face, dark and strained, as he stroked powerfully into her, felt the muscles bunching and rippling in his broad, scarred back—but then she gave herself up to the fire that was building between them.

They were no longer bitter enemies. Merely two bodies straining to become one. Two hearts clashing in passionate need.

She took his weight, his raging need, as they climbed to the verge of another shattering climax, and when the explosion came at last, neither of them knew who was the conqueror, who the vanquished.

Chapter 17

For two full days and a third night, Ranulf remained sequestered in his chamber with his newest mistress. He spent the entire time pleasuring Ariane, and teaching her how to pleasure him.

Serfs delivered their meals directly to the solar, along with fresh bathwater and wood for the hearth fire. No one else dared defy the lord's orders for privacy or risk the Black Dragon's uncertain temper by disturbing him. Payn alone was permitted an audience with Ranulf for half an hour each morning and evening, and then was expected to deal with the vassals and household officials who demanded the lord's attention. All others were turned away.

When Ariane flushed in embarrassment and complained that Ranulf was shaming her with his lascivious attentions, he replied with an dismissive shrug, "I am lord here. I do what I please."

And what he pleased at the moment was to enjoy her body and the incredible delight she stirred in him. He could scarcely recall a more satisfying time with a wench. Ariane was a swift learner, and the token resistance she offered each time he took her in his embrace melted after the first few heated kisses.

He liked having her melt in his arms. He enjoyed overcoming her defiant pride. He savored watching every nuance of her expression when she reached pleasure beneath him, relished seeing her eyes soft and hazy with lovemaking afterward. As now.

Just now—the second afternoon of their enforced intimacy, while a blustery spring rain beat against the window panes—she looked well ravished as she lay replete and panting for breath in his arms in the big bed. Her hair was a wild tangle spread across the breadth of his chest, her slender, silken limbs entwined with his.

Ranulf's large hands stroked her naked back as he strove to collect his own breath. The storm of passion they had just weathered within the bed had been as fierce as the tempest raging outside the tower. The powerful shudders that had convulsed him moments ago still resonated throughout his body, leaving behind a sweet languor and a bewildering contentment. It startled him, how much he enjoyed the warm cocoon of closeness that enveloped them. He was unaccustomed to lingering in his lover's embrace, yet he found himself entirely unwilling to release Ariane. This urge to touch her and hold her when he was well sated was beyond his experience. Not that he would allow her to know how profoundly she affected him.

"As you see, lover," he said hoarsely when he could speak, resuming his role as carnal tutor, "your powers of endurance are greater than you imagined."

Lacking even the energy to open her eyes, Ariane murmured something in reluctant agreement.

"What said you, sweeting?"

"I said . . . you forced me against my will."

He laughed, a low sexual laugh filled with male triumph. " 'Twas not *force* that made you cry out my name and plead with me to end my possession."

No, Ariane thought in vexation, her cheeks flaming at the truth of his accusation. Ranulf had never needed to resort to force with her. Each time she resisted him until his exquisite caresses drove her beyond all reason, until her defenses were swept away in a storm of need, and then she responded with a wanton urgency that shocked her.

"If I pleaded, 'twas from simple boredom," she mumbled into his shoulder. "I grew weary at your attentions and would end them."

He chuckled at her brazen lie. "*Boredom?* You find this boring?" With sensuous fingers he plucked at her nipple, making her gasp. "I suspect instead you are piqued because you have no control over your traitorous body."

"If I am piqued . . . it is because your tactics are unfair. And wicked. 'Tis heathen, what you do to me."

"Heathen, aye. I learned the skill from a Saracen courte-

san, who learned it in an infidel brothel in the Holy Land.
The sexual arts of the East have much to recommend them,
would you not agree?''

''They are depraved and unseemly,'' she retorted in
disgruntlement.

''But effective, admit it.''

Sweet Mary, they were indeed effective, Ariane thought
sleepily, remembering the shattering impact his scandalous
ministrations had on her senses. Yet Ranulf had no need to
add such arts to his personal arsenal. His prowess with
women was overwhelming enough without them. ''I admit
naught, except that your conceit knows no bounds.''

''You wound me mortally, wench,'' Ranulf replied,
amused, holding his heart in mock pain.

Ariane roused herself from her lethargy long enough to lift
her head from his shoulder and peer up at him. The light
dancing in his eyes took her aback. This was not the first
time the feared dragon had teased her, yet she had never seen
him in so strange a mood—blithe, almost playful. ''You do
not look wounded, my lord. You look . . . smug.''

''Have I not reason to be? I predicted you would submit
to me willingly, and here you are.''

In irritation, she twisted her fingers in his chest hair, making him wince.

Catching her hand, Ranulf grinned and brought her fingers
to his lips. ''You like your play rough, wench?''

''No . . . you know I prefer gentleness.''

His eyes darkened. ''As do I. I learned long ago that gentleness can win over a wench where force cannot.''

Bristling at his impossible arrogance, she pulled her hand
from his grasp. ''You think women weak, simply because
our bodies are more fragile than yours.''

Ranulf grunted, his good humor fading. ''I have good
cause to know a woman's strength—and viciousness. Your
sex has weapons no man would think of wielding.''

Ariane hesitated at hearing the harsh scorn in his voice,
remembering Payn's tales of the scandals that had haunted
Ranulf's life. She wondered if he would divulge any more
about his past, or if it pained him too much to dwell on
it. ''Did some woman use her weapons against you?'' she
asked quietly.

Bleak pain flared in his eyes and died so swiftly she wondered if she had imagined it. Frowning, Ranulf absently twined his fingers in a lock of her hair. "I have no wish to speak of it."

A few days ago, Ariane might have retorted with a stinging reply, but that was before she had learned of his torment. Now, helplessly, she pressed her mouth against an old battle scar on his chest, feeling his heart beating sure and strong beneath her lips. His beautiful body was like a blade of the finest Damascene steel, forged by the sufferings of his past. And yet, even a sword could be broken.

Unaccountably, Ariane felt a fierce wave of tenderness assault her, an almost desperate urge to draw this strong, vital man into her arms, to hold and protect him and keep him safe from harm.

She raised herself fully upon one elbow, searching his harsh, handsome face, trying to read his features. Even as she looked down, his gaze slid to her mouth and darkened.

She recognized that heated look—an expression of his insatiable lusty appetites, and yet there was more to it this time. A question, a wariness, lay in the amber depths, as if Ranulf had suddenly recalled who she was, a noblewoman who could never be trusted not to deal him more hurt. She wanted desperately to erase that doubt from his eyes.

Even as she had the thought, though, his hand rose behind her head to capture her nape, his fingers twining in her hair to draw her mouth down for his kiss.

Weakness and warmth flooded Ariane at the tender pressure of his lips, at the sensual thrust of his tongue. Trembling, she struggled against the fierce wanting, denying herself as much as him. Her hands came up to resist him, her fingers spreading against warm flesh, softly furred. "My lord . . . have you not had enough?"

"Enough? Nay. I will never have enough of you, wench." When still she hesitated, he raised a skeptical eyebrow. "Do you deny that you want me, lover?" Ranulf demanded softly, knowing the answer already.

She could deny him nothing. Her need for him during the past two days had grown into an urgent clamoring that could only be quelled by his lovemaking. Even now, after a wanton excess of passion, her body throbbed, while the moist haven between her thighs ached for him, for the ecstasy only he could give her.

He had branded her his own in these past few heart-shattering days, marked her forever. For all her tender girlhood fantasies of Ranulf, she had never guessed how devastating the reality would be. The Black Dragon had seduced her very soul from her body.

And yet she could not allow Ranulf to know how deeply he affected her. She would be his slave in truth, then. No, she could only try to hold her own with this magnificent, self-assured warrior and pray it would be enough to keep her safe.

Boldly, Ariane reached down to cup his groin. She smiled at his sharp inhalation as she took his swelling manhood in her hand, her slender fingers curving around the pulsing crest as he had taught her. "Do you deny *you* want *me,* my arrogant dragon?"

His eyes blazed with fire. To her startlement, though, he rolled over her, pinning her with his weight. Kneeling between her legs then, he slipped his arms beneath her thighs, drawing them nearly up to his shoulders, opening her to his view. His golden eyes gleamed as he scrutinized her succulent pink flesh, still slick with the seed of his last possession.

"No ... Ranulf ... please ... I cannot bear any more...." She shook her head as if to deny her need, but her own voice betrayed her, and her words caught in a gasp as he lowered his head and tongued her.

She dared not look down to where the dark crown of his head was moving between her thighs. *Wicked,* Ariane thought as the sensual stroking of his mouth made her shudder. *Sinful.*

And then she had no more thought to waste on shame or sin or pride, but gave herself up to the tender, pagan assault of her dragon lord and the blazing heat he kindled in her anew.

When Ranulf finally, reluctantly, emerged from the solar the following morn, leaving Ariane to sleep off her exhaustion, he resumed his duties as lord with a vengeance. To atone for the sloth of the past days, he put his men through a strenuous practice in the training field that had even his most seasoned knights drenched in sweat and gasping for breath, as well as covered with mud from the recent spring rains.

"I had hoped you would burn your fever for the lady from your blood," Payn rasped as he bent over his sword, chest heaving, "but I can see your lusts are as hot as ever. Your loins yet drive your head."

Ranulf grinned, refusing to be provoked, and wiped his sword with his leather gauntlet before sheathing it in its scabbard. "My lusts are no excuse for these lazy whoresons to grow fat and unfit. King Henry may summon us at any moment, and I would be ready."

"We will be, unless you kill us all first," Bertran grumbled.

"Mayhap we should beg the lady to take him back so he will show us mercy," someone else chimed in, a comment that was met with ribald male laughter.

"Aye, a far more pleasurable pastime awaits you in your solar, milord."

"—where you can use your sword to better effect."

Ranulf accepted his vassals' good-natured ribbing with equanimity—until hours later, when he and Payn were quenching their thirst over flagons of ale at the high table.

"So ..." Payn asked casually, "will you let the betrothal stand?"

"Stand?"

"Will you wed the Lady Ariane now?"

Ranulf frowned. "No."

"No?" Payn's mouth curved in a lecherous grin. "There can be no doubt that your union has been consummated. The entire castle bore witness to your incarceration with her these past two days. And it is unlikely Rome will grant an annulment after you have so thoroughly sampled the lady's charms."

"Rome does not have to know."

The grin faded from the handsome knight's features. "Have I permission to speak freely, lord?"

Ranulf eyed him warily. "You know you do."

"Well then ... Are you not being overly harsh with the lady?"

"*Harsh?*" Ranulf stiffened defensively. "Time and again I have gone to heroic lengths to stay my hand and show her

and her rebellious supporters a leniency they ill deserved—
and now you say I am harsh?''

''I speak of the betrothal contract.''

''A contract that has been dissolved.'' Payn fell silent,
while Ranulf grumbled into his ale. ''As long as I have a
breath left to draw, she will not profit from her greed.''

''Are you certain it was greed, Ranulf?'' the knight
asked quietly.

No, he was no longer certain. There were times when he
wondered if he could possibly have misjudged Ariane, if her
motives were as innocent as she claimed.

The look he shot his vassal, though, was obdurate. ''You
saw for yourself her treachery. She falsified evidence of our
coupling, claiming I had ravished her when I had done my
damnedest to keep my hands off the wench.''

''Mayhap she thought it her right to require you to honor
the contract. And she told me ...''

''*What* did she tell you?'' Ranulf demanded when Payn
hesitated.

''That she would have given you her heart. I think ... she
wanted a true marriage.''

Ranulf stared a moment, then shook his head. He could
not believe Ariane's trick with the bedsheets had aught to do
with a desire for a true marriage. She could not have so
easily forgotten the contempt she held for him, nor could he.
A baseborn pretender ... without principle or honor ...

''She was serving her own mercenary interest,'' he replied,
keeping his tone curt so Payn would never suspect the doubts
he harbored, or guess the sway Ariane had begun to hold over
him. ''As my wife, under my protection, she could escape the
consequences of her father's treason. I would be responsible
for her actions then.''

''She claims her father is innocent.''

Ranulf's eyebrow shot up. ''She would, to save his skin—
and her own.''

''Perhaps ... but she could as easily disavow him. More
easily, in truth. She *would* disavow him if she were the jade
you claim. Such loyalty is admirable, you must admit.''

He shook his head stubbornly. ''Her show of loyalty to
her father could be as false and opportunistic as her lies about
our union—her support of Walter and his rebellion merely a

desire to maintain control of Claredon and avoid being held as a political hostage. If she is at all like the other highborn wenches of my experience, she would sell her soul to the highest bidder. And she would not hesitate to betray her sire if she found it to her benefit.''

''Aye, but what if she is different?''

Ranulf's eyes narrowed in reproof. He would not allow himself to consider that possibility, or to believe Ariane's claims to innocence. Yet he was not overly surprised to hear Payn championing her cause. She had bewitched everyone around her; why not his chief vassal? But it vexed him sorely to have to defend himself to his most trusted friend.

''She is no different. After three weeks in her company, I think I have her measure. Certainly I have had a taste of her nature. *If* I wanted a bride, which I do not, I would not choose a tart-tongued, defiant vixen who thinks to thwart me at every turn.''

''You agreed to wed her once.''

''Aye, when I thought her an heiress—a meek, submissive maid who would do my bidding without a battle royal.''

Payn laughed. ''Come now, Ranulf. I know you too well. You would be bored to tears with a meek maid. You enjoy the challenge of taming her, admit it.''

'Twas true. He did enjoy the challenge Ariane presented, enormously. In her company he was never, ever bored, and often he found himself relishing the sparks that flew between them, and eagerly anticipating more. With her, he needed to keep his wits about him, his reflexes keen and sharp. She was as tempestuous and unpredictable as a battle, and even more enjoyable.

''I have never had so difficult a time of bringing a wench to heel,'' Ranulf muttered.

''Or so pleasurable.''

''Very well! Or so pleasurable.''

His lips pursing, Payn refilled their tankards and appeared to choose his words carefully. ''There are advantages to wedding her, even if you already possess her castle and lands.''

''What advantages?''

''She could give you sons.''

She could give me sons now, Ranulf thought with a strange surge of delight. *But they would be bastards.*

"And if the past days are any indication, you will not find the marriage bed lacking."

His groin stirring at the hot, sweet memories of those past days, Ranulf did not reply.

"It would not hurt to think on it, Ranulf. You have earned a respite after all these years of driving yourself. You could settle back on your estates, raise your heirs, enjoy the fruits of your labors for a change."

"Settle back?"

"Aye. You would still owe Henry military service, but forty days is not much out of each year."

"Good God, what would I do if I forsook soldiering?"

Payn grinned. "I told you, administer your estates."

His lord's mouth curled in disgust.

"Do you mean to say you have never considered another sort of life for your waning years?"

Never till of late. "Seldom." Ranulf frowned. "Have you?"

"Aye. Sometimes . . . I confess there are times when I find myself weary of war and fighting and wenching."

"Wenching?" Ranulf snorted in disbelief. "The day you tire of wenching, my friend, is when your body is buried half a rod beneath the earth."

"True," Payn said thoughtfully. "But whoring is not the same as having a wife. Of late I find myself yearning for . . . something more . . . for the softness of a warm and loving woman at my side."

Softness. A warm and loving woman. Uncontrollably Ranulf thought of Ariane and flinched inwardly. There had never been any softness, any luxury or ease in his life. He wanted none. Ease led to weakness, weakness to defeat. His days were filled with fighting, just as he liked it. If sometimes he yearned for a settled life, for something more than conflict and combat to fill the long hours of each day, to ease the bleak solitude of the longer nights, he ruthlessly crushed the urge. He needed no woman's softness. He needed no woman.

"I know what it is," he observed cynically. "You are going soft in the head. Or mayhap the swordplay this morning addled your wits."

Payn raised a penetrating gaze to his lord. "Have you

never had a yearning for one special woman to share your dreams and sorrows?''

Unable to repress a sudden surge of bitterness, Ranulf looked away. He had too few dreams to offer a woman, and too much sorrow.

Payn's quiet voice continued relentlessly. "Have you never felt the press of loneliness deep in your soul?''

Ranulf scowled into his ale. He had felt the ache of loneliness all his life, even if he never allowed himself to acknowledge it. The darkness that had claimed his soul had left him empty, hollow, cold as ice inside. No woman could warm him, or erase the bleakness from his soul. Especially not a grasping wench of noble blood.

He gave a short, hollow laugh. "You talk like a ballad singer.''

"Have you?'' Payn repeated insistently.

"I learned long ago never to dream of anything but vengeance.''

"Vengeance is a cold bedfellow, my good friend. And once you achieve it, what is left?''

What indeed? he wondered. Perhaps he was getting old. Too often of late he had felt an aching weariness deep in his soul, his spirit drained by the constant struggle to prove himself. Too often he found himself questioning whether the fight held any meaning. There were times he even envied the peasants, whose sole ambition was to own a pig or a cow. They seemed satisfied with their lot. Somehow they found happiness in their simple existence. . . .

Realizing how morose his thoughts had grown, Ranulf made a soft, frustrated sound. "God's bones, if I wanted to bare my soul, I would have called for the priest!''

The intensity slowly left Payn's features, and he nodded, exhaling a soft sigh. "Well, then . . . if you refuse to wed the Lady Ariane, the honorable course would be to set her free—permit her to wed elsewhere.''

No, Ranulf thought with a fierce surge of jealousy. Ariane belonged to him. He had claimed her as his, and what was his he kept.

"She is your hostage, and a beauty. She could bring you a tidy sum, even if slightly tarnished by your usage.''

Ranulf frowned, not liking to consider what his usage had

done to her future. Yet her lack of virginity would not decrease her worth so much that she could never find a husband. She still possessed pride and grace and a haunting loveliness that would do any lord credit, and an allure that made a man burn. A discerning man might take her to wife, even without wealth and lands.

Ariane appeared just then in the hall, and Ranulf caught his breath at the sight. Her blue silk bliaud molded her tall body, defining and praising every feminine curve and emphasizing her firm, lush breasts, while the golden girdle, worn loose about the waist, draped the slender hips that had succored him so delightfully for the past several days. Her glorious hair, plaited and wound around the crown of her head, made him yearn to free it and bury his hands and face in the silken mass.

Then she turned her head, and their eyes met in a long silent moment. The seething pulse of desire that leapt between them made Ranulf's entire body clench.

It vexed him that she could make him want her so powerfully, that she could seduce him merely by being. He had thought that once he slaked his lust, he would have no trouble dismissing Ariane from his mind, and yet his damnable craving had increased tenfold. He had claimed her body as his due, without consideration for her pride or feelings, simply to prove to her and to himself that she meant naught to him. But his plan was failing wretchedly.

Ranulf cursed beneath his breath, scorning himself for his weakness. It was madness to feel as hungry and obsessed as he did. He could not allow himself to need her like this. Surrendering himself to her power could prove as perilous as turning his back on an enemy on a battlefield.

Forcing his gaze away, he took a long draught of ale, remarking to his vassal, "She is my leman, nothing more."

And she would remain nothing more to him, Ranulf swore fiercely to himself. He might use her delicious body, but he would not wed her. He might desire her, but he would not permit himself to fall deeper under her spell than he already had. He dared not risk the consequences. Never would he give any woman the power to destroy him, the way his despised father had been destroyed.

* * *

His manner bewildered Ariane. By night Ranulf played the sensual, passionate lover of her dreams; by day a near stranger.

She watched him at every opportunity, trying desperately to understand the bent of his mind, and more crucially, the hidden secrets of his heart. Toward his men and dependents, Ranulf was good natured and mild tempered, often exhibiting evidence of the formidable charm Payn had spoken of. She could see clearly why his leadership commanded their obedience and esteem, and why his magnetism drew the attention of so many eager women, unwed or wed. He was a proud, dynamic warrior, vital and charismatic, with the ability to inspire admiration and awe. His just rule and skilled administration had begun to sway even his harshest detractors. William, the young page Ranulf had promised to train, frankly adored him, but one by one, others followed suit.

Her half-brother Gilbert continued to rail against Ranulf for the shaming role he had forced upon her, and still spoke of suing him in civil court, but Claredon's villeins had accepted the new lord's authority fully, while her father's vassals had come to offer Ranulf a grudging sort of respect and even deference.

Toward her, however, his manner remained cool and detached, except when she shared his bed. That he still did not trust her was abundantly clear. Ranulf gave of himself physically, but he seemed determined to guard against any deeper form of intimacy.

His aloofness seemed calculated to keep an emotional distance between them. Was it an attempt to keep his heart safe from her? To defend that wounded organ from further hurt? She thought Payn's supposition might be accurate: Ranulf had shielded his heart with impregnable armor to keep it invulnerable. And as yet she had discovered no way to pierce it.

Observing him at arms practice with his men or at ease in the great hall, Ariane found herself envying the camaraderie they shared. When Ranulf laughed aloud, the deep, rich tones resonated with congeniality and made her hurt inside, for she realized how huge a gulf existed between them. They were enemies still, despite their physical closeness. She cherished those moments of intimacy, of reluctant tenderness, when they were alone together.

Not that she objected to the physical aspect of their relationship. Far from it. Of late it seemed all she could think about was having Ranulf between her thighs. And he *knew* it, the devil smite his arrogance.

The first time he caught her in a blatant scrutiny of him, Ariane blushed bright red. She had been admiring the way his tunic pulled tight across his broad back and shoulders, but when his bold gaze met hers, a heated memory instantly assaulted her—of Ranulf taking her last night, of his hips thrusting hard and rhythmically as he ground against her. From the scorching look he gave her, she could tell he was recalling that same moment.

His thoughts were frequently occupied in that manner, she was certain. When Ariane tried to draw him out in conversation, Ranulf avoided giving direct answers and somehow managed to turn the subject, most often distracting her with pure carnal desire. His remoteness shattered then, to their mutual satisfaction.

And then there were the times he deliberately tried to provoke her into losing her temper. She suspected he took pleasure in testing the limit of her control, for then he could use his formidable powers of persuasion to subdue her. He had merely to touch her and her body turned to flame. His caresses left her moaning and pleading with him to take her.

It frightened Ariane, how powerless she had become, to know she had been reduced to a helpless, wanton creature, craving naught but the touch of her lord. Her hunger frightened her. This need to be with him was a strange and constant ache within her. Her own vulnerability disturbed her almost as much as Ranulf's determined aloofness. She had vowed to bring him to his knees, but she was no closer to that goal now than she had ever been. And lamentably, she had few defenses against his relentless assault on her own heart; she could summon but a feeble resistance.

Even so, even though she had only her intuition to rely upon, her instincts warned her not to refuse whatever Ranulf wanted of her.

What he wanted was *her,* in his bed, willing and eager. The one time he gave her respite was during her monthly flux, which came the following week—and even then he scarcely curtailed his demands. He still required her to pleasure him as he had taught her, with hands and mouth and tongue.

His lust was insatiable, it seemed; his powers of endurance remarkable. Ariane found it nearly impossible to turn his mind to other pastimes. And unless she could manage to distract him, she knew she had no hope of controlling her own wantonness. In desperation one evening, she brought out her father's intricately carved chess pieces and polished wooden board.

Ranulf's eyes brightened at the sight, then turned doubtful. "Do you play?"

"I am credited with a measure of skill. I played regularly with my father."

And so they began a new sport in the evenings after the dinner entertainment concluded. Ranulf trounced her four out of every five matches, but Ariane defeated him often enough to make the competition challenging. In truth, the mental battles lent spice to their already spirited physical relationship.

And yet she wanted so much more. It was not simply physical desire she felt for him. Absurdly she wanted to please Ranulf, to become the instrument of his happiness. She craved his respect and trust more than anything else. She desperately wanted him to regard her with tenderness, for his eyes to soften with love.

She wanted to comfort him, wanted to prove she could be a good wife to him. She had been trained from childhood to run a vast, noble household and knew how to make his life more comfortable, if only he would permit it.

Yet Ranulf resisted her attempts to serve him willingly and see to his needs. She had to struggle for every hard-won victory, much as she'd always had to fight to gain her father's regard. Yet Ranulf was worse even than Lord Walter. He viewed her motives with suspicion when she simply asked permission to have the great hall cleaned.

"Why?" he demanded warily.

"Why?" Ariane repeated in amazement. She swept her gaze over the smokey hall, remembering how it had looked when her mother had ruled. Lady Constance would never have tolerated such filth for an instant. "Because it needs cleaning. The rushes have not been changed since before your arrival. And the rain has dampened them enough to make them smell."

"Someone else can see to it."

"No one else will be as particular as I. Serfs often carry out their duties in a haphazard fashion, and neglect the worst dirt."

"Ah, a crime indeed," Ranulf observed, his amber eyes warm and teasing as he pulled her against him.

Ariane felt her temper rising at his flippant mood. It vexed her sorely that he was trying to avoid acknowledging her competence, just as her father had always done.

Hands pressed against Ranulf's chest, she presented him an ultimatum. "If you wish me to share your bed, my lord, you will allow me to put the hall in proper order. I will not tolerate filth."

The gleam in his eye told her clearly he saw her threat as a challenge, and his lips claimed victory for the nonce.

And yet later, Ranulf yielded the skirmish. With his permission, Ariane organized the castle serfs to carry the soiled rushes out to the bailey to be burned and to gather new ones. The wooden floor was swept and scrubbed with vinegar, then sprinkled with pennyroyal to eradicate fleas and chamomile and lavender to sweeten the air and quell odors.

When she had seen to the cleaning of the floors, she ventured to suggest a more ambitious proposal—to whitewash the walls of the great hall to mask the soot and smoke stains of the past winter.

"I fail to see the need," Ranulf replied, scrutinizing the darkened walls.

"Men rarely do," Ariane retorted. "But it will freshen and brighten the hall. You will appreciate the results, I promise you."

"Had I any faith in your promises," Ranulf murmured cynically, "I would not be required to remain at Claredon to ensure its submission."

"*My* promises? You are the one who disavowed our long-standing betrothal."

"And you were the one who turned traitor and closed the

gates against me in defiance of the king's orders, and then refused to swear allegiance to me.''

It raised Ariane's hackles to be held solely at fault when Ranulf bore the greater blame. "What have you done to earn my allegiance, my lord, besides claim my father's demesne and turn me into your whore?''

Ranulf scowled at the term. "You are not my whore.''

"Your leman, then, which is the same thing.''

They broke off the discussion, both of them smoldering, with Ranulf digging in his heels and refusing to consider her request to paint the walls.

When the following day Ariane hinted she be allowed to run his household, their dispute evolved into a major argument.

"It would be less burdensome if I held the keys to the castle,'' she asserted that morning when Ranulf grumbled that she was overly concerned with castle affairs. "I could put the place to rights without having to ask your permission for every little task.''

Ranulf's eyebrows rose in disbelief. "You think for one moment that I would turn over the keys to *you?* My hostage?''

"Mayhap you intend to play chatelaine, my lord?'' Ariane responded dryly. "Somehow I cannot envision you in the role.''

His lips twitched, yet he strove to keep his expression cool. "I need no one to run my household. For that I have a seneschal.''

"Who needs supervision. A *woman's* supervision.''

Ranulf frowned suspiciously. "Would you, perchance, be trying to weasel your way into my good graces, vixen? Is this an attempt to persuade me to wed you?''

He had hit too close to the truth, but Ariane managed a casual shrug. "Claredon has been my home all my life, my lord. I do not care to see it fall to ruin. Besides, I need employment. I am bored to tears during the hours you are away from the keep.''

His mouth curved slowly, suggestively. "Then I shall have to lessen the hours I am away—and see that you remain occupied.''

'' 'Tis not what I meant, as well you know!''

When he bent to nuzzle her neck, Ariane drew away sharply. Ranulf's expression turned cool. "Denying me is hardly the way to persuade me, demoiselle. If you are wise, you will be done sulking when I return."

Ariane had been trying to comb her wild hair after a particularly passionate bout of lovemaking, and the ivory teeth snagged in a tangle with such force that it brought tears to her eyes. She very much wanted to throw the comb at his stubborn head, but she refrained, schooling herself to patience. She had known Ranulf would not relent easily.

And yet that very afternoon, he sent a cloth merchant to her so that she could choose silk threads for her ladies' embroidery, and provided the coin to pay for it.

She was moved by the gesture, and thought perhaps she might eventually succeed in wearing down his formidable defenses, if only she kept at it long enough.

She still had not determined how to solve her most crucial dilemma, however. Her twice-monthly visits to the forest had been curbed entirely and she was now weeks late. There had been time, before Ranulf's capture of Claredon, to make only a brief foray into the eastern wood to aid the inhabitants there. By now their situation would be growing grim, and they would be desperate for food.

There was no one she could entrust with such a mission, either, save for perhaps Gilbert, and she could not be certain about him. Only she and two others were privy to the secret of the haunted Claredon forest—her father and her father's chief vassal, Simon Crecy, and both men were gone. It was left to her to see to the task—and she could wait no longer.

The solution came to her one afternoon, toward the end of Ranulf's first month at Claredon, when she visited his injured squire to satisfy herself that Burc's shoulder wound was healing. The lad was still bedridden and feverish, and still in pain. The wound showed signs of putrefying, the surrounding flesh streaked with red, with yellow pus draining from beneath the scabs.

Ariane spent the afternoon in the herbal, pounding and steeping herbs to make a tea to reduce the fever and mixing a poultice to draw out the poison from the wound. But then she had to seek Ranulf's permission to administer them.

A frown darkened his features when he discovered she had

visited his squire, and his tone turned intimidating. "What meant you by defying my express orders?"

"I merely wished to see how Burc's wound fared. I feel somewhat responsible for his injury—"

"You should. You *are* responsible."

Setting her jaw, Ariane meekly lowered her gaze. "My sole wish was to help him."

"My leech can see to the boy."

"Your leech had already had his chance," Ariane retorted scornfully. "Burc desperately needs a cure. His arm will rot off, if he does not die first!" Her hands went to her hips. "And I have no intention of letting him die and giving you one more mark to hold against me."

Seeing Ranulf visibly wavering, she softened her tone. "Can you not trust me this once, Ranulf? He is suffering needlessly. I do not intend him any harm, I swear it."

"Very well," Ranulf muttered gruffly.

But he scrutinized her work, watching closely as she cleaned the wound and applied the poultice, then bandaged the boy's shoulder.

"There. He should sleep now," Ariane said quietly when she had finished.

She looked up to find Ranulf watching her with an odd expression in his eyes. "You have a gentle touch," he murmured.

His mood shifted, however, as soon as they had left the chamber and entered the solar. "I would feel your touch, wench." Ranulf drew her hand over the bulge in his tunic. "Soothe my fever, Ariane. . . ."

He kissed her then, and as always, she forgot whatever thoughts had occupied her mind . . . forgot her very name.

And yet when their passion was spent, her vital mission came rushing back to trouble her. She had to find a way to visit the east wood. Her supplies of medicines was running low. Most of the plants she needed would not mature till summer, but there were a number of shrubs and wildflowers that could be harvested now. She would ask Ranulf's permission to conduct the spring herb gathering, which would give her a legitimate excuse to leave the castle grounds. She would even offer to take her guards. Surely she could outwit them long enough to see to her errand.

That evening, when she sat across the chessboard from Ranulf, she took a deep breath, girding herself for the risk. "If I win tonight, my lord, may I ask a boon?"

"You may ask," he replied, studying the ivory pieces. "I may not grant it."

It took all her concentration and skill, but she won the match. As casually as possible, she asked permission to gather herbs in the forest.

"You wish to leave the castle grounds?" was Ranulf's first question.

"I will not attempt to escape, I give you my word."

His expression became an enigmatic mask, as if a shutter had suddenly closed. "Is this the same forest the Claredon serfs believe to be haunted by spirits and plagued by wolves?"

Abruptly Ariane lowered her gaze, not wishing him to see the lies in her eyes. "Aye, my lord."

Ranulf refrained from answering at once, conflicting emotions warring within him as he studied her serene face. *Had* he been too harsh on Ariane? Was it time to give her the chance to prove herself? Could he trust her enough to leave the castle grounds on such an innocuous errand? Or was she intent on some more nefarious purpose? . . .

"I shall be away from the castle on the morrow," he said finally, without inflection. "If it does not rain, you may go then. You will take an armed escort for safety, lest you come upon a wolf with a fancy for lovely flesh."

She was surprised Ranulf had given in with such ease, and that he had made no mention of rebels or lovers, but she would not permit herself to question her good fortune. If, for the remainder of the evening, he seemed quieter than usual, if occasionally she caught him glancing at her intently, she told herself it was purely her imagination.

The following morning she watched with relief as he rode out with a company of knights. She was grateful for his absence, for although she might outmaneuver her guards, she knew Ranulf's vigilance was another matter entirely.

She dressed in one of her oldest woolen gowns and mantle and had her palfrey saddled, along with cobs for two of her tirewomen and the castle midwife. While the women were loading the panniers on the packhorses with baskets and pottery jars and cloth bags, Ariane prepared two baskets of food-stuffs—bread and cheese and roasted meat, as well as vegetables and dried fruits. Leather flagons of wine complemented the victuals, and she included another flagon for her Norman escort.

It seemed overly cautious to be so heavily guarded by armored knights and archers on so beautiful a morning. The rains had stopped, leaving the air fresh and cool, the spring breeze scented with growing crops and wildflowers that grew in sweet profusion.

The entourage wound its way past patchwork fields of green and brown and across meadows abloom with spring flowers and wet with dew, before coming to a halt at the edge of the eastern forest.

For much of the morning, Ariane pretended to participate in the herb gathering, but as the other women spread out, she wandered further afield, venturing into the wood itself.

Ariane's heart was pounding by the time she was able to slip away from the party. No one followed her, she was certain, but she hurried nevertheless, her footsteps almost silent as they trod a carpet of moss and humus.

When she came upon the cotter's hut hidden among a tangle of birch and hawthorn, she came to a halt, her vision blurring with tears. Hazy spears of sunlight cast the clearing in a golden glow, giving it an almost heavenly aura, yet she knew, to her great sorrow, the inhabitants were afflicted by Satan's curse. Brushing the moisture from her eyes, Ariane forced herself to go on, knowing she could not afford to indulge in her own anguish.

She performed her duty and emerged from the wood some quarter hour later, her heart heavy as always when she paid her visits, and yet lighter than any time since Ranulf's capture of Claredon.

The sudden silence that greeted her when she reached the meadow disturbed her. There was no sign of her women, or of the escort Ranulf had forced upon her. They were all gone.

In their place, at the far edge of the meadow, a powerful knight in full armor sat silently astride his warhorse.

Ariane halted abruptly, staring in horror. The Black Dragon awaited her, his piercing gaze fixed on her. His helmet shielded much of his harsh face, concealing his expression, yet even at this distance, she could sense his seething fury.

"You no longer need work at all, except to fulfill your duties as leman—and it ... sharing my bed and being

Chapter 18

"Mother of God," Ariane breathed, her face draining of all color.

Ranulf sat motionless on his massive black stallion, his right hand resting on the hilt of his sword. The dark image he presented struck her as vengeful, pagan, ruthless.

The cry of a wild hawk keened over the meadow, but Ariane scarcely noticed. She stood frozen as Ranulf nudged his destrier and rode slowly forward. A constricted feeling of terror welled in her chest as he halted before her.

"What do you here, wench?" he demanded, the menace in his tone making her shiver.

She forced her reply past the dry swelling in her throat. "G-Gathering herbs, my lord."

"You were absent a long while. You should have a bountiful yield to show for your efforts. Show me the contents of your baskets."

Too paralyzed to move, she simply stared at him, sick dread twisting her insides.

"Do as I say!"

With trembling hands, she pushed back the lids of the two baskets she carried. But for a few twigs and leaves, they were empty.

Ranulf's face hardened even more, if that were possible. "My men say your baskets were filled with food. Have you mayhap been providing sustenance for my enemies?"

"N-No ... of c-course not ..."

"Do not lie to me, wench!"

Ariane flinched in fear. His face had darkened to a thundercloud, while his piercing eyes had turned to shards of ice. It had been mad to think he would believe her lame excuse, witless to have planned so poorly. She had not even prepared a proper alibi. She should at least have refilled her baskets with plants after leaving the food at the cottage.

"Know you the punishment for aiding a rebellion?"

"I was n-not attempting to aid—"

"Then what do you so far afield? Were you not plotting treachery? Consorting with traitors? If I ride into yonder wood, will I find Simon Crecy?"

She stared at Ranulf, desperately searching her mind for a reply. "I swear on my life, it has naught to do with rebellion."

"A tryst, then? The serving wench, Dena, tells me you go frequently to the woods to meet a lover." His voice was hoarse, guttural, even bitter.

Ariane sucked in her breath at the falsehood. " 'Tis a lie! I have no lover!"

His icy expression never faltered. "I wondered when I gave you leave to come here if you would act. I granted your boon—*I trusted you*—and this is how you repay me. With guile and betrayal."

She shook her head frantically. His accusations were erroneous, yet she was terrified that Ranulf would discover the truth. That he would uncover the secret she had vowed on her life to keep safe. Stupid fool! She knew how little Ranulf trusted her, but she had fallen blindly into his trap. It seemed clear now that he had lain in wait for her—and she had witlessly led him directly to this place.

"Nay, Ranulf . . . it is not what you think . . ."

"Nay?" he repeated on a harsh bark of laughter. Savage pain caught him unaware. He did not want to hear her lies. He did not want to think, to reason, to feel the terrible bitterness cutting into his heart at her betrayal. He had been willing to trust her, to give her the chance to prove her intentions, but she'd meant to deceive him from the first, plotting her furtive mission here with cunning and guile, thinking she could conceal her scheming from him. He should have relied on his intuition

"I swear to you, there is no rebellion, no lover."

He refused to believe her denials. Her fear was too real, her reaction too forced. And his sick fury too strong.

He fought the feeling desperately, struggling to overcome the suffocating pounding of his heart. She was protecting something or someone—Simon Crecy the most likely culprit. But by God, he would discover her secret if he had to comb every inch of these woods.

His violent emotions nearly strangling him, Ranulf deliberately drew on the one weapon that had stood him in good stead all his life: rage. The kind of rage that destroyed.

"Come here."

The velvet-honed voice of steel brooked no defiance, yet Ariane could only stare at him.

When she hesitated, Ranulf's eyes narrowed like twin lances. "*Now*, wench. Do not force me to pursue you."

She took a faltering step backward, her throat closing with fear.

His fury breaking, Ranulf threw his leg over the pommel and dropped to the ground. In two strides, he had reached her and caught her in his imprisoning grip, making her drop her baskets. His leather gauntlets dug into her arms in his desire to shake the truth from her. "Do not defy me, wench! I am a scant instant from striking you where you stand."

Ariane gave a cry of alarm and tried to twist from his grasp, but her resistance became a futile struggle for balance as she stumbled and fell backward. Her gown tore with a rending sound as Ranulf refused to release her. His heavy, mail-clad body followed her down, his powerful torso pinning her panting chest beneath him, his thighs spreading hers. When Ranulf drew his head back, their gazes collided, hers terrified, his hard and glittering.

Ariane whimpered. His heavy hauberk was crushing the breath from her, the links of chain mail pricking her tender flesh painfully. Tears sprang to her eyes. "Ranulf . . . you hurt me. . . ."

Fingers like steel manacles curled around her wrists and forced her arms above her head.

"Nay, I beg you. . . ."

"Aye, beg me, wench. Beg me to forgive your lies, your deceitful heart, your futile professions of innocence."

Her breath caught on a sob.

"You weep?" Ranulf demanded furiously. "I will give you something to weep about."

Pinned helplessly beneath him, Ariane tried desperately to avert her face to escape his punishing assault, but Ranulf took her mouth with hungry violence, his tongue thrusting brutally between her lips, his steel-clad hips grinding her into the unyielding ground. All she could do was endure.

When finally he raised his head to stare down at her, his breathing was harsh. Through the red haze of rage, he saw the tears brimming in her gray eyes that turned them to pools of silver, saw her bruised mouth tremble, heard her shallow gasps for air. . . .

With a violent curse, Ranulf squeezed his eyes shut. God's blood, what had come over him? What devils had invaded him that he should treat her with such brutality? He had used her roughly, might even have raped her. He had broken his own vow never to be driven to violence with a woman.

Still cursing, he rolled off her abruptly and climbed rigidly to his feet. His fists clenched, he stood over her. "Rise, damn you!"

Still finding it difficult to breathe, Ariane stared up at him fearfully. "What . . . do you mean to do?"

"I intend to search this wood, every inch of it, till I find your cohorts."

God's mercy, Ariane thought as panic welled within her. She had to do something to stop him!

She resisted with all her might as Ranulf pulled her to her feet and scooped her into his arms. But when he had set her on his destrier, an idea born of blind desperation struck her.

Without thought, with no time to consider the consequences, Ariane reacted. Catching up the reins, she whirled the stallion toward the direction of the castle and dug her heels in fiercely.

"By the hounds of hell!"

She heard Ranulf's violent oath, but never paused, not even daring to look over her shoulder to see if he followed.

The stallion fought her, unaccustomed to carrying so light a weight, but desperation lent her strength. She knew she could not hope to escape Ranulf's retribution for long, yet her mad action would serve to distract him and perhaps buy her some time. If she absconded with his horse and left him stranded far from the castle, he would be so furious at her that he might not investigate the forest. And on foot he could not search the wood as easily. She prayed to God that the delay would somehow give her the chance to warn the inhabitants to flee.

She galloped back to Claredon as if a thousand devils were on her heels, and clattered across the drawbridge, alarming the guards at the gates and causing them to blare their horns.

When she came to a plunging halt in the inner bailey, a dozen men immediately surrounded her, all demanding answers at once.

"Were you attacked?"

"The lord? What of him?"

"How many assailants?"

"Is he still where we left him with you, milady?"

Ariane dared not admit to his knights and men-at-arms that she had stolen Ranulf's warhorse. If she made him a laughingstock, he would be all the more livid. But she had to give some explanation for her frantic arrival and dishevelled appearance.

"No, no . . . nothing like that," she murmured breathlessly. "'Twas an accident, merely. I fell and caught my tunic on a branch. . . . Lord Ranulf sent me back to change. He will be along presently."

Disbelief warred on their faces, but they did not challenge her account, except to ask if their lord was on foot.

"Yes," she answered reluctantly. "Someone should take him his mount."

Several of the men stepped forward at once.

Ariane did not wait for any further questions, but accepted aid in dismounting from the huge destrier. With dread curling her stomach like acid, she went in search of Gilbert. She desperately hoped her half-brother could be trusted to do her bidding without question and carry a warning for her. She would make him swear as she had sworn. . . .

To her dismay, Gilbert was nowhere to be found. She searched the keep from top to bottom, but could find nary a sign of him. Told that he might be with the steward tallying rents, she ran back down to the bailey to search the storerooms, the chapel, the stables, the smithy, anywhere Gilbert might logically be found.

She had given up hope and was about to return to the tower and beg one of her trusted ladies to carry the warning for her, when she saw Payn FitzOsbern striding across the yard toward her. Ariane came to an abrupt halt, her heart sinking with despair at the stern look on his handsome features.

The big knight stopped before her, searching her face intently. "What is this I hear of an accident?"

She hated to lie to this man. "Not an accident, exactly. Ranulf . . ." She paused, letting him draw his own conclusions.

He frowned as his gaze went to her torn gown beneath the edges of her mantle.

"I took his horse," Ariane added lamely.

"A grave mistake, lady."

"I know, but he would have . . ."

The expression in Payn's eyes was serious yet puzzled. "I know Ranulf. He would not have harmed you without severe inducement. There must be more to the tale."

He waited patiently for an explanation that Ariane had no time to give. She twisted her fingers together in agitation. She desperately needed to find someone to carry her message of warning—

The gatekeeper's trumpet heralded the approach of another party just then, making Ariane's heart clench. Had Ranulf returned so soon?

"I must go . . ." she exclaimed and started to turn away, but Payn's hand shot out to forestall her.

"I think not, my lady."

Ariane went white. "Sir Payn, I beg you—"

"My oath is to Ranulf. I will not side with you against him. In any case, you may as well await him here. You will not escape him, you know."

She shook her head blindly. Payn had mistaken the cause of her fear. She knew she could not hope to hide from Ranulf; he would hunt her down did she even try. She was more afraid of the consequences should he learn her secret than of the Black Dragon himself.

The choice was taken from her by Ranulf's vassal, however. Unable to escape Payn's imprisoning grasp on her arm, Ariane stood trembling beside him, taking faint comfort from his nearness.

Moments later the Black Dragon rode through the gates

of the inner bailey before a silent crowd that had gathered to watch.

Coming to a halt beside Ariane, Ranulf slowly dismounted, keeping his gaze trained solely on her. His expression was cold, harsh, unforgiving, as he stood before her, a towering, vengeful figure.

Ariane quaked, knowing she was in imminent peril of death. His eyes were savage, so dark they were nearly black. She could almost see the hate simmering there.

"I will ask you but once more," Ranulf said with lethal softness, his tone devoid of all emotion. "Whom did you think to meet in the wood?"

"I cannot tell you," Ariane returned in a voice trembling with anguish. A life was at stake, the life of someone she held dearer than her own. She could not trust Ranulf's mercy enough to risk divulging her precious secret. "I swore a sacred oath. You may beat me, imprison me, threaten me with death, but I cannot tell you."

At the alternatives she presented, bleak pain flared in Ranulf's eyes for a fleeting instant, but it vanished as a mask slammed down over his features. His duty was suddenly abhorrent to him, but he could no longer allow such defiance to go unchallenged.

"Your disobedience, your willfulness, must be punished, then. Payn, you will escort this hostage to the dungeon, where she will be incarcerated till she makes a full and truthful confession and gives up the rebels she seeks to protect."

"Nay! You cannot!" The cry came from a young man who pushed through the crowd of spectators.

Gilbert, Ariane realized in despair. If only she had found him a few moments earlier.

The boy was determined to come to her defense, it seemed. "You cannot imprison my lady. I challenge you, milord! I challenge you to single combat!"

"*You* fight *me?*" Ranulf's mouth curled in disbelief as he stared down at the slightly built youth. "I will not be driven to murder a weakling still wet behind the ears."

"Coward! Black-hearted coward!"

Ranulf froze, while a collective gasp rose from the crowd. His jaw hardening, Ranulf gestured to one of his sergeants.

"Fetch him a sword. And a helm and hauberk. If he is so anxious for a fight, I will give him one."

"Sweet Mary, no!" Ariane's plea went unheeded as Ranulf watched his command being carried out and the items fetched. She tried again, this time more desperately. "My lord ... I beg you. Your quarrel is with me, not Gilbert."

"Why do you tarry?" Ranulf asked Payn coldly. "Take her to the dungeon."

"Aye, my lord," his vassal replied.

His grip on her arm tightening, Payn drew Ariane toward the tower as her defiant younger brother was fitted with a heavy tunic of chain mail.

She had to be forced up the outer steps of the keep, for she kept trying to watch over her shoulder as Gilbert bravely donned the steel helmet and accepted a knight's sword.

When Payn had led her inside the hall, Ariane put a hand over her mouth to stifle a whimper. "Ranulf will kill him. . . ."

"No, he will only teach the fool boy a lesson."

She shook her head. It was *her* fault that Gilbert's life was at risk; that his stubborn loyalty had driven an unskilled youth to challenge a mighty warlord in combat.

"The boy's discipline has naught to do with you," Payn said quietly, as if reading her mind. "He was mad to defy Ranulf like that, especially before his liegemen and serfs. A lord cannot allow his authority to be undermined so flagrantly."

"I know," Ariane whispered hoarsely. "But I am the one Ranulf should punish."

"I expect he will, demoiselle," Payn admitted in a troubled tone. "I have rarely seen Ranulf in so dangerous a mood. When he is angry he bellows and blusters and knocks heads together. When he is furious he is deadly calm."

She did not need Payn to tell her that her situation was dire.

He came to a halt at the head of the stairwell, looking down at her somberly. "I cannot help you, my lady. Your best course is to tell Ranulf what he wishes to know—the full truth. He despises dishonesty, in women most of all."

"I never lied to him," she said weakly, her heart aching.

"Have you not, my lady?" Payn replied, his tone cool.

He lit a rushlight from a burning wall torch and used it to illuminate the descent past the kitchens and down a narrow flight of stone steps. The Claredon dungeon was little more than a dark hole beneath the tower kitchens—cold and damp and crawling with vermin. Ariane shuddered as Payn stepped aside to allow her to enter the tiny cell. She had to stoop to keep her head from brushing the ceiling.

She sank to her knees and drew the edges of her mantle protectively about her, watching gratefully as he lit a torch for her. At least she would not be imprisoned in the dark.

"I am sorry it came to such a pass, truly. I had more faith in you."

She heard the disappointment in Payn's tone, the quiet censure, as he turned to go.

Ariane hung her head in despair, unable to answer. The heavy door slowly swung shut, leaving her a prisoner, alone with the echo of her own thudding heartbeat and her prayers for her foolishly loyal brother.

Outside in the bailey, Ranulf forced himself to deliver the boy's punishment. Gilbert had refused to withdraw his challenge, even when offered an opportunity to reconsider his rashness.

Ranulf had to give the lad credit for courage. Gilbert fought like one possessed, though his lack of skill was pitiful.

Holding the unfamiliar sword with two hands, the boy swung wildly, most often swishing air instead of encountering steel. Struggling under the unaccustomed weight of the hauberk, he seemed barely able to keep his footing.

Ranulf had no difficulty defending himself, easily eluding his opponent's awkward blows. He struck back with the flat of his blade, never cutting, hitting mailed thighs or torso and drawing back swiftly. The boy's body would be covered with painful bruises on the morrow, but he would live to tell the tale of his armed combat. And this youth deserved to be taught a lesson in obedience to his overlord.

The confrontation did not last much longer. Ranulf's overwhelming superiority only seemed to increase the boy's fury, but he allowed only one concession to pain; he cried out once when Ranulf's sword struck his ribs. Soon, however, Gilbert was staggering with exhaustion. Eventually he stumbled to his knees, allowing Ranulf to act. In an instant, Gilbert found a sword point pressing at the vulnerable hollow beneath his chin.

Undeterred by the blade at his throat, he glared with hate-filled eyes as he knelt in the mud, just as Ranulf remembered glaring at his despised father.

"If you harm her," Gilbert vowed hoarsely, "I will kill you! I swear, I will make you pay!"

"Are you an imbecile, boy?" Ranulf replied in an icy tone. "Or mayhap you simply have a death wish."

"A death wish, aye. I wish you dead!"

One of Ranulf's vassals stepped forward with clenched fists, as if to strike the lad. "Curb your witless tongue, insolent cur!"

Ranulf pressed the point harder against the boy's flesh.

Gilbert grimaced in pain, but kept his blazing eyes focused on Ranulf, his anguish and fury spilling out. "What kind of knight is it that makes war on women? A coward! I have the right to defend my lady sister! You forced yourself on her, dishonored her—and now sentenced her to the dungeon, and all for naught!"

He practically spat the words, ignoring the dangerous stillness that had come over his lord. Clenching his sword hilt, Ranulf inhaled a steadying breath, knowing he had to shut the boy up or deliver a more severe punishment merely to maintain his authority—if he did not wind up killing the whelp first.

Before he could decide how to act, though, Gilbert continued his blind tirade. "I tell you she is innocent! She protects no rebels!"

Ranulf went rigid, his gaze sharply focusing on Gilbert's face.

Wondering what the boy knew, he glanced grimly around them. "Leave us." With a curt gesture, Ranulf dismissed the crowd of gawkers, scattering them like sheep and sending his men about their business.

Lowering his sword point from Gilbert's throat, he grasped a handful of the boy's fair hair and forced his head up. "You know where she goes in the forest?"

"Aye . . . but I will never tell you!"

Physical threats would not break the lad, Ranulf knew. Not

when he had worked himself into such a frenzy. "Mayhap your tongue will loosen if I flog your lady before your eyes." His threats to harm Ariane were false, but if the boy believed, he would more readily divulge the secret she was keeping.

Gilbert swallowed convulsively, his eyes showing fear for the first time. After a long hesitation, he asked, "If I tell you . . . you will spare her the lash? You will bring her out of the dungeon?"

"Do not think to bargain with me, boy! Tell me what you know and we shall see."

"You can take her word as true," Gilbert muttered, lowering his gaze.

"Whom does she meet? Rebels or lover?"

Curling his bleeding mouth, he made a scoffing sound. "She knows no rebels—and you are her only lover."

"God's teeth, how can you possibly make such a claim?"

"I was the one who brought her the calf's liver to stain the bedsheets with 'virgin's blood.' "

Ranulf stared at him a long moment, knowing instinctively the boy was telling the truth. "Whom does she meet, then?" he repeated tersely.

"I know not, but 'tis not rebels. For several years she has been making those visits."

"How know you that?"

"I . . . I followed her one day."

"You spied on your lady?"

"I . . . worried for her safety. That day . . . she went alone. Usually our father, Lord Walter, accompanied her."

"I am waiting," Ranulf said warningly when the boy fell silent.

"I have kept her secret these many years." Gilbert hung his head. "She will never forgive me if I tell you."

"I will never forgive you if you do not," Ranulf replied grimly. "Or her."

A long pause followed. "She goes . . . to a hut in the forest."

"To meet someone," Ranulf prompted.

Gilbert nodded slowly. "They are women . . . two of them, I think. I was only afforded a brief glimpse. Their faces were veiled, their hands bandaged. Milord, I fear . . ." He looked up, his voice tinged with horror. "I fear they are lepers."

Chapter 19

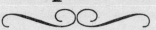

The quiet footsteps outside her cell door roused Ariane from a despondent stupor. Her head came up sharply as the heavy bar was lifted. It seemed like an eternity since Payn had left her to her cold prison, but more likely it had been scarcely an hour.

With her back rigidly pressed against the cold wall, her arms wrapped around her knees, she stared in trepidation as the door slowly swung open.

The young man who peered through the entrance was a squire of Ranulf's, Ariane realized with wary relief.

"Lord Ranulf bade me bring you to him."

"W-What . . ." she began in a croaking voice. Stopping, she swallowed the dryness in her throat and tried again. "What does he want with me?"

"I know not, my lady. I only know what he commanded. If you will come with me?"

"Please . . . could you tell me . . . my brother Gilbert. Do you know of his fate?"

"I do not believe he was harmed, but my lord had him confined."

Vastly relieved, Ariane climbed to her feet and followed the young man.

Preceding her up the narrow stone stairway, the squire led her, not to the solar, as Ariane expected, but through the great hall and outside to the bailey. Ranulf awaited her below at the foot of the tower steps, astride his destrier. She blinked at the sight of him in the bright afternoon sunlight, but forced herself to descend. He looked prepared for battle. He still wore his mail armor, with a sword belted at his waist and a shield bearing his black dragon device attached to the saddle.

Beneath his helm, his features remained expressionless,

enigmatic, as he silently reached down to her. He was offering his hand, evidently expecting her to mount before him. Ariane shivered, despite the warmth of her mantle and the balmy spring afternoon, but she obeyed, not daring to speak as Ranulf settled her sideways before him and set his warhorse in motion.

He offered no explanation as they rode through the gates and across the drawbridge, but when he turned the charger toward the east, her apprehension turned to dread. The forest! He was taking her there, she knew it. He would force her to betray what she held most dear. Sweet God in heaven . . .

"My lord . . . please . . . I beg you to turn back."

He made no reply.

"Please, Ranulf . . . I *beg* you."

"You beg me?" he repeated softly, his voice edged with ice. "Why should I listen to your pleas after the treachery you have shown?"

"It was no treachery, I swear! I will do anything you ask, give you anything you ask, if only you will not press this—"

"What have you left with which to bargain, wench? Your demesne is mine, you are mine."

His harsh retort permitted no argument. Her fingers clenching in the horse's mane, Ariane fell helplessly silent, knowing further entreaties would be futile. She could feel the steel mesh of his hauberk at her back, as cold and rigid as the man himself.

Tears of anguish slipped heedlessly down her face, tears to which Ranulf paid no heed. He hated the look he had put into her eyes—haunted, agonized—yet he forced himself to disregard it. The witch had deceived and betrayed him, and might very well be seeking to destroy him. He would not let himself soften; he did not dare, or she would exploit his weakness for her.

He needed no direction from her, but seemed to know precisely where he was headed. They crossed the meadow where Ranulf had discovered her that morn, and plunged into the wood. Sunlight speared through tall oaks and birches, the branches adorned with the new leaves of spring.

Ariane's terror grew with each step they traveled, a terror that communicated itself to their mount. The horse snorted

and pranced, requiring Ranulf to resort to the sharp discipline
of bit and spur.

The glade grew thicker the deeper they rode, until finally
it seemed to close around them. Ranulf pressed on, through
a narrow opening in a dense thicket. When the cotter's hut
came into view, he drew the destrier to a halt.

The hovel was old and shabbily constructed of wattle and
daub, with a thatched roof that badly needed patching. Shuttered, it had a look of desertion about it, an aura of death.

"What is this place?" Ranulf demanded quietly.

Ariane could not speak. Her breath was trapped in her
lungs by a terrible constriction; a vise gripped her heart like
a gauntleted fist.

She was sobbing mutely now, yet Ranulf hardened his
heart against her tears. He would not permit her to sway him
with such ploys, or to manipulate him into clemency. She
could protect herself with such tactics no longer. He drew
his sword.

"You there within the hut! Show yourselves or face the
wrath of the lord of Claredon!"

His demand was met with silence at first. Moments later,
however, a hinge creaked as the dilapidated door swung
inward.

Ranulf's hand tightened around his sword hilt as a shadowed figure stepped out into the light, gowned in black.

She was tall for a woman, and carried her slender form
with a familiar regal grace. Her face was veiled, her hands
wrapped in dark bandages.

"My lord Ranulf," she said in a sweet, low voice, sweeping him a deferential curtsey. "How may I serve you?"

Ariane choked on a strangled sob and bowed her head.
"Dear God, forgive me," she whispered.

"Do not blame yourself, daughter. It was only a matter of
time before we were discovered."

Raising her hands, the woman lifted her veil to expose her
face. The aging features must have been beautiful once, in
her youth. Yet her ravaged skin showed the unmistakable
signs of leprosy.

Ranulf recoiled at the sight, feeling as if a fist had plowed
into his stomach. Even battle-hardened as he was, he could
not be sanguine about the dread disease. And yet it was not

the affliction that shocked him to the core, but the identity of the woman herself.

She had been present at his betrothal five years earlier, seated at a place of honor at the dais. He had known her as the lady of Claredon, then. The wife of Lord Walter, the mother of his intended bride.

"My Lady Constance?" he breathed when he could find his voice.

Ariane's mother smiled faintly. "As you see, my lord. I regret I could not greet you under ... happier circumstances."

"They told me ... you were dead."

"I am—to the world. I live hidden here in the forest, with my tirewoman."

"But ... why?" was all Ranulf could think of to say. His head reeled, not only from the startling truth, but from the implications. Was this the secret Ariane had kept from him?

Another dry smile touched the Lady Constance's lips. "Because I would not be welcomed elsewhere. You are aware, I am certain, of the treatment lepers receive at the hands of the unafflicted."

Yes, he was aware. The malady was so feared, the unfortunate victims were often hunted from their homes and cast out from civilization, some even stoned to death.

She gestured graciously at the hut behind her. "I would invite you into my humble abode to partake of a glass of wine, my lord, but such close contact would not be wise. In truth, I usually do not allow Ariane to come as close as you are now, for fear of contamination."

Ranulf shook his head mutely in an effort to clear it. All he could focus on was Ariane—and what her forays here meant.

He stared down at her bent head, but with her sitting sideways in the saddle before him, all he could see was her profile. Catching her chin in his gloved fingers, he turned her face around to his, gazing intently into her tear-filled eyes. "This is your secret?"

Swallowing a sob, she nodded, trying earnestly to stem her weeping. Yes, this was her terrible secret: that her mother had not perished years before as the world believed, but suffered from a disease that roused horror and dread among villeins and nobles alike.

"I had to come. They needed food. . . . It had been so long . . . their need was dire."

A huge constriction lifted from Ranulf's chest; the anger, the pain, the bitterness, began to unravel. He felt shock and pity that so lovely a lady as Constance of Claredon had been ravaged by so terrible a disease, yet his relief was greater, more fierce. Relief that Ariane had not betrayed him. She had made her secret forays to this wood to succor her mother, not to consort with rebels or tryst with a lover. *She had not betrayed him.*

Forcibly he returned his attention to her mother, recalling the person Constance had once been. He remembered a gracious gentlewoman, a lovely soft-spoken lady whose kind smile radiated a sweetness and warmth he did not think contrived. He had felt then as if he could almost trust her, she who trusted no woman. He recalled foolishly reflecting how different his life might have been had his own faithless mother resembled Lady Constance.

"How came you to be stricken?" he made himself ask.

"Nursing my son, my lord. Jocelin returned from the Holy Land with the affliction, and I could not desert him. A mother's love knows no wisdom, I fear."

A mother's love? He had never known such a thing.

"Some say leprosy is God's punishment for mortal sin."

Ariane made a choked sound of protest. "Then God is blind and cruel!" she retorted passionately, not caring if her words were blasphemous. "My mother was guilty only of the sin of caring too much. And my brother . . . he went on holy pilgrimage as God's servant. Was *that* a sin?"

"Ariane," Lady Constance said gently.

"Did Jocelin die of the disease?" Ranulf asked. "I understood he was killed in battle."

Pain flickered in the Lady Constance's gray eyes, so much like her daughter's. "Yes, in battle. He was a soldier, his father's son, who chose to end his young life honorably in combat rather than endure his wasted body. Would that I had the same choice."

"No, Mother!"

Constance's chapped lips curved in a sad smile. "Bless you, daughter, you have been my strength. If not for you, I could not have borne it." It was said sweetly, without much bitterness. "In truth, it is harder to lose a child than to face one's own mortality. I have had a good life. I am prepared for God's kingdom."

Ariane's voice caught on a sob.

"There are two of you who live here?" Ranulf asked quietly.

"My woman, Hertha, a loyal servant. Another blessing. If not for her, my life would be very hard indeed. Hertha?"

An elderly, gray-haired crone, stooped with age, emerged from the hut, supporting herself with a cane, and made a deep curtsey to the new lord of Claredon. She did not seem to be suffering from the dread disease, Ranulf noted.

Constance explained. "My husband, Walter, was loath to condemn me to a leper's life. He allowed me to take refuge here, while telling the world I had been slain by outlaws during a journey. And reports were put about of a haunted wood—to protect me from the villeins. They would drive out anyone suspected of being a leper, even if I was once their lady."

Ranulf remembered the tale Ariane had once offered him of a haunted wood, a tale he had scorned as false. And yet the threat of evil spirits would be highly effective in keeping superstitious serfs away.

"And so . . ." the Lady Constance murmured, "now that you know our secret, my lord, will you banish us from your demesne?"

Slowly, Ranulf sheathed his sword, even as Ariane turned pleading eyes to him. "Ranulf, *please* . . . I beg you for mercy. She will die if you turn her out! I will do anything you ask, if you will only spare her."

His mouth tightened momentarily. How could she believe he would condemn this poor soul to so cruel a fate? Life in a hellish leper village would be far worse than the miserable existence she endured now. Her husband and daughter had gone to great lengths to protect her, and he would not be the one to destroy their efforts.

"I wish you no ill, my lady," he replied softly. "I see no reason the secret must be revealed. Or why you cannot go on as before."

At his answer, he felt Ariane's taut body sag against him in relief, while she buried her face in her hands. Attempting to disregard her display of emotion, he gazed at her lady mother somberly.

"Your daughter may bring you food, if she has a proper escort to the edge of the forest. I do not like the notion of her roaming freely, for she might come to harm."

"We would be grateful, my lord. Our supplies have run low since ... since your arrival," Lady Constance concluded tactfully.

Since his seizing of Claredon, she had meant to say, Ranulf knew. "I regret that I can do so little for you," he observed truthfully. He would have liked to aid this gracious lady in her valiant struggle. She was a brave woman facing a terrible fate, alone in the world but for one loyal servant and a devoted daughter.

"It will be enough that you permit my daughter to visit occasionally. We seldom receive company."

Ariane's expression of appreciation was far more fervent. "Ranulf ..." she rasped, "my lord, I thank you." Her husky voice shook with relief, but it was her accompanying gesture that startled him: she clutched at his gloved hand and drew it to her lips.

Ranulf extricated his hand uneasily. Such abject gratitude disquieted him. He was grateful himself when Lady Constance spoke.

"Ariane tells me you have assumed control of Claredon," she said quietly. "Can you tell me, my lord ... has there been any word of my husband?" For the first time since this disturbing interview began, she appeared less than stalwart.

Ranulf did not want to reveal the harsh truth, and yet there was no point in withholding it and raising false hopes. "I regret, my lady, that Lord Walter has been charged with treason for conspiring with Hugh Mortimer and is presently being besieged at Bridgenorth by King Henry."

She bit her lip. "I know little of politics, I fear, but I do not believe my husband to be a traitor."

Ariane had said precisely the same thing about the man, Ranulf reflected, feeling an unfamiliar pang of envy. Two such loyal woman were novel in his experience. "Henry is a just ruler. He will not act without reasonable proof of guilt."

Lady Constance nodded in resignation and surprised him with her next words. "I regret that circumstances required

the cancellation of your betrothal to my daughter. I would
have been honored to call you my son by marriage.''

She seemed sincere, Ranulf realized with startled awareness. Would she view him so favorably if she knew how he
had dealt with her daughter—forcing Ariane to serve as slave
and leman?

"We should be on our way," he said, more gruffly than
he intended.

Lady Constance smiled a little. ''As you will, my lord.
But please accept my heartfelt gratitude. Take care, my
daughter.''

Ranulf reined back the destrier and turned toward Claredon
Keep. He was keenly aware that Ariane gazed back over his
shoulder until they had passed through the concealing thicket
and were well out of sight of her mother. Then, with a small
sniff, she wiped her damp eyes on her sleeve and faced
forward.

They rode in silence for a time, the horse's hooves quietly
plodding along the forest floor, while Ranulf's thoughts
whirled. He was conscious of a searing relief welling
within him.

There was no band of rebels plotting his overthrow. Ariane
had no secret lover. Her sin was one of devotion and loyalty,
not betrayal. He understood now why she had remained silent, refusing to reveal her secret even under threat of imprisonment. She had not been truthful, yet neither had she lied
to him. She had said she could not break a sacred oath.

Ranulf's mouth twisted bitterly. If Ariane considered sacred oaths inviolate, she would be the first lady of her rank
to do so. In his experience, most would think nothing of
sacrificing their dearest kin for political expediency or personal gain.

It was some moments longer before he heard her say quietly, ''My lord, did you truly mean it? You will not banish
her?''

Ariane turned again in the saddle to gaze up at him. Ranulf
had agreed to keep their terrible secret, yet she needed to
hear his assurances once more, so the sick dread would leave
her. So she could be rid of the gnawing fear that had shredded
her nerves over the past weeks. She could bear anything if
only she could be certain her mother was safe.

He drew the destrier to a halt. They had reached the edge of the wood. Beyond lay a green, sun-warmed meadow carpeted with May wildflowers and splashed with color: pale daisies, purple speedwell, jonquil celandine, and daffodils.

His golden eyes were soft and muted as he gazed down at her. "Why did you hide the truth from me? Why did you not come to me? I have shown you lenience in the past, when you asked."

"I dared not risk it. I could not be certain. . . . You might even have wished her dead."

Ranulf's mouth curled faintly. "Have the tales you heard of the Black Dragon painted me so vicious?"

Ariane hung her head. "I could not chance it, my lord. And I had sworn an oath. . . ."

"You could not trust me."

"No, my lord." The words were a mere whisper.

Ranulf bit back a reply. It struck him as ironic to be chastising her for a lack of trust when he had shown her so little.

Her fingers clenched in her woolen tunic, twisting the fabric. "God is cruel. My mother never deserved such a terrible fate. She is the kindest, most gentle . . ." Ariane's voice broke on a sob. Turning her face into his massive chest, she pressed her forehead against his chain mail hauberk.

Ranulf could not reply. He had long ago learned not to rail against the heartless capriciousness of fate. Ariane was weeping again, softly. His arms came around her tentatively. He felt choked with tenderness and pity and despair. Her very forlornness touched his heart as nothing had in years.

He did not understand what drove him to try and comfort her. He had thought every trace of gentleness exorcised by the years of anger and bitterness. But perhaps he was wrong. The burst of emotion that surged through him now was so strong it took his breath away.

For a long moment, he simply held her, until her shuddering breaths subsided, until her body quieted. Slowly then he drew off his left glove. His hand rose to her cheek, caressing gently, his thumb stroking softly, tantalizingly, over her trembling lower lip.

Drawing a shaky breath, Ariane raised her gaze to his.

Her luminous eyes were swollen and tearful, filled with doubt, with pain. He badly wanted to ease that pain, to soothe her doubts, to comfort her. He had never touched a woman merely to offer comfort, without lust driving him. He did not know how. Yet he would like to try. With his head and much of his face encased in steel, though, he knew not if he could even kiss her.

Despite the confining restriction of his helm, he bent his head.

Her lips were petal soft, full and lush, trembling and warm.

"Ranulf . . ." she breathed.

Ariane closed her eyes. She was so grateful to him, so thankful. She needed to show her gratitude. She needed him to hold her, to drive the awful aching emptiness away. She needed to be with him.

Reaching out, she captured his hand and drew it to her breast.

Ranulf inhaled sharply at her action, a swift, hoarse intake of breath. Ariane had never initiated their lovemaking. He had always been forced to rely on his sensual skill to compel her surrender. Yet he knew now, as she met his questing gaze, that she would need no persuasion. He could feel her nipples beneath the wool of her torn tunic, peaked and pebble hard with desire, could see the heat of need in her shimmering eyes, could sense the sudden urgency quivering though her body as she reached for his helmet.

With anxious hands she tried to lift it from his head, but succeeded only in knocking it askew. Her clumsiness touched Ranulf unexpectedly, and he smiled—his beautiful, heartbreaking smile.

"Allow me, sweeting." Tearing at the helm himself, he drew it off and then tugged back his mail coif.

At once, Ariane raised her mouth to his, eager for his kiss.

Startling tenderness assailed him, a sweet balm after the wealth of raw anger, of bitter fury, of agonizing doubt. He would not deny her need, or his. He wanted her, more than he had ever wanted any woman. He wanted to feel her warm and soft in his hands, wanted to make her respond to him with passion. He ached to touch her, to have her touch him. And yet he wanted to draw out the moment. She was offering herself to him fully, and he wanted to savor his victory.

He held back, meeting her questioning gaze, relishing her

beauty, treasuring the way the sunlight filtered through the arch of trees above them to kiss her lovely face.

"Ranulf . . ." she murmured more urgently.

His hand cradled her cheek as he bent his head again. The quiver of her mouth beneath his sent little shocks of pleasure rippling through him. Her body, soft and yielding in his arms, filled him with desire. Yet still he held back. Gentling his kiss, he slanted his lips over hers, gliding his tongue into her warmth, stroking the soft openness.

Ariane gave a faint moan of frustration, impatient with his delaying tactics. She pressed against him, straining toward his seeking mouth, blindly searching. It was only when she fumbled beneath the split skirt of his hauberk that he broke the embrace.

"Ranulf . . . please . . . take me . . . here . . . now . . ."

"Aye, sweeting . . . presently."

Urging his horse forward, he found a patch of grassy meadow partially surrounded by a wooded copse, sheltered from prying eyes. It seemed an idyllic setting for a lovers' tryst—fresh and sweet and tranquil. Above in a gentle blue sky, fleecy clouds floated by, while the melody of a thrush serenaded them sweetly.

Dismounting, Ranulf set his helmet on the ground, then turning to Ariane, reached up for her.

She came willingly, eagerly, into his embrace, her mouth finding his unerringly as her arms encircled his neck.

Her naked urgency made Ranulf shake his head as he whispered against her lips, "Go slowly, sweeting . . . We have time . . . all the time we need."

Ariane took a deep, steadying breath as she allowed him to set her on her feet. She did not think she could wait or find the discipline to go slowly with this fierce craving burning inside her, but she would try.

Quelling her need, her turbulent emotions, with supreme effort, she forced herself to concentrate on the difficult task of undressing Ranulf . . . helping him to remove his heavy mail armor, and then his clothing beneath. Yet when his undertunic had been tossed aside, she couldn't deny herself the pleasure of pressing her lips against his chest, relishing the powerful expanse of naked flesh. Beneath the soft whorls of hair, she could feel his hot skin, the tightly curving muscles.

She felt his body tighten, and gazed up at him longingly. His thick raven hair glinted with blue highlights in the sun, while the harsh angles of his face had softened with tenderness. His amber eyes seemed warm as melted honey, deep enough to drown in.

Her trembling fingers loosened his braies and drew them down over his narrow hips and strong thighs. Finally, at last, he stood naked before her, detailed by the probing sunlight. Beautiful, pagan, powerful. All rippling muscle and sinew. His erection swollen thick and thrusting. Ariane drew a sharp breath at the sight.

He reached for her then.

" 'Tis my turn now," he murmured, his voice a husky, erotic whisper.

And yet to her frustration and dismay, Ranulf seemed content to draw out the process. First he unclasped her mantle and laid it on the grass to make a pallet. Then he slowly, sensually, attended to her clothing. It was long, long moments later before he had partially completed his task and she stood clad only in her filmy chemise.

He turned his attention to her hair next, taking down the coiled braids. His eyes uncharacteristically soft, he combed his fingers slowly through the luxuriant tresses, till it gleamed a glorious, shimmering mass of pale copper, falling around her shoulders in lovely, wanton disorder.

How can a man so harsh, so ruthless, be so gentle? Ariane wondered dazedly.

For a moment Ranulf gathered her close and simply breathed in the fragrance of her hair, his fingers continuing their stroking. Presently, finally, he bent to catch the hem of her chemise and drew the garment over her head, leaving her completely naked.

He began touching her elsewhere then, everywhere, caressing her skin ... the fine-boned curves and hollows of her face ... the thickly beating pulse in her throat ... the delicate lines of her body ... the gently trembling limbs ... rising again to her breasts.

Almost reverently Ranulf cupped the soft, graceful swells beneath his palms. They were high, firm, made as though to fit in a man's hand. His fingers spread, fanning over her breasts in deepening strokes, his thumbs passing in scorching circles over her nipples.

Ariane lost pace with her breath. Blindly, her hands caught in Ranulf's hair, pulling his head down to hers. "Kiss me . . . please, *please* . . ."

He complied . . . but only for a tantalizing instant. His mouth brushed hers fleetingly, and then drew back . . . even as he skimmed his palm downward over her flat belly. His hand lightly cupped the rise of her silky curls, his sensitive fingers discovering the warmth below. Ariane moaned.

He barely touched her sex, barely brushed the moist flesh, and yet the effect was like a jolt of lightening, inciting a throbbing ache in her lower body, teasing the feverish flush of her skin. Her breathing deepened in quick and steady arousal, while her hips strained against his hand, seeking release from the fiery sensations streaking through her.

This time he allowed it when she dragged him back into the kiss, when she arched into him, her seeking mouth insistent and urgent. And yet he refused to give in to her demands. He maintained control, defining the pressure and rhythm.

His restraint was pure torment.

Her fingers clenched in Ranulf's hair until finally he deepened the kiss with satisfying force. The sweetly probing eroticism of his tongue elicited small involuntary whimpers from her throat. His lips stroked against hers, drinking in her desperation, feeding the fire flowing between them. Ariane shuddered helplessly. His fingers were moving on her back, sending cascades of shivers through her.

"I crave you. . . ."

When he spoke the words against her lips, she answered him thickly, her head swimming. "Yes . . . yes . . ."

Her cheeks were hotly flushed, her knees weak. When he broke from her, she was trembling so badly that he had to support her with his hands.

With unhurried grace, Ranulf led her to the bed he had made with her mantle and settled himself there, then reached his hand up to her. Shaken by the pleasure-promise in his keen golden eyes, Ariane sank to her knees beside him.

Perhaps it was the breath of spring breeze that cooled her fevered skin, perhaps it was the bright look of male triumph in Ranulf's eyes, but somehow she found the will to temper her desire, to control her fierce need.

Dragging in a shuddering breath, she pressed her palms against his naked chest, urging him backward, to lie on the mantle. She desperately wanted to please him, wanted to give to him.

The scent of spring grass and wildflowers rose up to meet them; the wash of sunlight warmed their skin. Ranulf lay back unprotesting, letting his senses feast: the soft wool beneath his scarred back, the cool cascade of her hair as she bent over him, the warmth of her lips as she scattered hot, open kisses over his chest.

Shutting his eyes, Ranulf let his head fall back. In all his experience, he had never made love like this. He had taken wenches in the fields, a quick frenzied coupling, the rutting of animals. But never had he known anything like this ... this sweetness and warmth, this gentleness. This aching need. This melding of desire between two people. The latent tenderness he felt was a bewildering, swelling pain within his chest.

Her hair tumbled forward to spill over him, and he clutched at it, his fingers twining in the silken tresses, as a drowning man clings to a solitary rock in the midst of a crashing sea.

Ariane felt his surrender, felt the hammering of his pulse beneath her lips as they pressed against a battle scar, felt the shudder that passed through him. The scent of his skin was intoxication, his heat a drugging lure.

Some ancient primitive force controlled her hands as she drew them over his beautiful body, feeling the hard lines of bone and muscle and taut sinew beneath her palms, caressing his burning skin. When she reached his groin, her fingers closed brazenly over his rigid member.

The thick length surged in her hand, hot and pulsing and iron hard.

Hardly daring to breathe, she bent closer and touched the thick column gently with her lips.

His chest muscles contracted harshly.

Her tongue gently flicked and circled the aching flesh.

His breathing sharpened.

At his helpless response, she became the aggressor, tasting, sampling, tormenting, using her lips and tongue eagerly, willingly. Reveling in the dark flush of passion on his harsh face, she sucked at him brazenly, first the huge swollen tip, then deeper, taking him slowly, fully in her mouth, driving him mad with need.

His chest rising harshly, Ranulf clenched his fists in the wool and arched his back, his hips straining helplessly against the velvet torment of her mouth, his blood pounding through his veins. In moments the tremors that racked his body, his fierce need to have her, became too much to bear. He wanted, *needed*, to be joined to her.

"Ride me," he whispered thickly as his grip tightened in her hair.

Urgently, with barely controlled passion, he drew her upward, till she half lay upon him, her lush breasts pillowed in his chest. Settling one leg over his hips, Ariane mounted him, lowering herself onto his pulsing arousal.

At the sudden penetrating sensation, she drew a sharp, shuddering gasp of pleasure that disturbed the quiet of the lengthening day. Astride his thighs, his powerful erection deep within her, she felt fulfilled, complete, infused with a great inner joy at the pleasure she knew she was giving him, at the pleasure he was giving her.

When his hands covered her aching breasts, her passion-hazed glance locked with his. He was so hard inside her, so fiery hot, an exquisite shaft of fire spearing through her. Her back arching gracefully, she rode him as he had taught her, rocking against him, trying desperately to ease the throbbing, fevered ache he had kindled deep within her.

His teeth bared, Ranulf lost his masterful control. Blindly, his hands moved from her breasts to grip her buttocks, working her up and down in rhythm with his thrusts, his hips pumping, his manhood surging deep into her sleek, hot sheath.

"Ranullllf . . ." Her exhalation was a jarring series of broken gasps as he thrust himself to the hilt, impaling her.

In only moments the rapturous shudders began. He convulsed first; his body contracted like a bow, catching Ariane in the wrenching release. His hoarse groan mingled with her rasping sob as searing ecstasy erupted between them.

When the storm at last subsided, Ranulf caught her as she fell weakly into his arms, holding her shaking body. Yet he scarcely had the power to breathe. His own body limp, drained, his chest heaving, he lay there with his eyes closed as the fierce explosions slowly faded.

His hand cradled her throat, soothing her thundering pulse-beat, while he attempted to make sense of the foreign emotions rioting through him. He felt a tranquility, a sense of utter peacefulness, that was completely alien to him. He had never known peace. Yet here, in the soft-dying day, with this woman in his arms, he could almost forget his cruel past, could almost believe his future held more than harsh reality.

Gently, reverently, Ranulf brushed away a sweat-dewed tress that clung to the curve of her jaw, his lips pressing against her temple. He heard her soft sigh, and his chest constricted.

It was the gentleness that startled him most. She made him want to shower her with gentleness. Tenderness ran through him, hot, honeyed, unfamiliar, loosening something inside him, melting the edges of the ice that had encased his heart for so long. He had comforted Ariane, driven away her tears with his passion, but her ardent, needy response had affected him in ways he could not begin to understand.

Pulling her close, his hand gentle on her back, Ranulf stroked her silken skin, drifting slowly up and down. What was it about this woman that turned his vitals inside out? That made him long to hold and comfort her? That aroused this strange yearning within him, a sense of wonder about what might have been, a hope for what the future might embrace? What made him hunger to draw out the blissful, soothing peace enveloping him now?

Ranulf exhaled quietly, in a deep sigh. Perhaps he was dreaming impossibilities, indulging in whimsical fantasy, but for now he wanted to believe that the peace of this moment could last.

Chapter 20

The peace lingered as the day waned. Her body cradled by his, Ariane and Ranulf lay entwined, loath to disturb the enchanted moment.

"I would that we could stay here always," she murmured on a sigh, voicing Ranulf's own bemused thoughts.

She wanted nothing to spoil the languor that had stolen over her, the cocoon of numbing warmth. Nestled in his embrace, his heat at her back, his muscle-corded arms wrapped around her, she could almost pretend they were not enemies. That he was not her vengeful overlord, she his powerless hostage.

His hand on her breast, absently caressing, was soothing rather than arousing as it drifted over her skin, a mere reminder of the quivering heights of ecstasy to which he had carried her a short while ago. How strange to think she had once feared those strong warrior's hands, when all they had done was give such pleasure. His hands could be relentless when they drove her to the peak of passion, yet they could be gentle, too.

She could not comprehend his current gentleness, though, could not fathom Ranulf in this present mood. He held her like a cherished loved one, as if she were something infinitely lovely, infinitely precious. As if his sole thought was to offer comfort.

Ariane accepted his solace thankfully. She had never dreamed it could be so wonderful to lean against someone else's strength. Her gratitude to Ranulf for his leniency was profound; her heart felt unburdened, now that she knew her mother would be safe from his reprisals. And yet it was his unspoken compassion that fortified her, that bolstered her courage and her will to endure, that renewed her resolve to prevail after the past tumultuous weeks of adversity.

"Have you attempted to find a cure?" he asked quietly after a time.

Ariane sighed again, knowing he was thinking of her mother's affliction. "We tried countless herbs and remedies over the years. My mother is skilled in the healing arts, and she taught me some of what she knows, but this disease is far beyond our skills. I fear it is hopeless."

Wearily she closed her eyes. There was no known cure for leprosy. Sometimes the malady improved on its own or by God's grace. More often, the victim's flesh rotted away, eventually ending in death.

"We had hoped ... prayed ... that here in this wood, protected from worldly concerns, she might recover, but as yet there has been no improvement. The only promising sign is that her condition has not worsened. Yet my lord father ..."

"What of your father?"

"He lost faith long ago. He became so ... bitter after losing both his son and wife. And as the years passed, he seemed no longer to care." Ariane hesitated, biting her lip. "How I wish that I had been born a son instead of a disappointing daughter."

"Disappointing?"

She nodded mutely, her cheek rubbing softly against Ranulf's arm, which pillowed her head. She had never signified much to her father, not a tithe of what his only son had meant to him. She doubted Walter was even aware of making her feel inferior for having been born female, and yet it had affected her every endeavor her life long. She had tried desperately to be a good daughter in all things, including her betrothal to Ranulf.

"I failed my father," she said in a low voice. "Since I was not a son, I could not think to assume his demesne, not without a husband to rule for me." Ariane gave a shallow laugh. "I could not hold his castle in his absence as he charged me to. I could not even preserve the betrothal he arranged."

Ranulf felt a swift stab of guilt at her quiet lament, yet he did not wish to dwell on his seizure of Claredon or his repudi-

ation of their betrothal. "It seems to me you have done well
by him, within the constraints of your gender."

"Aye, I suppose. I have striven to do my best. Yet it is a
man's world, ruled by men. I would that I were one."

He heard the quiver of hurt and regret in her voice, a hurt
that echoed keenly the feelings locked deep in his own heart.
He could hear what she had not said; how she had tried to
be the perfect daughter, holding herself to impossibly high
standards in hopes of attracting her father's notice.

Raising himself on one elbow, Ranulf cupped her chin
and turned her face up to his. "I am glad you are not a
man, *chérie*."

His smile, soft and poignant, failed to hearten her. Seeing
the look of bleakness in her eyes, Ranulf stroked the delicate
line of her jaw, wishing he could ease her despair. He felt a
primal, almost savage protectiveness toward her, an emotion
he had never felt for any woman but her.

Just then the sinking sun descended behind the gnarled
oaks that arched high over the verge of the meadow. Ariane
shivered as the lengthening shadows probed the bed where
they lay. Solicitously Ranulf drew an edge of the mantle over
her and wrapped his arms more tightly about her.

Resting his chin lightly on her hair, he gazed unseeingly
out across their quiet haven. Ariane had confided her fears
for her mother, confessed to her strained relationship with
her father, arousing painful memories of his own past. Like
she, he knew the futility of yearning for something he could
never have. As a boy, he had desperately wanted the man
who was his father to look at him once, just once, without
hatred, without cursing him as "devil's spawn." It was not
even affection he coveted, just simple acknowledgement of
his existence.

"I once wished," Ranulf murmured tonelessly, "that I
could be anyone but who I was . . . the adulterine whelp of
a faithless wanton . . ."

His voice was low, remote, devoid of feeling, and yet Ariane could hear the quiet ache of things left unsaid. She sensed
in him a loneliness even greater than her own, a bleak despair
that had festered within his soul. She went still, wondering
if he would say more.

The silence stretched out between them. When he did not speak, she said softly, "Tell me."

Disengaging himself from their embrace, Ranulf drew away, rolling onto his back. Ariane felt the absence of his warmth keenly.

Her own woes forgotten, she turned in his arms, gazing at his harsh, handsome face. His eyes were closed, one corded forearm resting on his forehead.

"I was no man's son," he said finally.

The quiet anguish in his voice made her yearn to thread her fingers through his hair and draw his head protectively to her breast. Yet she was far from certain he would accept comfort from her. Tentatively she reached up, her fingers stroking his face, tracing its harsh angles and planes. She felt him tense for an instant, but he did not reject her touch.

"You were born at Vernay?" she prompted gently.

"Aye. I never knew my lady mother. She has been dead these twenty years. I was taken from her and given into a nurse's care at my birth."

"That was when your father imprisoned her?"

The corners of his mouth twisted. "Who told you such?"

"Sir Payn. He said ... your father abused you sorely when you were a child, in retribution for your mother's sins. And ... I have seen the scars ... touched them."

"Ah, yes, my scars. The sign of my purification." His chest moved with quiet laughter, bleak and bitter. He could still recall the terror as he knelt trembling before his father, as he fought back screams of pain. "My earliest memories are of my father's beatings. They were intended to punish my mother for her adultery, to drive the devil from me, her son."

Beatings, Ariane thought with silent anguish, which had left cruel scars on Ranulf's soul as well as his body.

"I thought him right to wish the devil from me."

"No!" Ariane cried softly. "You were but a child, a defenseless innocent. A helpless pawn at the mercy of a cruel monster!"

"Aye, I was defenseless. My lordly sire was bitter and hate filled and maddened with rage."

He stared into the fading light above her head, his eyes dry and burning, his chest and throat tight with a familiar pain. "I was sent to foster with another lord when I was six.

God's blood, how glad I was to escape my father! I hated him. I cannot count the times I wished him dead.''

"But . . . you did not kill him when the chance came.''

Ranulf's jaw hardened reflexively as he remembered the years when he had lived and breathed for revenge, the deprivation that had fired his determination to become more powerful than his despised father.

"No, though I craved to. He refused to give me my due, casting me off like so much offal. So I pledged my sword to Henry and gained sanction to recoup what was taken from me. I fought for what should have been mine by right, and defeated my own father in combat.''

Ranulf laughed softly, humorlessly. "I pretended to feel no guilt for my revenge, but I could not escape it. I could not kill him. *I stayed my hand.* After all he had done to me, I still could not bring myself to strike the final blow.''

Ariane's throat tightened with a fierce ache. "My father always said . . . it takes a valiant man to show mercy to his bitter enemies.''

"Valiant? Is it valiant to wish your sire dead?''

"You had good cause!''

Ariane watched Ranulf with sorrow and helpless despair, knowing that with every word he bound himself more firmly in her heart. She could only imagine what he had endured, the terrible guilt he had been made to feel for his mother's sins, the desperate loneliness of his life as a despised outcast. Yet he had no need to tell her of the pain inside him, the helplessness, the fear; she felt them.

She was filled suddenly with such tenderness for him that she ached with it. She buried her face in his neck, her arms holding him tightly because she thought she might weep. He was a man in pain, and she only wanted to help him heal.

"You were not to blame for your mother's sins,'' she whispered hoarsely, "or your father's madness.''

Extricating himself from her embrace, Ranulf sat up abruptly, turning his back to her. His chest felt tight and full, welling with too much emotion.

Why had he confessed his most private anguish?

Because you wanted her to understand, a mocking voice whispered in his mind. *You wanted her to know the demons*

*that shaped you and made you into the man you are now,
hard, ruthless, devoid of softness.*

He felt her slim arms encircle him, felt her cheek press
softly against the naked scars of his back. He hated being
touched there. He would have cast off the embrace, but he
could not bring himself to refuse her warmth, her tenderness,
the comfort she offered. His body rigid, he held his breath,
feeling as if he might break if he moved a single muscle.

"You are not to blame!" Ariane repeated fiercely, her
voice catching on a sob.

He felt the tender brush of her lips against his bare back,
felt the dampness, the trickle of moisture from her eyes.
Tears. His chest tightened unbearably. She was weeping ...
weeping for him.

He turned in her arms.

"Ariane ..." he whispered, revealing for one unguarded
moment the yearning in his soul. *I need you.*

In poignant response, her lips raised to meet his, offering
solace, the same exquisite tenderness he had showered on her
a short while earlier, the same hunger.

Ranulf groaned, a sound of passion and surrender, an acknowledgement of his own loneliness. He felt a desperate
need to accept her comfort, to bury himself in this woman
and forget, just forget everything, save her. Urgently he
pressed her down, fitting his naked body to hers.

With a soft gasp at his penetrating thrust, Ariane opened
to him, wrapping her legs around his thighs, taking him into
her body, drawing him close. He gripped her buttocks
fiercely, violent in his need, yet she welcomed his frenzy.
She could feel the surging power in his thrusting body, his
straining muscles, feel the vulnerability and pain inside him.
She held him with a fierce and primitive protectiveness, letting him use her body as a vessel for his release, while his
own arched and convulsed around her, within her.

His shudders took a long time calming afterward. Ranulf
buried his mouth in her hair, unwilling to face what he had
done.

He felt too vulnerable, too raw, to speak. Unaccountably,
he had laid his soul bare to this woman who should be his
enemy. It disquieted him, the weakness he had shown.

He had meant only to comfort her, not to rail against his

fate, not to let her probe his past and the darkness that had claimed his soul. He had not meant to give her such an advantage over him.

And yet, she was stroking his hair now, caressing his nape gently, as if he were a mere babe. As if she knew the devastation within him, understood what drove him.

Still, his weakness dismayed him, as did his lapse of control. Ariane had felt no pleasure in their fierce coupling, he knew. He had used her hard, as if she were no more than the whore she claimed he had made her.

"We had best return," he muttered tersely, his voice yet hoarse from the wrenching climax he had endured.

At his abrupt change of mood, Ariane's hand stilled in his hair.

Ranulf raised his head, gazing around him, looking anywhere but into her eyes. "I will accompany you here on the morrow, on the pretense of a lover's tryst. Our dalliance will provide a pretext for your venturing here, to visit your lady mother. No one will question it."

Ariane sighed inwardly. Ranulf was once again the cool, remote stranger, a stalwart warrior who had no room for softness. He regretted his gentleness, regretted opening himself to her, she knew.

And yet she took heart, if faintly. He had begun to soften toward her. He was wary of giving his love or trust to any woman, especially to her, but she had made a beginning.

Ariane rubbed the chilled skin of her arms as Ranulf rose to his feet, watching his hard, beautiful, scarred body. He was wrong, she reflected. He did possess a heart, buried somewhere beneath a terrible burden of rage and hatred.

The Black Dragon of Vernay might be a mighty warrior, but he was a lonely and vulnerable man as well . . . a man who needed her, though he did not yet know it.

Chapter 21

The interlude in the meadow affected Ranulf more than he cared to admit, for it was then that his doubts began to haunt him: He began to question seriously his belief that Ariane was no better than the faithless, highborn damsels he had always known.

He strove to remain on his guard. His relief that Ariane had not betrayed him was profound, but not so overwhelming that he would forswear his defenses.

And yet, if he had wronged Ariane once, the possibility existed that he might again mistake even her innocent actions for treachery. Admittedly his judgment when it came to ladies of her class was slightly slanted in her disfavor.

Thus, Ranulf watched her closely, noting small things he had refused to acknowledge before. Ariane was demanding but well loved by her people, he admitted reluctantly as he observed their interplay. Their loyalty had been fully earned; her spirit, her wit, her beauty, her caring nature all commanded their allegiance. His squire, Burc, sang her praises for her tender and successful ministering of his wounds. She had even won the respect and admiration of some of his own vassals, most pointedly Payn FitzOsbern, Ranulf remarked with disquiet.

She had courage, certainly. She bore the indignities visited upon her with a regal grace, asking no quarter. Once, when Ranulf caught her gazing out the solar window to the east, her look wistful and poignant, as if longing for happier times, she shrugged off his inquiry with a wry smile and a shake of her lovely head, refusing to dwell on her sadness or bid for his sympathy.

In truth, Ranulf could not find much fault with her demeanor. Her practical, perceptive nature was quite feminine and pleasing, even if her sharp tongue and rash defiance at times infuriated him.

Her physical response to him was pleasing, as well. Incredibly so. He had never had a woman who so completely satisfied his carnal needs. In his bed, the regal maiden turned lusty wench, fulfilling even his most demanding passions, to the point that he no longer desired any other lover.

Yet he could not explain his hunger for her in terms of mere lust. He felt a fierce possessiveness toward Ariane, true, but he could not deny there was something more.

Her presence filled his senses, his every waking thought. He was truly bewitched, Ranulf concluded with dismay. At the most inopportune times, he would find himself thinking of her, remembering the sweetness of her taste, the silky softness of her body: during dull discussions of profits and rents, while settling disputes among his villeins, even in the midst of a mock melee while facing armed opponents—a dangerous moment to be letting his mind wander. He could not explain the soft feeling that would flow through him at odd moments, so unexpectedly that he had no defense against it ... a new and strange emotion that he refused to examine more closely. A threatening sentiment he knew he needed to fight with all his might. He could not allow Ariane within the barriers he protected himself with.

He could not allow himself to completely dismiss his suspicions, either. For all he knew, she had deliberately set out to ensnare him, wielding her woman's weapons against him with methodical calculation. In truth, she seemed softer, more sweetly responsive toward him, since the day in the meadow—although that could be rationalized by gratitude. He knew his lenience toward her mother had won Ariane's indebtedness, if not her trust.

Her lack of trust annoyed Ranulf. He had shown her mercy in other instances; she should have had more faith in him than to think he would condemn a poor soul to almost certain death. And yet he had to remember how little faith *he* had placed in *her*. He had mistrusted Ariane so greatly as to accuse her of betrayal, when she had only endeavored to protect her beloved mother.

He could recognize and even admire the loyalty Ariane had shown her mother. When it came to those she loved, the vixen reacted with the courage and ferocity of a lioness. If he found himself wishing he could command such devotion for himself, however, Ranulf dismissed the notion as madness. He would never allow himself to lose his heart.

As for Ariane's mother, Ranulf kept his word, escorting her daughter back to the cotter's hut the following day with abundant provender for the afflicted woman. He regretted he could do no more to aid the Lady Constance. Acting on a compassionate impulse, Ranulf dispatched one his most trusted knights and a contingent of men-at-arms to Vernay in Normandy, with an urgent summons for the Saracen concubine, Layla, who possessed skill in the Eastern healing arts. He said nothing of his plan to Ariane, though, for fear of raising her hopes needlessly.

He also banished the serving wench, Dena, from Claredon, sending her to one of the manor houses to serve. He disliked the spite and deceit Dena had shown, and would not tolerate a serf who held so little loyalty for her mistress.

Ariane's half-brother, Gilbert, Ranulf set free, with an admonition to curb his reckless defiance or face a drubbing again. His sister's release from the dungeon, however, went much further toward curbing the boy's rash outbursts than any threat could have done. When Gilbert earnestly begged her forgiveness for divulging her secret, Ariane even forgave him, Ranulf was aware.

It was two days after his discovery of Lady Constance that he received a missive bearing King Henry's seal.

"A summons?" Payn asked when Ranulf had unrolled the parchment and perused the contents.

"Nay, a mission," he replied almost grimly, handing the sheepskin to his vassal to read. "The Lady Eleanor requires an escort to reach the king's camp at Bridgenorth."

"And she asked for her favored knight as escort," Payn surmised with an edge of amusement.

Ranulf grimaced. "You overstate the case. Far from favoring me, the queen doubtless acts to spite me. She has never forgiven me for spurning one of her ladies at court two winters past, and knows I would far rather be engaged in battle than attend her retinue. But one does not question the king's command. Tell the men we ride for London in three days."

That night Ranulf lay awake long into the night, regretting the distasteful task ahead of him, reminded of what he despised most in noblewomen. Queen Eleanor was a master at ruling men and their desires and compelling them do her bidding, but her loyalty was to herself. She had contrived an annulment from Louis of France after bearing him two children, and then wed young Henry of Normandy in her search for power. Eleanor had half of the civilized world at her feet, attracting foolish poets and sycophants like flies to honey with her beauty and wit, which *was* extraordinary. Her court was a hive of intrigue and scheming, and the lovely queen not only encouraged it, but led the charge.

He could devise a hundred missions he would prefer over this one, Ranulf reflected. And to his surprise, he begrudged the time he would spend away from Claredon. It would be his first absence of any length since his arrival nearly five weeks ago, his first time away from Ariane.

He did not want to leave her. The thought startled Ranulf.

She murmured a soft protest when he woke her from a deep sleep, but he ignored it, drawing her back against him, nestling her soft buttocks against his throbbing loins. Her breathing quickened when his arm wrapped around her hips, his fingers seeking and massaging the tender bud between her legs to slickness. And when he probed within her, coaxing her body to receive him, she soon was whimpering in pleasure.

His buttocks tightening, he thrust into her sleek hot passage from behind, pushing his burgeoning rod deep, closing his eyes and pretending to ignore the exquisite sense of completion he felt when joined to her, telling himself he needed her merely to slake his lust. She was simply a warm female body, a means to relieve his male ache, to ease the loneliness for a short while.

And if he lied to himself in the panting darkness, if he deceived himself as his shuddering body sought the ecstasy only she could give him, he was not prepared to acknowledge it.

He rose early the following morning, before Ariane awoke, and hastened to the arms field, where he drove himself to the point of physical exhaustion in an effort to obliterate his damnable obsession with the wench. Haplessly, he failed.

After unnecessarily leading a patrol over the demesne for countless hours, Ranulf returned late in the evening to find Ariane awaiting him in the solar while she worked her stitchery, with wine and food to ease his hunger and a warm fire burning in the hearth. At his entrance, she immediately set aside her simples and gave him a soft smile of welcome.

Ranulf stilled at the sight she made. Her pale hair glimmered like molten copper in the firelight, while her ivory skin glowed with an unearthly beauty. She looked for all the world like a mural rendering he had once seen of the Virgin Mary before the birth of her Son.

A dangerous image formed in his mind, a picture of Ariane swollen with his child. It filled him with such longing that he was shaken by it. He had to turn away to keep from betraying his weakness. For all that he had vowed to protect his heart, he felt the formidable shields of ice and steel threatened.

Ariane would not want to bear his child . . . would she? Would she care tenderly for a babe of his, nurturing it with the affection he had craved his life long but never known? He had heard tales of love between noble mother and child, but dismissed them as romantic fantasy, believing only peasants showed their offspring such affection.

And yet Ariane's mother had demonstrated by example that such unselfish love did exist among women of her rank. Lady Constance had risked her very life to nurse her only son. And she had also taken in her lord's bastard, Gilbert, to provide him a better life.

Would Ariane be willing to do the same with *his* bastards? Ranulf wondered. Would she raise his children at Claredon if he asked it of her?

Not that he would ask. He would not take his children from their mothers and bring them to a foreign country, exposing them to loneliness and scorn, simply to gratify his own need for their company. They were well provided for now, their futures assured. They would be better off where they lived—

"How fared your day, my lord?" Ariane asked softly,

interrupting his thoughts as she rose to aid him out of his armor.

Missing his children, reminded of the need to resist the warmth in her gray eyes, Ranulf answered tersely, his tone almost harsh. "Well enough." When he saw the searching look Ariane gave him, he renewed his vow to close his heart and mind against any soft intrusions.

Ariane was forgiving of his foul mood, though. Since her release from fear over her mother's plight, she had been too overwhelmed with gratitude to take umbrage at Ranulf's occasional brusque manner or his usual detachment. And with the freedom from fear came hope. Hope that in time Ranulf would cease regarding her as a bitter adversary and come to look upon her as someone meaningful, even vital, to his happiness.

That day in the meadow, she had been given a glimpse beyond the impregnable barrier he had erected between himself and everyone else. She had touched the vulnerable core of him, the tender center he always kept guarded and remote. He had shown her a gentler side to his nature, baring his mail-armored heart for the fleetest of moments, and she would not rest until she had rent the whole shield. She wanted passionately to free him from his unyielding defenses, to divest him of his protective armor. She wanted Ranulf to reach for her again in tenderness, in trust. To ease this constant ache in her own heart.

It was the following morning, though, when Ariane realized how very far she was from earning Ranulf's trust.

The day began badly, for she had to hear from Payn that Ranulf was being sent on the king's business, and that no less a personage than the new queen of England, Eleanor of Aquitaine, might pay a visit to Claredon.

Disgruntled by Ranulf's lack of consideration, Ariane hastened to inspect the keep—both the tower and the castle grounds, making mental lists of the countless tasks that required attention. She had a thousand and one details to see to, even if Ranulf had forbidden her to take a hand in the running of the castle. Under no circumstances short of imprisonment would she allow the queen of England to see Claredon at less than its very best.

When Ranulf came in for the midday meal, the keep was

ahum with activity as the castlefolk prepared for his departure
and Lady Eleanor's possible arrival. Ranulf scowled at all
the bustle as he ran up the steps to the solar, regretting the
nuisance of preparing for royalty, as well as wary of the
enormous expense. Royal visits had been known to beggar
many a hapless host.

When he entered the solar antechamber, though, he came
to an abrupt halt, feeling as if he had taken a blow to his
midsection with a lance. Ariane and Payn stood with their
heads together before the solar door, both laughing.

The sight of Ariane gazing up so sweetly at his vassal sent
a sick stab of jealousy streaking through Ranulf. Her gray
eyes were alight with amusement and more: admiration for
the tall, handsome knight.

"What find you so humorous?" Ranulf demanded, making
them both jump with his harshness.

Sobering, Payn and Ariane glanced briefly at each other.

"It was naught, Ranulf," Payn said evenly. "The Lady
Ariane was telling me of the time King Stephen paid a visit
to Claredon—"

"Can you not find a more worthwhile occupation than
listening to tales and dallying with my leman?"

Stiffening, Payn looked as if he might refute the remark,
but he merely gave a brief bow. "As you wish, my lord."

When he had gone, Ranulf turned his piercing gaze on
Ariane, a muscle in his jaw flexing ominously. "Do not seek
to win Payn over with your artifices, wench. You will not
succeed."

Her eyes widened at his hostile tone, and at his implication.
Apparently Ranulf had mistaken her growing friendship with
Payn FitzOsbern for a flirtation and had reacted with unreasoning jealousy. "We engaged in merely a harmless conversation, my lord, only that—"

"You think to seduce my vassal, and you call it
harmless?"

"Seduce? . . . Are you *mad?*" Ariane retorted in disbelief.

Ranulf's fierce gaze never wavered. His heart thrummed
against his ribs, his chest rioting with the devastating emotions that threatened him. "I have your measure, wench. And
I will not permit you to gain an advantage with the stratagems
your sex is so fond of employing."

"And I will not dignify that absurd accusation with a reply!"

She made to brush past him, but a cruel hand forestalled her flight.

His fingers bit into her wrist as he ground out between his teeth, "You belong to me, Ariane. I advise you not to forget it!"

Her chin rose, her eyes flashing dangerously, yet she kept her voice low. "I am quite aware I *belong* to you, my lord," she returned, her scornful tone all the more emphatic for its softness. "But as far as I am concerned, I consider myself your *wife,* not your leman. As for having my measure—you are as wrong as you are blind. Your suspicions are completely unfounded. And even if you do not trust me, you should be ashamed of accusing your friend of dishonoring you. Sir Payn is an honorable man—and entirely undeserving of such shameful charges. It only proves how unworthy you are of his devotion, if you can think so little of him—"

Interrupting her biting castigation, Ranulf hauled her against him, his look almost frightening as he glared down at her. Ariane gasped at his violence, then stilled.

The air was suddenly charged with something more than Ranulf's fury. Beneath his tunic, she felt him tightening, hardening. She could read the flicker of lust in his eyes, a promise of retribution; within those glittering golden depths a molten fire burned hot and searing.

Abruptly Ranulf released her, but only long enough to turn and propel her into the solar. Kicking the door shut behind them, he strode to the bed, pulling a startled Ariane in his wake. In merely an instant, he had pushed her down upon the mattress; in another heartbeat he was upon her, his hands holding her wrists, stretching them above her head. His thighs were like granite upon hers, pinning her down, while his amber eyes glittered with heated fury.

"I will not abide your criticism, wench." Yet his irrational response had little to do with her censure, Ranulf knew. She had terrified him, showing such amusement and affection toward his vassal, and he was punishing her for it.

Keeping her wrists imprisoned with one hand, he shoved up her skirts, baring her lower body to his gaze. His eyes darkened with the hot gleam of lust; his nostrils flared at her scent. She lay spread before him, open for his taking.

He thought she would fight him, yet once she had absorbed the shock of his sudden assault, Ariane made no attempt to struggle or evade his ravishment as he poised above her. She had *wanted* Ranulf to desire her enough to lose that icy control, and now he was teetering at the edge of an explosion ... as was she. She could feel her pulse beating wildly, the throbbing ache between her legs echoing in her blood, her body readying itself for his claiming.

She watched, unresisting, as Ranulf raised the hem of his own tunic and tore at the laces of his braies, freeing his male length that thrust thick and full from his groin.

He bent over her, his face dark and strained with arousal. "Open your legs," he commanded harshly.

She yielded instantly, humbled by her need, whimpering with pleasure when he crowded inside her. He was large and magnificent; she was hot and eager. She gasped at his heat, at his exquisite hardness. It was like being penetrated by inflamed velvet steel, and with the first stroke she was halfway to ecstasy.

He showed her no tenderness. He moved roughly in and out, pumping his fury, claiming her triumphantly. And yet Ariane wanted no tenderness, no holding back. She arched wildly against him, reveling in the mark of his possession.

He was a dark fire, igniting a raging inferno within her as he branded her his own.

It was only moments later that she cried out, a high, keening pleasure sound, a cry that merged with his hoarse groan as he convulsed with the force of his seed spurting from his body.

They lay spent and panting afterward, their flesh still joined.

Finally, without a word, Ranulf eased off her and stood to adjust his clothing. His manhood hung thick and flaccid and wet, Ariane saw as he covered himself.

"Know that you are mine," he said tersely.

"I do know it, Ranulf," Ariane replied with quiet conviction, needing to assuage his doubts, to melt his enmity and suspicion. "I belong to you. I want no other man ... lover or husband."

He gazed at her warily for a long moment, before turning away.

The fierceness seemed to have left him, but the coldness remained. He made no apology for his outburst of violence—not then, nor later when they descended to the hall for the meal, or indeed, at any time as he prepared to leave for London the next day. It was as if he preferred to pretend his insane jealousy had never existed.

And yet remorse and chagrin ate at Ranulf. He could not find the words, though, to explain how difficult it was to cast aside the ingrained fears and convictions of a lifetime, or to express the apology that trembled on his lips.

And so he said nothing.

It was a strained leavetaking at dawn the following morning, with silence reigning between Ariane and Ranulf. He had her body once more before calling his squire in to help him dress, and then he spoke to her only to give her his parting orders. He responded with merely a brief nod to her wishes for a safe journey, not entirely trusting that she meant it.

And yet at the last moment he turned back to her, unable to leave without tasting her sweetness once more, without having one final kiss to sustain him on the journey ahead.

Ariane saw the desire in Ranulf's amber eyes as he drew her into his arms, felt the heated need in his powerful body, in his fervent lips. Yet his mask of coolness had descended again when he released her. And he had no kind word of farewell for her, no word at all.

Thus it was with a heavy heart that Ariane let him go. She watched from the solar window as Ranulf, clad in full armor, mounted his mighty steed and clattered across the drawbridge at the head of his retinue. Behind him streamed a pennon of crimson silk emblazoned with his feared device, the black dragon rampant.

When they were long out of sight, Ariane let her breath out in a sigh. Infuriatingly, she already missed Ranulf. Illogically, she worried for him. There were countless dangers awaiting unwary travelers—brigands and miscreants, mercenaries and other powerful knights greedy enough to challenge all comers—but it was absurd to worry. Ranulf was a seasoned warrior who had survived nearly three decades of war and strife without her assistance. And it was the time-honored lot of women to await their men when they rode away.

Ariane sighed again. She knew she would count the days till Ranulf returned safely to her. Despite the cold indifference he continued to show her, despite his recent unfeeling treatment of her, she still had hopes of someday gentling him to her touch, of somehow overcoming the haunting vulnerability she had seen in his eyes.

Chapter 22

The distant blare of the watchman's horn made Ariane tense as she sat embroidering with her ladies in the weaving rooms. *Ranulf!* Had he returned?

Trying unsuccessfully to quell her excitement, she followed the chattering women to the window to see what had caused the commotion. A single rider approached the castle gates, bearing a pennon with the royal colors of King Henry.

"The queen!" Gleda squealed, voicing the thrill all of them felt.

"No need to screech like an alewife," Maud scolded. "Mayhap 'tis only a messenger."

Yet the rider did appear to be a herald announcing the arrival of the queen's entourage, for he carried his own trumpet, which he sounded long and frequently. The watchman at the gatehouse apparently considered him friend rather than foe, for the screech and clatter of chains soon reverberated throughout the keep as the drawbridge slowly lowered across the moat.

Calling one of her tirewomen to her, Ariane hurried to her own chamber and quickly changed her old brown wool bliaud for a much finer one of red cendal. She had moved her belongings here to her quarters, and Ranulf's as well, so that the solar could be readied for Queen Eleanor and her ladies. Only the best accommodations would serve for so important a personage.

Her stomach felt tied in knots as Ariane smoothed her gown's folds one last time and made her way to the tower entrance. As Ranulf's hostage, she had greatly overstepped her authority in making preparations for the queen's visit, although she had done no more than any chatelaine would have—conferring with the steward and head gamekeeper as well as the kitchen staff; ensuring adequate stocks in the storerooms, pantry, larder, buttery, fishponds, dovecotes, and rabbit warrens; supervising the gathering of herbs from the garden and ordering spices from the spice merchant in the village; instructing the household serfs in matters of service—the myriad details that would help the visit run smoothly.

And Payn had given her a free hand, after all, trusting her judgment in such feminine matters, knowing she would do naught to shame Claredon.

Ariane's tension rose as she left the tower to wait with Payn at the head of the outer entrance stairway. The newcomer had indeed been a herald for the queen, and now, beyond the castle walls, Ariane could see an advance guard riding toward the gates, their armor glinting in the late afternoon sun. The bright crimson banner that fluttered at the head of the troop looked to be bearing Ranulf's dragon device.

" 'Tis Ranulf, my lady," Payn murmured at her side.

Even as she watched, a single mailed horseman on a black charger broke from the retinue and approached at the canter. Ariane felt fresh anticipation curl within her. Ranulf had been gone more than a week, and she had missed him sorely. She craved his touch and the feel of his fierce embrace, and even the sparks that flew between them when they were at odds, which was nearly always. Their strained parting had left her feeling anxious and disheartened, wondering if he would ever again treat her with the tenderness he had shown her that magical afternoon in the meadow.

She was not surprised to find herself trembling as, with Payn, she descended the long flight of steps to the yard to await the returning lord. In only moments, Ranulf rode briskly into the inner bailey, his destrier's hooves striking a heavy rhythm in tune with Ariane's suddenly thudding pulse.

Drawing his charger to a plunging halt on the hard-packed earth, Ranulf greeted his vassal with an easy informality, which Payn returned while Ariane held her breath. Ranulf's conical helmet with its steel nasal descending almost to his lips hid much of his face, but she could feel his golden gaze shift to her.

His eyes seemed dark and intense as he searched her face. Then he drew off his helm and pushed back his mail coif, to reveal raven hair drenched in sweat and several days' growth of beard stubbling his hard jaw.

Joy flooded her at the sight of those harsh, handsome features. Joy and a fierce surge of heated excitement. Even sweat and dirt could not detract from the aura of a powerful, intensely sexual male animal.

Emulating the graciousness of her lady mother, Ariane swept him a low curtsey. "My lord, be welcome."

Surprise kindled in Ranulf's eyes at the warmth of her greeting, yet he forced himself to respond neutrally, not wishing to create a scene for the crowd forming in the bailey to gawk at. It was all he could do to prevent himself from leaping off his horse and hauling Ariane into his arms. Yet he merely nodded, acknowledging her welcome, then returned his attention to his vassal, trying to ignore the distracting wench who had preyed on his mind incessantly during the past interminable week.

"How went the journey?" Payn asked just as a page ran out to claim the lord's charger.

"I have enjoyed better," Ranulf replied dourly as he dismounted. "The Lady Eleanor possesses the stubbornness of a mule."

Ariane was surprised to hear him disparage his queen. To her further surprise, he said nothing about finding her acting the role of chatelaine, nor did he demand that she hide herself away. Instead he seemed to disregard her entirely as he quizzed Payn on the happenings at Claredon during his absence.

Long moments later, a troop of riders dashed through the inner gates, led by a laughing, fair-haired lady on a snow-white palfrey, whose saddle and bridle were trimmed with silver bosses and tassels.

Ariane had heard tales of the headstrong duchess who was now queen of England. Eleanor of Aquitaine's beauty was said to be breathtaking, as was her wit. She was also credited with being a superb horsewoman—all assertions Ariane could readily believe as she watched Ranulf aid the lady down from her saddle.

"Faith! I thought we would never arrive," Eleanor said with a careless laugh.

"Welcome to Claredon, my lady," Ranulf replied so stiffly that Ariane could sense the discord between them.

Payn stepped forward just then to bow over the queen's hand. "I greet you, noble lady."

"FitzOsbern! Just the man to soothe my wounded sensibilities. Your liege lord has the manners of a field ox."

"Mayhap, your grace," Payn replied with a smile. "But an ox upon whom you can depend to serve you well."

She gave a delicate snort. "I vow Lord Ranulf would have wrapped me in swaddling had I allowed it. He required me to remain lazing in that stifling contraption until I could not bear another minute." She sent a glower at the gilded, silk-curtained litter that was just then lumbering through the gates. Abruptly, her blue eyes moved on to Ariane, surveying her curiously. "So this is the heiress I have heard tell of?"

Ariane bowed in a deep curtsey. "You do us honor, your grace."

"Do I? A strange reception from the daughter of a man charged with treason against my husband the king."

It was Ariane's turn to stiffen. "*Charged*, I believe is the applicable term, my lady. Not convicted. Fortunately for my lord father, King Henry is said to be a just ruler, who will judge a man's guilt or innocence based on proof and not mere rumor."

Eleanor's eyes flickered with new respect, while her lips curved wryly. "And so he is."

"We have made every effort to arrange for your comfort," Ariane continued coolly. "I trust you will find all to your liking."

"We shall see," Queen Eleanor replied, turning to flash Ranulf an arch smile that was at once both mischievous and challenging. "I perceive you have had your hands full subduing Claredon, if this lady is any indication."

Without waiting for a reply or for assistance, the queen swept regally up the stone steps, leaving her attendant knights and their ladies to follow as they would.

Ariane thought she heard Ranulf sigh in disgust, and found herself sharing his sentiments. Raising the hem of her skirts, she preceded him up the stairs and into the great hall, where varlets passed silver goblets of wine spiced with cloves.

"My lord," Ariane murmured to Ranulf, "I have given

the queen and her tirewomen your solar, and moved your belongings to my old chamber. I hope that meets with your approval?''

Ranulf bent his head to hers, so close she could feel the warm rush of his breath on her cheek. ''Any chamber will do, so long as you share it with me, wench.''

Ariane could not restrain the fluttering of her pulse at the heated promise in his tone. From his earlier conversation with Payn, she had gathered that Ranulf would remain only the one night; early on the morrow he would continue to ride escort for the queen's cavalcade, as agent of her safety, conducting her to her royal husband's camp to the northwest. But that one night it seemed he intended to spend with her—at least insofar as his duties as host permitted.

''You will sit at the high table with me this evening,'' Ranulf surprised her by adding. He left her then, accompanied by his squire, in order to bathe and change. Ariane remained busy arranging baths and accommodations for the important guests—a score in all—and did not see Ranulf again until he returned to the hall for the supper feast she had ordered.

Ariane thought him devastatingly compelling with his harsh features clean shaven, though he had dressed plainly in a black tunic with a crimson undertunic. The visiting knights and their ladies wore more costly and better adorned garments, but the Lord of Claredon possessed an imposing presence that mere cloth could not confer.

When Queen Eleanor appeared, however, her gorgeous attire put the entire company to shame. The long, bell-like sleeves of her bliaud were heavily embroidered with gold thread, while the tight, long-sleeved undergown of gold-shot samite shimmered in the torchlight. A gold cord encircled her head, holding in place a small square of linen, completing the image of a regal ruler.

Eleanor took the place of honor at the high table next to the lord, sharing the same wine cup and thick trencher of day-old bread as Ranulf. On his order, Ariane had placed herself at Ranulf's other side, to share with Payn.

The tempting viands she had ordered arrived in courses: venison, shoulder of wild boar, roasted swans, minced meat paste made with breadcrumbs and herbs, pigeon pasties, fresh mullet, eel pies, all accompanied by hot sauces spiced with pepper or ginger or mustard, with stewed fruit and cheeses at the conclusion. A harp-playing minstrel began the entertainment then, while a fresh round of honeyed wine was poured.

Queen Eleanor had kept up a gay chatter throughout the meal, interspersing her comments with compliments on the fare, so that it seemed that the feast was progressing well. Thus Ariane was startled when halfway into the third song, the queen rose and addressed her. "I should like a word with you, Lady Ariane."

Ariane cast a worried glance at Ranulf, who was frowning into his goblet, but she dared not refuse a direct command. When Eleanor was attended from the hall by two of her ladies, Ariane followed reluctantly.

She watched silently as the queen was undressed down to her shift and her long hair taken down.

"Leave me," Eleanor then said to her women. When they were gone, she took up a polished hand mirror and a silver-backed brush, settled herself on a stool, and presented her back to Ariane. "Will you assist me?"

Realizing what was expected of her, Ariane came to stand behind the queen. Accepting the brush, she began running it softly through the golden mass of Eleanor's hair.

"I gather you find yourself in a difficult position," Eleanor said musingly, watching Ariane in the mirror. "First your father's treason, then Lord Ranulf's repudiation of your betrothal."

Ariane remained silent.

"I confess it disturbed me to hear of your treatment at Lord Ranulf's hands. To force you to his bed without benefit of marriage ... well, I find it reprehensible."

Ariane had no need to ask how the queen had learned of her difficulties. Castle gossip was swift and brutally explicit. Eleanor would have discovered all she wished to know from the servant hierarchy within moments of her arrival.

A blush rose to Ariane's cheeks at such frank speaking, but she refused to be drawn into a discussion of Ranulf's faults.

"I do not care to see any woman mistreated," Eleanor prodded. "Men hold far too much of the power in this world, and frequently misuse it."

"I have no complaints regarding Lord Ranulf, my lady."

"You hold a tendre for the man, is that it? I could not help but notice how you watch him."

"Does it show so clearly?" Ariane asked in dismay.

"To some, it does—to me, yes. I find myself intrigued by matters of the heart, so I pay closer attention than most. When you look at him, your face holds a softness, a yearning. . . ."

Ariane knew it was true—that what she felt for Ranulf was strong enough to show on her features.

"I think I can understand the attraction. I knew Ranulf at court, and several of my ladies were wild for him, though he would have naught to do with them. Despite his atrocious manners, he always acquitted himself skillfully in tourney and battle. A renowned knight who has served my lord husband admirably . . . powerful and well-landed . . . It is a pity that he will not wed you."

In complete accord with the queen's thoughts, Ariane made an absent murmur of agreement.

"But I think I can provide a way out of your difficulties . . . by offering you a position in my service as one of my ladies. If you join my court, I can extend you my protection, which is no small matter."

The brush stilled in Ariane's hand, while her eyes widened at the generous offer of refuge. As lady-in-waiting to the queen, Ariane knew she would be safe from whatever repercussions her father's actions generated.

Eleanor expanded on the compelling argument. "Henry is yet besieging Mortimer's castle at Bridgenorth. When the siege is successfully concluded, your father will be tried for treason for supporting the rebellion."

Ariane bit her lip, thinking that Eleanor would make a cunning political adversary—or benefactor. If she accepted the queen's protection . . . But then she shook her head slowly. She could never abandon her father, or her mother, or Claredon's people, merely to save herself. And then there was Ranulf. . . .

"You are all that is kind, your grace. Please accept my sincere gratitude, but I must decline. Claredon is my home, and I have some hope . . ."

When she hesitated, Eleanor prodded, "Yes, you have hope . . ."

"That one day Ranulf will come to view me as . . . someone he can trust. Perhaps you know he does not give his trust lightly.''

"You have fallen in love with him." It was not a question.

"Yes," Ariane admitted to herself for the first time. Against her will, against all reason and judgment, she had fallen in love with Ranulf.

She was suffering a lovesick passion worthy of some languishing maid. Ranulf possessed her heart. In truth, he had ensnared it years ago with his tender smile, when she was but a nervous, tongue-tied girl. She did not often see that smile now—an expression so rare as to be almost priceless— and yet she had fallen deeper into Ranulf's snare, perhaps for the very reason that made her crave to ease the suffering of other wounded, helpless creatures; because she had glimpsed the bleak vulnerability beneath the warrior's hard exterior. She had seen his pain.

"I fought against loving him," Ariane murmured, "but I found it hopeless."

She had tried valiantly, futilely, to stop herself, but she could not love by half-measures, holding back in self-protection. In that respect she was like her parents, who loved deeply.

It was mad, though, her yearning for Ranulf. He treated her no better than a serf, his personal possession. He was unlikely ever to acknowledge her as his wife, let alone his love. Yet she cherished the hope of one day overcoming his blind, pigheaded mistrust, of penetrating his impregnable mail-armored heart.

"So be it," Eleanor said brusquely, her tone somewhat curt. "But do not think to apply to me should your troubles deepen."

Their eyes met in the hazy surface of the hand mirror, and Ariane knew that the discussion had ended.

"Aye, your grace."

She had refused the queen's offer of support, and now she must live with the consequences.

Ariane deeply regretted her confession to the queen regarding her feelings for Ranulf, for she could not absolve Eleanor of possibly trying to stir up mischief. But there was no use lamenting what was done.

After her dismissal from the queen's chamber, Ariane returned to the great hall to find many of the guests already in their cups. The lord, however, appeared sober enough to be almost grim.

"What wanted the Lady Eleanor with you?" Ranulf demanded as she slipped into her seat.

She met his brooding look with a forced smile. "She required me to brush her hair." Ranulf stared at her for a long moment, but fortunately did not press her to expound on her conversation with the queen.

"By your leave, my lord, I would like to retire."

"Retire, aye," he said, his voice dropping to a husky baritone, "but not to sleep. I expect a sweet welcome, wench."

A fierce surge of heat and excitement swept through Ariane at the promise of passion in his gaze. "As you wish, my lord. I shall await you in your bed."

She was rewarded by a flare of heat in his amber eyes as bright as a torch flame.

He came to her shortly, as if unable to contain his impatience. Ariane scarcely had time to undress before Ranulf was there, standing before her, as she sat brushing her own hair.

A fire burned low in the brazier, and by the faint glow of embers, she could see that his eyes were hard and bright and hungry—and so hot that she felt seared by their molten heat.

He did not reach for her at once, though, but took the brush from her and set it aside. With a gentle finger under her chin, Ranulf tilted her face up, letting his gaze caress her hauntingly lovely features and the full, gleaming mane that fell thick and gloriously unkempt over her shoulders. Her ivory skin glowed with the translucence of a pearl, her bright hair glimmered, the waving tresses threaded riotously with flaxen and gold and copper.

Eagerly Ranulf plunged his fingers into the incredible softness, letting the warm weight of it pour over his hands like molten honey as he sought her sweet mouth.

He could have had his pick of women this eve. Half the castle wenches would be tumbled by the visiting knights, while his own men would have the others, but as lord, he could have chosen first. Most would have been eager to share his bed.

But there was only one woman he wanted, needed to be with. He yearned for Ariane's company. He could not account at all for the sense of banishment he had felt when he had been gone from her, nor could he comprehend the bewildering gentleness he felt when she was near.

Capturing her mouth in a kiss, he drank of her sweetness, thrusting his tongue deep into her inviting warmth in a bold imitation of the carnal act, stroking her bare body to urgent arousal. In only moments Ariane was arching against him, the tips of her breasts hard and aching under his curving fingers.

Yet they both craved more than mere caresses. Her own hands trembling, Ariane undressed Ranulf, not stopping until he stood before her naked, magnificent, looking like a dark, pagan god. When brazenly she closed her fingers around the strong root of him, she could hear his breath quicken harshly in her ear.

And still she was not satisfied. Her body was already so vibrant with yearning that she thought she might die unless he eased the ache. Refusing to release him, Ariane drew him to the bed and lay back upon the sheets in invitation, spreading her legs wide for his claiming, aching for him.

Joining her on the soft mattress, Ranulf settled between her eagerly parted thighs and thrust deep, capturing her cry of pleasure with his mouth. Without speaking, he stroked and inflamed and coaxed her body to new heights, bringing them both to a shattering peak of ecstasy.

Ranulf recovered first from the wracking pleasure, to find himself collapsed limply upon Ariane, her arms clasping him loosely. Her awareness followed more slowly, gradually growing conscious of the damp warmth of his skin, the crushing heaviness of his powerful body.

She did not mind his weight, though; somehow it gave her primal comfort. Sighing, Ariane clung to him more tightly. Ranulf had come home to her, no one else. She had given him welcome of the basest sort, but she had also provided shelter for his guarded warrior's heart—a feat she was certain no other woman had ever accomplished.

He was gone by dawn's light, riding escort for Queen Eleanor's retinue. They were a dozen leagues from Claredon when the queen first deigned to speak to him. Riding along-

side Ranulf on her palfrey, Eleanor broached the subject of
Ariane in a manner that set his heart lurching and his mind
skittering.

"I must confess I was pleasantly surprised by the Lady
Ariane. I spoke to her at length last night. I could not help
but be affected by her plight."

"Her plight, your grace?" Ranulf asked guardedly.

"My Lord Ranulf, let us not mince words," the queen
said sweetly. "You have taken full use of the girl, when her
rank should have protected her. An honorable knight would
make reparations."

His eyes narrowed and darkened. "Did she claim I had
dishonored her?"

Eleanor's musical peal of laughter was like the chime of
crystal bells. "Nay, she would say naught against you. I had
to learn of it from my ladies. It pains me to see any gentlewoman so ill used, though, so I offered her refuge at the
royal court as one of my ladies-in-waiting."

Ranulf felt a jolt of panic like a knife in his belly. "Did
Ariane ask your protection?"

"No, but I offered it just the same. The lady refused."

"She refused? . . ." Ranulf stared blankly at Eleanor.

"Yes. She claimed she had no wish to leave her home,
despite the terrible difficulties she faces. Such devotion is
admirable, would you not agree?"

Relief flooded Ranulf like sweet wine. He knew not why
Ariane had decided to remain at Claredon; he was just happy
she would not leave him.

"You have found yourself a prize in the girl, my Lord
Ranulf, if you would but see it."

Ranulf turned to stare at the queen.

"You could do worse than to wed her."

His jaw hardened. "It seems you take uncommon interest
in my affairs, my lady."

Eleanor smiled sweetly, the expression that had brought
kingdoms to her feet. "You are your own man, my lord. I
would never presume to advise you. I will merely say what
many gentlemen of my acquaintance have discovered to their
sorrow: a sword makes a cold wife."

With that parting arrow, Queen Eleanor tugged on her reins
and turned her palfrey back toward her own knights, leaving

Ranulf alone to ponder his whirling thoughts and to wonder why Ariane had refused the queen's offer of refuge.

With faint success, Ranulf tried to push from his mind the suggestion that he marry Ariane. To himself—solely himself—he was even willing to admit the true cause of his reluctance to consider the proposition: his fear. For all his courage in battle, he was afraid . . . afraid of the pain Ariane could cause him, afraid of being hurt again, of giving his bewitching temptress even more power over him than she already wielded.

The strength of his feelings for Ariane disturbed and bewildered Ranulf, as did his reluctance to leave her. Never before had he regretted riding away from a wench, nor had he ever missed one or longed for her presence.

God's wounds, he should be eagerly anticipating joining King Henry's siege. War and strife were his lifeblood, his reason for existence. He was a warrior, a professional soldier, a knight for whom military vassalage was a way of life. Ariane's ability to sway him from his purpose should be a warning to him.

Yet he had been a fool to think he could share her intimate secrets and not pay a price himself. Making her his leman was not the wisest course he could have taken. Were it only her body he craved, he could have sated himself and been done with it. But it was more. She had touched a weakness in his spirit, he acknowledged with dismay. And now she threatened to break through the barriers he had carefully erected over a lifetime.

He did not intend to deny himself her body now, though. Simply, he would have to guard himself with more care. He had to renew his resistance, strengthen his defenses, to prove to himself—and to Ariane—that she had not become vital to him.

Chapter 23

A thoughtful frown scored Ranulf's brow a week later as he surveyed Claredon's great hall from his position at the high table. His welcome home this morning had been nearly as elaborate as the previous one which had honored Queen Eleanor's visit, yet this time there was no queen to warrant such painstaking preparations, or to justify the dinner banquet they were about to enjoy.

A great deal of trouble had obviously been expended. The walls were brightly whitewashed, the rushes sweetly scented, and the silver and pewter polished to a high sheen. Everywhere cleanliness and order reigned.

He could see Ariane's fine hand at work here.

"She has overstepped her bounds," Ranulf murmured in an undertone loud enough for Payn to overhear.

"I for one consider it an improvement to a bachelor's existence," the knight said, grinning. " 'Struth, I had forgotten what it is like to have a well-run household."

Ranulf grunted. "That wench has taken advantage of my absence—and your soft-hearted command. You failed to curb even the worst of her excesses. You well know I would rather spend coin on armor than this tunic she gifted me with."

This morning Ariane had met him in the bailey and presented him with a fine overtunic made by her own hand—saffron silk with sleeves and collar exquisitely embroidered with black and gold thread to match his hair and eyes. Joy and pleasure at her gift had leapt within Ranulf before he could arm himself against them.

He liked the garment well enough; what did not sit well with him was her motive for giving it. Ariane was clearly determined to undermine all his defenses, and to force the issue of their marriage. It was customary for a wife to greet

328

her lord with a gift of welcome upon his return from a journey, and Ariane had behaved as if she were his lady in truth—a position Ranulf had vowed she would never hold.

Against his better judgment, he wore the tunic now, girded by a wide belt studded with amber stones. He had been unable to refuse without seeming the veriest churl. Even his squire had conspired against him to insure he donned her gift. Burc had recovered enough from his shoulder wound to help his lord dress, and the fool lad had not ceased singing Ariane's praises as a healer the entire time, nor refrained from championing her cause.

"The fabric was on hand," Payn said now in her defense, "purchased three winters ago as a marriage gift to you. And the thread you yourself recently gave her permission to buy."

Unmollified, Ranulf stiffened at the reminder of his broken betrothal. "Mark me, she is up to mischief, if not something more sinister."

His vassal laughed outright. "It is hardly sinister to wish the lord to be handsomely attired."

Ranulf shook his head, refusing to be swayed. But even more disturbing than her scheming was the apparent conspiracy that others seemed to be waging against him. Burc, Payn, Queen Eleanor, even the king himself, all seemed eager for him to wed the lady.

Ranulf had delivered Eleanor to Henry's camp as commanded, without incident, and tarried two more days to discuss his sovereign's future plans. King Henry, a man known for his violent disposition, was in a rage over the slow progress of the siege of Mortimer's castle, but the arrival of his queen soothed the royal temper somewhat. At Eleanor's persuading—and in order to please her—Henry had proposed reinstating Ranulf's betrothal.

The queen's attempt to force his hand annoyed Ranulf, and perversely strengthened his resolve to resist. Not even a king could force a man to wed against his will, but Henry *could* make his life a misery if he chose. And it would be political and perhaps financial suicide to defy the king's wishes.

The most disturbing aspect of the matter, however, was the profound relief Ranulf felt at Ariane's decision to continue on at Claredon. She had refused Eleanor's offer of protection, and thus remained in his hands, under his control. His spirits could not help but be lighter—but he resented the feeling. It should not matter so much to him whether Ariane stayed or went.

"Mean you to say," Payn asked lightly, "that you do not enjoy the comforts the Lady Ariane has provided you as lord?"

Ranulf's frown darkened. He enjoyed the comforts too much, that was the trouble. He could grow addicted to her softness if he did not take care. Already—for the first time in his life, in truth—he found that the pleasures of war and fighting had dimmed. After living in luxury at Claredon for a few short weeks, he was no longer quite so eager to return to the harsh existence he had always known. His sojourn at Henry's camp had been a portent. Sleeping in tents on the damp, hard ground, enduring boredom and rain and vermin-ridden victuals, had lost its appeal—which was what came of allowing softness and ease into his life.

"Methinks you undervalue the benefits a wife can offer," Payn suggested with a grin.

"God's teeth, you sound like Queen Eleanor."

"Did she press you to wed Ariane?"

"She hinted strongly, and incited the king to support her view."

"Perhaps you should heed her."

Ranulf sent his vassal a look that would have pierced him fatally had it been a lance.

"Perhaps you *should* give wedded bliss a try," Payn prodded, undaunted. "If your husbandly duties become too much for you, you can always send her away to another of your castles."

Ranulf involuntarily jerked his wine cup and sent the dark liquid sloshing over the rim. "I will not wed, only to banish or lock my lady away!"

"Then . . ."—Payn's features suddenly grew sober with concern—"should you not let Ariane go?"

"I am careful of what is mine," Ranulf muttered defensively.

"I think you need not worry she might put horns on you, Ranulf. She has eyes for no one but you."

Ranulf looked away. They had never spoken of his false suspicions regarding his vassal's relationship with Ariane, but evidently Payn had forgiven him for his unwarranted jealousy.

"I believe she can be trusted," Payn asserted quietly. "And that her virtue is above reproach. You would see it yourself if only you would judge her fairly."

Forcing himself to control his rising temper and to relax his rigid grip on his goblet, Ranulf gave a dismissive shrug. The discussion was ended. He would not honor Ariane as his wife.

He was satisfied with the current state of affairs. Ariane had not left his demesne when given the opportunity, and while she remained, she would fulfill the position of his leman. Until he'd had his fill of her, he would not let her go. He *could* not let her go.

With all her might, Ariane wished Ranulf could come to trust her and care for her. It seemed unlikely. Since his arrival home three days before, he had shown little sign of lowering his vigilant guard. Yet unaccountably she was filled with hope.

Perhaps her optimism was due to the change in the weather. Spring had come to England in full force, with trees and blossoms bursting into vivid bloom. The sun warmed the earth by day, while gentle rains nurtured the fields by night, creating the conditions for a bountiful harvest.

It was a season of renewal, of peace and promise. A time for lovers to rejoice in the sheer beauty of life.

Her lover, however, seemed determined to keep dark clouds hovering over the horizon.

Ranulf's reaction to her gift, for example, had sorely disheartened her. Ariane had taken fierce delight in the pleasure of his expression when she first presented him with the finely stitched tunic—a pleasure that was all too fleeting. The wonder and elation on his features had abruptly disappeared, to be replaced by suspicion and mistrust—a look she was coming to recognize with loathing.

In truth, she was coming to better understand Ranulf. She no longer quailed at his harsh scowls or flinched at his cutting remarks, yet it distressed her to know he still regarded her as his enemy.

She had done everything in her power to prove her worth

to him, to show that she would make a capable chatelaine and a good wife.

She had willingly endeavored to make Ranulf's life more pleasing, to make herself indispensable to her lord's welfare. With effort she had even kept control of her sharp tongue, remembering the advice her mother had given her: that it fell to women to charm and civilize their men and teach them to curb their warlike inclinations.

Regrettably, Ariane could only mark her progress in minute increments—a heated glance, a smile, a tender touch, manifestations that Ranulf bestowed upon her all too rarely. 'Twas not fair! The Virgin save her, he could trample on her heart by merely smiling at her, while remaining coolly aloof and distant himself. He refused to acknowledge her endeavors or recognize her merit as a helpmeet.

Yet she refused to abandon hope. Ranulf needed a wife, needed her. It remained to convince *him* of that.

One evening when she was battling him over the chessboard, Ariane attempted to plead her case and found herself unwisely arguing again over possession of the keys to the castle.

"I cannot see why you object to my resuming the duties I have held for these four years past," she remarked dryly. "Perhaps you fear the responsibility will overtax my intelligence."

"In truth," Ranulf retorted with a dry humor of his own, "I fear it would overtax your oath to me. Were you to be given the keys, you might feel encouraged to let more of my prisoners escape, as you did Simon Crecy."

Ariane was surprised by his teasing tone, and answered in kind. "I thought my action fully justified that night. I daresay you would have done the same in my position—to try and foil an invader."

"I would never have been in your position, for I would not have betrayed my king."

"I did *not* betray King Henry."

"Your sire did, which is the same thing."

The seriousness of the charge, even expressed lightly, made her stiffen. " 'Tis not true. My father is innocent."

"Lord Walter joined Hugh Mortimer with a troop of knights and men-at-arms merely for a lark?"

"It was his duty to provide knight's fees for his liege."

"It was his duty to support his king, just as it was yours to obey the king's orders and surrender Claredon to my control. Your actions then were proof enough of your disloyalty."

Ariane clenched her teeth. "Loyalty must be earned, my lord. What have you done to win mine?"

Ranulf moved a wooden knight across the board to take one of her pawns, refusing to be provoked into a full-fledged quarrel. "I have no need to win it. As your overlord, it is mine to claim by right."

Ariane shook her head. "You have readily proven you can take almost anything from me—my possessions, my body, my oath of obedience—but my loyalty cannot be commanded. It is mine to give as I choose."

Dismissively, Ranulf fixed his attention on the carved wooden chess pieces, yet he saw her point—and was struck hard by a thought. If he wholly won her loyalty, he need not fear her betrayal. A reflective frown turned down the corners of his mouth.

While he mused, Ariane pressed the issue. "I cannot comprehend your obstinacy. Perhaps I overestimated *your* intelligence. I had the absurd notion that you would be pleased to have your castle put in order."

He made a dry sound in his throat. "Forgive me if I find myself suspicious of your efforts to please me."

"Why? What have I done to deserve your suspicions?"

His gaze lifted to search her face. "Does your memory escape you so soon? You bloodied my bedsheets with your false virginal stains and tried to force me to wed you, for one."

Ariane colored, wishing he had not so unforgiving a memory. "I was in error, I admit it. I wished to make you honor your promise to wed me, but I chose the wrong way to go about it."

Barely mollified, Ranulf studied her. "And you think now that by engaging in wifely tasks, you can persuade me to make you my wife in truth, and thus better your lot."

Ariane lowered her own gaze to hide her pain. That had

indeed been her strategy at first, but she had not counted on falling in love with this stubborn, hard-hearted lout. She shook her head, achingly aware that she was not loved by Ranulf in return.

"Not only my lot, but the people of Claredon's—and yours as well."

Ranulf's brows shot up in disbelief that Ariane cared a whit for *his* welfare.

"A castle needs a lady," she insisted. "And a lord needs a wife."

"I have managed well enough without one till now."

"Have you?" Her tone was dubious. "I hear tell that Vernay is a cold, hostile place that provides you so little cheer, you refuse to live there."

It was Ranulf's turn to stiffen. "I collect Payn has been filling your head with nonsensical tales."

"Are they nonsense, my lord? Or do you simply refuse to see reality? A wife could benefit you greatly."

Willfully Ranulf returned his attention to the chessboard. "Good servants can see to my comfort, while any wench will satisfy my carnal needs. What need have I for a wife?"

That stymied her momentarily. "To provide sons, for one thing."

"I have sons, half a dozen children scattered from Normandy to Poitou."

"*Legitimate* sons, who are unconstrained by the bonds of serfdom. Members of the nobility. What of them? Have you never wished for heirs?"

Ranulf shifted uneasily on his stool. There were times in the past when he had thought wistfully of noble sons to follow him, youthful images of himself whom he could raise to knighthood. He would teach them gentleness and compassion, not the cut of the lash. . . . Yet noble sons could only be gotten from the loins of a noblewoman, and he had never met one yet whom he would trust to be the mother of his children . . . not until Ariane—

His mind shied away from that disturbing thought. "My wishes are hardly your concern," he muttered. "And I believe it is your move."

"A moment past, you demanded my loyalty," Ariane retorted in frustration, "and yet when I offer it, you tell me to mind my own affairs!"

He could sense her growing vexation, and for some inexplicable reason it appeased him. Silently Ranulf vowed to give in to at least some of her demands regarding the running of his household. In truth, Ariane *was* a fine manager, and if reinstating her duties would sweeten her temper and win her loyalty, then he was willing to make concessions. Not that he would announce his surrender just yet. . . .

Aloud, Ranulf said, "I know you can well manage a household, wench, but that is scarcely a reason to wed you. I need you only to ease my lonely nights . . . and days." He flashed Ariane a wicked grin. "You do have your uses. I confess I find you entertaining."

"Entertaining!"

"Aye. Your temper is amusing to watch. Your sharp tongue arouses me. . . ." His gaze swept over her, coming to linger on her breasts. "As does your lovely body. I like the challenge of a saucy, comely wench."

"You . . . you . . ." she sputtered.

Her ire rising to the breaking point, Ariane picked up a wooden bishop and threw it at Ranulf's broad chest. It bounced off and clattered to the floor.

He laughed at her outburst, the warm, rich sound filling the chamber. The knave actually had the audacity to laugh!

Her eyes flashed sparks as she reached for another piece, but Ranulf was quicker. With a sudden lunge, he moved around the table and caught her in his grasp, pinning both her arms to her sides. In a single, easy motion, he bore her down to the furs before the hearth.

Ariane struggled against his embrace, but Ranulf subdued her with ease. When finally she ceased squirming to glare at him, panting, he grinned down at her, his eyes bright. "You have challenged me and lost, demoiselle. Now you must pay a forfeit."

Before she could catch her breath or even protest, he covered her mouth roughly with his. His kiss was hungry, lusty, and when he finally raised his head, his eyes smoldered with need. "Ah, what you do to me, wench . . ."

He gazed down at her silently for a moment before shaking his head. An intimate, amused warmth entered his voice as he remarked, "And yet your methods of persuasion seem wanting. Why do you not try to use your womanly arts to stir my passion and sway my judgment instead of forever fighting me? A wise leman knows well how to bend a man to her whims—with honey, not vinegar."

"I am not like your lemans," Ariane said stiffly, refusing to be provoked further by his teasing.

In truth, she was like no other wench of his acquaintance, Ranulf reflected, and yet she was a woman, with a woman's needs. It occurred to him, not for the first time, that he would do better to take the offensive, to use passion as a weapon in order to compel Ariane's loyalty and bind her to him.

His lips curved upward in anticipation. He had enjoyed their fight, but he would relish her surrender more.

He bent to nibble at her lips, murmuring in a voice suddenly grown husky, "And I am not like other lords. Indeed, I am inclined to show you lenience and devise a penance you will enjoy."

Ariane pushed futilely against his broad shoulders, deploring the way her senses throbbed at Ranulf's gentle, arousing kisses. "I will derive no enjoyment from being mauled, you conceited oaf! I find no pleasure in your touch."

"None?" His slow-growing smile was a sensual caress. "Methinks you are untruthful, wench. Shall I prove it?"

He had no need to prove his expertise, Ariane thought with despair. Ranulf well knew he could command her body's every response. She twisted beneath him, but with his weight holding her down, she could not break free.

He did not bother to undress her, but merely tugged down the bodice of her tunics and shift, baring her beauty to his gaze. His golden eyes kindled. For a heartbeat, he buried his face in her breasts, drinking in the sweet warm fragrance of her skin. "Can I make you hot for me, I wonder?"

In answer to his own question, his mouth dipped to her repeatedly, tasting and kissing her erect nipples . . . until she whimpered.

He smiled against her skin. "That is how I want you, sweeting . . . pleading for me . . ." Reaching down, he drew up her skirts and slipped a probing hand between her thighs. "Show me where you want me to caress you."

She tried unsuccessfully to elude his searching fingers. "Ranulf, please. . . ."

"Please?" His teasing grin held an intimacy that made her heart twist. "Truly I like that word on your lips."

"Nay, Ranulf! 'Tis indecent."

He laughed, a low sexual laugh that made her hurt inside. "You claim modesty after all we have been to one another?"

"What have I been to you?" Ariane retorted bitterly. "You said I mean naught to you."

"No, wench, you mean a great deal to me."

"You want only my body."

"And your body wants me," he murmured huskily against her throat.

"No . . ."

In answer, he rubbed his thumb along the wet, swollen lips of her sex, finding the tender nub that was the seat of her passion. "This bud is plump and juicy—evidence of your desire, sweeting. Can you honestly claim you dislike being stroked here?" Her muted whimper made him smile. Probingly, he slid two fingers into her sleek passage, making Ariane draw a sharp breath. "So you feel no pleasure at my touch, at having my flesh buried within you?" His fingers thrust deeper, while his thumb caressed.

Her choked gasp was the only answer he needed.

"I crave a taste of you," he announced softly in satisfaction.

Shifting his weight, Ranulf moved his mouth downward over her body, to her womanhood, his strong hands spreading her naked thighs for his enjoyment. When he lowered his head to her, Ariane clenched her teeth, trying desperately not to respond to each delicately provocative thrust of his tongue, but the sweet agony was too much to bear. Her hips strained against his mouth of their own accord.

When a moan dredged from deep within her throat, Ranulf stopped to gaze up at her in triumph. His lips, wet with her dew, curved in a tender, arrogant smile.

Without haste, he raised his tunic and tugged at his braies, freeing himself. Then he slowly lowered himself upon her, sighing with pleasure as he entered her.

"I may not give you rest until the dawn," he whispered as he began to move urgently within her.

With a soft moan, Ariane closed her eyes in surrender. And when the shattering ecstasy came moments later, the pleasure was more intense than anything she had ever known, while the heartache was greater than she thought she could bear.

Ranulf desired her only for her body, while she desperately needed and craved his love.

When it was over, when he was holding her trembling form in the aftermath of passion, she felt the helpless tears well in her eyes. One spilled over, despite her effort to quell it and the terrible ache in her heart.

"Ariane?" Ranulf raised himself on one elbow, his eyes dark with concern at the sight of her weeping. "Did I hurt you?"

Yes, she wanted to cry, yet she sniffed and dashed away the moisture, determined to give him no cause to think she was employing feminine wiles. "No, it is naught."

With a puzzled frown, he brushed her damp cheek with his thumb, tracing downward to her trembling mouth.

"Just hold me . . ." Ariane whispered, pressing her face against his chest.

Uncertainly, Ranulf wrapped his arms around her and gathered her close, comforting her silently with his embrace, offering her tenderness in the only way he knew how.

Chapter 24

Ariane sighed as she watched the display of knightly exploits in the practice yard. Even from her position at the solar window, she could distinguish Ranulf from the scores of helmeted, mailed horsemen. He was the most powerful, the most dominating, the most compelling warrior of them all. And he had vanquished her as easily as he conducted his military triumphs.

She had fallen helplessly, hopelessly, in love with the unfeeling lout.

It was vexing, infuriating, and entirely unjust. Whenever she remembered Ranulf's teasing laughter, her blood simmered. He claimed to find her *entertaining!* She provided sport for him, only that. He used her merely to slake his lust and to relieve his boredom.

She could not forgive him for his insensitivity, despite his recent carnal tenderness.

In the fortnight since his return from King Henry's camp, Ranulf had shown her a passion that left her gasping and weak. Yet passion was no longer enough. Ariane wanted far more. No longer was she content merely to aspire to become his wife, or to await crumbs of attention tossed her way. Somehow, someway, she vowed to make Ranulf love her.

Regrettably, she had hit upon no suitable strategy to help her achieve those ends. As May had ripened into June, she'd marked little progress in her attempts at winning his love. Ranulf remained invulnerable, invincible, while he held the power to wring her heart dry.

At times—chiefly when she was in his arms—he seemed to soften toward her, raising her hopes that he was coming to care for her, even if he would not admit it. But more often he treated her with cool indifference. She could not count the minor concessions he had made regarding the running of the castle. Ranulf had turned several domestic matters over to her, placing the kitchen and tower staffs under her control, yet he had not given her back the keys to the castle or access to the household accounts. He had come no closer to honoring her as his lady, nor had he exhibited the least inclination to return her love.

"He regards you with all the tender concern of an ox," Ariane muttered to herself, gazing after Ranulf's distant figure in frustration.

Even his occasional tenderness was suspect. Three days before he had even gifted her with a costly bauble, the kind of present a lord might give his lady. The jewelled broach that pinned the front of a mantle together was carved of onyx in the shape of his device, a dragon rampant, with rubies for eyes and studded around with the same precious gems.

When Ranulf had first presented it to her, a warm glow had swept through Ariane—until she realized the significance of the gift: it branded her as his property.

"Is it not to your liking?" Ranulf asked.

"Nay . . . I mean . . . it is lovely. I am well pleased, my lord." But she had been untruthful. She would rather have an avowal of affection from him than all the jewels in the kingdom.

She was preparing to turn away from the window when the watchman's horn announced new arrivals at the castle gates. Ariane waited as a small party rode across the drawbridge and through the outer bailey. A strange sense of foreboding curled in her stomach when she realized one of the newcomers was a woman.

Veiled and cloaked, the woman urged her palfrey toward the practicing knights. When Ranulf saw her, he broke away from his men and rode toward her at an eager gallop. Coming to a plunging halt at her side, he apparently offered greetings. Ariane would have given a year off her life to hear the exchange between them—until the veiled woman bowed low and kissed his gloved hands.

A shaft of pain streaked through Ariane, so fierce it took her breath away, yet she forced herself to move away from the window. She would not allow herself to jump to foolish conclusions. Doubtless there were reasonable explanations for such a fawning display. Many people kissed the lord's hand—supplicants for his favor, for example.

Trying unsuccessfully to repress the knot of apprehension inside her, Ariane made her way below to the great hall, where the new arrivals were just entering.

One of Ranulf's younger knights, Richard of Lorne, approached Ariane at once, escorting the woman. "May I present Layla of Acre, milady, summoned from Vernay upon the lord's orders. Lord Ranulf bids you find her private accommodations."

Acre in the Holy Land? Vernay in Normandy? *Private?* Such disjointed thoughts flashed through Ariane's mind, but she could only focus on the last. It was unusual for any but the highest-ranking guests to be afforded privacy, since a castle had few chambers and hundreds of people to shelter.

Just then, Layla raised her veil and Ariane caught her breath at the woman's stunning beauty. Obviously from the East, Layla was sloe-eyed, with heavy black brows and lashes, full ruby-red lips, and darkly golden skin that seemed to glow with vitality. Lush and sultry, she possessed a figure that would entice any male ... especially a lusty, sensual, physical male like Ranulf.

Was the beauty Ranulf's leman? A Saracen from the East? Brought here from Vernay for what purpose?

It was all Ariane could do to nod civilly in acknowledgement of the imparted command. The thought of Ranulf rousing any other woman to passion scalded her with sick jealousy, but the realization that he had summoned his leman the vast distance from Normandy to take *her* place made her feel as if her heart were slowly being ripped from her breast.

She did as she was bid without speaking, not trusting herself to say a word without losing any semblance of dignity or control. She led Layla to an alcove off the women's dormitory, a small chamber with a bed built directly into the wall, curtained with rich hangings, all the while enduring sly looks from the Saracen beauty. When Layla expressed her thanks in heavily accented French that was both sultry and musical, Ariane nodded, still reeling from the blow. In a haze of pain, she returned to the solar to nurse her bleeding heart.

When sometime later, Ranulf came in with his squire, Burc, directly from the training field, Ariane stood at the window, her back to him, her stance rigid as glass. She felt brittle, fragile, perilously unstable: if he touched her, she would shatter; if he spoke, she would explode.

"Did you welcome Layla?" Ranulf asked as he unbuckled his sword belt, blithely unaware of the tension emanating from Ariane in waves.

"I did as you ordered, my lord," she replied quietly, carefully, straining to keep any emotion from her voice. "She is your leman, is she not?"

"She *was*. Her story is a wretched one. My lord father bought her from a brothel in Acre. She had been torn from a good family and sold there by slavers. My sire rescued her"—Ranulf's tone turned sardonic—"in order to save her heathen soul, and brought her to Vernay, where I inherited her upon his . . . abdication."

Ariane felt her heart whither a little further at Ranulf's explanation. She no longer harbored any doubts that he had brought his beautiful Saracen concubine here to service him. *Any wench will satisfy my carnal needs*, he had claimed only recently, yet he had been dissatisfied enough with *her* to desire a foreign beauty in his bed instead, even at the expense of summoning the wench from another country.

If Ranulf thought she would meekly accede to his plans, though, Ariane vowed, he could think again.

Her fingers suddenly clenching into fists, she turned to confront him. Her face was set like flint, but the pain shimmering in her eyes was unmistakable.

Not normally thick witted, Ranulf paused in the act of pulling off his tunic, then cast a dismissive glance at his squire. "I desire a moment alone."

When Burc had gone, Ranulf raised a concerned eyebrow at her. "What is amiss, sweeting?"

"*Sweeting?* You bring your *whore* into my home to replace me in your bed and then shower me with endearments?" Ariane's voice trembled with scorn and fury, while she looked as if she might again throw something at him.

Glancing at the chessboard, Ranulf took a precautionary step backward. "You are mistaken. I have no intention of replacing you with Layla."

"You intend to enjoy both of us together, is that it?" Her

voice lost its careful control. "You plan to practice your wicked perversions on *two* of us at once?"

Offering her a rueful smile, Ranulf shook his head. In the past he had been known to enjoy such sport, but asking Ariane to participate in such licentiousness was the farthest thing from his mind. He had no desire to bed Layla—or any wench other than Ariane, for that matter.

Hoping to calm her, he raised his hands, palms out, but she was too heated and hurt to notice.

Her eyes kindling, she pointed at the door. "I will not share you, do you mark me? Certainly not with that . . . that heathen creature!"

Ranulf's conciliatory smile faded, while his eyes narrowed. It was one thing for him to overlook her sharp tongue because he enjoyed the spice of their spirited exchanges. It was another to let her rule him with ultimatums.

She ignored his look of warning entirely. "I will not endure such despicable treatment from you!" Ariane declared. "I will not share you!"

Ranulf stared in amazement as she stamped her slippered foot. With her stormy eyes both flashing sparks and sparkling with tears, she was the picture of defiance and wounded outrage. He had never seen such an outburst from her.

"What is this, sweeting?" he said slowly. "From your shrewishness, I could almost suppose you jealous."

"Jealous!" She skewered him with her eyes. "I care not how many women you have! You can take your lust elsewhere—anywhere—it matters not to me. But I will not be subjected to the ridicule of everyone in this keep."

"This keep and everything in it is mine, including you, wench. Think you to tell me whom I will and will not bed?"

"I would not *dream* of depriving you of your pleasure, my lord," she retorted witheringly. "In truth, I would be delighted to be relieved of your lascivious attentions."

He stared at her a long moment, seeing the hurt shimmering in her eyes, hearing the echo of tears underlying the hysterical note in her voice. Some of the heat left Ranulf's expression. Ariane possessed pride aplenty, he had always known that, but her outburst had been due to more than wounded pride, he would stake his life on it. Despite her denial, he could not help but believe she lied. She *was* jealous. She was jealous of a wench who meant nothing to him.

A slow smile of male triumph stretched Ranulf's lips at this twist of events. Ariane was at fault this time. *She* had been the one to erupt in a foolish, unwarranted fit of jealousy, while he had kept his calm. She was jealous! His self-satisfied smile broadened into a grin. He rather liked the idea of Ariane's possessiveness.

His good humor, haplessly, had the same effect as pouring oil on flames. "You dare laugh?" With a shriek, Ariane clenched her fists in impotent fury, wishing she could strike him. "Oooh, you ... you cur!" Trembling with rage, she wielded the only weapon at her command. "Must you be reminded that the Church considers adultery a *sin?*"

"Adultery!" The smirk faded from Ranulf's face.

"Yes, adultery! When a man fornicates with someone not his wife, it is deemed a sin!"

Suddenly sober, Ranulf crossed his arms over his chest. "You are not my wife, wench. May I remind you that no vows were ever spoken between us?"

"The Church may view the matter differently!" Ariane retorted scathingly. "Your petition for annulment may not be granted."

The corner of his mouth twisted with mockery. "Methinks your denunciation of adultery rings false, sweeting. I have never known a lady of your station to put principle above personal ambition."

Her fury exploded. "I am nothing, *nothing*, like the noblewomen you have known, you blind, thick-witted ox! I value honor and loyalty and virtue as much as you—more so! I always have! And I will not countenance your hypocritical standards any longer—or your despicable treatment. If you wish to lie with your strumpet, you will no longer lie with *me!*"

Determined to force the issue of who between them was lord—and to drag an admission of jealousy from her if he could—Ranulf fixed her with a menacing look. "What right have you to dictate to me?" he demanded. "Perhaps you have a reason for your possessiveness?"

"You desire a reason? Because I am a stupid fool! Because I *love* you, you wretched lout!"

For a long moment afterward, utter silence reigned. Ranulf could hear the slow thud of his heart as he stared at Ariane in startled disbelief.

She *loved* him? Love, as in affection? As in tenderness and soft-hearted concern? As in witless obsession?

Ranulf shook his head dazedly, doubting her claim, refusing to believe her profession of love. His entire life he had been betrayed and manipulated by nobly born women like her. Though he had begun to hope Ariane was different, he could not help but wonder if her motive was only mercenary. She had tried to trick him into formalizing their union once before. Perhaps this was merely another attempt at forcing his hand.

Deliberately keeping his features blank, Ranulf leaned a muscular shoulder against the oaken bedpost. "Are you quite finished?"

Ariane felt as if he had slapped her. She had just bared her soul to Ranulf, declared her love for him, yet his expression remained cool, his eyes neutral. No, not neutral. There was doubt there, even suspicion.

And he seemed determined to ignore her declaration—as well as to change the subject.

"Sheath your claws, vixen," Ranulf said abruptly. "I sent for Layla, not to act as my leman, but as a healer."

Her dismay faltered, to be replaced by confusion. "A . . . healer?"

"Aye. I summoned her because she is skilled in the medical arts of the East. She originally comes from a family of physicians—physicians whose knowledge is far more advanced than any our leeches possess. I had hopes Layla might be able to aid your diseased mother."

It was Ariane's turn to stare in shock. "You brought her here . . . to cure my mother?"

"To *attempt* a cure, yes. You yourself said that a successful treatment for leprosy is unknown. Layla cannot be expected to work miracles, but if she can ease your lady mother's plight, then I will consider it worth the expense."

When Ariane remained mute, Ranulf continued. "I ordered Layla to bring her medicine baskets from Normandy without revealing why. At the time, Burc was still ailing from his wounds, so it will be assumed that I summoned her to tend him. No one else knows the true reason. And I expect most will think Layla my leman, just as you did. It would be wise to foster that mistaken assumption if we wish to keep your mother's secret."

Stunned, Ariane could only gaze at him wordlessly.

"I had thought you would be pleased," Ranulf said dryly, "but instead you rant at me like an alewife."

"I am pl-pleased," Ariane stammered. "And grateful ... immensely grateful, my lord." Mollified, greatly chastened, she bowed her head. "Forgive me, my lord ... for my outburst. I apologize ... most humbly."

Uncrossing his arms, he strode over to her and put a finger under her chin, forcing her to meet his gaze. His amber eyes had kindled with a heat she recognized so well ... and something else that she could not name.

"Save your gratitude for Layla. You can repay me in services rendered. Now, I suggest we confer with her to see what is best to be done with your mother."

"But ... will she even minister to a leper?"

"I have no doubt the wench is greedy enough," Ranulf said cynically. "If she can help, I intend to reward her with her freedom and fund her return passage to the Holy Land."

"Ranulf ... " A huge lump in her throat choked Ariane, making her voice quaver. Unable to speak, she reached for his hands and bent to kiss them, as she had seen Layla do.

Ranulf withdrew his hands abruptly, looking supremely ill at ease. "Come, assist me to wash, and then we will summon Layla."

Layla showed no surprise at being summoned to the lord's solar in the presence of another beautiful woman, even the previous chatelaine of the castle and a lady far above her in rank. Indeed, Layla's sensual, catlike smile when she glanced at the huge bed expressed anticipation rather than dismay.

Evidently the Saracen woman had reached the same conclusion as Ariane regarding the reason for her presence at Claredon: that they were rivals for the lord's carnal attentions. Ranulf, however, quickly disabused Layla of the notion, and explained his proposition.

Her response could be read in the emotions that flickered across her exotic, expressive features: disappointment, feminine pique, shrewd resignation, and finally, burgeoning delight. She seemed to regret Ranulf's indifference to her charms, but truly eager to win her return passage to her homeland. With scarcely a moment's hesitation, she promised to devote her best efforts toward helping the poor, afflicted woman. Ariane felt hopeful that Layla would at least make a sincere attempt.

It was hours later, after they had journeyed to the eastern wood so that Layla might examine the Lady Constance, when Ariane allowed her hope full rein. Layla seemed confident she could concoct a treatment that would at least slow the ravaging effects of the disease. In additions to potions and perfumed lotions for the skin, she claimed to possess a certain green mold made from stale bread and the juice of pomegranates that multiplied when left in moist, warm darkness. At present she had too little of the mold to prepare more than a few applications of a poultice, but in time, she thought she could grow enough for Lady Constance's needs.

Ariane tried not to let her hopes swell too high. She wanted too desperately to believe a cure for her beloved mother was possible. Yet for the first time in a long, long while, she felt a spark of true joy at the promise Layla's remedy held.

She was genuinely grateful for the Saracen's presence, and surprised herself by actually feeling sympathy for a beautiful woman who was in truth a potential rival. Layla had doubtless led a wretched life; it must have been terrible, being sold into slavery in a strange land.

Yet when Ariane was lying in Ranulf's bed that night, her worries regarding the beautiful concubine returned full force. Ranulf claimed he did not mean to replace her with his former leman, Ariane knew, yet he had scarcely spoken a word to her throughout the evening meal. And when they retired to the solar, he had not made love to her, nor even touched her. Instead, he had turned away, lying on his side, giving her his scarred back.

Ariane sensed that his withdrawal was not mere indifference; in truth, he seemed almost ill at ease with her. If she did not know better, she would have thought him *nervous*. Perhaps her avowal of love earlier had disturbed him. She regretted now blurting out the truth in so rash a fashion. She had wanted to tell him, to admit her feelings, but not in such a manner—not shouted in anger.

"Would you rather your Saracen leman share your bed in my place?" Ariane asked Ranulf quietly, and then held her breath, awaiting his answer.

"I told you, she holds no interest for me."

"She is very beautiful," Ariane murmured almost inaudibly.

"Layla's bounteous charms cannot compare to your attractions, if that is what you ask."

"Then why do you turn away from me? Have I done something to displease you?"

With a sigh, Ranulf rolled over and gathered Ariane in his arms. She nestled against his naked heat gratefully, and yet even this comforting closeness was unsatisfying. Ranulf was absently stroking her hair, yet he remained silent, uncommunicative. He seemed distracted, deep in thought, hardly aware of her presence.

In truth, Ranulf was brooding over her earlier profession of love. Ariane's admission had terrified him. Could it be true? Could she believe herself in love with him? Or was this merely another scheme of hers to win his surrender? He *wanted* to believe her.

A pale copper lock of her hair curled around his fingers, sleek and vibrant, with a life of its own. Ranulf stared at it a moment, then raised it to his lips.

"Ranulf?" she murmured in the silence. "I meant what I said earlier. . . . I love you." Abruptly she felt him stiffen against her.

"Do you?" The cynicism in his tone clearly conveyed his doubt.

Ariane drew back, trying to see his face. "Why can you not believe me?" she asked softly. "Because of your mother's betrayal so long ago?"

Reflecting reluctantly on his bitter past, Ranulf raised his gaze, his mouth drawn in a rigid line, his eyes bleak. "Aye . . . I suppose . . . in part. I hated her . . . the noblewoman who gave me birth. She lay with her peasant lover in sin, and defiled the honor of Vernay. Because of her, my life became a living hell."

"Perhaps she allowed her heart to rule her head. It happens, sometimes, when feelings become so strong that naught else matters. Love makes fools of us at times."

The curling of his lip told her clearly how strongly he scorned the notion of love.

"Love?" he murmured softly. "The word holds no meaning for me." He had never known a woman's love, never wished to. Love was the villain in too many tales for him to suddenly wish to embrace it.

Sorrowfully, her heart aching, Ariane searched his face. After his experiences, she could understand why Ranulf would be disdainful of love. Why he would hold little belief in its power. Why he could not believe any noblewoman could be faithful to her vows. "My lord, will you condemn all of us for the sins of a few?"

He remained ominously silent.

"You have my love and loyalty," Ariane vowed softly. "As God is my witness, I give it to you freely, and with all my heart."

Searchingly, desperately wanting to believe, Ranulf returned her gaze. In the dim light of the bedside candle, the gray of her eyes looked silver and softly luminous—and totally honest. He could almost, almost believe her.

And yet the harsh lessons of a lifetime could not be forgotten. He had spoken true. He knew nothing of love. After so many years of hate, he doubted he was capable of it.

His mouth twisted with a bitterness he could not hide. "I cannot return your love. I have no heart."

She placed her hand on his bare, muscled chest, splaying her fingers against his breastbone, feeling the steady, rhythmic beat beneath her palm. "I think you do, my lord. It wants only nurturing to be freed from its shell of armor."

Her own heart felt as if it were breaking when he gently caught her wrist and drew her hand away. And yet he did not release her completely. Instead, he regarded her bleakly, his eyes tormented.

"What am I to do with you?" he murmured almost to himself.

"Can you not simply trust me, Ranulf?"

He squeezed his eyes shut. Trusting her would be like baring his breast for a sword thrust. The depth of his mistrust for women of her kind was exceeded only by his hatred for his father.

Feeling somehow brittle, he lowered his head, pressing his face to her breasts, as if seeking solace. His very uncertainty struck a tender cord in Ariane. She held him gently, her fingers stroking his dark hair, not pressing him to give assurances he could not give. She had known how difficult winning his heart would be, how deeply afraid Ranulf was to love or trust her.

Silently, tenderly, she tilted his head up and drew his lips to hers for a kiss, renewing her vow to make him love her. If only she could prove her loyalty to him, she might be able to overcome his fear of betrayal. But somehow, someway she intended to heal this man who had lived too long with demons from his past.

If only he could believe her, Ranulf thought the next morning as he sat watching Ariane speak with the serfs at the lower end of the hall. Something of his feelings for her must have shown on his face, for his vassal remarked on it.

"You are smitten by her, admit it," Payn murmured, satisfaction in his tone.

Ranulf dragged his gaze away from Ariane. Smitten, aye. The wench had tied him into knots. She had taken hold of him in a way he could no longer control, and the thought terrified him. He was bewildered by his feelings, plagued by doubts—and he knew it was futile to try to hide his turmoil from his closest friend.

"She is the lady of Claredon in all but name, my lord," Payn observed. "You may as well make her lady of it in truth."

Ranulf stared into his wine cup. Already he had made so many concessions to Ariane that she practically ran his keep. Against his better judgment, he had yielded to her ambitions, even though he knew he risked betrayal.

Betrayal, that was the rub.

"How can I *know* if I can trust her?" Frustration marked his words, while his fists clenched around his chalice.

"You cannot, Ranulf," Payn replied solemnly. "You must simply have faith that she will be true to you. I think that with the Lady Ariane the risk will not be too great."

But what if it were? Ranulf reflected. He knew himself well enough to predict his reaction. He would never countenance an unfaithful wife. He would slay her first in a jealous rage—or imprison her. Could he do that to Ariane? What kind of husband would he make her, a man with his brutal past? He knew nothing of love or tenderness; he had none to give her.

Yet what if his vassal was right? Ranulf reflected in a turmoil of agitation. He *had* changed in the past weeks. Despite his austere self-discipline, he was coming to appreciate the comforts of a settled life. He *liked* having a gentlewoman at his side, looking after his needs.

Upon occasion he had even let his thoughts stray. What would it be like having Ariane as his wife? The pleasure of waking up in her arms each morning? The joy of having her beneath him each night? The possibility of having children by her?

He closed his eyes, recalling last night when he had finally made love to her. The fierce sweetness of it had possessed him totally, leaving no room to doubt her sincerity when she professed to love him.

And yet in the cold light of day, his doubts returned to torment him. Could he ever come to forget his bitter past? Would it ever be possible for him to begin again ... fresh and clean and new ... with Ariane at his side? Would she fight with him against the world, if need be?

And what of Ariane herself? She claimed to love him now, but what if she had mistaken her heart? Could he watch her turn from him in indifference and scorn? Was it even possible that he could make her happy?

Looking up, Ranulf sought her out with his gaze—and frowned at what he saw. The lad, Gilbert, was accompanying Ariane from the hall.

Repressing the jealous urge to follow them and discover their intent, Ranulf forced himself to attend to his meal. He would not question her loyalty. She had asked for his trust, and he would give it ... this time. And yet it was hard, harder than riding unarmed against a legion of enemy knights.

Adjacent to the hall, in a dark alcove, Ariane was eying her half-brother quizzically. Though surprised, she had been relieved that Gilbert had sought her out. She had seen little of him in the past weeks since his challenge of Ranulf; in truth, he seemed to be avoiding her, as if afraid to face her after betraying her mother's secret to the new lord of Claredon, even though she had given her forgiveness.

Gilbert looked at her now grimly, sparing a brief, stealthy glance at the shadows that surrounded them. "My lady, I have a missive for you. A serf brought this onto the castle grounds, and entrusted me to give it directly into your hands, none other."

He withdrew a scrap of parchment that he had tucked in his belt, and offered it to her with a bow.

Curious, and with a growing sense of unease, Ariane accepted the note and quickly scanned the two brief lines.

"Mother Mary in heaven," she whispered, her heart suddenly pounding.

"What is it, my lady?" Gilbert asked anxiously, with a show of his former impassioned concern.

"Simon Crecy has returned." Looking up, she gazed at her brother with dismay. "He desires me to meet him in the forest."

Chapter 25

For much of the day Ariane agonized over torn loyalties, divided between her allegiance to her father and Claredon and her pledge to Ranulf.

She desperately wanted to prove her loyalty to Ranulf. Were she truly devoted to the new lord, she would turn over Simon's missive to him and allow Ranulf to deal with it. What better proof than to deliver his enemy into his hands? Yet by betraying Simon, she might be sending a good man to his death. Ranulf had been furious at Simon's escape and the subsequent ambush all those weeks ago, and would be more so to discover his foe skulking in the forest. More damning, if she were caught harboring a fugitive, Ranulf would see her action as a betrayal—more treachery on her part.

And yet Simon might have word of her father. Or he might have returned to Claredon to seek aid for Walter's cause. And Ranulf would put a swift end to any hopes she had for her father's deliverance.

But no, Ranulf was a fair and merciful lord. Surely he would not condemn Simon without a hearing? Surely he would permit her the opportunity to learn of her father's fate and assist him if she could?

Mother of Christ, what course should she take?

Anguish showed in Ariane's eyes when she at last approached Ranulf as he came into the hall from the tiltyard.

"What is amiss?" he demanded, concerned by her obvious agitation.

She forced herself to cease twisting the cords of her girdle between her fingers and found the courage to answer. "I would speak with you, my lord . . . on a matter most urgent."

"Yes?"

353

"In private, if I might."

Nodding briefly, Ranulf led the way to the solar. When they were alone with the door firmly closed, he turned to Ariane with a probing look and was startled to see the tears that shone in her eyes.

"There is something I would tell you," she murmured, her voice quivering. "It may concern my father. But first ..." A tear rolled down her cheek. "I wish you to know, Ranulf ... my allegiance belongs to you now . . . even if it means my father's death for treason. I place his fate in your hands."

Confounded by her declaration, Ranulf regarded her intently, waiting.

Ariane swallowed against the ache in her throat. "My father's vassal, Simon Crecy, has returned to Claredon and ... and asked to meet with me."

She could see Ranulf's expression darkening and exclaimed, "Ranulf, I beseech you! Hear me out."

For a long moment he stared at her, not speaking as he willed himself to calm. Taking a slow breath, he searched Ariane's upturned face, gauging her look of entreaty. The gray depths of her eyes held no secrets, no deception, only a quiet anguish. "Very well. You have my undivided attention, demoiselle. What passes? Tell me, does this Simon plan an assault on Claredon Keep?"

She shook her head. "I have no knowledge of his intentions." At Ranulf's skeptical look, Ariane handed him the scrap of parchment she had received from her brother. "I tell you true, Ranulf ... I have had no communication with Simon, other than this message."

He scanned the note quickly, before again favoring her with his penetrating regard. Ariane thought that he looked as if he wanted to believe her, to give her the benefit of the doubt. Certainly, he would know she had taken a grave risk by coming to him. He could order Simon captured and imprisoned without thought to justice or compassion.

"What is it you wish of me?" asked Ranulf finally.

Hope welled within her at his rational tone. "If you would accompany me to meet Simon ... I could discover what news he has of my father."

"Why should I do so, demoiselle? How can I know your vassal does not lie in ambush to slay me?"

Ariane shook her head again, her tears spilling over. "Simon is a brave and loyal knight, my lord, qualities you value highly. When he escaped Claredon, he planned to ride north to Mortimer's castle, his only intent to work for my father's good. I cannot believe he played any part in the raid on your troops."

"Has he other men with him?"

"I know not. This message is all I was given."

"Given by your sibling, Gilbert?"

She nodded reluctantly, not liking to implicate her brother in a conspiracy, yet unsurprised by Ranulf's discernment. His sharp eyes missed little, doubtless because he was prepared for betrayal from every quarter.

He was silent for a long moment, saying finally, "Very well, I will accompany you. But I shall take along a troop of knights to be equipped for any eventuality."

"I thank you, my lord," Ariane said with fervent gratitude. "Yet . . . Simon might flee if he sees so many of you."

"Then he will be pursued and captured," Ranulf replied coolly. "You must needs be satisfied with that, demoiselle." His voice was courtesy itself, but she had learned to recognize the commanding note of finality in that tone. Nodding, Ariane swallowed her tears and fetched a mantle to shield her against the damp of the blustery day.

Ranulf followed her belowstairs uneasily. In truth, he was wary of her motives, knowing Ariane could have devised a trap to lure him into his enemy's clutches. It went against every painful lesson experience had ever taught him, every cautious instinct, to accept her tale on faith.

Then again, she could indeed be telling the truth; he had wronged her before by accusing her falsely. If so, then it presented him with a troubling dilemma. She had entrusted him with the lives of those dear to her, and counted on him to deal with them mercifully. What if he were forced to act otherwise? He could not let a traitor remain free. What if he were compelled to slay Simon? Could he bring himself to cause Ariane grief? Could he betray the trust she had placed in him?

The gray day was waning by the time he rounded up

enough of his knights and men-at-arms to form a rear guard. The lengthening shadows would aid in an enemy ambush, Ranulf noted grimly.

Ariane, riding beside him on her own palfrey, was keenly aware of Ranulf's silence. Armored in chain mail tunic and steel helm, he seemed the embodiment of an invincible, relentless warrior, and she knew he would not hesitate to lash out with all his formidable might should he be threatened.

They rode toward the east, to the forest where her mother's hut lay hidden.

" 'Tis not much further, my lord," she murmured as they reached the meadow where she and Ranulf had made love so tenderly that one enchanted spring day.

With a long, level look at her, Ranulf raised his hand and commanded his troops to await him there. Alone, he and Ariane entered the gloom of the forest. After a long moment, near a dense copse of oaks, she drew her horse to halt.

"Simon?" she called softly. "I have come as you requested."

The unmistakable sound of steel whispering against a scabbard greeted her words and sent panic leaping through her veins. In an instant, Ranulf had his sword battle-ready in hand, prepared to fight, even as Ariane cried out, "Nay, Simon! Hold! We mean you no harm!"

In the resulting silence, she could hear her heart pounding. "I have vouched for your innocence to the new lord of Claredon. If you draw sword against him, you declare yourself his enemy."

When no response was forthcoming, Ranulf added gruffly, "Show yourself, Simon Crecy. No man of honor skulks in the shadows."

Grim-faced, his hand resting on the hilt of his sheathed sword, the tall knight stepped from behind the thick trunk of an oak tree. Every measure of his stance bespoke wariness, mistrust, and yet he faced the powerful Norman warlord without flinching.

Shifting his gaze from Ranulf, Simon shot Ariane a reproachful glance. "My lady, I expected more discretion from you."

"I have no secrets from my lord Ranulf," she replied

quietly. "He has agreed to hear you out. How fare you, Simon?"

The knight eyed Ranulf once more. "Well enough, my lady."

"You can speak freely," Ariane assured him. "Have you any word of my father?"

"Word? Aye. But no success to report. I failed to gain access to Bridgenorth Castle, and so can recount only rumors."

"What did you learn?"

"I have no proof, my lady. Merely suspicions."

"Tell us," she urged.

"The siege of Bridgenorth is taking a toll on the defenders," Simon replied, keeping his attention on Ranulf. "King Henry was preparing to move war machines against the walls when Hugh Mortimer commissioned his envoy to sue for terms. When Mortimer's agents met with the king, I was able to question a page briefly. The boy said that Lord Walter is being held prisoner in the tower dungeon by his liege for refusing to declare against King Henry."

"Prisoner? He *refused?*" A fierce surge of hope welled within Ariane. If true, it meant that her father was no traitor!

Overjoyed by the possibility, she started to question Simon further, but he held up a cautioning hand. "Walter is said to be ill, my lady. If he opposed Mortimer, there is every likelihood he is being punished for his defiance ... starvation, even torture. Mortimer is known to be ruthless in his anger."

She turned to gaze beseechingly at Ranulf. "Ranulf ... *please,* you must allow me to go to him. His condition could be grave."

Ranulf's amber eyes showed no sign of weakening resolve. "Your father has been charged with high treason. You expect me to believe in his innocence without proof?"

"I swear to you," Ariane vowed in anguish, "when he rode for Bridgenorth, he was not contemplating treason. You heard Simon. My father is Henry's man."

" 'Tis true," Simon added solemnly. "Walter once considered declaring for Stephen's bastard son, William. But he realized his error the more he learned of the young man. He knew England needed a strong ruler and was prepared to support the new king fully."

"Yes," Ariane said earnestly, remembering the late King Stephen's reign—a time of greed and anarchy in a land rife with lawlessness. "My father was sickened by the strife that had torn England apart, and welcomed a ruler who could give us peace."

"And yet Walter supplied Mortimer with knights to aid the rebellion," Ranulf reminded her. "Do you deny the truth of that?"

She shook her head. "He took only those knights he owed for the land held in fief of Mortimer, as he was bound by honor to do."

At her impassioned defense, Ranulf frowned in contemplation. Ariane had always maintained her father's innocence, and in truth, it made little sense that Walter would join the revolt against Henry when he had striven to hold an even course in the tumultuous political seas of two decades. It would be the height of foolishness to declare against a powerful new king who already had many of England's great earls in his camp—and Walter had not struck him as being a fool. Far from it. The lord of Claredon had seemed as shrewd as they came.

Reluctantly Ranulf found himself swayed by Ariane's fervent defense of her father. The ambitious Hugh Mortimer had reason to rebel against Henry; as a powerful baron and supporter of the late Stephen, Mortimer doubtless harbored illusions that he could emerge victorious in a battle of wills. But there was every possibility his vassal Walter was innocent of treason if he was being held hostage to Mortimer's demands.

While Ranulf deliberated, Ariane dug her nails into her palms, waiting anxiously for him to come to a decision. "My father is not guilty," she repeated finally in a low, imploring voice, "and somehow I must prove it."

Ranulf raised his gaze to hers, but she could not read his expression.

"I could go to Henry and plead my father's case—"

"No." Ranulf shook his head slowly. "I know Henry well. He would not hear you. He means to break the back of the rebellion and make an example of those barons who challenged his rule."

Ariane bit her lip hard. She could not remain passive

when there was a chance she might save her father. "Ranulf, please ... I *beg* you, allow me to go to him."

Taking his time, Ranulf slowly sheathed his sword, before finally answering. "No."

"No! But—"

Raising his hand, he cut off her cry of protest. "I will ride north for the king's camp and speak to Henry directly. He will at least hear me out."

Ariane stared at him, hardly daring to believe Ranulf would trouble himself so for her sake.

"However, if Walter is found guilty ..." he added in warning. His amber eyes held hers intently. "If so, there may be naught I can do for him, but I will petition the king for leniency."

Her hope soared; her love for him swelled till she thought her heart might burst. "You would do that for me, my lord?"

Abruptly Ranulf looked away. "For justice," he muttered untruthfully. "I like not to see an honorable man condemned unjustly."

Eager to change the subject, he turned his attention once more to Simon. "You will surrender your sword to me, and give me your oath of fealty."

Simon bowed his head. "I will yield my sword, my lord, and vow never to raise a hand against you, but I cannot give such an oath."

Ranulf's brows snapped together. "Do you deny my right to fealty as your liege?"

"I deny not that you are lord here," Simon replied quietly. "You have control of Claredon, and are not likely to ever relinquish it. But I will not swear fealty to you, my lord. I am Walter's man, his sworn vassal, and I count my oath to him sacred. As long as he lives, I will not forsake him."

The grim set of his mouth relaxing, Ranulf nodded, respecting a man who would stand by his principles even at the risk of his own life. He would have done the same in Simon's place.

"My lord," the knight added, "if you would permit me to keep my sword, I might use it on my lord Walter's behalf. I had hoped to raise a force to aid his defense, but if you mean to go ... Will you permit me to ride under your banner?"

"Aye," he agreed. "You will be welcome."

"I would return to Bridgenorth as soon as may be. Time could be of the essence."

"We will leave on the morrow," Ranulf assured him. "Now come, return with us to Claredon so that you may brief my men on the state of the siege."

Ranulf and Ariane waited while Simon fetched the horse he had tethered beyond the copse, and then the three of them rode together toward Claredon.

All remained silent. Ariane's thoughts were too wrapped up in her hopes regarding her father for her to make idle conversation, while Ranulf brooded on his possible course of action.

He had promised to aid her father, but the odds were still great that he would fail in his mission, that Walter would not be exonerated as Ariane so desperately wished, that her fate would be sealed by her father's sentence. As a convicted traitor's daughter, Ariane would suffer untold indignities, would lose all rights to land or property, any claim to the king's mercy. She would be rendered destitute, without a dowry even the poorest nunnery would accept.

Unless he intervened. There *was* a way to shield her.

Ranulf took a steadying breath. If he made Ariane his wife, he could protect her from the consequences of her father's treason. In truth, his own honor demanded that he make some sort of reparation, Ranulf admitted with an unsettling twinge of guilt. He had waged an unrelenting war against her in his determination to free himself from their betrothal, treating Ariane as an enemy to be crushed. It had been an unequal fight, and she, a vastly weaker opponent, despite her courage and her people's stubborn support. No knight worthy of the name would violate the codes of chivalry as he had done.

More damning, he had used her body—for his own pleasure and as a weapon against her. He had shamed and dishonored Ariane by forcing her to his bed.

And in the end, she *had* yielded to him, had pledged her loyalty to him as her liege, and in so doing, had made him responsible for her welfare.

He would be departing on the morrow, though, leaving her alone for weeks, perhaps longer. He would have to act now, tonight, if he acted at all.

Ranulf could feel his heart pounding as he came to a decision. He would take Ariane as his wife. Now, tonight, before he could change his mind. If his action would also bind her to him irrevocably, it was a consideration he refused to examine too closely.

His heart was still thudding unnaturally when they reached the hall where many of the castlefolk were engaged in the evening meal. Ariane started for the stairs, saying she would leave him to consult with his men, but Ranulf forestalled her with a hand on her arm. "Stay, lady." Turning to summon a serf, he commanded the man to fetch the priest.

She gave Ranulf a quizzical look. "Is something amiss, my lord?"

"No." He returned a brooding glance. "You will at last get your wish, demoiselle," he replied cryptically.

Her confusion increased. "My wish?"

"You sought to become my wife. Before I leave, I mean to formally wed you."

Her mouth opening, Ariane stared at Ranulf in shock, in disbelief. *"Why?"* she asked finally, her breath a rasp of sound.

"Why?"

"Why would you agree to a formal union between us after all this time? After standing so firmly against it, against me, for so long?"

Ranulf looked away, reluctant to meet her gaze. "Because King Henry wishes it. When last I saw him, he urged the marriage. If I am to seek his favor, I prefer not to face him from a position of weakness."

"Is that all?" she asked quietly. "Is that your sole reason?"

It was not the sole reason, nor even the most important one, though it *was* true he could strengthen his position by acceding to Henry's wishes regarding the marriage. But Ranulf was disinclined to confess his feelings of remorse to Ariane, or to divulge his need to protect her, or to expose his weakness for her, the desire that had become a raging obsession.

" 'Tis reason enough," Ranulf replied gruffly instead.

"No, my lord," Ariane said finally, shaking her head. "It

is not enough. Not for me." She took a deep breath. "You may choose to wed for political expediency, Ranulf, but I cannot. I will not speak the vows to become your wife. I will not wed you."

Chapter 26

It was Ranulf's turn to stare. Had he misheard her? "Are you saying you *refuse?*"

"Aye, my lord," Ariane replied quietly. "I will not wed you."

Bafflement, disbelief, doubt all warred in Ranulf's mind. Never had he considered her possible refusal. Yet perhaps Ariane was being coy, pretending to spurn his magnanimous offer in order to win further concessions from him.

Irritated by her ploy, he favored her with a quelling stare, one that never failed to make the most courageous of men quake in their boots. Instead of flinching, Ariane returned his gaze somberly, her expression one of incredible sadness.

"You once thought political expedience an adequate reason to wed," Ranulf pointed out—quite reasonably, he thought.

"That . . . was before I came to know you."

His scowl faded, to be replaced by true uncertainty. "What mean you, 'before you came to know me'?"

"I understand you far better now, Ranulf. And that understanding weighs more with me than any politics." She looked away, unable to meet his gaze further, and clasped her hands together to stop them from trembling. "The original reasons for an alliance between us no longer exist. I agreed to an arranged marriage to please my father, and to provide Claredon with a strong lord when he eventually passes from this life. But as you have often reminded me, you already are Claredon's lord. And my father, in his present danger, doubtless has more vital worries to occupy his thoughts other than which suitor I wed."

A sinking sensation assaulted Ranulf in the pit of his stomach, though he ignored it as he strove to follow her rationale. The circumstances between them had indeed changed radically—but there were still reasons for the marriage, certainly on his part. He had initially agreed to the betrothal to further his own interests, and his original justification still had merit. He wanted heirs of Ariane. And the political basis was still sound, especially with the king pressing for the union. Both were reason enough to marry—or so Ranulf tried to convince himself. He did not want to examine too closely his eagerness to wed Ariane now. It was enough that he was willing to honor her as his lady wife.

"I will make the contract terms generous, if that is what concerns you," he said finally.

Ariane drew a steadying breath, summoning every ounce of courage she could muster, knowing she was taking the biggest gamble of her life. "I thank you my lord, but I must decline."

He still could not believe she meant to refuse. He had expected her to leap at the offer. She had *won* the battle between them, by the Cross; he was willing to give Ariane exactly what she had been demanding for weeks.

Ranulf felt irrationally betrayed by her sudden, inexplicable reversal. Yet unable, unwilling, to recognize the feeling as pain, he took refuge in anger. He had opened his mouth to deliver a scathing reply when he noticed the crowd that had gathered around them, awaiting his orders.

"We shall discuss this in private," he muttered so that only Ariane could hear.

"There is no need to discuss it further, my lord."

His temper kindled. Grasping her arm, Ranulf propelled her toward the stairwell. "The solar—*now,* wench, if you have a care for your skin."

They ascended the steps without speaking, the only sound their footsteps and the clinking of his spurs.

"Now, what is the meaning of this nonsense?" he demanded in irritation when he had shut the door behind them in the solar. "For weeks now you have harped at me to make you my lady."

"I have not harped at you," Ariane replied quietly. "Nor is my position nonsense. I no longer wish to wed you."

"Whyever not?" Ranulf exclaimed, torn between incomprehension and frustration, hurt and anger.

Her own gaze held anguish. "Because you will say I

tricked you, that I forced you into a union that is repugnant to you. I will not compel you to accept a marriage that is so distasteful to you, my lord."

He stared at her a long moment. "It would not be distasteful to me," he admitted finally, grudgingly.

"It would. I will not force you to marry against your wishes."

Curtly Ranulf shook his head. "Were you attempting coercion, wild horses could not compel me to wed you. But that is hardly the case. I am reconciled to the marriage. I will be acting at my king's behest—"

"King Henry's wishes are not a good enough reason for me," Ariane repeated stubbornly.

Muttering an oath, Ranulf shook his head again in disbelief. "I agree to honor you as my lady wife, and you refuse? No, I cannot accept it, wench. You will wed me tonight as planned, so that I may leave tomorrow with a clear conscience."

Her chin lifted. "There, you see, Ranulf? You call me 'wench' in that scornful tone, as if I were dirt beneath your feet."

Ranulf looked taken aback. "I mean naught by it. I call all females 'wench.' "

"I know." The ache in her throat made her voice quaver. "But I wish to mean more to you than other women. I want more, far more, my lord. I want to be accepted as your partner in life, the mother of your children, your true love—not your chattel, your leman, your slave."

He stared at her, appraising her expression, noting her deadly seriousness. "You ask much, wen—demoiselle."

"Not so much, my lord."

His lips compressed. "Would you see me on bended knee? Is that what you want from me?"

Ariane shook her head sadly.

"Then *what*, by the Saints?"

"I want a husband who can trust me, for one."

"Trust?" Ranulf's brow furrowed. "What has that to say to the matter?"

"Everything, my lord. You believe noblewomen cannot remain faithful to their vows; you think we have no honor, no scruples. But I consider a vow sacred. I intend to remain faithful to my lord husband until the day I die.''

Warily he searched Ariane's beautiful face, realizing the truth of her commitment. He knew the value she placed on vows; he had seen proof of it in her devotion to her parents, her people. Indeed, that conviction was why he had at last risked surrender, why he was insisting now that she wed him. Her oath to honor and obey him she would hold sacred—but now she was refusing even to consider a marriage between them because of some nonsensical notion about trust.

Taking a steadying breath to control the tension rising within him, Ranulf decided it wiser to emphasize the advantages of the union. ''Must I spell out what your dower rights would be, demoiselle?''

''No, I care not what they would be.''

''You care not?'' His mouth curled skeptically. ''What if I should die? I will be riding into an armed camp, to a castle under siege. I could be killed by a spent arrow, or assaulted by robbers on the road, for that matter. As my widow you would have certain rights to my estate.''

She flinched at the thought of Ranulf dying, but refused to look away. ''You mistake my character,'' Ariane said softly, ''if you believe considerations of wealth and power are why I wish to be your wife.''

''Well, then . . . as my wife you would have more influence over the disposition of your precious Claredon,'' he pointed out.

''Perhaps . . . but Claredon will survive without me. You will rule it justly, I have no doubt.''

His eyes narrowed. ''If I manage to free your father, then will you reconsider?''

''My decision has naught to do with my father. I am profoundly grateful for all you have done—and will do—for my family, Ranulf. More grateful than I can ever say. But your generosity toward my parents will not sway me in this matter.''

A unfamiliar feeling of panic rose in Ranulf, but he managed to ward it off by summoning fresh anger. ''Perhaps you have forgotten an important detail, my lady,'' he said tightly. ''We may already be wed. Your trick with the bedsheets may have cemented our union, whether you will it or not. Rome may very well have refused to dissolve the contract.''

''There is as much likelihood the annulment has been granted,'' Ariane countered softly.

''If the Pope has not acted yet, I shall withdraw my petition. I no longer mean to seek an annulment.''

She would not reply.

His jaw clenching, Ranulf grasped at another argument. ''Have you considered the consequences to yourself if you refuse? If your father is found guilty, you will be stripped of rank and possessions, forced to beg for your very bread. You will become a ward of the crown—and likely be forced to wed a man of Henry's choosing.''

''That is preferable to the alternative. King Henry will give me to a man I cannot love or perhaps even respect ... but I would rather that than have you come to despise me.''

At her quiet declaration, Ranulf felt suddenly faint, stunned, as if he had taken a sword thrust to the gut but could not yet feel the pain.

The blow she had dealt him showed on his features. Dismayed by his reaction, Ariane moved toward him, reaching out an imploring hand. She had to make Ranulf understand that she was not rejecting *him*. She was leaving him free to choose, giving him the chance to decide what he truly wanted.

Her features softened in entreaty as she gazed up at him. ''You still do not understand, do you, Ranulf? I *want* to be your wife. But if you cannot admit your deepest feelings to yourself, if you do not know—truly *know*—deep in your heart that I can make you happy, that I can complete your life as you could mine, that our two hearts would be as one, then I must refuse your offer of marriage.''

He looked away, saying stiffly, ''You want me to ply you with sweet words, but I am a soldier, not a poet.''

''No,'' she replied earnestly. ''I care not what words you use, although if you truly loved me, you would not hesitate to shout it from the castle walls. What matters only is what you *feel* for me. If you cannot trust me, if you think I have trapped you into wedding me, you would come to hate me. Ranulf ... I could not bear it if that happened.''

''I could never hate you,'' he said rigidly, his voice low.

"But you do not love me."

There was a long, pregnant silence.

Ariane gazed at him sadly. "Now, at least, you desire my body. But when you grow tired of me, what then? Will you set me aside? Will you turn to another woman for comfort? Will you seek pleasure from your Saracen leman and forget me? I could not bear to lose you that way. My heart could not bear it. 'Tis better that I not wed you at all."

Ranulf stared at her, aching to deny her accusation. She was mistaken on one score. He wanted more than Ariane's body; he wanted *her,* all of her. He wanted to bind her to him unalterably in marriage. And he wanted to believe her. He wanted desperately to trust her, to know that she would not betray him. He wanted to bare his heart, to release the fear inside him. He *wanted* to love her. But he could not force the words past the tightness in his throat.

The ache roughened his voice. "You have secured the offer of my hand. Must you have my soul as well?"

"Nay, Ranulf," Ariane said softly. "Not your soul. Your heart. I want your love. Nothing else will do. If and when you can say freely that you love me, then I will proclaim my vows before God with all the love in my own heart."

How could he admit to a love when he had no heart? Ranulf wanted to cry. How could he give what he did not possess?

When he remained silent, Ariane smiled sadly. "You are a good man, Ranulf, worthy of my love and devotion. But you cannot believe me worthy of yours. You cannot trust me. And until you can, till you can say truly that you love me, I cannot be your wife."

She read his answer in the bleakness of his eyes.

"I thought not," she murmured, her heart aching.

She reached up to touch her fingertips to his cheek. Ranulf flinched as if burned.

"You ask too much of me," he said almost bitterly.

"Perhaps. I hope not."

Gritting his teeth, Ranulf turned away and went to the door. "This issue is not settled between us," he flung over his shoulder, before he let himself from the room, shutting the door hard in his wake.

"I devoutly pray not," Ariane whispered to herself, won-

dering if she had made a terrible mistake. She would take
Ranulf on any terms, if only she could believe that by mar-
rying him she was not sentencing him to a life of misery.
That one day he might come to open his heart to her without
reservation, without bitter wariness or treacherous doubts.
Love could not survive without trust.

Am I a fool for wanting your trust, my love?

She sighed, knowing she could not allow herself to give
up hope. Someday, God willing, she would penetrate the
armor around the dragon's heart and claim her most cherished dream.

Dazed, feeling as if he had taken a lance blow directly to
the chest, Ranulf descended to the hall and called for wine
as he took his rightful place at the high table.

"Is something amiss?" Payn asked, taking one look at his
liege's troubled features.

"She refused my offer of marriage," he said numbly.

Payn looked startled. "She refused?"

"Aye, she will not wed me, can you credit it? She says I
do not trust her enough."

His vassal watched him in silence, saying finally, "*Do* you
trust her, my lord?"

"Enough to marry her. What more can she ask of me?"

Payn was a long time in answering. "I suppose I can
comprehend her position."

"*Can* you?" Ranulf shook his head bitterly, trying to deny
the emotion warring within his soul. He should be pleased
Ariane had refused him. For weeks now—years—he had tried
to elude a marriage to her. Why then did he feel this pain in
his gut, in his chest? Why did he feel this gnawing fear? It
was fear, not of committing himself to Ariane, but of losing her.

"Then perhaps you can explain her answer to me," he
retorted grimly. "Never will I understand the workings of a
woman's mind."

"I fear that is the dilemma, my lord. The Lady Ariane is
not like others of her kind—and you will not see it."

"She said much the same," Ranulf replied, his tone suddenly bleak.

Payn's expression turned grave. "Can you not give her the trust she asks for, Ranulf?"

He stared down at the table. "What matters it if I do or not?"

"I think it matters a great deal ... to her. Several times recently you have suspected the Lady Ariane of wrongdoing—yet each time you doubted her, she has proven your suspicions false. But you will not absolve her of treachery and deceit. She has ample cause to be wary of placing her fate in your hands."

It was true, Ranulf admitted; he had wronged her unforgivably. And yet when he had tried to make amends, she had thrown his gesture back in face. He had laid himself open to her, had bared himself to this pain, for naught.

"Do you love her?"

Ranulf gave a start at the question. He could not answer that with any certainty. He could not put a name to the madness he felt for Ariane, the nameless emotion that flooded his heart whenever she was near, whenever he simply thought of her. "Truthfully ... I do not know."

Payn nodded in sympathy. "Then I advise you to consider carefully what you feel for her, my lord. Search your heart, your conscience. If you feel anything for her besides passion, then tell her. A woman likes to hear these things—"

Priest John came hurrying up to the dais just then, his aging features showing concern. "You summoned me, milord?"

Ranulf's reply was almost a growl. "I was in error. Go back to your flock," he ordered bitterly. "It seems I have no need of your services after all."

No wedding ceremony was held that night.

Unforgiving, steeped in his own dark reflections, Ranulf scarcely said two words to Ariane throughout the evening meal, and then he remained in the hall with his men until well past midnight, delaying the moment when he would have to confront her again.

When at last he came to her, disturbing her warm body from slumber, he made no mention of the turmoil that was in his heart. But he made love to her with a fierce urgency that bordered on desperation. For no matter what else stood between them, his desire for her had not diminished. His passion was unquenchable.

She accompanied him to the bailey the next morning as Ranulf prepared to leave for Henry's camp. His war stallion pawed the ground impatiently while he gave final instructions to his vassals who would remain behind, including Payn.

He saved his farewell to Ariane for last. When finally Ranulf turned to her, he could not utter the fateful words she yearned to hear.

"I will do my utmost for your father," he said stiffly as he tugged on his leather gauntlets.

She searched Ranulf's harsh, impassive face, aching to be in his arms, wishing she could put things right between them. His remoteness made her sick with longing. "I thank you, my lord."

He did not touch her, did not hold her or embrace her or kiss her as Ariane yearned for him to do. She stood there unmoving, her heart hurting, as he mounted his destrier without speaking.

But even as he gathered the reins, Ranulf made another concession to her. In a voice strong enough for all to hear, he addressed her clearly. "My lady, I charge you to keep this castle safe for me. Hold it well until my return."

Ariane felt a sob catch in her throat. Ranulf had let it be known he was leaving his castle in her hands. He trusted her that much, at least. She could only hope he would someday come to trust her with his heart.

With a tremulous smile, she nodded solemnly, accepting the charge. "As you will, my lord."

She thought he would leave without another word, but she was blessedly mistaken. Without warning, Ranulf muttered a curse and bent down to catch her about the waist. Lifting her up, he covered her mouth fiercely with his, startling her with his violence, his need. Yet Ariane clung to him with all her might, returning his passion, tasting regret, sorrow, despair in his kiss.

Just as abruptly as he had begun, Ranulf released her and set her on her feet. His amber eyes were enigmatic as without another word, he turned his destrier and cantered to the head of the column of mounted knights and men-at-arms.

Through a blur of tears, Ariane watched as he rode away without a backward glance, his dragon's banner snapping tauntingly in the spring breeze.

Chapter 27

It was a disturbing ride for Ranulf. His thoughts hounded him the entire journey north, while his vassal's counsel echoed in his mind with a relentless, pounding urgency: *Search your heart, search your heart, search your heart....*

What did he feel for Ariane? What, beyond passion, lay hidden in the depths of his heart?

Her generous nature, her spirited defense of her people, her devotion to her loved ones, her passionate caring, all pointed to someone who was trustworthy. Women were not often noted for their faithfulness and high principles, but within Ariane's shapely breast lay a heart of honor, with the courage and honesty of a valiant knight. She was a warrior's woman, worthy of any ruler. Far more worthy than he, Ranulf concluded bleakly.

He had been so blinded by prejudices, his view so twisted by bitter experience, he had refused to see, had stubbornly refused to admit even to himself, that he was losing his heart to her. He could not arm his heart as he could don a coat of mail, he had discovered painfully. And now it was ensnared by silken chains.

God's teeth, he hoped, *prayed,* Rome would not grant an annulment. If so, he would have no legal claim to Ariane.

Could he give her up then? The question was absurd. He could not face the bleak emptiness of a life without her. He could not, would not, relinquish her. Yet the price of her acceptance was his heart.

Ranulf took a deep breath, squeezing his eyes shut against the images that tormented him: Ariane challenging him to look beyond his bitterness and hate. Ariane laughing. Ariane making love to him ... her soft breasts pillowed on his chest, her cool hands encircling him, stroking him. Ariane refusing his offer.

If you do not know—truly know—deep in your heart that I can make you happy, that I can complete your life as you could mine, that our two hearts would be as one....

Aye, he *knew.* He could give her his heart. Had given it. He desperately wanted her to love him. And he loved her. His desire went beyond blood, beyond a fever of the flesh. It came from deep within him, within his soul. She had touched something in him he had not known he possessed. He loved her.

Opening his eyes to the gray day, Ranulf stared wonderingly out at the rolling English countryside, savoring the words on his tongue. *I love her.* The rightness of it echoed through his mind, resonated through his body, his very soul.

He threw back his head and laughed, startling his men. For the first time in his life he felt released from the burden of bitterness he had always carried. He felt like a newborn babe, helpless, innocent, marveling at the world around him.

He loved Ariane, needed her—a need as pure and strong as his need for air. If she were his, he would ask nothing more of life than to be allowed to stand between her and the world, protecting her from all sadness and harm; he could ask for no greater boon. Yet knowing the woman she was, Ariane would refuse to meekly accept his protection. She would stand with him against the world, fighting at his side, as his equal, his soulmate.

Ranulf shut his eyes, remembering. No woman had ever offered him the generous, unselfish tenderness she had shown. No woman had ever dared defy and challenge him as Ariane had, either.

A rueful smile tugged at Ranulf's lips as he thought of their tempestuous encounters ... a smile that swiftly faded. He had tried to crush that spark of fire in Ariane, that precious spirit, when he should have cherished it.

But no longer. He had broken the chains of his past, and he would honor her as she deserved.

Yet there was work to be done, Ranulf reminded himself, suddenly sobering. He had vowed to aid her father. For Ariane's sake, he prayed Walter was innocent. He could not bear the thought of her grief should her father be hanged for treason.

But it would not come to that, Ranulf vowed. He was the king's man, but he was prepared to go to great lengths for the woman he loved. If need be, he was prepared to battle even his king for her father's life.

Henry's camp was a familiar sight, teeming with military purpose. Tents and pavilions spread over a vast acreage, with banners waving at each entrance and great destriers tethered nearby. Everywhere there were crowds—knights and archers, squires and pages, cooks and camp followers, smiths and armorers, as well as couriers riding to and fro.

Ranulf eyed the commotion with little enthusiasm. How profoundly he had changed in the past months from the eager warrior he once had been. He had battled, feasted, reveled, and whored with the best of them, yet now all he wished was to return home to Claredon, to Ariane.

The royal tent was the largest of the lot, but even Ranulf, as high ranking and valued a knight as he was, could not gain immediate entrance. He was made to cool his heels outside for the better part of ten minutes, awaiting the king's pleasure.

The delay, however, allowed him to learn of the events that had occurred in his absence since escorting Queen Eleanor here. It seemed Henry's efforts to bring the rebellious barons to heel was nearing success.

"They have sued for pardon," a fellow knight informed Ranulf jovially. "Their resources are so depleted, they would make terms with the Devil, I trow."

Ranulf nodded in approval. Henry had been reluctant to storm Mortimer's castle and lose valuable men by ordering the walls destroyed, and so had chosen to starve the inhabitants with a lengthy siege. But it was clear the campaign to crush the rebels was nearing the end. At this very moment, Henry was in council with his earls, who had conducted the terms of surrender.

When at last he was bid entrance, Ranulf found Henry pacing the ground as was his wont, surrounded by his high-ranking knights, as well as stewards and servitors, all in a gleeful mood.

Pressing through the crowd, Ranulf went down on one knee and kissed the king's hand. "My lord king, I congratulate you on your victory."

"Ah, Ranulf, best of my knights! You come just in time to partake in the spoils."

The youthful, red-haired ruler of England and Normandy was not overly tall, but he bristled with a fierce energy that, in addition to his broad shoulders and powerful body and booming voice, gave him a commanding presence second to none. Henry also possessed a fiery temper that was the stuff of legends, yet at the moment, his famous fits of rage were nowhere in evidence. Instead, he was grinning broadly.

Ranulf let out a breath he hadn't been conscious of holding. In such an expansive mood, Henry would be more amenable to a subject he would doubtless find unpleasant; Walter would at least be afforded a hearing.

Ranulf kissed the king's hand again and rose. "I have no need to share the spoils, sire," he said carefully. "In truth, I have but one boon to ask of you. That you lend me your ear as a merciful and impartial judge. See you, I think there is good reason to believe Walter of Claredon has been falsely accused of treason."

That night the terms of surrender were accepted and Mortimer's castle at last fell to the siege. Ranulf was one of the first inside the keep, but while others searched the tower for stray rebels, he and his men headed straight for the dungeons.

He received no protest when he commandeered the keys from the jailer. Opening the heavy, metal-banded door, he gestured for his squire, Burc, to follow with a torch, and nodded permission for Simon Crecy to accompany them. Then he crouched to enter the pit.

The stench was almost overpowering. Within, there was barely room to stand erect. Ranulf held his breath as he searched the dismal chamber.

A dozen figures—thin, filthy, ragged—stood chained to the walls, bodies slumped, heads lolling on weakened necks. Ranulf's throat tightened with pity for these poor souls who once had been men. He would not wish this fate on his worst enemy, and yet he prayed Ariane's father was among them.

"I seek Walter of Claredon," Ranulf said quietly, compassion roughening his voice.

One man's head slowly came up, his chains clanking as he lifted his arm and tried to shield his eyes from the blinding torchlight.

"I am Walter," he whispered hoarsely. He held himself proudly, despite his suffering, a courageous knight even in torment.

Ranulf swallowed hard. "I am Ranulf of Vernay. Remember me, my lord? I am here at your daughter's behest."

"Ariane?" the hoarse voice rasped.

"Aye, Ariane," Ranulf said humbly as he moved to release Walter from his chains. "Your daughter, who never forsook you. Who never abandoned faith in your innocence."

Walter of Claredon was a free man. He had been found imprisoned in the Bridgenorth dungeon, just as rumor purported—a circumstance that went a long way toward supporting his claim of innocence. His wretched physical condition attested to the tortures he had suffered. And with a dozen knights willing to vouch for his refusal to join the rebellion and his defiance of Mortimer, Walter received the king's full pardon while lying in an invalid's bed. He had suffered no debilitating wounds other than starvation, and God willing, with time and sustenance, he would recover fully.

It was a full fortnight, however, before he regained enough strength to stand before the king and swear fresh allegiance. No longer considered a traitor, Walter was reinstated to the king's good graces and his lands restored. Additionally, he was granted a gift of another handsome fief for his unwavering loyalty.

"You have served me well, Walter of Claredon," Henry declared before ordering a clerk to bestow on Walter a writ proclaiming his new barony.

As for the other rebellious warlords, the rift with their king was not mended without blood. Hugh Mortimer was hanged for his treachery, as an example to future insurgents, and many of his followers imprisoned for life.

Too weak to travel, Walter remained at Bridgenorth for another fortnight. Ranulf stayed as well, refusing to return to Claredon without Ariane's father, not daring to face her otherwise. He had dispatched messengers regularly to her with reports of her father's progress, and had received two replies, expressing her gratitude. But gratitude was no substitute for love.

Summer was spreading its nourishing warmth over England by the time they at last made preparations to return to Claredon. They made the journey on horseback, in easy stages, for Walter refused to ride in a litter. Even weakened as he was, the aging knight possessed a spirit that bore a decided resemblance to his beautiful daughter's; Ranulf could clearly see from whence Ariane gained her stubborn streak.

As the cavalcade drew closer to Claredon, though, Ranulf alternately chafed with impatience and gnawing fear. He wanted desperately to know his fate, and yet at the same time, wanted to delay as long as possible the moment when he would have to confront his uncertain future.

He had once been too craven to confront Ariane when he thought her a mere child bride. And now that he knew the steel she was made of, he was doubly afraid.

She had no reason to wed him now. Her father was free, her inheritance restored. And after the trials she had endured at his own hands, Ariane ought very well to wish him in Hades.

Chapter 28

The waiting was the hardest. At times Ariane wanted to scream with impatience as she awaited the outcome of events at Bridgenorth. The fate of the two men she loved most in the world hung in the balance, as did her own.

With the failure of the rebellion, at least her fears on one score diminished. Her father's release from imprisonment and his full pardon by the king made Ariane weep with relief. She could look forward to Walter's return to Claredon with joy and anticipation.

Her mother's situation, too, was cause for hope. Layla had begun administering treatments of mold to Lady Constance's skin, although it was far too soon to predict the result. Gilbert, who had been shocked and distressed to learn the identity of the leper in the woods, faithfully provided escort for Layla on her missions of mercy, eager to aid the generous, loving Lady of Claredon who had raised him from serfdom.

It was her relationship with Ranulf that still frightened Ariane. Would she ever have a future with him? Would he ever come to love her? To trust her? She had trusted Ranulf to save her father if he could; she did not trust him to know his own heart. More damning, in his absence a messenger had arrived from Rome with an official document bearing the Pope's seal. Whatever that scroll contained would decide her fate, Ariane knew, struggling against the urge to open a missive meant for Ranulf.

When one fine summer's afternoon in July, the watchman's horn announcing visitors at last sounded, Ariane fairly flew to the window of the ladies' bower. She could see two banners flying over the party, and even though she could not make out the devices, judging from the colors of the two fields, she was certain one boasted her father's hawk, the other a fearsome dragon.

Joy filled her at the sight. Joy and apprehension. Her father was safe. And Ranulf had returned. She had greatly feared he might stay away forever; he was no longer lord here now that Claredon had been restored to her father.

My beloved, have you come for me at last?

Summoning her ladies to her at once, Ariane hurried to change into a gown of forest green samite so that she might present the best possible appearance.

Her heart was pounding by the time she raced down the stairs and took her place beside Payn in the bailey. She scarcely had time to regain her breath or her composure before the party of horsemen rode through the inner gates. Trembling with nerves, Ariane clasped her hands before her in an effort to hide her trepidation.

She could not take her eyes from the two lead knights. They appeared so tall and formidable as they sat their powerful destriers, although Ranulf was the larger of the two. Her gaze shifting anxiously between them, she fervently wished she could tell what Ranulf was thinking, and found herself cursing the helm that shielded his expression.

Only with effort did she tear her gaze from him as Lord Walter was aided from his horse by his squire and his helm removed.

"Father," she murmured, tears filling her eyes as she offered him her hands. He seemed to have aged ten years in the months he was away, and his face was far thinner and drawn with fatigue. "Welcome home."

To her surprise, her father embraced her tightly, nearly crushing her against his mailed form, as if desperate to hold her. "I thought I might not see you again," he whispered hoarsely.

He held her thus for a long moment, and when at last he stood back, Walter smiled down at her. "You did well, daughter. My lord Ranulf tells me you defended Claredon bravely and championed me when all the world spoke against me."

Her father's unfamiliar praise stunned Ariane, making tears of pride and happiness slip unheeded down her cheeks. Ranulf, waiting quietly to one side for her attention, felt a stab of envy at the obvious closeness father and daughter enjoyed at this poignant moment. He longed to share that closeness. *He* wanted the right to hold Ariane, to be the one she greeted with love and devotion shining softly from her gray eyes.

In truth, he could not take his own eyes off her. She was a breathtaking vision with her long, pale copper hair hanging loose under a gold circlet, her carriage as regal and graceful as a queen's.

He yearned to take her in his arms, to ease the pounding of his heart that was like a huge drum of fear inside him. Without Claredon in his possession, he no longer held any power over Ariane. With both her father and her inheritance safe, she could easily forswear him. When at last Ariane glanced at him, their eyes met and locked in a question.

Her expression held uncertainty as she searched his face. "Ranulf . . . my lord. How can I ever repay you for aiding my father?"

His smile held a bleakness he could not hide. "I do not wish your gratitude, demoiselle." What he wanted, what he needed was her love.

Payn took the opportunity to break the tension by slapping Ranulf on the back and bowing to Walter. "My lords, come inside the tower and celebrate this glad day with wine. The Lady Ariane has been preparing for days for your arrival, and plans a feast tonight to honor your homecoming."

Walter nodded approvingly and patted the chain mail covering his stomach. "A splendid notion, daughter. I could do with a good meal to put some flesh on this bony form. I trow a green babe could unhorse me with a feather."

With a flush of pleasure at his approval and concern at his condition after his long imprisonment, Ariane accepted her father's raised hand and led the way up the stairs and into the great hall, where many of the castle retainers waited eagerly to greet the returning lord.

The celebration that followed lasted well into the evening. The duties of chatelaine occupied much of Ariane's attention, giving her no opportunity to speak privately with Ranulf as she yearned to do.

Ranulf, too, chafed at the delay, watching her with possessive eyes as she sat at her father's other side—too far from him, he thought. He ate sparingly and drank very little, caring naught for food. He wanted only to sweep Ariane up in his arms and carry her above stairs at this very moment, to lay her down and cover her with his body, to capture her mouth with his and drink from her sweetness. Yearningly he looked at that beautiful mouth, his lingering gaze hungry, wistful, as he recalled her adamant refusal to wed him. *If you know in your heart* ... He *did* know, and he was prepared to admit it to her, to bare his soul to her if that was what she wanted, even though it would be one of the hardest things he had ever done.

Even then he could not be certain Ariane would accept him. He could perhaps force the issue of their union, Ranulf knew. Her father would give his daughter's hand in marriage to the man who had championed his innocence and won the king's pardon.

Yet he would never make such a demand, Ranulf vowed. He would not compel Ariane to wed him. He had treated her too harshly in the past to revert to such coercion. In truth, he never wanted to force her again. He wanted Ariane to come to him freely, of her own will, because she loved him.

He would have to woo her this time, he realized, yet even that effort might fail. Ranulf thought of the gilded coffer he had ordered delivered to her chamber shortly after the banquet had begun. A knight who sought to win the hand of a lady would bring her gifts to win her favor and sweeten her regard. He had spent a small fortune buying goods from cloth merchants and goldsmiths, praying that such riches might sway Ariane. Now all that was left was to put his most fervent hopes to the test.

The evening was well advanced, a lively entertainment by traveling minstrels underway, before Ranulf summoned the nerve to rise from the table and approach Ariane's chair. Bending, he murmured in her ear, "Might I have a private word with you, demoiselle? In your chamber?"

"Aye, my lord, as you wish," she said rather breathlessly, sending his hopes soaring with the quizzical smile she bestowed upon him.

Excusing herself from her father and the company, Ariane lit a taper and led the way upstairs to her chamber. Ranulf followed her, his demeanor uncharacteristically humble, his heart beginning to pound again.

His momentary optimism had plummeted by the time he closed the heavy door behind them. He did not take her in his arms as he yearned to. Instead, he stood regarding her silently in the candlelight.

"You wished to speak to me?" she asked uncertainly.

"I brought you a gift," Ranulf said finally, lamely, pointing toward the coffer his squire had placed just within the door.

Puzzled, Ariane went to kneel before the chest and raised the lid. Her breath caught in a gasp at the treasures glittering in the candlelight. With trembling hands, she withdrew a gold-linked girdle encrusted with rubies and a gold chaplet studded with the same precious stones. Beneath lay ells of costly silks, samites, cendals, and damasks, as well as pelts of ermine and sable.

She turned questioning eyes to Ranulf. "What mean you by this, my lord?"

"I could think of naught else to give you," he replied in a voice so low it was barely audible. "Your father's demesne has been restored to him. Your inheritance remains intact. Your precious Claredon is safe from me."

Ariane held her breath, waiting, yet no further explanation was forthcoming. "I need no riches from you, Ranulf."

"I know," he said bitterly. "You have no need of me at all."

She could not fathom his mood, or comprehend what he was trying to tell her. But there was another crucial matter that clamored for attention.

Slowly Ariane rose and on leaden limbs went to another chest, where she withdrew the rolled parchment with the papal seal intact. "This came from Rome in your absence."

Stark fear rippled through Ranulf as he eyed the document she held out to him; despair rose higher within him, shoving at his throat. "Know you what it says?" he asked hoarsely.

"No. I would not pry into your personal affairs."

"It doubtless concerns you as well, demoiselle. Were you not even curious?"

"If you do not believe me—"

Ranulf shook his head abruptly. "Nay, I meant no accusation. Your word is your honor and I will not question it."

Ariane stared at Ranulf, knowing how much it had cost

him to say those words. Finally she crossed to him with her offering.

Accepting the roll reluctantly, he turned away from her intense scrutiny and moved over to the brazier that had been lit even in summer to take the chill from the tower stone. For a long moment he stood there, his back to Ariane, staring down at the smoldering coals.

"Will you not open it, my lord?"

Ranulf voiced a quiet oath. He wanted to burn the vile thing, to tear it asunder without reading it. But he needed to know what he faced.

With hands that trembled slightly Ranulf broke the seal and unrolled the missive. His heart thudded in slow, painful strokes as he tried to make sense of the Latin that blurred before his eyes. Yet there was no mistaking the import of the document. It was confirmation of his worst fears.

His shoulders slumped, his head bowed. The decision had been taken from him.

"The annulment has been granted," he whispered.

"So . . . now you are free of me," she said tonelessly after a while.

"No, you are wrong, Ariane." There was an edge of bleakness in his response. "I could never be free of you."

At her long silence, Ranulf glanced over his shoulder at her. Her face was pale, her eyes stricken with the same terrible anguish that was tearing him apart inside.

His mouth twisted with bitterness. "Are you not pleased, demoiselle? Now you will have the opportunity to make another alliance for your house. With Claredon restored, your hand will be coveted by richer, more powerful lords than I— a castoff pretender to nobility who has ill used you and claimed your virtue and stained your honor."

She shook her head. "I want no other lord than you."

He went still, afraid to move, afraid he had misheard.

"Are you not pleased, my lord? Was not an annulment what you devoutly wished for?"

"No."

"Then . . ." She searched his face. "What *do* you want?"

Ranulf averted his gaze, unable to meet her eyes. "I want you, Ariane. . . . I want you to be my wife in truth. I want a future with you at my side. I want to settle on my estates and raise fine sons to manhood. To watch my daughters grow to be beauties like their mother.''

Her breath caught; her head whirled. Ariane raised a trembling hand to her temple, not daring to believe he truly meant it. ''You wish to settle down? I thought . . . you preferred soldiering.''

Ranulf exhaled a deep sigh. ''Once I did. But I am tired of fighting. I grow weary of constant war. I've had a bellyful of blood. My lands are barely known to me, and I would change that.''

''Will you return to Vernay?''

''No,'' he replied sharply. ''I despise Vernay. I intend to remain in England.''

''Here, at Claredon?''

''Not here. I do not belong here.''

''Then . . . where?''

''Henry has given me new lands in the west, with orders to build a castle to defend the marshes. I could make a fresh start there. I want an end to the loneliness, the hatred, the battles. I want my life with you. . . . If you will have me.''

''What of trust, Ranulf? I could not bear to watch our marriage destroyed by mistrust and suspicion. I want a husband who can believe in me.''

''I trust you, Ariane . . . as much as I can trust anyone.''

She realized the risk Ranulf had taken with his heartfelt admission. ''And love?''

Turning his head, he glanced over his shoulder at her, forcing himself to meet her gaze. ''My love is yours, such as I have to give. If what I feel can be called love, then, aye, I love you.''

''What *do* you feel, my lord?''

He thought of the powerful, poignant emotions welling inside him. ''I feel helpless,'' he whispered hoarsely. ''Afraid. Afraid that I have lost you through my own blindness.''

The pain in his eyes sent a wave of tenderness surging through her; it hurt her to see her fierce dragon suffering.

Her throat aching, Ariane moved toward him. From behind him, she wrapped her arms around Ranulf's powerful form, pressing her cheek against his back, against the scars she knew were hidden beneath his tunic. "You have not lost me, Ranulf."

Slowly, he turned in her arms, gazing doubtfully down at her. She searched his proudly sculpted features, seeing the vulnerability, the uncertainty, in the golden depths of his eyes.

"I will not press my suit if you refuse me," he added bleakly. "The choice is yours."

"No, my lord. The choice was taken from me long ago." She watched as a spark of hope flared in his eyes.

"From me, as well, my lady," Ranulf whispered. "You bewitched me from the first."

"I too am bewitched," she said softly.

Taking her hands in his, he stared down at their interlaced fingers. "I know not how to love, Ariane. Will you teach me?"

"Yes ... willingly, gladly." An immeasurable joy flowed over her when his tentative smile reflected hers. "But are you certain, Ranulf? Truly certain?"

"More certain than anything in the whole of my life. You are my life. You are in my blood."

"I am not the wife you wished for."

He shook his head. "What I ask for in a wife is courage and honesty and loyalty. You have proven those in ample measure."

Her smile struck him with the force of a lightening bolt. Ranulf felt suddenly breathless, as if his heart might burst from his ribcage.

Yet Ariane seemed intent on teasing him. "Do you not wish for obedience and docility, my lord?"

His mouth twisted into a bold grin. "What I crave is a saucy wench who will challenge me and nag me and force me to love."

"I do not nag!" Ariane exclaimed indignantly.

With a husky laugh, he drew her close. "I care not if you do. I want you just as you are."

Unmollified, she pressed her palms against his broad chest. "Not so quickly, my fine lord. Ask me for my heart."

"Very well." His expression suddenly sobered. "My lady ... my love . . . Ariane . . . could you, would you, give your heart to this humble, battered warrior?"

Her gaze softened. "It is yours, Ranulf. I pledge you my love, for always."

A smile blazed across his face, bright and dazzling like hot sunshine, while a flame of joy spread through him. "And your hand? Will you wed me and be my lady?"

"Aye, my love. I will wed you eagerly."

He glanced at the parchment he still held. "This grant of annulment . . . I have no need for it, have you?" To her shock, he tossed the document in the brazier, watching as the flames slowly licked at the parchment.

"What will Rome say?" she wondered.

"I care not what Rome says." He threw back his head and laughed, a full-bodied guffaw of delight.

It was that laughter, ringing with happiness, that convinced her. Ranulf truly wanted her as his wife. She had waited nearly half a lifetime for this moment. For her dream lover to come for her in tenderness and love.

Yet Ranulf was too overjoyed to remain still. Impulsively he caught Ariane up in his arms and whirled her around, till she was laughing and breathless.

"Ranulf, stop! You make me dizzy!"

"Not as dizzy as I feel!" But he ceased his exuberant motion and set her on her feet, although he kept her imprisoned within the circle of his arms. "I feel like shouting from the battlements." Suddenly he stared down at her, his heavy brows drawing together in mock warning. "I shall have a petition of marriage drawn up at once, so that you cannot withdraw your acceptance."

Her eyebrow rose in amused protest. "*I* am not the one who delayed the marriage for five years, my lord. *I* am not the one who repudiated our betrothal."

His smile faded. "No, I am. Because of my stupidity, my blindness, my compulsion to believe the worst. Can you ever forgive me?"

She could see the uncertainty in his eyes, the sweet vulnerability that reflected his newly acknowledged feelings.

In answer, Ariane reached up and joined her lips tenderly with his. He had doubted and mistrusted her for too long. But never again, Ariane vowed solemnly. As long as there remained a breath in her body, Ranulf would never have cause to doubt her love.

Chapter 29

The wedding between Ariane of Claredon and Ranulf of Vernay was cause for rejoicing all around. The ceremony to sanctify the marriage was held on the doorstep of the demesne church rather than the castle chapel, so that all of Claredon's people might participate in the celebration.

The morning sky glistened a rich summer's blue for the joyous occasion; the clear air resonated with minstrels' jubilant music as the long procession wended its way from castle to church. At its head, with her lord father at her right hand, Ariane rode a white palfrey whose scarlet saddlecloth was emblazoned with fierce dragons and whose breastplate tinkled with tiny bells, a faint echo of the ecstatic peal of church bells.

Ranulf had hoped the fabrics he had brought her would prove suitable for a bridal gown, and indeed they did. For her wedding vestment, Ariane wore an undertunic of brilliant scarlet samite, overlaid with a bliaud of the finest white paile—a tissue of embossed silk woven with gold threads. Around her hips she had fastened Ranulf's gift of the exquisite double girdle, and at her throat, the heavy gold torque collar he had given her weeks ago, the morning after claiming her maidenhead. Her women had plaited her luxuriant hair into two long ropes entwined with scarlet ribbons and gold lace, and on her head rested the gold chaplet studded with rubies.

The path to the church where her bridegroom awaited with peasant and noble wedding guests alike was strewn with bloodred roses, whose sweet perfume filled the air. Ranulf looked resplendent in scarlet and black and gold, his attire richly embroidered around the neck, sleeves, and hem. Even without mailed armor, he looked every inch the powerful warrior. The sword buckled at his waist boasted a jeweled hilt and scabbard, while around him, his vassals carried shields and pennants bearing his feared dragon device.

He watched with possessive eyes as his beautiful bride came to him. It was rare for a man to want the woman who was his wife, yet he wanted Ariane with a passion that shook him to his soul. He loved her, and he meant to spend the rest of his life honoring their union and her.

With a humble reverence, Ranulf reached up to assist his bride down from her mount.

"My lady," he murmured for Ariane's ears alone. "I pledge my oath to you: You will never have cause to regret this day."

She gave him a radiant smile, full of joy and promise. "I know, my lord Ranulf. And I make the same vow to you."

Love and pride swelled in Ranulf's chest, fierce and overwhelming, before he turned to lead her up the short flight of stone steps to the church door. There they halted before the priest, Father John.

A hush fell over the crowd. The actual marriage would be held here, under the summer sky, the later ceremony within the chapel but a final formality. Numerous noble guests had been invited to witness the wedding: Claredon's knights and their ladies, Ranulf's vassals and men-at-arms, neighboring lords and their families, as well as the craftsmen and freemen and serfs who served Claredon's demesne. The guests gathered around to listen as Father John ascertained that there were no impediments to the marriage according to the stipulations of the Church. There being none, the good father asked if the affianced man and maiden gave their free and solemn consent to the union.

When Ranulf and Ariane answered in heartfelt agreement, the priest read out the property rights of both parties. The lord of Vernay pledged his lady a dower right, a third of his holdings after his death, while the bride's parent, the lord of Claredon, assigned to her a dowry: gifts of clothing, linen, utensils, furniture, and generous parcels of land.

Ariane scarcely heard a word. She felt dazed, wrapped in a cloud of joy, too distracted to concentrate on such material matters.

The next rite was delivered in Latin, the surrender of the

bride by her father and mother. Ariane felt a bittersweet ache in her throat because her beloved mother could not be present for this moment, yet she was comforted by the knowledge that Lady Constance awaited her within the church, hidden in the chapel gallery. Her mother's progress was alone cause for rejoicing. Layla's strange remedy seemed to be having at least a modest affect on Constance's ravaged skin, and the Saracen was optimistic that a full recovery eventually was possible.

Ariane was further gladdened by the note of pride in her father's voice as he presented her to Ranulf, saying, "To you I confide my daughter Ariane. Keep her well."

"Before God, I promise to shelter her," Ranulf responded, clasping her ungloved hands and gazing deeply into her eyes.

When Father John had consecrated the ring, Ranulf slipped the small circlet of gold progressively over three fingers of Ariane's right hand, before moving it to a final resting place on her left hand, where it would remain till her death, a pledge of faithfulness and fidelity. The metal, warmed by his touch, gleamed no brighter than the gold of her beloved's eyes, she thought dazedly.

"With this ring I thee espouse," Ranulf vowed solemnly to her in Latin, "with my body I thee honor, with my goods I thee endow."

Only then did they enter the church, where the marriage was solemnized before God. As she prostrated herself on the floor of the nave beside Ranulf, Ariane felt her mother's love surrounding her. Disguised behind a veil and a concealing curtain, the Lady Constance watched secretly from the chapel gallery. She had given the couple her blessing days before, and on the morrow, Ranulf had promised Ariane they would visit her mother in her forest dwelling.

A mass followed, and after making a generous offering to the Church, the bride and groom knelt to receive the solemn benediction of the priest.

Finally, at last, Ariane was led from the church by her lord husband, where a chorus of joyous shouts and cheers and pealing bells greeted them. She could see her half-brother, Gilbert, among the crowd, as well as Ranulf's trusted vassal and friend, Payn, their broad smiles reflecting her own gladness.

As was the custom in a wedding celebration, Ranulf set her upon his steed and mounted behind her. To the accompaniment of blaring trumpets and flowing silk, they led the procession from the church to the bridegroom's home—or in this case, Claredon Keep.

Secure in his embrace, Ariane leaned back against Ranulf's broad chest, cherishing the feel of his powerful arms wrapped around her.

"So ... are you satisfied, wench?" Ranulf asked with amused affection lacing his voice. "You have finally achieved your ends."

Ariane felt a glow of happiness at his tender teasing, but she shook her head saucily. "You may address me as madame in future, my lord husband. I am not your *wench*, nor even *demoiselle* any longer. I am your *wife*."

"Wife," Ranulf murmured thoughtfully. "I like the sound of that."

Laughter bubbled out of her, full and joyous, and Ranulf found himself wanting to join in, to laugh and shout with joy himself, at his long-delayed admission. For too long he had resisted surrender; for too long he had fought against the inevitable.

"Very well, sweet wife. I shall call you madam in future. Unless you misbehave, which is highly likely—in which case you will revert to *wench*. Do you accept these terms as fair?"

"Fair enough, husband."

When Ariane turned her head to gaze up at him, he saw in her eyes the same all-consuming love he knew shone in his, and knew himself to be blessed. He no longer harbored any doubts. She had claimed his heart irrevocably—and he intended to prove it to her, for all the days of their lives.

The festivities ensued through the entire day and half the night. Lord Walter had provided a wedding feast to rival a king's, holding it out of doors in a nearby meadow, so that the huge crowds could be accommodated.

The nobles banqueted within shaded pavilions, with the newly wedded couple and most important guests occupying the dais of honor. The long trestle tables outside groaned with both standard fare and delicacies: venison, whole roast boars, partridges, thrushes, peacocks and swans, fish and lampreys, all swimming in highly spiced sauces, with cheeses and sweetmeats for the final courses, as well as innumerable pastries sweetened with honey and glistening with costly imported sugar.

The celebration began with toasts for the bride and groom. "Will you share with me, my lady?" Ranulf asked huskily, offering Ariane wine from an ornate silver chalice embellished with dragons. When she had sipped, he took it from her and, holding her gaze, turned the goblet so that his lips touched the rim where her mouth had been. His sensual smile afterward caressed her with warmth, clearly proclaiming his desire for her.

Ale and wine flowed freely, and by late afternoon those who could still stand participated in the games and the dancing and the mock tournaments.

Ranulf played his role as bountiful lord, dispensing gifts to the wedding guests, but primarily he watched his beautiful bride enjoy the festivities and thought impatiently of the evening ahead. Tonight Ariane was going to come to him of her own free will, in love, as his beloved. In the church this morning, they had exchanged pledges and sacred vows, but only in their marriage bed would those vows be sealed. She would belong to him fully then. He felt the heat in his loins surging to match the fire in his heart.

His longing had grown to a fierce need by the time dusk settled softly over the countryside and huge bonfires were lit to illuminate the night. Ranulf cared naught for what festivities remained. He wanted only Ariane, alone, in their bed.

By torchlight the wedded couple was escorted to the castle, into the tower, and up to the bridal chamber—Ariane's former rooms that would be hers and Ranulf's as long as they remained at Claredon. It was customary for the wedding guests to help in the disrobing for the bedding ceremony. Thus the chamber was crowded and filled with gay chatter, until everyone hushed for another solemn moment.

The wooden floor was strewn with roses; Ariane and Ranulf knelt among them as Father John blessed the nuptial bed. Then, with a last, lingering glance at his wife, Ranulf reluctantly accompanied the men below while, according to custom, the women undressed and put the bride to bed. When at last she was ready, they closed the bed curtains around her and retired.

Moments later Ariane heard his knights bearing Ranulf to his marriage bed amid much laughter and ribald comments. The jesting only grew coarser as his sword and garments were stripped from his body, but at last the door slammed shut behind the men and blessed silence reigned.

Ariane was surprised to find herself trembling. She had yearned for this moment for so long, it seemed like a sweet dream. Her dream lover had come for her, to her, at last.

"Ariane?" Ranulf murmured into the silence.

"I am here," she replied unsteadily.

His lips curved upward in a grin when he heard the slight catch in her voice. It seemed that *she* was as nervous as he. He closed the distance to the bed. His heart pounding, he parted the drawn curtains to find his bride lying in wait for him, her pale copper hair cascading across the pillows, the covers turned down invitingly. She wore nothing but a wedding garland of roses, and Ranulf inhaled sharply to see her slender white body gleaming in the soft glow of candlelight. Arousal flared within him, insistent and urgent.

Controlling his fierce need with willpower alone, he turned away to pour a silver goblet full of wine. Returning to the bed, he sat beside her, settling a tautly muscled flank against her hip. His position reminded Ariane of the first night Ranulf had alarmed her by invading her bedchamber, and yet this time, she was not frightened of him, only of the powerful, overwhelming, helpless way he made her feel.

She drank in the sight of his beautiful, scarred body, with its rippling muscle and sinew, his broad chest with its furring of raven hair. . . . Her gaze lowered to the goblet, hesitating quizzically.

"I scarcely drank a drop the entire day," Ranulf explained, "and I find I have a great thirst." Yet from the smoldering flames in his eyes, she did not think his thirst had aught to do with wine.

"Perhaps you intend to ply me with wine," Ariane suggested with a teasing glance, "in order to render me more malleable."

He smiled that rare, tender smile that she loved so dearly. "Ah, no, never, my lady. I wish you to be in possession of all your senses tonight. I mean for you to feel every nuance of everything I do to you." His sensual, provocative tone made her pulse skitter. He glanced down at her lips. "I thought we would begin with a lesson in wifely conduct."

"Indeed?" She smiled uncertainly. "What sort of lesson?"

"One on how to please your husband. I am your husband now, am I not?"

"Yes. . ." Ariane answered breathlessly.

Ranulf's hand slowly rose to touch her cheek. Holding her gaze, he began to caress her, his long fingers tracing the delicate line of her jaw, the smooth column of her throat, the ridge of her collarbone, stroking lightly, clearly intent on seduction. Ariane responded to his touch like a blossom opening to the sun; beneath his sensitive fingertips, she felt her flesh ripple with warmth.

"Will you drink, sweeting?" he asked as her passion-heavy eyelids began to drift shut. Bringing the goblet to her mouth, he let her sip for a moment. Then taking it away, Ranulf slowly bent and, covering her mouth with his, drank the wine from her lips.

Ariane gave a soft moan from deep within her throat at the delicious taste of Ranulf mingled with wine. Yet he would do no more than let her taste.

Drawing back, he slowly dipped his forefinger into the cup and brought it back to her parted lips, gliding over the moist surface till her mouth was red and wet and dewed with wine. Ariane could be acquiescent no longer. Urgently, she captured his hand and pressed a kiss against his palm.

"Yes, Ranulf," she whispered. "Teach me how to please you."

"You do. . . . You please me greatly, dearling."

The endearment warmed her heart, even as his scorching look warmed her flesh and sent the blood racing through her veins. But he would not allow her to participate in her own seduction.

"Lie still," he urged huskily as his fingers splayed gently over her throat, his palm resting on the thickly beating pulse.

Weakly, she nodded, prepared to give Ranulf his way—at least until the ecstasy became too unbearable.

She lay completely still as once more he dipped his finger and trailed it indolently down her throat to her left breast, making the nipple tighten and contract with sensation as the cool liquid touched her heated flesh. Then, with exquisite care, he bent to lick the drop off the taut peak with the tip of his tongue.

Ariane whimpered at the spark of fire that fanned through her—and whimpered again, as his mouth closed over her nipple and sucked gently. She did not want gentleness. She wanted fierceness, wanted his powerful body thrusting hard into hers, wanted Ranulf's desire to match her own.

Her fingers twined in his thick ebony hair to draw his head closer, while her back arched, offering her aching breast to him willingly. And still Ranulf would not rush the moment. His hot mouth and rough, wet tongue pleasured her unhurriedly, almost lazily, evidently intent on driving her mad with wanting. They played passionately over her straining nipple, tugging the crest, deliberately arousing, his slow, erotic suckling bringing her to a feverish pitch.

Hot and shivering, Ariane gritted her teeth and moved her head restlessly on the pillow. Her cheeks were flushed, her breath coming in soft pants, by the time he at last drew back.

With a smile that held a wicked promise, Ranulf dipped his finger again into the wine.

She knew what pleasure came next, even before he sought the hidden recess between her thighs. At his exquisite touch, her senses went wild. Her hips arched helplessly in agitation, until Ranulf's husky command came again, telling her to be still. His brow furrowed in concentration as he properly attended the woman's flesh exposed to his gaze ... stroking her tenderly ... rubbing the wet nubbin with wine ... boldly parting the quivering folds ... gliding his fingers deep, deep within her ... encouraging her soft moans of passion.

Flames shot through Ariane, radiating heat through her, heat that centered around his probing fingers in an intense pool. Gasping and shuddering, she clamped her legs around the caressing hand that tortured her so exquisitely.

Finally, as if sensing how near she was to the edge, Ranulf bent to set the goblet on the floor and then leaned over her, his hot, open lips pressing into the musky warmth beneath her breast ... her flat, trembling belly ... the silken curls that shielded her womanhood.

"Ranulf ... please ..." she begged in a gasping plea as her hips thrust wantonly against his hot mouth, craving his possession.

Parting her legs wider, he kissed her there, relishing the slick, swollen sweetness, inhaling her fragrance, letting his tongue stroke and explore and caress her to madness.

"I love your pleasure sounds," Ranulf whispered against her moist, heated flesh. "I love the taste of you. I love *you*, Ariane . . . my own."

She could not answer. The hurting, painful need was too fierce to be borne. Hot and feverish beneath him, nearly desperate, Ariane reached for him, her trembling fingers seeking . . . closing over his arousal . . . cherishing the tantalizing feel of his throbbing male power . . . delighting in the feel of him pulsing and burning in her hand.

Ranulf went rigid at her touch, suddenly unwilling to continue the game of torment any longer, *unable* to continue. His breath growing short, his control tenuous and ragged, he stretched his long frame over her and sank slowly between her parted thighs.

Ariane gasped with pleasure as she felt the enormous heated strength of him ease within her, deep within. His hard flesh filled her, possessive and commanding. Through a sensual daze, she looked up at him.

The planes of his harsh, magnificent face were shadowed, but his hot, intense gaze was unreserved, trusting. Ariane smiled tremulously at her golden-eyed, glorious lover, and wrapped her legs tightly about his hips. Desperate to draw him closer, she let her fingers move blindly over his scarred, muscular back, murmuring soft, meaningless words of love and need.

Beneath her caresses, Ranulf trembled with a leashed desire that shook his powerful frame. And when Ariane whispered, "Ranulf . . . my love," against his lips, a new, more violent flame seared his heart. He groaned in tender anguish as he increased the rhythm of his taking, his thrusts fiery and urgent, till she was writhing and shuddering beneath him.

She gave a sob of joy as she strained against him in frenzied abandon. And then the relentless climax began. He felt her shattering release burgeon an instant before his own body exploded savagely into hers. In a frenzy of need, Ranulf cried out her name, surging with the passionate strength coiled within him, forced to surrender as she was surrendering.

Long, long moments later, he came to his dazed senses to

find his sweat-dampened body still shaking in the aftermath. Laboring for breath, he tried to ease his weight from Ariane, but she murmured in protest and tightened her arms around him. For another moment, he remained where he was, listening as his thudding heart slowed to something resembling normalcy.

"Ariane, my love," he whispered into her hair. "I will crush you."

"Mmmmm ..." Her mouth curved in a dreamy smile. "Am I truly your love?"

"Aye, always."

"Tell me again."

"My love ... my beloved ... my heart ..."

In reply, she raised her lips to his for a kiss that spoke eloquently of her own love.

The exertion expended her remaining energy, however, draining Ariane of strength. When finally her grip loosened and she allowed him to move, Ranulf shifted his weight onto his side and tenderly gathered her limp, unresisting body in his arms. The wild longing he felt for her was still urgent and raw, yet he reminded himself there was time enough to appease his desperate need. They had the entire night ahead of them, an entire lifetime of wedded bliss.

Bliss. With a grateful humbleness he had never before felt, Ranulf nuzzled his face into her rose-scented hair. The passion he shared with Ariane was far more fulfilling than mere coupling, the desire more than bodies straining together or the slaking of lust. It was pure rapture. Before Ariane he had not known what rapture was. Never had he experienced this profound, incredible feeling of completeness, of oneness.

Wife, he thought dazedly. *My ladylove.*

He held and cherished her, unwilling to relinquish her. Tenderness ran through him, hot, honeyed, filling him with wonder and something akin to awe. He felt strong, unassailable, kindled with new purpose. With her at his side, life would hold a richness and fulfillment he had never before known. No longer would he battle alone. The bleak loneliness had been vanquished. His bitter hatred, his need for vengeance, washed away, his soul purified.

Ranulf's gaze drifted lower, over their entwined legs. This was their marriage bed. He hoped Ariane would conceive here. He wanted a son—or a daughter—any child of her loins. And yet if she somehow proved barren, he would be disappointed but not distraught. Ariane meant more to him than just a breeder of sons. He wanted her, *needed* her, with a desperation he had never felt.

Somewhere in the darkest recesses of his soul, he had always known it. She was made for him, his heartmate. She belonged to him, just as he belonged to her.

Ranulf shut his eyes, frightened by the depth of the love he felt for this woman. He would lay down his life for her without regret or scruple. He would give up all his worldly possessions—in truth, whatever she asked of him. And in return, she would give him her heart. She would teach him to love, would teach him gentleness.

Already she had influenced him profoundly. Ranulf's mouth curved ruefully as he realized how easily even a powerful warrior could be brought to his knees by love. He had surrendered in love to her. And in attempting to win Ariane's loyalty, he had given his own. In truth, he was grateful for the profound sense of tranquility Ariane had given him, for freeing him of his demons.

He was done with fighting, at least for the moment. This time of peace in England would not last, he knew. And he would always owe his overlord, Henry, the requisite forty days knight's service, as well as innumerable other fees for the fiefs he had been given. But never again would he purposely go seeking battles to win, victories to achieve, challenges to overcome. He would be satisfied to build a dynasty here, in this new country, with Ariane as his lady, his wife, his love.

His arms tightened around her. She was so dear to him. And for the first time in his life he could say he knew what happiness was. Their past had been stormy and troubled, their battles tempestuous, but the hope he felt for the future was burgeoning in his breast, like a clamoring drum.

"Dear one," he murmured as he sought her lips once more.

His kiss was filled with incredible tenderness, startling in its wonder.

Rousing herself to wakefulness, Ariane gazed up at him adoringly. His golden eyes were melting into honey, full of love, of softness. "I love you," she whispered with heart-felt joy.

"And I you," Ranulf replied reverently. "I never thought to feel this way."

"What way is that, my lord?"

His fingers closing over her slender hand, he brought her palm to rest on his breast, directly over his heart. "As if I would die if you left me. 'Tis you who lights the fire in my loins. You who commands my heart. I need you as I need air, sunlight, fire in winter."

Her eyes blurring with tears, Ariane smiled at him. "I will never leave you, my love. I swear by God to keep faith with you against all others, forever and always."

"And in return I give you my life, yours to keep till the day I die."

They sealed their pledges tenderly with yet another kiss that began to evolve into something more passionate. . . until to Ariane's surprise and dismay, Ranulf suddenly ended the embrace.

"One moment, sweeting."

Drawing back, he reached over the edge of the bed to retrieve the wine cup. To Ariane's further surprise, he spilled a measure of wine on the sheets in the middle of the bed, watching with satisfaction as the dark red stain spread and was absorbed.

"There," Ranulf said with satisfaction. "That should allow us to display the requisite bleeding on our sheets on the morrow."

"I fear it does not look much like blood," Ariane mused, eying the splotch skeptically.

"What matters it?" he said with a wicked grin. "Twice before you have stained the sheets with your 'virgin' blood. And if I say our marriage was consummated tonight, who is to prove otherwise?"

When her cheeks pinkened with chagrin at his reminder, Ranulf laughed softly, at her, with her, delighting in the flush that suffused her skin.

"Will you never allow me to forget that incident, my lord?" Ariane asked ruefully.

"No, never, my lady." His laughter turned husky as his amber eyes darkened. "And I intend to demand penance from you regularly, for the rest of our mortal lives. You may begin appeasing me now. Kiss me, wench, before I lose patience.''

"As you wish, my lord," she replied with false meekness. Her eyes shining with love, Ariane obediently reached up to twine her arms around his neck and embrace her lord husband.

Epilogue

Marsden Keep, England: May 1158

The warm lips nuzzling his bare skin no longer had the power to arouse him, nor did the cool, silken hair trailing provocatively over his naked back. Ranulf lay sprawled on his stomach upon the musky linen sheets, sated and spent, his body glistening with sweat after his exertions. Pleasing his lusty young wife taxed even a man of his strength and stamina.

In a benumbed state of repletion, he had no energy left to respond to Ariane's erotic caresses. He did not move a muscle, even when she pressed her lips tenderly against the savage scars on his back, for her soft, loving kisses held the power to heal his wounds, both without and within.

Only the sudden plaintive wail from the cradle near the hearth had the ability to make Ranulf stir immediately from his delicious lethargy. If it was not one wench demanding his attention, it was another, he thought with laughter warming him inside.

"No, wife, permit me," he said when Ariane started to rise.

Easing from the bed, he went to the hearth to attend to the latest fruit of their love. The new keep at Marsden had been completed in time for the birthing of their daughter, Blanche, although their two-year-old son had been born at Claredon. Having grown too large for his cradle, Alain slept in the adjacent antechamber in the company of his nurse.

Ranulf murmured soothing endearments as he picked up his fretful daughter. With infinite tenderness he rocked her against his chest, silencing her cries.

Watching from her reclining position on the bed, Ariane

smiled to see the broadest pair of shoulders in all Christendom sheltering such a fragile bundle. Never in her fondest
dreams had she pictured Ranulf thus—cooing over his tiny
daughter and reverently stroking her silken head with its curling thatch of raven hair, the strong hands that could wield a
battle sword with deadly power and precision caressing with
incredible gentleness. Ranulf was devoted to his son and
proud as any father could be, but, as sometimes happened
with strong men, he positively doted on his baby daughter.

Eventually he caught Ariane watching him and lifted a
dark eyebrow. "What find you so amusing, dearling?"

"You, my lord. I was merely remembering the fearsome
dragon who took possession of Claredon. You scarcely resemble that fierce warrior any longer."

Ranulf's mouth curved in a grin as he recalled the bitter
man he had been. He could scarcely believe how profoundly
his life had changed in a few short years. He had a family
now, a home. He was surrounded by people he loved, who
loved him—a wife and children as well as loyal retainers and
vassals. He no longer needed war and conflict to feel fulfilled.
Instead he knew a fierce contentment—a contentment that
Ariane vowed he would always retain.

Just then Blanche let out a wail lusty enough to bring the
rafters down. Wisely, Ranulf carried her at once to her mother
so that Ariane might nurse her. Joining them on the bed, he
watched appreciatively as she settled their hungry daughter
at her breast. Noblewomen usually called up wet nurses from
among the serfs, but Ariane had chosen otherwise. She was
devoted to their children, just as he was.

His marriage had proved the end of his wenching. To the
dismay of many a female heart, the lord of Vernay and Marsden was too attached to his beautiful lady wife to take any
interest in the castle wenches—or any other woman.

Ranulf's gaze lifted momentarily to survey the solar, which
had become the center of his life. Ariane had made their new
castle a true home, decorating this chamber for their comfort,
adorning the stone walls and wooden floor with colorful
silken tapestries and fur coverlets and woven rugs.

The past years had been bountiful. As a reward for a
knight's loyal soldiering, King Henry had given Ranulf the

handsome fief of Marsden to hold, with orders to build a castle there to provide a base loyal to the crown.

He was never in residence at Vernay, which held such bitter memories for him. Indeed, he had returned to Normandy only once, for a short while, and then only to oversee his lands and to give Payn FitzOsbern the castellanship of Vernay for his years of devoted service—a prize any knight would covet. Ariane had embraced the plan with as much fervor as Ranulf. She had stood by him with the courage and loyalty of a warrior's woman, executing her duties as lady with grace and gentleness, making no complaint when he was called away for feudal service. With reluctance, Ranulf had participated in the king's campaigns in Wales, but he had returned home eagerly, barely in time for his daughter's birth.

His features softened as he gazed down at his nursing daughter, a fierce love swelling in his chest. She was tiny and perfect and beautiful, so beautiful he did not even wish to consider the countless hearts she would break when she was older.

Aye, he had mellowed, Ranulf thought contentedly. Payn would tease him unmercifully could his vassal see how thoroughly he was ruled by the women in his life—although by all reports, Payn had recently found a lady of his own who was leading him on a merry chase.

When Blanche had finished nursing and fallen into a doze, Ranulf returned his daughter to her cradle and called for her nurse, who changed the babe's napkin and dressed her in a fresh tunic. Even after the woman had gone, though, he loitered, tucking Blanche warmly beneath the coverlets and watching her sleep.

"Ranulf," Ariane called finally, "do you mean to return to bed before the fall harvest? I am cold."

She could not possibly be complaining about the temperature of the chamber, he knew; not with the fire in the hearth and the mildness of the fine spring weather.

His eyes were warm and teasing when he joined her in the bed and gathered her naked body in his arms. "You command, beloved, and I obey. I am but a humble knight wishing to please his lady."

Ariane muffled a spurt of laughter against the heated skin

of his furred chest. "You are the *least* humble knight I know, my arrogant lord."

With feigned pain, Ranulf clutched at his heart and sighed heavily. "I am sorely afflicted."

"Are you indeed?"

He bent to kiss her lips, her throat, her bare breast. "Aye, afflicted with desire and love. Every part of you is so dear to me. . . ."

Those were the last words he spoke for a long while. With eagerness and joy, Ariane closed her eyes and lay back, giving herself over to the lazy worship of his lovemaking.

Her cup of happiness was filled to overflowing. Within the week, her parents would arrive at Marsden to pay their first visit to their grandchildren. Lady Constance, though somewhat scarred and no longer in possession of her former beauty, had been cured of her terrible disease, a feat for which Layla had been lavishly rewarded with her freedom. Ariane would always be grateful to Ranulf for the service he had done both her mother and father.

Indeed, she would always love him, deeply and irrevocably. She could not have chosen a better lord and husband had she searched the whole of England and Normandy. Ranulf had gentled under her touch, becoming as tender, as passionate, as any woman could wish.

Breathlessly arching against him in response to his erotic caresses, Ariane smiled up at Ranulf through a shimmering haze of pleasure and pure joy. She had tamed her fiery, golden-eyed dragon, turning him into the lover of her dreams.

Avon Romantic Treasures

*Unforgettable, enthralling love stories,
sparkling with passion and adventure
from Romance's bestselling authors*

CAPTIVES OF THE NIGHT *by Loretta Chase*
76648-5/$4.99 US/$5.99 Can

CHEYENNE'S SHADOW *by Deborah Camp*
76739-2/$4.99 US/$5.99 Can

FORTUNE'S BRIDE *by Judith E. French*
76866-6/$4.99 US/$5.99 Can

GABRIEL'S BRIDE *by Samantha James*
77547-6/$4.99 US/$5.99 Can

COMANCHE FLAME *by Genell Dellin*
77524-7/ $4.99 US/ $5.99 Can

WITH ONE LOOK *by Jennifer Horsman*
77596-4/ $4.99 US/ $5.99 Can

LORD OF THUNDER *by Emma Merritt*
77290-6/ $4.99 US/ $5.99 Can

RUNAWAY BRIDE *by Deborah Gordon*
77758-4/$4.99 US/$5.99 Can

If you enjoyed this book, take advantage of this special offer. Subscribe now and get a

FREE
Historical Romance

No Obligation (a $4.50 value)

Each month the editors of True Value select the four *very best* novels from America's leading publishers of romantic fiction. Preview them in your home *Free* for 10 days. With the first four books you receive, we'll send you a FREE book as our introductory gift. No Obligation!

If for any reason you decide not to keep them, just return them and owe nothing. If you like them as much as we think you will, you'll pay just $4.00 each and save at *least* $.50 each off the cover price. (Your savings are *guaranteed* to be at least $2.00 each month.) There is NO postage and handling – or other hidden charges. There are no minimum number of books to buy and you may cancel at any time.

Send in the Coupon Below

To get your FREE historical romance fill out the coupon below and mail it today. As soon as we receive it we'll send you your FREE Book along with your first month's selections.
